A CHAIN OF VOICES

A CHAIN OF VOICES

André Brink

faber and faber

First published in 1982
by Faber and Faber Limited
3 Queen Square London WC1N 3AU
Set by King's English Typesetters Ltd, Cambridge
Printed in Great Britain by
Fakenham Press Ltd, Fakenham, Norfolk

British Library Cataloguing in Publication Data

Brink, André
A chain of voices
I. Title
823[F] PR9369.3.B7

ISBN 0-571-11874-7

This one is for
TIM

History is always and above all a choice and the limits of this choice

Roland Barthes

Every man is an abyss; you get dizzy when you look down
Georg Büchner

History makes itself in such a way that the final result always arises from conflicts between many individual wills, of which each again has been made what it is by a host of particular conditions of life . . . What each individual wills is obstructed by everyone else, and what emerges is something that no one willed . . . (Yet) each contributes to the resultant and is to this degree involved in it

Friedrich Engels

ACT OF ACCUSATION

In the criminal case of Daniel Denyssen, Esquire, His Majesty's Fiscal at the Cape of Good Hope, acting ratione officii *by prevention, versus*

1. GALANT *(age 26 years, born in the Cold Bokkeveld), formerly slave of the late Nicolaas van der Merwe;*
2. ABEL *(age 28 years, born in the Cold Bokkeveld), slave of Barend van der Merwe;*
3. ROOY *(age 14 years, born in Swartberg) and*
4. THYS *(age 18 years, born in Swartberg), both Hottentots formerly in the service of the late Nicolaas van der Merwe;*
5. HENDRIK *(age 30 years, born in the Warm Bokkeveld), Hottentot formerly in the service of the late Hans Jansen;*
6. KLAAS *(age 40 years, born in the Cold Bokkeveld), slave of Barend van der Merwe;*
7. ACHILLES *(age approx. 55 years, born in Mozambique), formerly slave of the late Nicolaas van der Merwe;*
8. ONTONG *(age approx. 60 years, born in Batavia), formerly slave of the late Nicolaas van der Merwe;*
9. ADONIS *(age 60 years, born in Tulbagh), slave of Jan du Plessis;*
10. PAMELA *(age 25 years, born at Breede River), formerly slave of the late Nicolaas van der Merwe;*
11. JOSEPH CAMPHER *(age 35 years, born in Brabant), Christian of the Cape Colony;*

be it hereby made known that it has appeared to His Majesty's Fiscal from a report dated the 8th February 1825 from the Landdrost of Worcester to the Government Secretary, and from further preparatory Informations obtained in this case:–

9

That the first prisoner Galant, who in one of the winter months of last year, 1824, had been guilty of deserting from his Master, the late Nicolaas van der Merwe of the farm Houdden-Bek in the Cold Bokkeveld, (but having afterwards voluntarily returned to his Master), and who further, during the time of the last harvest, which must have been in the latter end of the month of December 1824, had formed the wicked intention, together with the other people in his Master's service and with the 11th prisoner Joseph Campher, a foreman in the service of the neighbour Jean D'Alree, to provoke his Master, while they were at work at the threshing-floor, by complaining of bad victuals, and then should their Master punish them, to murder him, but which intention they did not carry into execution, in consequence of their Master when they told him that they could not eat his victuals having merely answered that he could not give them better, without his having said anything further or attempted to punish them, availed himself of the opportunity that offered, by his Master taking him with him when riding round to visit his friends after the Harvest was got in, to draw into his Interest the people of several places where his master stopped and especially those of his father-in-law Jan du Plessis, among whom was the prisoner Adonis, slave of said Du Plessis, from which time he communicated to and persuaded some of those people to join in the plan he had framed to attack the places and effect a general effusion of blood among the Christians, and in this manner to get possession of the farms as far as should be in their power, and finally to repair to Cape Town; or in case they might not be safe within the Colony, to proceed beyond the boundaries to the Great River and join a number of Bastards who had collected there. —

That the 1st prisoner Galant, both previous to and on his said journey and also after his return to the place of his Master, got some of the people in the neighbourhood to join in his plan, and in particular those of his own Master, namely the prisoners Rooy, Thys, Achilles and Ontong; likewise the prisoner Abel, belonging to the place Elandsfontein of Barend van der Merwe, elder brother of the late Nicolaas van der Merwe; also the prisoner Hendrik *who, on the day before the murders, i.e. on the afternoon of Tuesday 1st February, had arrived with his master Hans Jansen from the Warm Bokkeveld on the farm Houd-den-Bek in search of a strayed mare; also some people in the service of the tailor and shoemaker Jean d'Alree, resident on a plot of ground on the farm of Nicolaas van der Merwe, among whom was the prisoner* Joseph Campher *and in all probability the convict named Dollie. –*

That of all the prisoners whom Galant *had persuaded to join in his said plan, the 2nd prisoner* Abel *took the most active part, by using his endeavours to get his fellow slaves to co-operate therein, and actually persuaded the prisoner* Klaas, *foreman or* mantoor *on the farm of Barend van der Merwe, to take a part. –*

That the night between Tuesday 1st and Wednesday 2nd February of this year 1825 had been fixed as the time for carrying their plan into execution, such decision having been taken on Sunday 30 January when the prisoner Abel *and his Master spent the night on Houd-den-Bek (i.e. after the late Nicolaas van der Merwe and the prisoner* Galant *had returned from their visit to neighbouring farms); that on the following day the prisoner* Abel *returned to the farm, upon the pretext of having forgotten a leather thong, in order further to consult with the prisoner* Galant; *and that on the evening of the 1st the prisoner* Abel, *in accordance with their agreement, set out for the place of the late Nicolaas van der Merwe, in order with the people of that place to commence the execution of their plan; where having arrived, he proceeded to the hut of the 1st prisoner* Galant *and his concubines, the Hottentot woman Bet and the 10th prisoner, the slave woman* Pamela *(the latter however not being present on that occasion, having been instructed by her Master, as was his habit, to spend the night in his house); and having found the prisoner* Galant *already prepared together with the prisoners* Rooy, Thys *and* Hendrik, *the latter having been persuaded earlier that day to join in the plan, accompanied them on horseback to the place of his master Barend van der Merwe; and having reached the place in the night, he and*

11

the 1st prisoner Galant *began their operations by rushing into the house, while his master was enticed out of doors by the sheep running out of the Kraal, and where they seized two guns together with the powder and ball belonging to his master. –*

That the 1st and 2nd prisoners Galant *and* Abel, *the former of whom acted as Captain and the latter as Corporal of the gang, divided the guns and the powder and ball between them, and being further joined by the 6th prisoner* Klaas, *they each fired a shot at Barend van der Merwe, who in the meantime had perceived treachery through the barking of the dogs, of which shots the one fired by* Abel *wounded him in the heel, but the other missed him; on which Barend van der Merwe ran into the house, but having shortly afterwards come out through the back door and taken flight through the quince hedge to the mountain, clothed only in his nightshirt, he was again fired at by the 1st and 2nd prisoners, but without effect. –*

That the wife of Barend van der Merwe, named Hester (née Hugo), having at the same time availed herself of the darkness of the night, also left the house and some time afterwards made her escape into the mountains accompanied by her children and assisted as it seems by a young slave named Goliath who had not joined the gang, after which the first five prisoners, augmented in their number by the 6th prisoner Klaas, *rode back to the place of the late Nicolaas van der Merwe, the 1st prisoner's Master. –*

That on their way thither, the first six prisoners, although it was their intention to murder Jean D'Alree, living about half an hour's walk on foot from the farmstead at Houd-den-Bek, they however did not call at the dwelling of said D'Alree in order that the late Nicolaas van der Merwe should not be put on his guard to defend himself by hearing the shots that they might fire there, but they nevertheless inquired on passing by the hut of the old Hottentot woman Rose if their fellow prisoner Joseph Campher *was at home, in order to take him with them as had been previously arranged; whereupon they were informed by Rose that the said* Campher *had gone to Worcester* in order to escort to the Landdrost the slave Dollie who had deserted a few days before. –

That upon being informed of this circumstance the said first six prisoners rode on to the place of the late Nicolaas van der Merwe, where they arrived in the middle of the night, and having dismounted and put up their horses, they proceeded to the 1st prisoner's hut, where it seems they were joined by the prisoners Achilles and Ontong, and where the 1st prisoner's Concubine Bet likewise was, who previously to their departure had been left bound and in the care of said Achilles and Ontong upon the instructions of the 1st prisoner, that she should not have the opportunity of informing her Master thereof. –

That while they were in the hut, a long discussion took place in the course of which it was agreed to wait there till nearly daybreak, at which time the prisoners Galant, Abel, Thys and Klaas proceeded to the farmhouse to take up their previously appointed positions under the peach trees, while Rooy and Hendrik were charged with the care of the horses, and Achilles and Ontong remained at the Cattle Kraal, there to await their Master's coming. –

That while they were thus concealed, the late Nicolaas van der Merwe, accompanied by the late Hans Jansen who had spent the night on the farm, came out of the front door of the house and went to the threshing-floor, on which the prisoners Galant, Abel, Thys and Klaas left their hiding place and ran into the house, when the prisoners Galant and Abel immediately proceeded to the Master's bedroom where they knew that he kept his two guns on a rack against the wall, having been thus informed by Galant's Concubine the slave woman Pamela, and while Van der Merwe's wife Cecilia (née Du Plessis) was still in bed, they each seized a gun. –

That Cecilia van der Merwe on seeing this, leaped up and got hold of the guns one in each hand, but of which the one held by Galant was immediately forced from her by him and given to the prisoners Thys and Klaas who in the interim had remained outside the bedroom door, on which Cecilia van der Merwe having used her utmost endeavours to force the other gun from

13

the prisoner Abel, *who it appears was assisted by* Thys, *she in this manner struggling reached the kitchen, when the other people called out to the 1st prisoner* Galant: *"Shoot!", the latter actually fired the gun that he had in his hand, which was loaded with shot, and most dangerously wounded Cecilia van der Merwe in the upper part of the left thigh, creating a wound of nearly 8 inches in diameter and from one inch to one and a half inches in depth, lacerating also a portion of the tensor vagina femoris muscle and exposing others, whereby she fell and was obliged to let go the gun that she had got possession of, and which* Galant *thereupon took up and brought out of the house. —*

That the 1st prisoner Galant, *being thus outside the door, was immediately followed by* Abel, Thys *and* Klaas, *and thereupon successively joined by* Rooy, Hendrik, Achilles *and* Ontong. —

That the two guns of the late Nicolaas van der Merwe, which had been taken away, one of which was without a lock, were distributed on that occasion by the 1st prisoner Galant, *the one to* Klaas *and the other without a lock to* Ontong, *while the 4th prisoner* Thys *was armed with a sabre that had been stolen from the house of Barend van der Merwe, and* Achilles *with an assegai which his master had purchased for him to take care of the sheep; the prisoners having likewise in their possession at that time the necessary gunpowder and balls, partly made from a quantity of lead which together with the bullet mould was stolen by the 9th prisoner* Adonis *from his master Jan du Plessis, father-in-law of the late Nicolaas van der Merwe, and given to* Galant *during his visit the previous weekend, and partly with other balls and slugs made of shot, all stolen from their masters. —*

That while the prisoners were thus outside the house, Nicolaas van der Merwe and Hans Jansen, having heard the shot that wounded the wife of the former, proceeded to the house, upon which the 2nd prisoner Abel, *whose gun was loaded with shot, fired at Nicolaas van der Merwe and wounded him in the left arm or shoulder, notwithstanding*

14

which however both Van der Merwe and Jansen got into the house. –

That after this took place, a short time elapsed, during which the gang prepared to attack and again rush in, which opportunity said Jansen availed himself of to get out of the house, mount a horse, and ride towards the place of Jean D'Alree, but which the prisoner Rooy having perceived and warned the other prisoners of, he at the order of Galant brought the horses to the house, and having mounted, he accompanied by Abel and Thys pursued Jansen, who was soon overtaken by Abel, who had a good horse, and driven back to the house of Nicolaas van der Merwe, into which he rode with the horse, when the door was shut after him. –

That the house having been thereupon surrounded by the first eight prisoners and each person's post assigned to him, they waited for the moment that they could execute their murderous plan against Nicolaas van der Merwe and Hans Jansen, as well as Johannes Verlee, the Schoolmaster who had arrived at Houd-den-Bek only three days previously together with his young wife Martha and their baby, in order to take care of the education of Van der Merwe's daughters; but the 1st prisoner Galant, who it seems was driven by impatience because the master would not open the door, had more than once resolved to set fire to the house, which however it appears he was dissuaded from by the prisoners Achilles and Ontong, because they said not only the women and children would be burnt but everything else in the house as well; while the 4th prisoner Thys made an effort, but without success, to get into the house by breaking open one of the window sashes. –

That the 2nd prisoner Abel however soon found an opportunity, while he saw Nicolaas van der Merwe endeavouring to reconnoitre through the window, to thrust in his gun and fire at him, which shot grazed the side of his head; upon which Van der Merwe opened the front door a little and begged and prayed the murderers to spare his life, but in vain, although the 2nd prisoner, who was within shot of him, hesitated a little, which caused the 1st prisoner Galant to call out to him with a curse:

15

"Shoot, Abel!"; on hearing of which Nicolaas van der Merwe having shut the door, the 1st prisoner placed himself in such a situation that he could shoot his master himself when the door should again be opened; shortly after which Nicolaas van der Merwe, having first said prayers with his wife in the bedroom, opened the door, whereupon the 1st prisoner Galant *gave him a shot in the head, of which he immediately fell dead. –*

That Hans Jansen, on seeing this, shut the front door and went to the kitchen whither Johannes Verlee likewise went, and to which the wounded Cecilia van der Merwe also made her escape from the bedroom, and endeavoured to conceal herself in the oven; which the gang perceiving went round the house outside to the kitchen, when the prisoner Galant *first broke a hole in the oven with an iron crow and thereupon together with the other prisoners fired, in consequence of which breaking of and firing into the oven, the widow of the late Nicolaas van der Merwe fell out of the oven on the ground covered with rubbish and clay; upon which the 1st prisoner* Galant, *having broken open the kitchen door with his crow, he and the other prisoners rushed in, just at the moment when Hans Jansen was employed to extricate Cecilia van der Merwe from under the rubbish. –*

That Jansen, seeing that his life was also aimed at, advanced towards the murderers and begged of them to spare him, saying that he was a stranger who had only spent the night on the farm, to which Galant *answered that no Christian should have pardon, for that the report had been that the slaves were to have been free at the New Year, but that it not having been done they would make themselves free, upon which without hesitation* Abel *presented his gun at said Jansen and gave him a shot in the breast, the consequence of which was his immediate death. –*

That about the same time, Johannes Verlee, who had laid hold of the muzzle of Abel's *gun after he had fired at Jansen, received a shot in the left arm from the 1st prisoner* Galant, *through which he fell, and as it would appear left the prisoners in the idea that he was also killed, which gave them time to search round the kitchen and elsewhere, whereby they got possession of a pair of pistols and some powder and ball that they found there. –*

That after the pistols were found, the 6th prisoner Klaas having perceived and informed the others of the gang that Verlee was still alive, the 2nd prisoner Abel gave him another shot in the breast, but Verlee still retaining signs of life, the 1st prisoner Galant gave one of the pistols to the 3rd prisoner, the youth Rooy, with orders to shoot Verlee dead, in these words: "Shoot him with the pistol that you have right on the button, for he is not yet dead," which order the said Rooy complied with. –

That while this took place, Cecilia van der Merwe found an opportunity to conceal herself under a table in the front room, where however being sought for and found by Galant and Abel, she heard the former give orders to the latter to shoot her; on which she came out from under the table and begged of Galant to let her live, as she was already severely wounded, whereupon he allowed her to withdraw into her bedroom. –

That the 1st prisoner Galant and his accomplices thereupon left the house, but returned shortly afterwards, during which intermediate time Cecilia van der Merwe made her escape out of the bedroom and round the house to a loft, where her children had earlier concealed themselves with Martha Verlee and her baby. –

That the 10th prisoner Pamela, the second concubine of the prisoner Galant, who from the commencement of these murderous acts to the time that her mistress took refuge in the loft, was in the house, remained all the time entirely passive, without affording her mistress any assistance; but after her mistress made her escape to the loft, she went to Galant's hut, where she met the abovementioned Bet (who that morning when Galant had first entered his Master's house had likewise come in, and had assisted her mistress and helped to bind her wounds before returning to the hut), and having informed her that all the men were murdered and that Cecilia van der Merwe and Martha Verlee had made their escape to the loft with the children, said Bet thereupon returned to the house. –

17

That on coming into the kitchen, she found the 1st prisoner Galant *there again, together with* Thys *and* Klaas, *to the last mentioned of whom* Galant *having given orders to go and see whether his Mistress and her children were not in the loft, said* Bet *interfered and begged of him to spare her, but with no other effect than that the 1st prisoner* Galant *threatened to shoot her because she spoke for her Mistress, in which however he was prevented by the 6th prisoner* Klaas, *who thereupon went to the loft, and seeing the situation in which* Cecilia van der Merwe *already was, told her not to be alarmed, for that nothing more would happen to her.* –

That the 4th prisoner Thys *did not scruple on that occasion to threaten the daughters of the late* Nicolaas van der Merwe *with his sabre; while the 1st prisoner* Galant *threatened to fire at them, but in which he was again opposed by* Bet. –

That the 1st prisoner Galant *prior to leaving the house of his murdered Master, broke open the drawer of the table, from which he took the lock of the gun that he had found without one, which having been screwed on, he gave the gun to the 5th prisoner* Hendrik, *and having drunk of his Master's wine with his accomplices, he thereupon accompanied by* Abel, Rooy, Thys, Hendrik *and* Klaas *left the place, leaving behind the prisoners* Achilles, Ontong *and* Pamela, *the latter of whom saw the child at her breast beaten with a gun by* Galant *before his departure; and after the said prisoners had ridden off the prisoner* Pamela *fled into the mountains there presumably to await the return of* Galant *in accordance with some previous arrangement, whereas* Achilles *and* Ontong *remained on the farm and were apprehended when the Commando under Fieldcornet* Frans du Toit *arrived later in the same day.* –

That the first six prisoners, armed with the four stolen guns and the two pistols, having ridden back to the habitation of Jean D'Alree *with the intention to murder him also, found his house deserted (*D'Alree *having already left to summon the Field-cornet after having been alerted to the plot by* Barend van der Merwe *who had arrived there at daybreak); and that they thereupon rode forward to the place of* Barend van der Merwe,

18

which they had left the night before, for the purpose of murdering him likewise should he come home; where having arrived, they found he was not there, but met two Hottentots named Slinger and Wildschut, with a slave named Moses, all in the service of old Piet van der Merwe of Lagenvlei (the father of Barend and Nicolaas), and belonging to a grazing place of said Piet van der Merwe, whither Hester van der Merwe had the night before made her escape; each of whom was armed with a gun, and who as it would appear were sent there by said Hester van der Merwe to assist her husband should it prove necessary. –

That these three persons however, perceiving the superior strength of the gang, were induced to join them, and after drinking some brandy with the others at Barend van der Merwe's place, they accompanied them to the grazing place of old Piet van der Merwe, where Moses having got away, he was pursued and found by the gang. –

That about this time a number of Christians, who had placed themselves under the command of Field-cornet Frans du Toit, on the report of those wicked deeds having pursued and overtaken the gang, Slinger, Wildschut, Moses and Goliath immediately separated from them, while the first six prisoners having mounted their horses resisted the Commando, in consequence of which shots fell on both sides, Galant and Abel in particular having fired at the Commando, but without wounding anyone; upon which having taken flight they were pursued and dispersed by the Commando, and thereupon apprehended, first the 5th and 6th prisoners Hendrik and Klaas, and afterwards the other prisoners successively, some of them with considerable delay, notably the 1st prisoner Galant who was apprehended on the thirteenth day after having wandered about in the mountains (spending some time in the company of the 4th prisoner Thys who, after first escaping to the Karoo, later returned to join his Leader), abusing his freedom to steal a sheep belonging to Jan du Plessis and firing a shot through the latter's front door, before he was finally discovered in the Skurweberg near the place of the late Nicolaas

19

van der Merwe, by a group of Hottentots to whom he delivered himself without offering any more resistance. –

All of which crimes, and each of them, in proportion to the circumstances that have accompanied them, are punishable corporally and with death, according to the existing laws, as an example to others; and therefore require that all the prisoners in this case should be tried this day before the full Court conformably to the 6th Article of the Crown Trial.

(Signed) D. DENYSSEN
Fiscal's Office
Cape of Good Hope
10 March 1825

PART ONE

MA-ROSE

To know is not enough. One must try to understand too. There will be a lot of talking in the Cape these days, one man's word against another's, master against slave. But what's the use? Liars all. Only a free man can tell the truth. In the shadow of death one should walk on tiptoe, for death is a deadly thing. Now I suppose it's easy to say I've seen it coming a long way, as one sees the clouds coming from far off, over the Rough Mountains which they call the Skurweberge, and all along the ridges and the farms, the hills and valleys, over the vineyards and the wheatfields and the orchards, growing darker as they come closer, darker and darker all the way, until they break out in a storm that beats you down and strips you to the bone. Easy to say, and yet not so easy. For how far back must one go? To Galant's childhood, or mine and old Piet's, or my mother's, or still further? The world is very old hereabouts. It was like this in my mother's time, and in her mother's, and I suppose in her mother's too, how am I to know? In the beginning everything was stone. And from the stones the great god Tsui-Goab made us, the people, the Khoikhoin, the People-of-people. And here in the Bokkeveld you can see it very clearly, for we live surrounded by stone.

If you go towards Tulbagh and climb the highest peak, you can see a long way in all directions. You can see fully seven days far, for that's how long it takes to Cape Town by wagon. You can see the Table Mountain of the Cape, even though it's so far you can't really be sure it's there, but it is; and you know that's where the Gentlemen live and where the ships come and go and where the cannon booms from the Lion's Rump; and you can see Paardeberg, and Contreberg, Riebeeck's Castle, Huningberg, all of them, all the way to Saldanha where the sea draws a shiny line, and that's shit-far, and Piquetberg, and the whole country of the Four-and-Twenty Rivers that I've known since my baby days. If you look straight ahead between sunrise and sunset, it's the Winterberg rising in front of you, with the green valley of Waveren behind, and to the right the narrow valley below the Witzenberg. That is the way to our mountains, the Skurweberge, as rough and fearsome as in the time of Tsui-Goab. Here the earth is a dark red as if it's bleeding inside, growing more yellow as you dig into it; and it's broken by the grey and black of rocks strewn about in the old days. There's the yellowy green and the brown-green of the scrub, proteas and milkwood, and the ashen wagon-trees with their pitch-black trunks. Patches of heather among the cliffs. Now you know you're coming the right way and no need to hurry. The grass turns harsh and tough and stubbly, with tufts and plumes in between, and the glow of red-grass against the sun, and rushes in the marshes. This is high country, and if you come up this way from Waveren it's as if you're moving right out of the world, and rising all the way. When at last the earth flattens the valleys remain narrow and spare, hemmed in with stone. Grey stone, a flaming red inside, broken from the cliffs and scattered about. Mottled with lichen, overgrown with coarse shrubs and bitter heather and sudden splashes of yellow or the tiniest blue starflowers; and high up in the mountains the black and the grey of the rocks are streaked with the white of thin waterfalls. Then it's pure solid stone again. Stone grows old just like a tree, it seems to me, and as it grows old it turns black or grey. Deeper down, inside, it stays red, as if its guts are glowing, as if it's still alive; but outside it is old and grey.

Indeed, our mountains are old, stretching like the skeleton of some great long-dead animal from one end of the Bokkeveld to the other, bone upon bone, yet harder than bone; and we all cling to them. They're our only hold. They shelter us from the sun and ward off the wind from the narrow valleys and inlets among the rocks, the fields and farms, the sudden whiteness of homesteads and walls, the grazing sheep and cattle. There is a settled look about the string of farms with their houses and outbuildings and kraals, Houd-den-Bek and Riet River and Wagendrift, Winkelhaale, Lagenvlei, Buffelshoek and Elandsfontein; but don't be fooled by that. One single great gust of wind and it's all gone as if it's never been here. The White people, the Honkhoikwa, the Smooth-haired ones, are still strangers to these parts. They still bear in them the fear of their fathers who died on the plains or in the forbidding mountains. They do not understand yet. They have not yet become stone and rock embedded in the earth and born from it again and again like the Khoikhoin. One doesn't belong before one's body is shaped from the dust of one's ancestors.

They're newcomers here, the White men, moving in from the Cape and the valley of Waveren, arriving in ones and twos through the years, since the days of Piet van der Merwe's grandfather, from what I've heard; but by that time we, the Khoikhoin, had been coming and going for innumerable winters and summers. We'd come and gone as free as the swallows that arrive in the first warmth and depart in the first frost—here one evening and gone the next morning, and who can stop them? And here they found us, the White men did, when they came to tame the land as they called it, digging themselves in, and building their stone walls. But it's no use. They know nothing of these parts yet and already death has come in among their walls.

We of the Khoin, we never thought of these mountains and plains, these long grasslands and marshes as a wild place to be tamed. It was the Whites who called it wild and saw it filled with wild animals and wild people. To us it has always been friendly and tame. It has given us food and drink and shelter, even in the worst of droughts. It was only when the Whites moved in and started digging and breaking and shooting, and driving off the animals, that it really became wild.

Not that we had an easy life. My mother used to tell me how our people had been as numerous as the stones of the

25

mountains, as countless as the swallows; but then, she said, there came a disease among us, in the time of my mother's mother's mother or thereabouts, when the Great Hunter Heitsi-Eibib was still young; and ever since we've been only a handful, and fewer with each new summer. And yet, until my mother's time we still continued to come and go like the swallows or the wind. Winters are bad here, so my people would trek to other parts; in summer they might come back, depending on the rains—there were always old people in our midst who could tell exactly when and where to trek. We used to stay over on Piet's farm, in the Low Valley he called Lagenvlei; but when the time came to go, no one would stop us from leaving; and then we would come back again. Only much later, after the death of my father and my mother, when there were very few left of us, I settled here for good. At first I lived on Lagenvlei, seeing Piet's sons grow up in front of me, Barend and Nicolaas both; and suckling them when they were small. Afterwards I moved to Houd-den-Bek with Nicolaas. But in the time of the last harvest, when old Piet fell ill so suddenly and lay in the big bed staring at the ceiling, unable to move or speak, I went back to nurse him, to feed him and turn him over and wash him: for I'd known him since he was a young man and I knew his needs and likes. Only his wife, the old woman Alida, didn't want me there—she'd always been jealous of me, and with reason—so she sent me back to Houd-den-Bek. She knew only too well that I'd known his body even before she had. Now he's small and wasted, lying in his bed like an old sick vulture making noises no one can understand; his hands like talons; his body thin and almost transparent, just bones and folds of skin; and then that poor little limp thing with its blue head, like a small naked bird in a tattered nest, and the small eggs sunken into the wrinkled bag. Now it's lifeless, but in his youth it stood up like the pole of a stallion, and whenever he got into me, neighing like a wild horse, I could feel the spasm coming right from the bottom of my spine all the way to my throat, and my eyes would turn up. He could pump away, all right. And I have a right to judge, I've

26

had all the men of these parts and from far away; for when I was young they all heard about me and came to have their marrow drained. Now I'm old and they think I'm useless, but I swear I can still milk the lot of them.

This is a hard land and women are scarce, and the men are lustful. And who am I to turn away from life? When the stallion approaches, quivering with stiffness, I open up. And the men need it, it keeps them sane; otherwise they get mixed-up and mad and try to break down the world. Look at Nicolaas. Look at Galant.

I can no longer be silent about him. I've tried to think about other things, but it's Galant I have to come back to. For I was the one who brought him up, and in a way I suppose you might call him my child, even though he's always had a streak of the devil in him.

His mother was Lys, she was much younger than I, a mere child with apricot breasts; and she was a stranger in our Bokkeveld. They said she'd come from a land across the sea, from Batavia, like Ontong—so he also tried to comfort her in his own way, the old goat. Yet men will be men, and more so when women are hard to find. Same with old Piet. I often saw him stealing across the yard at night, mostly on his way to my own hut; but often to little Lys. And then she began to swell. She was the youngest ripe girl in our parts, and pretty too, although that cannot be seen in the dark, but she was; and she had something about her that seemed to lure the men, as Ontong said, by saying: *Come, bruise me*. And they couldn't resist it—the way some people cannot enjoy a flower without plucking off its petals; the way they cannot pass a young anthill without kicking it to bits. That was how it was with Lys, Lys of the apricot tits; and all the men from far and wide came to pluck her, the way they used to come for me, except I didn't mind; but it made her wild, and that made them desire her even more. She was a fruit, green but sweet, and they ate her. And so she began to swell.

Lys had a bad time with the birth. I was with her, she refused to let anyone else come near. At first I thought the

27

child was stillborn, so I put it aside to tend to her, for she was in a bad state; and after a while I called Ontong to dig a hole and bury the baby. But suddenly he came back, ashen with shock, carrying the little thing stiffly in his palms, standing there shaking in the light of the candle and saying: "Look at it, Rose, it's alive." And then I saw it stirring, wriggling like a puppy. I took it from Ontong and bathed it and put it to my breast, for I was flowing with milk after the death of my own baby and I was also feeding Nicolaas who was then a few months old. The little creature blindly nudged me with its small puppy-head for a while; then it got hold of the teat and started drinking, as tight as a tick. Spoiled him from the first.

Just as well I was in milk, for Lys refused to take him. She was all set against the child, refusing even to look at him, to say nothing of holding him. Lay there crying day and night until I thought she was going down. "Don't take it to heart so much," I told her at last. "I'll feed him, I got milk enough." That seemed to calm her down, but she remained ill for a long time. I think she was scared of getting well, scared the men would start again. One night Piet came in, demanding: "How's the slave girl? It's getting time. I've got the feeling tonight." He was wearing his night shirt so I could see how things were with him; but Lys turned her back, drawing up her knees to her chest and started whimpering, not like a woman but like a dog. Piet wanted to force his way past me to her, and it was his good right of course; he was her master, and he was a big man, with that wagon-pole of his. But as he came past me I lifted his shirt and gave him some of my breath on his man-thing, and as he turned towards me I got hold of him properly. I have a way of holding a man that comes from way back. And after a while I pulled him down on me, and with a sigh he moved into me; and then the earth came to life again in a big storm. Deep in the night I milked him once more, just to make sure he wouldn't bother Lys; and when it was time for early coffee and prayers in the front-room, as the morning-star came out, he staggered outside, a weary man; there's no weariness like that, ask me.

28

In the same way I kept the others from her too. My body is deep and I am marsh enough for herds to wallow in; and if I could help to spare Lys, so much the better for all of us.

But Piet was getting annoyed and in the end I had to speak to him straight. "You take Lys again," I told him, "and it will be the death of her. She'll drown herself in the hippo pool." I'd seen that look in her eyes whenever he came our way. And I suppose that's why he sold her to the man from the Karoo who passed Lagenvlei on his way to Cape Town with his produce wagon.

It worked out all right for the child. The man who'd bought Lys didn't want to take the baby too; and since Lys wasn't interested in having him anyway he stayed behind with me. He was perched on my arm as we stared after the wagon, Lys sitting in a small heap at the back like a bundle of washing that might fall off at the first jolt—odd that I should have thought that at the time, for when the wagon came past the farm again on its home journey a month later, the man told us that she had indeed fallen off and the wheel had gone over her and she'd died; he wanted his money back, but Piet refused and there was a bad quarrel on the farm that day, it even came to shots before the stranger left—anyway, the baby was sitting on my arm, his tiny round head erect like a meerkat's. I couldn't help laughing. "Look at this," I said to Ontong. "Gallant little fellow." And that is how he got his name Galant.

Ontong helped me to bring him up. The child was the only thing he'd ever had to think of as his own in this land. And maybe it really was his, who knows? But he might have been anyone else's too, any one of the many who'd come from far and wide to lie with Lys, some of them faceless in the night and gone before daybreak. So, if you think of it, he might just as well have been Piet's. In which case he and Nicolaas would have been the lambs of one ram pumping my dugs. Who am I to say? Galant has many fathers. No one is his father, and everybody is. That's the answer I always gave whenever I was asked. But they gave up asking long ago. Now I'm old and

29

worn and weary. Every winter I feel I'm going down, this Bokkeveld is fearsomely cold. But in summer I seem to sprout again, every time anew, like a thing growing. My body swells and withers with the seasons, but my roots are deep and sure; I'm rooted in rock. Piet and I have grown old together. But he's had it, and I still have life in me.

PIET

Dumb. That's what they bloody well think I am. Just because I'm lying here and like this. Because I cannot move my tongue in my mouth to speak they think I understand nothing. What do they know about the thoughts running like an underground watercourse? Think I'm senile, they do. This is no place for the old or the very young. They think we're difficult or obtuse. In the beginning I cursed them as I lay here. Shouting in silence, in fumes of sulphur. They didn't even know. Old Rose, maybe. She'd always had a way of looking at me and understanding. But Alida sent her away and except for the day of the funeral I haven't seen her again. Now I'm left to lie and die. I've given myself over into Alida's hands. What else could I do? There's no window on the mountain side. Pity. I'd have loved to cast mine eyes up to the hills. All I have to look at is the bleak veld sloping down from the house, a monotonous grey in the summer drought. In Grandpa's day the plains were abundant with game. Predators too. Even in my own youth, when I trekked back to these parts. And when the boys were young, the unexpected lion marauding on its own. But that was the last. There are still jackals in the mountains at night, or the occasional whoop of a hyena. Then Alida snuggles closer against me. After all these years she's still not used to our Bokkeveld.

"If we'd lived in the Cape this would never have happened." That was her sole reproach after Nicolaas's death. Must have been hard on her.

To think that Galant did it. Grew up with my own sons. But it goes to show. You can never really trust them, never really tame them. Like a jackal cub you bring back from the veld. You rear it like a dog. Tame as anything. Suddenly, when you least expect it,

31

it snarls and bites your hand. There's a wildness there you can never really subdue. And still I thought.

My God, can you imagine: Barend running off like that into the night when it happened, leaving wife and children behind? Hester and Alida were standing at my bedside discussing it. Thought I wouldn't understand them. Think I'm dumb. But I heard every word, scorching like live coals. Barend is thirty. But if I'd had my strength I'd have thrashed him for it. Running off into the mountains in his nightshirt. Much rather dead like Nicolaas. And I swear to God.

Is it something I did wrong? God has raised His arm against me that day He struck me down on the wheatfield. Everything going black, the world plucked from my grasp. And when I woke up I was like this. Paralysed. And they carried the ark of God in a new cart out of the house of Abinadab: and Uzza and Ahio drove the cart. And David and all Israel played before God with all their might, and with singing, and with harps, and with psalteries, and with timbrels, and with cymbals, and with trumpets. And when they came unto the threshing-floor of Chidon, Uzza put forth his hand to hold the ark; for the oxen stumbled. And the anger of the Lord was kindled against Uzza, and He smote him, because he put his hand to the ark: and there he died before God. I don't mean to reproach You, Lord, but it does seem unjust to me. The man only tried to help. But You struck him with Your lightning.

All my life I've tried to keep Your commands. You can ask my wife. And my remaining son. And my daughters-in-law, Hester and Cecilia. Ask all the slaves, everybody from my household. Didn't I read Your Word to them and prayed for them every evening of my life? Didn't we sing hymns together? Did I not teach them the Ten Commandments and set an example to them?

I have never had other gods before me nor made unto me any graven image; never had time for such nonsense. On this farm it's a matter of working from dawn to dusk and beyond. I've never taken the name of the Lord my God in vain, except when they made me bloody mad and then I had good reason. I have remembered the sabbath day and kept it holy when my work allowed it. And my father and mother I've honoured, You are witness to it. I have not killed; not needlessly. A few marauding Bushmen in my youth, but they tried to steal my sheep. A few other times I came close to it when slaves made me angry. But I always knew where to stop. Adultery? Ever since I took Alida I've never been with another woman. At least not a white one and God said nothing about others. They were made to give us a bit of sport in a hard land, otherwise it would all be labour and sorrow. I have never stolen anything, so help me God, and false witness I have never borne against my neighbour; in fact, I've always tried to stay as far away as possible from my neighbour to avoid trouble. I have never coveted anything belonging to him. His wife and his ox and his ass and his maidservant were his own concern. I had maidservants of my own.

So where did I sin against You? I must have an answer to this question when I appear before You.

Today I lie helpless; and Alida must feed me soup with a spoon. But it was different before. The world was different. In Grandpa's time. Pa's time. Even in my own. I often think: There were giants in the earth in those days, when the sons of God came in unto the daughters of men and they bare children unto them. The same became mighty men which were of old, men of renown. Why has it changed then? One generation passeth away, and another generation cometh: but the earth abideth for ever.

A hundred years ago, this I have straight from Pa's mouth, Grandpa Van der Merwe trekked away from Tulbagh and moved in here, after a quarrel with the Landdrost; and staked out a farm to his own liking, galloping on horseback from sunrise to dusk. Some time afterwards messengers were sent to summon him to the Drostdy. Then came a detachment of dragoons, but Grandpa shot them off his farm. "In this place your word counts for nothing," he told them. "No one but I have the right to speak here." And so he called the farm Houd-den-Bek, which means Shut-Your-Trap. In those days it comprised not only Lagenvlei and what is now Houd-den-Bek but stretched all the way to Wagendrift and round the bend to Elandsfontein.

But a few years later there was a severe drought and some of the children fell ill, so Grandpa loaded his wagons again and moved away to Swellendam. In our family, however, talk about this distant valley high in the mountains never stopped: the freedom they'd known here, the fertility of the soil. In the tales of the old people it came to sound like Paradise, and this image was rooted in my mind. I'd become attached to Houd-den-Bek long before I'd ever set foot there. It was a place destined to be mine, ordained by God and my forefathers. And that was why I eventually returned here from Swellendam, to drive off the intruders who'd settled here in the meantime, and buy out the rest (only Wagendrift remained in strange hands), to rebuild the broken walls and plough the fields again. That was after Hendrina's death. I'd married her in Swellendam, a girl Pa had chosen for me; but since she'd died in childbirth I didn't feel a need to remarry for many years. Only after I'd come back to this place and started the farm anew, I felt the time was ripe to find myself a new wife. It was not good for a man to be alone; in the Garden God had created woman for his comfort and delight. So I rebuilt the house and reploughed the lands and pruned the old trees and started my grazing places, and then I loaded two wagons and drove to Cape Town to fetch a wife and buy slips and cuttings for trees—peach and plum and apricot, pear and fig, quince and pomegranate; and vines; but also oak and willow and poplar for shade in the dry land.

One of the wagons broke on the road down the Witzenberg. We had to reload everything on the remaining one. Two teams of oxen in front. Rear wheels removed for the steep descent. Took us ten days to the Cape. Towards nightfall we outspanned beside the Salt River, and in the early dawn drove in to the Farmers' Square. I gaped in amazement. Even in those days the Cape was a big place. At least twenty streets, crossing at right angles, and paved with stone. The oaks of Heerengracht, all the way to the Mountain. The rough-cast white houses, cornices and high stoeps where people gathered in the shade to talk or smoke or drink *sopies*. The market-place. Grapes and melons, pears and figs and guavas, walnuts and almonds, chestnuts. I'd brought a bushel of cherries from the old trees on the farm: those were scarce in the Cape and fetched a good price. Two ships in the harbour, sails flapping in the wind and masts creaking. Gulls. Sailors strutting about on stiff legs and offering wads of dollars for rolled tobacco and brandy, if you could smuggle the kegs past the hawk-eyed agents of the East India Company. There was a fair at Green Point. Cape carts on the green grass. Races. Women in outlandish clothes. Hottentots clustered on one side, smoking and staring through narrow eyeslits.

It was Alida who took me there. A niece of uncle John de Villiers whose name Pa had mentioned long ago. ("Well, Alida, aren't you going to show Piet the town? I'm sure he hasn't seen it before.") Delicate, delightful little creature. Eyes shy yet mocking under the parasol. On the point of getting betrothed to a swaggering young foreigner; D'Alree in his natty clothes. Soon sent him packing. Poor man crawling on all fours in the front-room, chewing up the carpet.

One night I stole her a bunch of roses from the Governor's garden. Stopped by the guard. Told them to go to hell and made my escape with the flowers. Next day, can you believe it, a detachment of soldiers arrived to take me away. Uncle Jan purple with indignation and shock. "Piet, how can you disgrace us like this?" Alida tried to hold me back, but I shook her off and broke through the cordon. That night I crept back. Just before nine the front doors were opened and guests came out to hurry home before the curfew. Lanterns bobbing away in all directions in the dark. Voices calling: "Good-night to you!" A few breathless Hottentots and slaves scurrying past to avoid the nine o'clock watch. Thud-thud, thud-thud the soldiers came marching past on the paving stones, farther and farther away. And at last only the sound of the sea remained, and perhaps an occasional night-owl in an orchard.

Gave her the fright of her life when I knocked on her shutters. Tried to stop me as I climbed over the low sill. I held her against me. Her dark hair loose down her back. The small painted lamp on a low table. The light shining pinkly through her ears as she turned her head. "Piet, we'll both go to hell for this."

35

I took her away with me. Luckily it was moonlight. Urging on the oxen across the Cape Flats. Alida sobbing in the wagon, hitting me with her small fists when I tried to comfort her; but I held them tightly in one hand and calmed her down. When she started crying again, it was a different sound. The wagon swaying and creaking under our bodies in the night, the single lantern swinging wildly under the canvas roof. Like a dream. All the time I expected to wake up and find her gone. When I did wake up it was daylight.

Months later a bailiff came all the way from Cape Town, instructed by Alida's relatives. I chased him off the farm. Perhaps it was a fortunate thing that just about that time the English took over the Cape; in all the commotion that came with it they must have forgotten about us. We allowed her family a year to calm down and resign themselves to the will of God, and then invited them to our wedding in Tulbagh, taking little Barend with us to be christened. What a wedding party we returned to. People came from everywhere. Many of them we'd never seen before. Horses. Carriages. Wagons. Some on foot, each with his gift of food and drink. A whole row of oxen on the spit. Lambs and pigs. Game: springbok, hartebeest, bontebok, pheasant, bustard, wild duck, any living moving thing, pure or impure according to Scripture. Lasted a full week. And when we were too exhausted to move we called Rose to dance her wild reels for us. What a body she had in those days. Strange race, the Hottentots: smooth and beautiful until they're twenty or thirty; then they grow old overnight. Less than ten years later Rose was an old hag. But at the time of the wedding she was still shining with smoothness, a half-wild female creature wearing only the briefest of karosses around her parts. And even that was soon shed as she danced naked among the men, breasts bouncing. Trembling with every move. The brandy was flowing in torrents; and the men taking turns with Rose, some of them on all fours. Even the chickens were drunk by the time it was all over. Two men left for dead in a wonderful free-for-all, and not a single instrument in the orchestra left unbroken. All the feathers from our mattress shaken out in the yard and most of the chairs and tables

36

broken. Even a haystack burned down. Verily, the hand of God was abundantly on us.

Then it was over. And from that day it's been only Alida and I in the fear of the Lord and the sweat of our brow, comforting one another as we proved ourselves fruitful, multiplying, and replenishing the earth, and subduing it. In those days whatever I saw was mine. Farm, grazing lands, mountain, hunting fields. We were masters here, my sons and I. Whatever we needed was provided by God, and our hands, and our guns, summer and winter alike.

There were regular trips to Tulbagh and Worcester across the mountains, to barter our ostrich feathers and eggs, and hides, and produce; to buy ammunition and clothes and whatever the town could provide. But we seldom returned to Cape Town. Once I took Alida with me, but I could see it wasn't good for her. She still had the sea in her blood, and it depressed her to return to it. I suppose we lived too far away to her liking. But she's always been a good and dutiful wife, and I'm not complaining.

One particular trip to the Cape I remember well. It was in October, I'm not sure which year, but Barend must have been about fourteen, Nicolaas ten; and Hester had already come to live with us. She stayed behind with Alida. We'd hardly reached the Cape when rumours started about slaves rising at Koeberg and in the Swartland. Instigated, it would seem, by two Irishmen who'd stuffed their heads full of wild tales of freedom. What else can one expect of foreigners? There were the most horrible rumours: thousands of slaves on the rampage, making their way plundering and murdering from farm to farm and heading for Cape Town, set on driving us all into the sea. Everybody had something more terrifying or extravagant to add. And then it all turned out to be so much chaff in the wind. All that had happened, if I remember well, was that a few ringleaders had rounded up their men, trekking from one farm to the other, binding or locking up the white farmers, stealing guns and ammunition, and gorging themselves with food and wine; and then this tattered, drunken army had set out on the road to Cape Town, to be dispersed and blasted to bits within an hour by the army. A miserable business. Some of the leaders were hanged afterwards, I heard; the rest were flogged or sent to jail, and that was that. And all the commotion over the single false rumour that the Government had decided to set them free: and when nothing had happened by the appointed date they broke loose. So ludicrous and unnecessary. And still I shall never forget that day.

The people massing in the street. The women with their parasols. The slaves with their carrying-poles. The coachmen stopping left and right. Like an antheap kicked open. In the shops people were forgetting about buying or paying or taking what they'd bought. Market stalls were abandoned to looters. And slowly the streets were drained of life. Small clusters of people remaining for a while in anxious discussion before they, too, dispersed. Soldiers trooping past on horseback. Hooves clattering. Doors bolted. Wooden shutters let down and barred. Silence came sliding over the town like the shadow of a cloud. As if an enormous invisible hand had erased a picture drawn in sand, in front of one's very eyes. One felt quite alien and out of place. Only in the distance, by the sea, could one still hear the gulls. Then even they seemed to fall silent.

I had no inclination to stay on. Not even when news came that it was all over and the people began to make merry in the streets. I ordered my sons to the wagons and we returned to the farm with what we'd bought and bartered in town—groceries and ammunition, chintz and baize, copper wire and ironware; and also the slave Achilles I'd acquired just before the turmoil had begun. A stiff price too, he cost, for what with the importation of new slaves being stopped by the Government, prices were going up to high heaven.

It is a hell of a road back to the Bokkeveld, but all the way, as I remember, I kept silent, not talking to either son or slave. For it was an awful thing that had happened, a blasphemy against God Himself who had decreed that the sons of Canaan should forever be the servants of Shem and Jafeth. In silence I sat on the wagon, my pipe clenched between my teeth, staring at the slow landscape. Somehow it seemed quite different from before, now that one had come so close to losing it all. The skull shapes of

Paarl mountain. Green valleys opening up on either side below the blue ridges of the mountains. The Old Kloof. The tollgate at Roodezandskloof. From the deep valley of Waveren up the impossible mountains, through the narrow strip of the Rear-Witzenberg, across the Skurweberg, into these remote highlands. Home. But even home looked strange. I barely recognized the frail woman with her dark hair drawn into a tight bun, who came out to meet us. As if a strange presence had touched it all and turned it all transparent, revealing veins and secret organs and the skeleton below.

I brushed Alida off when she came to greet me. There was something more urgent I had to attend to first. I ordered the *mantoor* to summon all the labourers to the yard, even those who'd gone far out into the veld with the sheep. I waited in silence for them all to come home. Then, one by one, I had them tied to the front wheel of the wagon and flogged by the *mantoor*, every one of them, man, woman and child; thirty-nine lashes for each grown-up, and twenty-five for a child. The *mantoor* was last; I flogged him myself. Only then, after they'd all had their share, did I speak. "Let this be a lesson to you," I told them, "should you ever get it in your heads to rise up against me. Now go back to your work and finish whatever you were doing." Then I went into the house, and kissed Alida, and sat down to eat.

I've never had trouble with slaves all my life. Now I've been shamed by my sons. And all because of Galant, brought up, one might say, like a child on my own farm. Lord, consider Thy Servant Job.

GALANT

High up in the mountains, in the solid rock, lies the footprint of a man. The mark of Bushman or Khoikhoin, says Ma-Rose, imprinted in the sunrise of the world when stone was soft; perhaps the mark of Heitsi-Eibib himself, the Great Hunter of her stories, or Tsui-Goab's, when he came down to shape men from stones. I dream about that footprint. Imagine leaving your mark like that, in stone, forever, come wind or rain. My own tracks cover the length and breadth of the Bokkeveld, the tracks of child and man. Across the farmyard of Lagenvlei and that of Houd-den-Bek, through the veld with its ditches and stone ridges, up the broken slopes and into the many mountains. Footprints marking my treks into the Karoo, with Ontong and Achilles and the sheep, in search of warmer winter grazing. Footprints in search of runaway sheep or hunting down marauders, including that one lion. Footprints up to the dam, mine with those of Nicolaas and Barend, and Hester's narrow ones. Barefoot, all four of us. Except for Sundays or visiting days, when their tracks show the marks of shoes.

"Ma-Rose, why do you and I always walk barefoot?"

"That's how it is."

"I also want shoes, for the thorns."

"Only masters wear shoes."

Tracks. Tracks. Across the mountains to Tulbagh, to Worcester, some of them marked with blood. Runaway tracks. Homeward tracks. Yet none of them visible, gone in wind and rain. They're there, but you cannot see them. No sunrise footprints these, forever marked in stone.

Look at my feet. Look hard, at every mark and crack and scar and callus from toe to heel, tough, hard as horn. It's all my wanderings through the Bokkeveld you can see here, summer and winter, and drought and frost. Here it is marked, grass and stone, mountain and plain, earth and water, house and hut, everything. With my feet I'm glued to this world, and there is no escape.

I cannot say: this—and then that—and then that. All the tracks run together. Look at my feet.

Always coming back to Ma-Rose. Ma-Rose smelling of dung-fire and buchu, warm as a kaross protecting you against the world, surrounding you like an attic filled with smells. Ma-Rose with her cure for every ill. Buchu for the bladder, touch-me-not for gargling, wild garlic for croup and honey-tea to cheer you up, bitter roots for colic, dagga for sore eyes, aloe for the stomach, little davids for constipation, something for everything. And stories for all occasions. There are the water-weeds you're not allowed to touch because they're the spirits of girls who offended the rain: and rain is to be treated with respect, otherwise it sends the lightning to kill you and turn you into a weed in the marsh. —There are the night-walkers running about in the dark accompanied by their owls and baboons: moving backwards, and carrying diseases to naughty children; it's the night-walker women who come to a man in his dreams and make him hard and draw his seed from him leaving him weak and weary in the morning; and it's the night-walker men who visit a woman in her sleep to plant the seed of dead children in her womb and turn her insides bitter so that she will never look at an ordinary man again. —There's Tsui-Goab who made the world and all the people, and rain and sun and wind and fire; and Gaunab who lives in the night and rules over all that happens in the dark. —And there's the Lightning Bird that scorches the grass where it settles to lay its egg which burrows into the earth in search of moisture. There it lies abiding its time, swelling and growing, until the clouds start thundering overhead again: then a new Lightning Bird is hatched. The lightning is its spittle, and the clouds its dark wings spread out over the world. —Such are the stories of Ma-Rose. And whenever I cannot sleep she holds me close to her, uttering the sounds of a mother-hen as she caresses me, taking my

41

small member in her hand and rubbing it, ever so gently, until my feet leave the ground and I begin to drift away like a cloud over the mountains, far away, beyond the Cape that Nicolaas has told me about, beyond everything, and I fall asleep.

Always Ma-Rose. Tied in a bundle on her back while she goes about her work, kneeling to rub the floor, or leaning over the open hearth to reach the copper pots and the black kettle, stirring me to sleep. She remains close even when I start helping her in the house, sorting knives and spoons from the wash-up tub, or filling with firewood the large square box beside the hearth, fetching and carrying under the watchful eye of the Mistress, the Ounooi Alida. Then out to the yard. Gradually my own footprints begin to mark the ground. The harness of the farm settles on me. "If you work well, we'll get along," the Oubaas says, "but if you're cheeky or neglect your work, it's the strap. Right?" "Yes, Oubaas." From now on it's no longer Ma-Rose but Ontong who supervises me and shows me the ropes. But she is always there to return to.

In the beginning the work is easy. Gathering wood or dung-cakes. Feeding the chickens and keeping them out of the vegetable garden. Chasing birds in the wheatfields and the orchards in summer: the sun blazing down until you can hardly see straight as you march up and down beating a bucket with a stick and shouting yourself hoarse. Long before sunrise the cicadas start screeching, going on till dark on one single note. Your shirt sticks to your back like an old tough hide. And when you stagger home at dusk it's time to give Achilles a hand with the milking. Not to mention the eggs. If the nests are full, there's no problem. But when the hens abandon the nests it means roaming about in search of eggs until it's too dark to see—only to find, very often, that they've been stolen by an otter or a leguan. With an aching body you drag yourself back to Ma-Rose's hut, its door ajar and a candle burning, dark-yellow, inside. You're almost too exhausted to eat. All you want to do is lie down and sleep. But more often than not there's no room for me because a man has taken my place on the mattress beside her; and I have to make myself comfortable somewhere else. Some nights it's the Oubaas who's visiting her, then I'm warned well in time not to come home but to take my kaross to Ontong's hut. In summer I simply bed down in the grass near the furrow, where one can lie on one's back and watch the stars above; sometimes the moon is so bright it seems to be shining right inside your head. Yet even before you have properly drifted off there's Ma-Rose's voice shouting:

"Galant, the morning-star is fading. Don't keep the Oubaas waiting."

When it's harvesting time I follow the reapers to pick up the stalks and ears dropped by the less experienced men. But soon I'm one of them, and this is no longer child's work. Bending, swinging your arm, swinging your whole body as you stride ahead with every swish of the blade, trying to keep up with the rest of the row; swaggering or bragging when the day is still young; when someone farts there's no end to the joking. But as the day wears on in that sun the men grow silent. It's gruelling work not to fall behind, and if you do the foreman's sjambok flicks over your buttocks or back—sometimes merely teasing, a brief warning, but if he suspects you of malingering that thin switch cuts a clean line right through shirt or trousers, leaving its burn till nighttime. Once the wheat is down, the wagon must be loaded, the tall stack expertly strapped down for the swaying journey to the shed, there to dry out properly over Christmas.

On the first windy day after New Year the threshing starts. It's what I prefer to all the other work on the farm. Watch your step with those milling horses or you're trampled right there with the wheat. Treading and grinding, up to their chests in straw, round and round, the great hooves thundering past. Until the Oubaas or the foreman decides it's time to break. Then the shout comes: "Take 'em away!" and as soon as they're out of the way there's another shout: "Turn over!" One's arms are almost torn from the shoulders, lifting and turning the fork with its heavy load of chaff and grain. The straw is worked out of the way with the long wooden forks, over and over, leaving the grain cleaner every time round, until it is ready for the shifters and winnowing-fans whose swooshing sound will persecute you into your very dreams at night. At last, the West wind now steady and strong, the

43

winnowing starts, the chaff forming small speckled clouds overhead, hanging in the wind before they drift off as the heavy grains rain down on the hard floor. Shovel and up and over, shovel and up and over. It's like dancing. Sweat prickling all over your body, as the faces of the men around you turn grey in the chaff, leaving only their eyes exposed, glistening moistly in the dust. Your throat gets dried out, but there's no time to rest. While the wind lasts the winnowing must go on, until the last dirt and chaffdust has been cleared away and the bags are filled and taken off to the wheat-loft. This is a final test of strength: and you're not a man unless you can walk up the stone stairs to the loft with a full bag on your shoulders. "Hup! Whoa!" And at last it is flung down and stacked with the rest.

It is at Lagenvlei that harvesting and threshing usually begin; from there we work our way round the mountain, past Houdden-Bek as far as the turn-off at Wagendrift. One farm after the other. When you've cut your way through them all you know you can do a man's work.

The harvest home, the year gradually quietens down, except for the bean-harvest and the vineyards; but in these parts there isn't much treading to do, nothing like across the mountains in the winelands of Tulbagh and Worcester. Oubaas Piet keeps just enough grapes for his couple of half-aums of brandy every year. And once the wine has fermented on the husks, buzzing and rumbling like a bees' nest, he personally takes charge. For two or three days he never comes home, even eating his meals beside the still, and sleeping there at night, if he sleeps at all. For the following week, while he tastes the new brew, he is worse than a wounded buffalo. But we have a good time all the same, for he is generous with the faints.

At this stage the beans have also been harvested and the fruit picked and dried; the swallows are gathering on the cliffs and the first frost is forming pale patches on the grass in the mornings, brittle underfoot. It is time to bring in great stacks of dung and wood—good hard *tkoin*-wood that will smoulder right through a long cold night—for winter descends very suddenly on the Bokkeveld; and the kraals and stables must be prepared for those

44

animals that will stay behind on the farm while we take the sheep to the warmer grazelands of the Karoo. The men who remain on the farm will weed out new lands and burn the stacks of dry shrubs; and before the cold North-wester has died down ploughing will start. And soon the whole familiar round begins anew, your footsoles cracked and numb with frost, and the drop at the end of your nose frozen into a permanent icicle. No respite. Yet it is wholesome too, winter and summer each at its appointed time and you in step with them, it's like a heartbeat going on and on. You can't break away from it; but it keeps you going. In a way every year is different, of course. One year a great thunderstorm or a flood; the next, a freak wind or a drought, or oxen breaking out of their kraal, or sheep freezing to death, chickens dying of sunstroke, a leopard coming from the mountains to drag off lambs or calves, a flock of springbok or hartebeest trekking across the farm in a cloud of dust, baboons devastating the orchards, a dam wall breaking, someone maimed or killed in an accident, a child falling into a pot of boiling water. Always something new, something different. But the broad course of the seasons runs unchanged. Pasturing and ploughing in winter; sowing in spring; harvesting in summer; bringing in the beans and grapes in autumn. And then the new beginning.

The Oubaas sees to it that I am broken in thoroughly, taking turns with all the different kinds of work to check my strengths and weaknesses. A few seasons in succession I'm sent to the grazing lands with the shepherds, across the Black Hills down to the shrubby plains of the Karoo. I go hunting with the boys, taking turns with the big gun, and hell to pay if you waste powder or lead. I'm tried out at leading the oxen; I'm even given a few turns at driving the wagon and wielding the long rhino whip. This is the province of Achilles; but it's Ontong who teaches me to ride and work with horses. I like the wagon—the joy when a mere flick of the long whip and a series of shouts urge the oxen into action, all straining together, yokes creaking and thongs stretched taut—but nothing can compare with the horses. From the very first day I think of them as mine; I can work with them for hours, and when I talk to them they seem to understand every word.

The big grey stallion. It is with a peeled eye that I watch him, ever since the drizzly early morning when, without Ontong to help me, I find myself thrusting an arm shoulder-deep into the mare to ease him out. A wild creature, the very devil of a horse, meant for veld and mountains, not for yard or stable. Looking at him I can feel my guts turn in desire. In my deepest sleep he comes galloping through my dreams, from nowhere to nowhere, as wild as the wind. But he's been set aside for Barend. Goddamit, why? What does Barend care about horses? That stallion will break his neck.

"Today we're going to break in Barend's horse," the Oubaas announces one morning. It's like lightning hitting me in the stomach, and I gasp for breath. Barend's horse? He's mine. My grey stallion.

A horse like that should be tethered to a tame one for a week; preferably he should have one on either side. But this stallion has never allowed anyone near him, so today it's all or nothing.

"You take him, Barend, he's yours," calls the Oubaas. Barend is shit-scared, anyone can see that, but he's keeping a tight jaw to impress his father. The grey is being held by four strong men, but almost effortlessly he pulls them this way and that, like half-filled bags. It takes Barend a lot of effort to mount and steady himself, but he's hardly hit the saddle when the stallion sends him tumbling through the air and ploughing a wet trail through the deep manure of the kraal.

"Come on, Barend, up you get."

The Oubaas doesn't let a man off so easily. This time the men try to hold on for a bit longer before they let go. Barend has time to pull up his knees and to dig his heels firmly into the great animal's flanks. But once again the horse pulls in his neck and kicks up his hind legs, throws him back into the dung, landing this time against the wooden gate which winds him.

"Come on, Barend, what's the matter with you?"

After the third fall Barend refuses to get up again, defying even his father's ready sjambok. Tears have formed white streaks in the green dung covering his face.

"You try, Nicolaas."

Nicolaas is four years younger, not nearly as strong as Barend, and almost before he's started he finds himself back on the ground, a sorry bundle. Now it's Ontong's turn, and he is an old hand at breaking horses, a knack they say he's brought from Batavia. But Ontong is also thrown, after a single raging gallop round the kraal; and before he can be caught again the stallion clears the wall in one wild bound and is gone. It takes two full days to track him down and bring him to the kraal again.

Once more the Oubaas orders Barend to get on the horse. And when he lands in the dung the first time, head first, his father wallops him with the sjambok on his up-ended unprotected backside. Another try; another landing with a thud and a skid. In spite of the sjambok Barend refuses to get up again. Then Nicolaas. Then Ontong. And each time a rider comes flying through the air something inside me jumps with joy and I feel like shouting: That's it, that's it, my beauty, throw the lot of them, for you're mine.

Suddenly the Oubaas says: "Your turn, Galant."

A rush of fear numbs me. I can feel my knees knocking together. How can anyone be expected to ride lightning or the wind?

"What does he know about riding?" asks Barend, still shaking with angry sobs and nursing a bloody knee.

"Let him try."

"It'll be the death of him," says Ontong, clearly upset.

"No. Let him try."

I scramble on to the back of the grey while they hold him tight, catching the rein round my wrist in a loop and drawing up my knees in a firm grip. My eyes are misty and I can feel my stomach rising to my throat, but somehow I manage to croak: "All right, let him go."

Like a blue flash he bolts with me. Holding on like a tick, thinking of nothing else except to stay put, I survive the first few bucking rounds in the kraal. For brief breathless moments it feels as if he's sprouted wings, as if we're soaring right across the wall and the mountains. Then it's down again, my arse hitting the saddle in a blow fit to crunch a backbone. Once I land on my

47

balls, sending a taste of green gall into my mouth, blacking out my eyes. Still I manage to hold on, thinking grimly: Even if you kill me I won't let go. Up he goes again. Then down, head drawn in, hind legs thrown into the air. It feels as if my arms are plucked right from their sockets. But I hold on.

He makes a rush straight at the gate, obviously intending to throw his full weight against it and crush me. Just in time someone flings it wide open, tumbling head-over-heels out of the way. And there we go. I've never known a horse to run like that. Thundering across the veld, drawing a stream of tears from my eyes. Very suddenly, he stops, nearly shooting me right over his head. Another bout of rearing and bucking. Then he sets off towards the dam, galloping madly, the booming of his hooves drowning out all other sound. All right, I think, drown me if you wish. I still won't let go. For now I've recognized the frenzy in him and I know he's scared too, and of me. We charge into the dam at full speed, spraying us with mud and water. If he decides to roll over now, I think, I'll be drowned. But I swear to all the gods of Ma-Rose and the Oubaas: if he does that I'll hold him under until he drowns with me.

At that moment, in the middle of his maddest madness, he suddenly stops dead. For a moment the great body remains tense. Then I can feel the muscles relax, trembling like water.

"Come on," I say gently. And when we reach the side of the dam, I say: "Hoho," patting him on the neck. His whole body stands shivering beneath me. He is flecked with foam, white with saltpetre. With wobbly legs I slide from his back and blindly pluck handfuls of grass to rub him dry. He makes no move, utters no sound, only stands there shivering as if in cold. After a long time I take the reins and begin to lead him back to the yard. In the distance I can see the men running towards me from the kraal. They must have expected to find me dead. As I reach them, they stand aside in silence to let me pass. I lead the grey to the gate of the kraal. But there is no feeling in me. It is as if something has died inside me the moment the fury left him. As meek as a donkey he follows me into the kraal, while a desperate urge inside me silently shouts at him to break loose again, for God's sake, and to

48

gallop away to where no one, not even I, will ever find him again. But the madness has gone from him. One can see it in his eyes, moist and round and mild as any cow's.

"Well done, Galant," says the Oubaas. "You've broken him in properly. You can have him now."

"No," I stammer bluntly, angrily. "It's Barend's horse."

Let him have it, I think as I stumble away from them. For I swear I'll never forgive the grey stallion for this. To have allowed himself to be broken in so shamefully. I walk back to the dam and hurl myself into the water, trying ridiculously to drown myself; then lying, panting, on the side to recover, wishing something would wipe out the memory of this miserable day. By the time Barend and Nicolaas come to join me there is no anger left, only a dull sadness which I will not share with them.

The dam has its own way of soothing grief; it is as motherly as Ma-Rose. Our tracks lie all over the farm; but it is to the dam we always return. A gritty mudwall on the lower side, a grass-covered slope above; and willows with the nests of weaver-birds hanging down almost to the surface of the muddy water. These nests are constantly raided: and more than once there's a snake curled up inside. Then you simply let go and tumble back into the water shrieking with exquisite fright. I'm always the one sent to scout for snakes before the others follow; likewise, I must test the springy branches to make sure they will support our weight. If one breaks, I am the one to fall, while they dance and roll about laughing. But it doesn't put me off. As long as the nests are there we will go after them. At other times we have mud fights, lasting until only the whites of our eyes are visible. Or we duck one another to see who can last longest, emerging more dead than alive since no one is prepared to give up first. Some days we take the dogs with us, the males, and hidden behind the mudwall reach for their pricks to pump them, feeling the tight muscle contract into a knob in our hands as each excitedly cheers on his victim, to see which will be the first to shoot: the tension heightened by a sense of danger, since some of them, as the spurting approaches, will snarl and snap at one without warning. Often, tired of games and swimming, we simply lie about naked

49

on the grass, chewing reeds or rushes and staring up at the clouds to see who can make out the most unlikely shapes: a cow with a huge udder, a team of oxen, a wagon, a face, a grasping hand, a shoe, a woman's breast, a heron, a hammerhead. Sometimes we linger so long that we forget about the work we have abandoned—birds are ravaging the wheatfields, and there are sheep to be rounded up, cows to be milked, wood to be chopped, a vegetable garden to be dug. And when we try to sneak back unnoticed, the Oubaas is there waiting.

Not that it scares one off for long. The very next day we are back at the dam. It is of course easier for Barend and Nicolaas who have less work than I. Mine never really stops, and Achilles or Ontong is always there to keep an eye. But no matter how hard the work, I always slink back to the dam. That is where most of the footprints of my childhood lead to. And it is always best when Nicolaas and I are alone, which happens more often than not, for Barend has outgrown us very soon.

One afternoon, still wet from swimming, the two of us start digging a hole into the earth wall on the lower side. At first we're looking for a rat we've seen burrowing. But soon the rat is forgotten, yet our digging goes on. Deeper and deeper into the sand, our wet shoulders touching. The earth is waterlogged and crumbling, quite different from the hard clay near the outlet. Our feet, soles turned up, still feel the sun; behind us lies the whole afternoon world of weaver-birds and water; but here we're burrowing into the gullet of the earth, as eager and untiring as worms.

But suddenly the tunnel caves in on us. One moment we're still digging and scooping: then there is a strange motion all around and everything is clogged with sand—eyes, nose, ears, mouth. Huddled together in shock, we try to push ourselves up into a kneeling position, to force open some breathing space. We're going to die like this, I realize; and I no longer know whether it's my body heaving and shuddering, or his.

When at last I manage to cough and throw up, it is daylight again and I can see Ontong's legs, and others, around us, standing like trees.

50

"Please don't tell Pa!" Nicolaas is pleading. "He'll kill us. Won't he, Galant?"

"He'll kill us dead," I say, spitting and spluttering.

Long after the men have left, the two of us remain there together in the darkening day, two boys who have discovered death together.

That is what I cannot understand. For at this very dam where our tracks merge they also run apart, his in one direction, mine in another. And all because of the writing, it seems to me. Their mother, the Ounooi, has been teaching them for a long time to read and write: I know, because they always talk about it at the dam. And one day Nicolaas flattens a patch of the clay, and smooths it with his palm, and with a twig draws a series of strange marks on it, lines and curls and squiggles like the tracks of some small animal. "What's this?" he challenges me. "How must I know?" I reply. "Looks like the spoor of a chameleon."

"It's my name," says Nicolaas. "See?—It spells *Nicolaas*." It still looks rather suspect to me. "How come," I say, "that you can be standing over there and your name is lying in the clay here?" He laughs again. "I tell you it's my name." He traces the separate marks: "Ni-co-laas." Then he wipes it out and draws a new row of marks: "This is Barend's name." Whereupon Barend starts throwing mud at us, and the lesson gives way to our more usual cavorting in the water.

But a few days later, when Barend is off into the veld with the Oubaas, I drag Nicolaas back to the dam. "Put down your name in the clay again," I tell him.

"Why?"

"I want to see."

He shrugs, and draws the marks as he did before. For a long time I sit on my haunches studying them, tracing their outline with one finger.

"Can you put down my name too?"

"Of course."

"Show me."

He smooths a new square and draws new signs in the wet clay. "Is that my name?"

"Yes. It says *Galant*."

I find it hard to believe. If you look down into a still pond you can see your own face looking up at you; and when you start moving to and fro, or pulling faces, that other you does the same. It's a strange thing to see, but in a way one can understand it. But these tiny tracks marking my name, *Galant*, confuse me.

"Leave it just like that," I tell him when we undress for swimming. And, having covered the marks very carefully with leaves and twigs, I let them lie undisturbed until the next time when Barend is also with us. Without giving him any warning I uncover the marks and ask him point-blank: "What's that?"

"Why, it's your name," he says. "*Galant*."

So I know it must be true.

"I want you to teach me to make those marks and to read them," I ask Nicolaas.

"All right," he says.

But Barend stops him rudely. "Why bother? He's only a slave boy. What use is writing to him? It won't help him to bring in the cattle or to cut wheat or chop wood."

"Will you teach me, Nicolaas?" I repeat.

He stares at me with a little frown between his eyes. Absently, with a shrug of annoyance, he throws a pebble at a frog. "I suppose Barend is right," he says at last. "Writing is no use to you at all, you know. Come on, see who's in the water first."

That night one of the Bokkeveld's wild thunderstorms breaks out over the farm; and when I return to the dam the next day there is no trace of the marks in the clay. It is as if they've never been there.

"They don't want to teach me to write, Ma-Rose," I complain to her. "Will you show me?"

"What do I know about writing? All my life I got on very well without. It's just looking for trouble. You keep your eyes open and you'll see: every time there's a newspaper from the Cape the Oubaas is out of sorts for days and days."

The Cape must be a wonderful place; and the newspaper is a truly wonderful thing. When they talk about it they call it the *Gazette*; and by the very name you can hear it doesn't belong to these parts. There's no telling when it will come, that depends on who's going to Tulbagh and for what. Sometimes there's only one; but when a long time has passed there may be a whole stack, all of them thin and mysteriously folded. Then the Oubaas puts on the small round glasses he uses to read the Book at supper, and he drags his chair outside the kitchen door, and there he sits reading, frowning and mumbling by himself, for many hours. It's better to stay out of his way on such days. Afterwards the newspaper is put away in a yellowwood *kist* in the front room, Ma-Rose tells me, so it must be very valuable. From time to time an old one, curiously yellowed, may reappear: in the wood-box beside the hearth, or for wrapping eggs when the wagon goes to Tulbagh. But mostly it is kept quite out of sight, and not to be touched by slave or Khoin, Ma-Rose warns, for it is a thing with a dark life of its own and she has no remedy for it.

In the past it has never bothered me. But this once, after Nicolaas has refused to teach me, I decide to do the unthinkable. For days, for weeks perhaps, I stay on the prowl in the yard, keeping a close watch on all the comings and goings, until at last the Field-cornet arrives with a new newspaper. After allowing the Oubaas enough time to read right through it and vent his bad temper on everybody in sight, I wait for a chance to slip into the house and filch it from its hiding-place in the front room. It is thin enough to wear close to my skin, under my shirt, for fully five or six days, until I'm quite sure they won't miss it any more. Then, at last, all by myself in the veld with the sheep, I carefully take it out and unfold it on a flat rock, straightening out the worst creases. With my fingers I nudge and prod the rows upon rows of small black tracks running like ants across the smooth paper; I even press my face against it to smell it. But it says nothing to me. And yet I know only too well it must be speaking of the marvels of the Cape.

Ever since their first visit Nicolaas and Barend are trying to outdo one another in their accounts of that distant, incredible place; and when they run out of stories I ply them with new questions, pumping their memories the way we pump the dogs behind the dam wall, until I'm left quite dazed with new thoughts and images. The streets crossing each other in straight lines, paved with flat stones. The Mountain, higher than any of ours, its top as flat as a table. The big dam they call the sea, endless, bigger than the whole Bokkeveld, its water alive and moving all the time. And ships taller than houses, arriving from lands beyond this sea, further than the horizon. Flags on the rump of the mountain, and a cannon booming every day at noon, scaring the pigeons in the streets. Horse races where one can win a fortune in a single day. People with splendid clothes and tall hats. Houses where you may buy anything you can think of. And even slaves, they say, are allowed to keep their own shops there and get rich; and although they go barefoot like us their clothes are as fine as any gentleman's. Once Nicolaas brings me a scarf from the Cape, of fine red silk; another time it's a conical hat; strange things I've never held in my hands before. Some place, this Cape.

"You wait," I tell Ma-Rose at night. "One day I'm going there to see for myself."

"Says who?"

"Says I."

"It's not for you to say. It's the Oubaas."

"The day I go to the Cape, Ma-Rose, I won't ask anybody. I'll just go. And I'll take you with me."

"I've seen the place before."

"Is it really like Nicolaas says it is?"

She sits staring through the open door of the hut to where the evening shadows are gathering. "Yes," she says at last, her voice almost too low to hear. "Yes, the Cape is truly a wonderful place. But it's not our place. It belongs to the Honkhoikwa, the White people."

"Why can't it be ours too, Ma-Rose?"

"That's not for you to ask."

And in the silence of that maddening newspaper, spread open on the flat hard rock, I hear those taunting words again: in silence the rows of black ants run across the paper, telling wild stories of the place that haunts my dreams. But all they say to me is: *It's not for you to ask.*

54

I start shouting abuse at them, but they give no answer. Here's a curse for the bloody cunt of your own mother! The small black tracks remain unmoved. In rage I start tearing the paper to shreds, crumpling the bits, trampling on them, hurling them against the wind, winnowing them like chaff so that they may blow to the end of the earth, back to the Cape they came from, into the blue flames of the Oubaas's own hell.

Yes, go to hell. I don't need your goddamned newspaper. And why should I write my name on clay? I know it without seeing its marks. Galant is my name.

And yet. If only someone would tell me. Show me. What have I done, what am I, to be kept in this darkness? A horse locked up in a stable. The darkness of an attic.

Why doesn't Nicolaas help me? He's different. No. He is like the rest. Whatever doubt I may have had is cleared away by the lion, although the lion itself remains a mystery. Down in the Karoo one sometimes still finds the odd marauding male, depending on the rains and the movement of game; but not in these parts, not in our Bokkeveld. Perhaps it is the drought, one of the worst ever, that has forced it so far away from its usual hunting fields, or the agony of age or of hunger. Whatever the reason, the lion is suddenly in our midst. The first we know about its presence is when sheep start disappearing from the kraal at night. Must be a leopard from the mountains, says the Oubaas. But the tracks are much too big for that. Then a slave child on a neighbouring farm is dragged from its hut one evening; and a great roar is heard in the dark. From all the farms in the Bokkeveld the men come down with their dogs and their slaves, a proper army on horseback and on foot, armed with guns and assegais and sticks, whatever comes to hand. The three of us are with them, Barend and Nicolaas and I; for we're not children any more, and Barend is soon to be married.

Now watch out, the Oubaas warns gravely, standing in the yard like a tree with the sun behind him, his hair like a great mane, and shining. This is a matter of life and death, he says; he's seen men maimed and killed before.

In the beginning the tracks run boldly through the open veld; it

55

seems only a matter of time before we run the lion to ground. But after a while they begin to curve back into the foothills where it becomes more and more difficult to follow them. The army is split up in small groups, each with at least one gun. Nicolaas and I are together, with a handful of slaves and Hottentots. Soon the others are out of sight.

The first hour or so one is very cautious and very alert. You notice everything on your way. Insects in the grass; lizards scurrying across rocks; a meerkat on its hind legs in front of its burrow; an anteater digging up a termites' nest; small quail and *kiewiets*; a secretary bird strutting along on stiff legs like the Oubaas of a Sunday morning; a small steenbuck and its ewe motionless in the dried grass; a speckled puffadder; a tortoise hurrying along slowly and deliberately on its way; a swarm of bees in a hollow tree; the specks of vultures circling in the distance; cobwebs glittering with dew. But as the sun grows warmer and the sweat starts trickling down your back, you become less attentive. In the silent heat you begin to feel drowsy. Which is why we get caught so unawares.

All of a sudden there is something moving in a patch of dry protea shrubs, barely a hundred yards away. It can be anything. But you simply know it's the lion, even though you've never seen one in your life. Nicolaas gives another step forward. The thing in the bushes utters a low, deep growling sound that causes the ground to tremble underfoot. The men with us drop their sticks and assegais in a wild stampede for the nearest shelter, a single thin dry tree. In a moment they hang from its branches as if a flock of large bats have swarmed into it. I find it so funny that I burst out laughing.

But already the lion is charging, head down, dark mane streaming.

"Shoot, Nicolaas!" I whisper excitedly.

I see him raise the gun. But his hands are trembling too much.

"Shoot, damn you!" I shout.

In sudden panic he throws down the gun, looks round wildly, and starts running towards the overloaded tree. For a moment I'm too shocked to move. The lion comes streaking past me, only a few yards away without even looking at me. There's no way Nicolaas can reach that tree in time. It's all over. Except that a great invisible fist seems to grab me, causing me to do things I don't even know about. The gun. The barrel trembling, then steadying itself. The sound of the shot, which sends me staggering back until my legs simply give way and I sit down in a thornbush. Madness. I could have killed Nicolaas.

Everything is dead quiet, as if a giant horse has suddenly been reined in. One moment I can still hear Nicolaas shouting something. Then the lion is on top of him. Both tumble down in a small cloud of dust. Then the men come falling and scrambling down from the little tree. Nicolaas sits up slowly and starts dusting himself very meticulously. I start running, my arms flailing. We grab each other, dancing and laughing in mad joy.

From all sides the other hunters come on running.

"Good God," the Oubaas says. "Well done."

"It was a near thing," I hear Nicolaas say. "He almost got Galant. I was just in time."

I stare at the others. Is no one going to say anything? All they seem to be able to do is grin stupidly, staring past me. Then they shoulder me out of the way to get closer to the lion, to kneel beside it and touch it and look at its worn and broken teeth, to comb their fingers through its knotted mane.

"On its last legs," the Oubaas says. "Probably couldn't catch buck any more. So he was driven from his pride and became a loner. Must have got desperate in this drought." He lights his pipe with a grin of satisfaction. "Watch out when you skin him. Don't want to spoil it. We'll dress the skin for Nicolaas."

When we are alone again at last I ask him: "Suppose I tell the Oubaas it wasn't you?"

"Why don't you?" he snarls. "You think he'll take a slave's word against mine?"

Now he really is one of them. I don't understand. Again the darkness, the attic closing in on all sides. Is there no light at all? Is there no one who will not betray me?

Hester?

Wherever our footprints lead, hers follow. Neither abuse nor

57

stones will drive her away once she's set her mind to it. Even the Oubaas and the Ounooi, I've noticed, get desperate with her at times. They try everything, including the strap, but she's a stubborn girl. Barend and Nicolaas often get mad at her if she insists on coming with us; they only relent if I offer to carry her on my back. I don't mind. She isn't much of a load.

What she seems to like most is to go to the dam with us, sitting in the grass or on the earth wall watching us, knees drawn up, chin resting on her hands; on such days we seem to go out of our way to show off to her. As she grows more used to us—her father, the foreman on Houd-den-Bek, is dead; she's come to live with the Oubaas and Ounooi—she becomes less aloof; in the end we're all splashing and swimming together.

Then, out of the blue that, too, changes. It's been a bad winter with early snow, and lasting longer than other years; on our way back from the Karoo with the sheep we lose countless lambs. And even after the swallows have come back there's a late heavy frost. So it's much later than usual when the weather turns warm enough for us to go up along the quince hedge, back to our dam. We all seem to have grown in winter; my clothes feel tight. And we're unruly as young foals sniffing the wind. On this first day of the new summer the girl is also with us, as before, after the unduly long break of winter.

But when we come to the end of the quince hedge Barend stops and looks very sternly at me: "Galant, we're going swimming with Hester. You can't come with."

"Why not? We always go together."

"From now on you stay away when she's there."

As I look in amazement from one to the other, Nicolaas butts in: "I heard Pa calling you a while ago. You'd better go and see."

Disgusted, stunned, I turn away, stopping again to watch them at a distance as they trot up the rise to the dam. In a flush of anger I pick up a stone and hurl it after them, but they're already out of sight. In the orchard I can hear bees buzzing. From the dam, as I strain to listen, I imagine their shouts of glee. And the weaver-birds. But there is a great silence between me and them, a silence following me all the way as I slowly walk up the mountain on my own. Looking down from time to time I feel an intruder here, a stranger arrived from elsewhere, and ill at ease among these mountains and ridges and plains, the young wheat in the distance and the patches of barley; although I know that, invisible, my footprints cover it all.

We've always been together, haven't we? They're my mates. What earthly difference does it make whether the girl is with us or not? It's like being part of a group of people and listening to someone telling a story; but halfway through you grow tired and fall asleep, to wake up again with a start much later and hear the same story going on: yet something is different now, you've missed out on something and now it's lost forever; and although everything seems familiar it is really altogether different and you no longer belong with them.

High above the farmstead I sit down on a boulder from where I can look out over everything that has just been denied me. I can feel the rage building up again, a horse inside me straining against the reins to break free. Pressing hard against one of the boulders poised below me I feel it shift slightly under my weight. Putting my full force behind it I push and heave, panting heavily, trying again and again until, at last, it gives way, balanced for a moment on the edge of the ridge below, then toppling over and rolling down, gathering speed, tearing smaller rocks and stones with it, in ever greater bounds, with a noise like thunder, and striking sparks from whatever gets in its way. Suppose the sparks set the grass alight? Suppose I start a mountain fire and it rages all the way down from here to the wheatlands of the farm below? Let it burn. Let it all burn down. I'll be the maker of thunderstorms!

How well I remember the other storm. It feels so close, I can clutch it like a stone. The drowsy Sunday afternoon, the Oubaas and Ounooi gone to visit neighbours, the three of us roaming the mountainside, shouting at baboons on the upper cliffs, scaring each other with the forged footprints of a leopard. Then the storm, the sudden thundering peal as if the mountain itself is crashing down on us. We scuttle down the slope in fear, Barend and Nicolaas far ahead, lightfooted, leaving me behind to cope with Hester.

"Let's stay here," she pleads. "I love thunderstorms."

"It'll kill us," I say. "Hurry!"

"No." She clutches my arm. "Stop. Please wait, Galant. Look: lift up your face like this. Feel the rain."

Angrily I tug at her hand. "If the thunder doesn't kill us, the Oubaas will."

"Look. Oh look. Did you see that flash?"

"If the Lightning Bird sees you you're dead on the spot. Now come."

"Galant, stay with me!"

Desperate, I pick her up to carry her down forcibly. She kicks and shouts at me, trying to break loose. We both fall down, grazing knees and elbows.

"Now look at what you've done."

"Just listen to that, Galant!"

But at last we're down the slope, where Ma-Rose's hut stands proudly apart from the others. We're soaked. I am too scared to face the Oubaas with this drenched child; and I know I can't count on the boys to shield me. My teeth chattering, and trembling as much with fear as with cold, I kick open the rickety door of the hut and we tumble inside, into the heavy smell of smoke and buchu and Ma-Rose.

"Look at you!" she scolds, but her voice sounds more comforting than angry. In her quick, matter-of-fact way she strips the clothes from us and spreads them round the fire to dry while we are bundled into a large kaross of dassie and meerkat and jackal skins. Then comes the smell of sweet bush-tea, and its fierce heat spreads through me as we sit huddled together, slowly giving way to the smelly warmth of the hut, close and safe and comforting as an attic.

Prodded by Hester, Ma-Rose begins to tell us stories to pass the time while the clothes are drying at the fireside. All the stories I've known from my baby days. The water-weed you're not allowed to pick; and the night-walkers, men and women, with owls and baboons as bodyguards; and Tsui-Goab; and the Lightning Bird that lays its eggs in the scorched ground. One story after another in that fragrant dark, the fire burning low on the *tkoin*-wood

60

coals, small blue flames flickering and dancing, breaking out in flurries of sparks like fireflies, while we sink away into the warmth of our large kaross—and the smell of tea and herbs, of buchu and lard and woodfire—our bodies huddled together as, once before, long ago, Nicolaas and I in our caved-in hollow; except that in this closeness I feel no fear, there is neither hurry nor need to get out; this is all I ever want, this secret dark warmth, with the girl-child sleeping beside me, her head on my shoulder, and my hand moving almost by itself under the kaross, caressing her in the way Ma-Rose puts me to sleep at night, gently and evenly, touching and exploring in the unforbidding dark, a world as secret and wonderful as the tracks of one's name on the smoothness of clay. Until I, too, drift off to sleep; and when I wake up, sometime in the night, the girl has gone and I'm lying beside Ma-Rose again, on the mattress in the corner, her soft warm body against me, her hand stroking me back into sleep.

Can it be true?

Galant, it is not for you to ask.

But it must be true. For my body remembers. Only, it makes it even more difficult to understand. Like the attic. Always back to that one dark moment. And why? There's nothing special about it at all—

Whenever we can find a reason we scramble up the ladder to the attic. Its unforgettable smells: bunches of onions hanging from the beams; pumpkins and pomegranates; the sweet-sour quinces in winter; the two yellowwood coffins filled to the brim with raisins and dried peaches and apricots; the all-pervading smell of bush-tea, plucked in the mountains and warmed in the baking oven to "sweat", then thrashed with whips and spread out to dry on the broad floorboards of the attic. Endless afternoons are spent up there, mostly Nicolaas and I; sometimes Hester too; or Barend. Only this once I am alone. I don't know where the others are; it doesn't matter. I've come here to be alone. I, Galant, in the house of the Oubaas. To see what it is like when they're alone down here. (Ma-Rose, why do they live in a house, and we in a hut?—Galant, it's not for you to ask.) I must know. There must be an answer.

I crawl along the beams to the front of the house, to the long narrow slit between two boards. From all the times I've been inside the house with Ma-Rose it has no secret for me; it's an easy place to come to know: the single long narrow front-room with a bedroom on either side; and the kitchen behind. The secret lies in what they *do* here when they are alone; in what they *are*. Today I must find out. The newspaper has remained sealed to me; but here I'm right inside the house, a rat spying on their deepest secrets.

They are in the bedroom, in the heavy heat of the summer afternoon.

The Oubaas on the edge of the big brass bed, bending over to untie his shoelaces and remove the boots from his curiously vulnerable white feet. A sigh as he rolls over on his back on the embroidered coverlet, for all the world like a tree that has been felled. The Ounooi sitting in a chair by the window, her needlework in her lap; but she isn't working. She sits there staring blindly through the window into the whiteness of the heat outside—erect and still, her hair drawn back in a tight bun, her back very straight, and turned towards the bed as if to deny it as she stares into the distance.

And that is all. Nothing more. There is no secret. There is no answer. Only the difference remains: they there, I here.

Ma-Rose, Ma-Rose. But she has no remedy for this ache. I am left alone. To whom else can I turn? If I had a father: perhaps—? He must be somewhere in the wide world. But who is he, and where?

ONTONG

The Oubaas appointed me to keep an eye on the child and teach him the farmwork. And he was a good learner. He might have been my own child; I'd known his mother, the girl almost too green to pluck; one always felt she would bruise easily. That, I think, he got from her. How often did I warn him: "Galant, it's no use resisting. Wood breaks, but rushes bend. Ask me, I know." I wanted to save him from that. But I could see he wasn't listening. I'm Malay; I can see things coming.

I had hoped that Rose would be able to teach him; a wise woman if ever there was one. But his aloneness, his aloofness, depressed me. There's no remedy for that sort. They pretend to be meek, but they belong to a breed of horse that refuses to be broken. When you least expect it they bolt. A pity. He had a good start, and it wasn't I who put ideas into his head. I never wanted to have any part in it. If only it had been possible to discuss it with the Oubaas in time. But ever since he fell ill that day during the harvesting it's been impossible to talk to him. No use discussing it with his wife either. Ounooi Alida has always kept herself apart from the people on the farm. Even more so after Nicolaas died.

ALIDA

He had been prised from me long before the fact of his death: I cannot grieve. All my life I have been in dread of losing husband and sons in violence, of being abandoned in this hostile land remote from the familiar Cape of my youth; nights of terror, by day an alien sun. Now I have lost my third-born—counting the dead one in between: I count them all—and Piet lies speechless, turning his pale eyes to follow me about. Yet there is hardly anguish, only serenity. In the obscurity of this death life has acquired a precarious lucidity. With nothing left to fear, no catastrophe can surprise me; I go about my business from sunrise to night unhurried and in control. There are slaves enough, I do not need to work but I do, and it gives me satisfaction. The urgency has gone, the compulsion to be occupied lest I yield to the despair of my condition, this existence, restricted and taut, with no room for individual desire or tenderness. Now I can take my time, I have acceded to the place prepared, invisibly, for me; and I am content amid the adequate truths of our landscape.

They brought the body on the wagon, rolled in a brown blanket and already washed by the old slave woman Rose. She'd come all the way, a proud bundle shaking with the jolts of the wagon, abandoned to the pace of the slow black oxen. She did not address me, but she remained beside the body, looking at me while I looked at him, my son, this Nicolaas, the artless boy become alien and opaque, but now in death restored to me, his young face in repose reconciled to his former transparency and to the impossibility of comprehending.

We buried him in the coffin that had been waiting in the

attic since the day of our wedding to contain Piet's recalcitrant
body; he will need another now, a smaller one. They all came,
not only from the Bokkeveld but from beyond the mountains,
the distant fertile valleys of Tulbagh and Worcester, for the
news had travelled far. Only Cecilia, of course, could not be
moved for her wound; and her father stayed away stubbornly to
tend her, implying perhaps we were to blame. They brought
the others too for burial within the squat walls, newly
whitewashed, of what will now be our family graveyard; it is
February and too hot for bodies to travel. The new schoolmaster Verlee; and Hans Jansen who, having come for his
stray mare, had shared their death. Jansen had no relatives
living close enough to attend. Verlee's wife Martha was there,
a small young pretty thing clutching a baby, herself a mere
child not yet recovered it seems from the dull surprise of being
deprived, through his death, of innocence.

The biggest funeral, they said, the Bokkeveld had ever seen,
and dust enough to return to. It took place at noon, so people
could leave after the big dinner on the trestled tables under the
trees; mutton, venison, potatoes and sweet-potatoes, yellow-
rice with raisins, pumpkin, beans. Close on a hundred people,
children included; yet, standing together in a hot throng
surrounding the three graves, dry holes broken into the
unremitting summer soil, we seemed a mere handful on the
hard hillside with the mountain behind us and the yellow
valley sweeping out below, trembling in a white noon haze;
the house on one side, where in stark uncool shade Piet lay
breathing and staring, tended I presume by Rose who was
taking the chance in my absence to reassert her old subversive
hold on him. We stood staring uncomprehending at these
graves, exposed to the violent simplicity of the landscape
around us, endless and monotonous, vast, patient, bare. We
must have appeared incongruous, a handful of grain forgotten
on a barren threshing-floor after the workers and the horses
had left and the wind had blown away the brittle dust of husks
and chaff. But it was not hostile. It had always been hostile,
threatening me not with obscure dangers lurking unknown,

unknowable, but with its very assertive emptiness; not with mystery but the absence of mystery. Now, for the first time, I felt I had a reason to be here. "Belong" would put it too strongly, no one "belongs" here. But through the death of my son and the imminent death of my husband—breathing and staring there, close by, tended by the dark free woman—I had acquired a responsibility towards the place, the landscape, ours, mine. My life is vested here, I shall be buried with the Van der Merwes. My extraneity has been strangely and solemnly resolved. In Nicolaas my flesh lies interred in this earth, and I am growing towards it.

The slaves were huddled beside the house, not daring to approach: dull placid faces hewn from dark stone, suggesting the cool of the earth as well as its secret heat. Will these too rise against us one day or night? Who are they? They move through our houses, lurk in our lives, but I know nothing of them. Who are we? In this hour of death our shared existences were unravelled and we were left separate, their group beside the house, ours assembled at the graves. Afterwards their men were summoned to fill up the holes while ours watched smouldering, with many guns at hand. Some of the younger ones, Frans du Toit among them, those who had been close to Nicolaas, were muttering in frustration; and Barend, overcome with grief and probably with shame for the nature of his escape, broke away from our group and raised a trembling gun at the men levelling the mounds, but I stopped him. Not on my farm, I told them. We are civilized people, we have standards to uphold, it is for us to set a Christian example. They complied, submitting I suppose to me not as a woman but as the mother of a murdered son.

After they had gorged themselves the people dispersed. Barend and Hester proposed to stay the night, but I preferred to be alone; I'd even sent away the slaves, out of sight in their huts. It was not easy to convince Hester. Thin and dark, she remains singularly close to me, closer than my sons had ever been allowed to be, contained as always in herself, yet now, I sensed, more vulnerable than before. After eight years of marriage to Barend she still had the hard and lean unyielding body of a girl, denying knowledge of the man who had taken her, a waif of fifteen, to himself. The large dark eyes unchanged, disconcerting in their nakedness, and hungry, yet refusing charity. But now, subdued it seemed by death—she'd always been close to Nicolaas as a child—she appeared matured, prepared for pain, as if a consummation of the flesh had finally taken place and at last she seemed ready to acknowledge ineluctable womanhood no longer as fate but as fulfilment.

In the room, after they had left for Elandsfontein, silence was shaped by Piet's breathing and by a single wasp droning against a closed window. The woman Rose still sat on the floor beside the bed, staring at him, unmoved by my presence.

I said: "Rose," meaning to send her away too, eager to repossess him and our solitude (the blonde girl Martha and her baby had gone back to the graves to gape in meek awe); but I stopped. There was no need. All these years she had been in the background, suckling our children, taking to her deep body my husband and others, abundant and accessible as any cow, fertile as earth, threatening my small decent authority with her voluptuous presence. When I died, I used to think, he would continue to sow and reap as if nothing had happened; his robust male need would find the female ready. But standing in the door that day—Piet breathing and the persistent wasp droning on the pane, the woman in humble dignity on the dung-floor, my son safe in his grave—I felt anxiety recede like a tide and leave me peaceful and in command. We were old, all three of us, beyond the urgency and exigencies of desire; the white house enclosed us in unthreatened harmony, and outside was the immensity of earth in which I now had a stake with them. In the silence death approached—age its burden and its mark—an ally inspiring confidence, extenuating suffering.

"You can stay the night," I said to Rose. "Tomorrow will be time enough to go."

Together, we washed him and changed his sheets and made

67

him as comfortable as we could, lavishing on him the care of our common motherhood, while outside the fierce day drew to its end and sunset sounds began to ease the silence into dusk. I fetched the blonde girl from the grave; Rose and I fed the baby and put it to sleep, then comforted the child-mother in her bed. She smiled and briefly kissed me when I tucked her in, cried for a little while, subdued by the gentleness of her ignorance, and slept.

Was I like that, once, a frail blonde doll, flirting with life? Less passive surely, more blindly defiant, high-spirited, head-strong: but then, I'd never had any responsibility to death at her age. Life in the Cape was frivolous and haphazard, there was no need to be involved; evasion sufficed. And how I loved it—the band playing in the Public Gardens of a Sunday, the parade of smart gentlemen and ladies, Malays in tall conical hats or turbans red or blue, red-sashed and agile as monkeys, laughter in the shade of the oak trees, slaves cavorting in their own exuberant dances; the masked ball at the end of winter, curtseying girls and dazzling men, dignitaries from passing vessels, music until the break of day; the throng on the quays when the ships came in, letters from abroad, Holland or Batavia, rumours of irrelevant wars and winters unbelievable in our temperate Little Paris. Without any warning the stranger from the interior arrived in our house, taller than the door, in his duffel jacket and sheepskin trousers, with his booming voice and boisterous laughter. The scent, the smart of the inordinate—in that whirl of gauze and ribbons and gaiety where tomorrow was of no concern and yesterday of no substance, where one's only responsibility lay in arriving home by the appointed hour and one's only sense of tragedy in a favourite blue dress torn or a small porcelain ornament—cat? dog? lady with parasol?—broken by a slave (duly punished). Only at night, but rarely, after the town-crier had passed on his rounds, when the distant almost inaudible low boom of an incoming tide insinuated itself into one's body in repose, there might be a stirring of uneasiness, a youthful pang of uncer-tainty, an intimation, perhaps—how can one be sure after so many years?—of something else, different, remote. All this vagueness of idle nights suddenly embodied in a man, expressed in a name: Piet van der Merwe. *Yes, I'll marry you. Yes, of course I'll run away with you.*

The Cape Flats had been my inland boundary—dune upon dune, bleak and pale, marked by tortoises and snakes and the footprints of scavengers—and crossing them sealed off not only familiar space but time as well, the past, making both irrevocable. Days in vaguely menacing territory, green but strange, defined only by the motion of the wagon and circumscribed by the terror following a reckless and un-redeemable transgression. There was a brief if irrelevant respite in the incredibly luxuriant valley of Waveren: but then came the mountains, those forbidding mountains. No man could possibly scale them, I was convinced; yet there were the tracks of wagons, and tossing and swaying we crossed them, the ultimate frontier and abandonment of hope, to break into a new dimension of intractable land, Africa. After the compliance of the Cape there was this new crudeness, simple statements of stone and narrow valleys: destiny assuming the shape of a cruel geography.

The very thought of returning had been crushed. For there had been, simultaneously, the other adventure, that other frontier crossed: impaled, terrified, humiliated, quickened—then left exposed and torn, trying in vain to enfold an aching new emptiness.

There was pride too, for having initially implied consent, even though at the time I did not fully know to what, I could not return to face either the rejection or the forgiveness of the righteous. I had to stay; I would be his wife. But I would not acquiesce. In this high forlorn region of mountains and men I saw all too soon the rare women reduced slowly to meek and pliant negative flesh, obtuse and coarse, bearers of children, mistresses of slaves. My survival was vested in resistance; I would live with him, but I would not lower my standards, I would patiently force a civilized way of life on this household. We would have our meals on time; we would be suitably

69

attired at table; our children would read and write; the house would be spotless, not the fly-ridden sties overrun by poultry and goats I had seen elsewhere; our slaves would be instructed in Holy Scripture. Piet thought it a joke and roared with laughter; I persisted. He flew into rages and threatened to break me in forcibly; I persisted. When he came home at the wrong hour there would be no food; if he refused to wash or to dress properly I would not serve him. In the end he submitted as, in other things, I yielded to his superior force. Water eroding stone.

Attrition. The body shows it. These hard, calloused hands, weary with overwork, once were supple and gloved, kissed by officers. The bent spine was straight. These lave breasts were tight and firm; Piet was addicted to them, laughing away my protestations of shame when he fondled them: the only rude tenderness he knew to show in what was possibly love.

Once, after our savage wedding and Barend's birth, he took me back to Cape Town. I was sick with joy. We were accepted with a show of formal goodwill by my family, but unsmiling forgiveness could not bridge the chasm. The Cape had become the past world of a girl who no longer existed: I had no place in the interior, but there was no possibility of return or rediscovery. The balls and races, the officers' parties appeared frivolous and irksome, not because the Cape had become British but because I no longer belonged. And yet, as soon as we had crossed our great mountains again, I was as lost as before: a bird exhausted with flying yet unable to settle on crippled feet. I missed the sea: yes, that indeed. But suppose he took me back to it, what would I do? Sit meekly on the sand, listening to the sound, rush into the breakers to soak myself and drown? There was no reason in it at all. And the next time he offered to take me with him I declined, not like a good Christian renouncing something dear for the salvation of his soul but in a small decisive way, accepting that I had foregone all hope of settlement. This I would not share with anyone, least of all with Piet. I became possessive of my own agony. No one should even suspect its existence. I would save face to spare us all the disgrace of incomprehension.

There were the children, of course; the only future I dared presume. The first was Barend, a large, strong baby torn from me and leaving me helpless; if Rose hadn't intervened he may not have survived. I could never reconcile myself with the thought that she'd suckled him, precisely because it had saved his life. He was the first thing I had ever owned for myself. From the moment I recovered I kept him with me night and day, except when he had to be fed; the effort wasted my body, yet I thrived on it. He was mine, a personal fulfilment, a bestowal of meaning on an ignominious act. The eighteen months after his birth was the closest I came to happiness since the carefree ignorance of my youth. A second pregnancy deprived me of that shortlived joy. I was constantly ill; without the ministration of herbs and horrible concoctions devised by Rose I might have died: I wasn't sure that I didn't want to. The child was stillborn, but the illness persisted; I'd lost much of my determination. Piet took over the care of the boy. "I won't allow my son to be a sissy. I'll teach him to be a man like myself." I intervened when I could but had to give up when I fell pregnant again. This time it was Nicolaas and I hated him for forcing my first-born Barend finally beyond my reach. Because he was a frail and sickly child he demanded constant attention almost as if, even as a baby and helpless, he willed me into overcoming my rancour; I exorcised guilt by devoting even more time and care to him than was perhaps necessary.

Barend was bewildered by it all. He had lost me to a sickly, constantly crying younger brother: after sharing intimately the shadow of happiness in my life he was thrust from it, exposed to the harsh demands of a father who knew only the sjambok and the thong to overcome resistance and instil fear where respect was impossible. When Barend crawled to me for comfort, sometimes sobbing in the night, he was torn from my arms by Piet and bundled away; and miserably I learnt to suppress my own burning love in order to save him from the punishment which his father, loth to take it out on me, inflicted on the child instead. I knew then that I had been

71

mistaken in trying to secure a future for myself through the children: I had served only to bring them into the world so that Piet could take them away in order to shape them to his own image.

In the end, broken in like a horse, Barend submitted. He became secretive in his ways, refusing to confide in anyone; learning to obtain by stealth what would undoubtedly be denied him in open confrontation. He did whatever Piet expected him to do, he even took pride I think in his father's obvious satisfaction with his strength and prowess; but a brooding sullenness remained, never openly expressed, but in its very muteness unnerving. Especially to me, as it became obvious that he bore me a particular grudge for having, as it must have seemed to him, abandoned him; and though I ached for him I knew very soon that I had effectively lost him.

Did I compensate by showing even more affection for Nicolaas whom I continued secretly to blame? Oh God, how agonizing and impossible it all was. To love, to hate; to loathe, to yearn for: how subtle the gradations of our suffering, the stations of our solitude, victims of our own condition. And how does one break out, how recognize the moment propitious for revolt? For us it never came. Perhaps there is redemption in submission; but sometimes even the distinction between heaven and hell seems blurred.

I clung to Nicolaas too, the more so since in Barend I could see what was in store for him. God, oh God, I often thought, how would he survive in Piet's world? It would be so much easier to be a dumb beast of burden, bending under the yoke and plodding on, unquestioning, like a slave.

By the time one breaks through to a perception of truth it is no longer true: one is always, inevitably?, too late: the wedding—the first child—the second—the third— Hester—and now this death and Piet's immobility.

That I would lose Nicolaas too, this delicate blond boy, that he too would be forced to progress from son to adversary, a member of "their" world hostile to mine, was never in doubt. But the transition was less violent than with Barend, possibly

72

because by that time Piet had already accepted Barend as "his"; there was less urgency to claim a younger frailer son. And for a long time, for years, after Piet had set to work on Nicolaas he would still come back to me secretly to confide or be cherished. Barend submitted grudgingly to my lessons of reading and writing, some arithmetic, and whatever I could recall of history or geography; but Nicolaas was an enthusiastic pupil and he used to spend hours with the Bible. Which was an embarrassment to Piet: by no means could he condone negligent work; yet it was difficult to reproach Nicolaas for occupying himself with the things of God. The solution lay in restricting the time for Bible reading to Sundays or evenings, leaving the daylight hours for work: six days shalt thou labour. Even so I noticed that, whenever Nicolaas was sent out with the sheep, he would take the heavy Bible or a more manageable hymn book in his knapsack to the grazing place. Sometimes, inevitably, the sheep would stray while he lay reading in the meagre shade of thorn bush or tree, and a jackal would get at one. Then Nicolaas would be beaten, one of those terrible floggings in which Piet spared neither slave nor son, going on endlessly, dull voluptuous smack upon smack penetrating to wherever I was trying to hide with the corner of dress or apron stuffed into my mouth to stifle the sobs of rage and helplessness; and salt would be rubbed into the open wounds; and at night I would have to spend hours trying delicately to detach the torn shirt from the coagulated blood disfiguring a back that once had been babyish and smooth and mine.

The strange thing was that Nicolaas seemed to bear it with more resilience than his brother. He may not have been physically strong but he was tough. In a way it may have prompted Piet to be even more harsh with him, but I believe he admired him too. And it was only later, at the time of Barend's marriage, that Nicolaas became obstinate in a different way, moody, aggressive, with flares of temper that provoked Piet to greater extremes of violence and brought on, in me, more of the blinding headaches that had become the bane of my life on the farm.

I never told anyone about them. It was given in my situation not to admit unnecessarily to frailty of body or mind, salvaging what I could of pride. I had neither wished nor willed this life, yet I had eloped with him; I would live up to that challenge and survive. That, perhaps, was one of the only ways permitted one to express love in this crude land: softness is out of place here, only the tough grow old. It has taken me many years, and much suffering, to realize this.

There were vulnerable hours, usually at night, when I dared to wonder: What would have happened had I refused to elope with Piet? What other life would have opened to me had I married my foreigner in his dapper suit and become Madame D'Alree? But I tried to avoid such sterile reveries. The alternative remained, but only as a shadow to the harsh light of my real existence—an impossible dream and perhaps not even desirable.

There certainly was a time, as I felt Nicolaas at last slipping from my grasp irrevocably to join the masculine world, when I nearly broke down. Hester saved me, saved my fierce diminished pride. A thin dark brooding child of six, she came to us. She was the daughter of Lood Hugo, who was Piet's foreman at Houd-den-Bek. In those days, before the boys married and took over, Houd-den-Bek and Elandsfontein were part of this farm, and Piet had foremen and a handful of Hottentots and slaves stationed on each to work the lands and tend the goats and sheep. Lood was a hard worker, uncommunicative but dependable. Of his wife we saw very little, he kept her to himself much as Piet did with me. Rose or some of the slaves occasionally said that she was unhappy—God knows how they come to hear these things; they have an uncanny way of perceiving the hidden lives of their masters—which I had no reason to disbelieve, since she was very young, barely fourteen if I remember well, at the time of their marriage; and she became pregnant within a month. Both mother and child barely survived the birth; Rose was sent to pull them through—that woman is everywhere—and for almost two years before she died Anna Hugo was bed-ridden. By that time an older sister of Lood's had come to live with them to look after the baby (though it was rumoured that, while she survived,

74

Anna clung to her child with a possessive love refusing to share her with anyone). The arrangement worked well for a few years, when the sister unexpectedly married a widower from Graaff Reinet or some other outlying district on his way to sell his produce in the Cape. They offered to take the little girl with them, but Lood insisted on keeping her. However, loneliness appeared to be taking its toll of him and he began to neglect his work, which Piet couldn't tolerate. They had a few quarrels. Lood took to drink. For days on end he would lie in his house in a stupor, or the slaves would find him in the veld and carry him home, an unworthy spectacle. What must they think of us if we do not set a proper example? We have rules of decency to live by; if these should be allowed to decay into disuse what would become of us? On one of these occasions the child was brought to us. When he was sober, Lood came over on horseback to take her back. Piet was reluctant as he no longer trusted the man; and I found it hard to give up the new child, a girl I could fondle without fear of losing her to the men around me; but I knew it was right for her to be with her father whom she obviously loved. It was bitter solace, after the humiliating quarrel with Piet, to see the thin hard man on the brown horse pressing the child poss- essively to his body, rigid in his wounded pride, as they rode off.

"I should have kicked him off the farm," said Piet.

"He needs another chance. He is a lonely man."

"Aren't we all lonely?" he said. "That is no reason for a man to break."

"He has a child."

"He doesn't deserve it."

But he gave Lood another chance. And I believe the man seriously tried; but in less than a month a shepherd came over from Houd-den-Bek to report that Lood had drunk himself into oblivion again and was lying mumbling and giggling in his room while the sheep were breaking out. Piet took his sjambok and mounted his horse.

"Don't do anything unreasonable," I pleaded.

"Have you ever known me to be unreasonable?" he asked, and rode off.

He came back at sunset, looking pale and stern, holding the girl in front of him on the horse. There was no sign of tears on her face, but in her eyes I saw the look I had witnessed once or twice when there was no way to avoid it in a lamb when its neck is drawn back taut for the throat to be cut.

"What happened?" I asked, although I knew.

"Given him the hiding of his life and left him to think it over."

"Not in front of the child?"

"Take her inside," was all he said.

The next morning the slaves from Houd-den-Bek brought news of Lood Hugo's death.

"How could you, Piet?" I said.

But it had not been Piet's doing. Unable to bear the final humiliation Lood had shot himself.

"A waste of powder and lead," said Piet.

"There has been an accident," I told Hester. "You must be brave. Your father is dead."

"That man killed him," she said, facing Piet, without raising her voice.

"No, please," I said, not daring to look at him. "Your father went out last night. To—to hunt. The gun went off by accident."

"That man beat him. I saw him."

"She needs to be taught a lesson," he said. "I won't have this in my house."

"You will not raise a hand against this girl," I said, interposing myself between the silent straight-backed child and his rage. "You have torn my sons from me. I have never interfered when you disciplined them, even if it broke my heart. But this one you won't touch. Not ever. She's mine now. I married you and I've borne the consequences every day of my life; I have never set myself against you. But if you do this girl any harm, I'll take her away with me and you will never see us again. I hope you understand that."

He stared at me with an expression I'd never seen before; and he uttered a brief, harsh laugh that sounded like a bark. He

76

didn't say a word. Turning on his heel he went out, and through the open door I could see him stalking furiously across the pale ochre of the veld, tall and defiant, immense in his solitude, and I knew defeated.

"Come," I said to Hester. "You're dirty, you need a bath," although she wasn't dirty and had had a bath the previous night before I'd put her to bed. But there was a different, dark need to fulfil now, an ablution as of a new-born, to establish her as mine, an affirmation of myself in her. There was nothing premeditated about it: I acted with the blind, savage instinct of the mother animal licking the wetness of birth from her young. And as I stripped the clothes from her to wash her in the tub before the kitchen hearth—naked she was a fragile bird-like little thing—I actually felt my breasts aching in a shocking but barren desire to suckle her. She stood unmoving, patient and indifferent to the urgent caresses of my cloth as I washed and washed the little bird-like body, the delicate shoulderblades, the straight back and tight exquisite buttocks, the narrow rib-cage and vulnerable soft stomach with protruding button, the shameless innocent cleft, the hard thin legs and bony knees: washing her limbs as if in those motions I were shaping them and giving them substance, forming them from clay as long ago and mysteriously I had shaped the others in my womb. There was no response when I pretended to tickle armpits or toes, no compliance when I folded her in the large cloth to rub her dry, and when I put on her clothes again—I undertook to sew new ones that very day—there was, at most, a small quick smile not to acknowledge my efforts but to express relief at being restored to herself.

A week later she ran away for the first time. A shepherd found her in the veld and brought her back: she offered neither resistance nor explanation, listened gravely to my gentle reprimand, and ran away again the day after. I had to thrash her to bring home to her the danger of such recklessness, the need for obedience. She didn't cry. She hardly ever cried in all these years, although upon occasion I saw her face contort in the effort to restrain the urge.

She went off again. It took much patience to establish that she

77

didn't have anything against us; that she only needed to return, from time to time, to her home at Houd-den-Bek. I lived in ceaseless dread that she might come to harm: hyenas, baboons, snakes, a leopard, God knows what; but I had to learn to accept it, there was no other way, unless she were to be kept tied or locked up. As she grew more used to us and resigned herself to us, she occasionally spoke about her wanderings, mentioning calmly that a snake had reared and spat at her but had gone away when she'd scolded it; that she'd seen a leopard stalking her but had chased it off; that she'd come upon hyenas attacking a lamb but had torn it from them. Piet got furious at her lies; I persuaded him she didn't mean it, that it was only her imagination and that girl-children were like that; and I urged her to be more careful and not to embroider too much on what had happened lest we begin to disbelieve her. It was disconcerting to learn from a shepherd, after the hyena story, that a badly bitten lamb had indeed been found, and signs of a struggle, and the tracks of scavengers; and occasionally some of her other wild tales were corroborated. But it remained difficult to distinguish event from imagination, and all it emphasized was what I had already painfully discovered: that in spite of all my efforts and my need to have her to myself, she would forever be solitary and independent. There was in her a quality of virginity that had nothing to do with the behaviour of men and women: she was accountable only to herself; what she shared with others would be munificence, decided by herself, but peripheral, never touching the essential.

And yet she was a companion to me. Whatever I decided to teach her she would learn: embroidery, sewing, reading, cooking; in everything she was quick, deft, precise, dissatisfied with whatever fell short of excellence. At the same time she showed a strange detachment, as if these things which occupied our days were really irrelevant: while there was no harm in doing them, and a certain satisfaction in doing them well, what really concerned her was her secret and would never be shared. So that her company, assuaging my need, also made my redundance more acute.

I loved to brush her hair, long dark hair reaching down to the small of her narrow back, and she would resignedly stand for what seemed like hours every night while I brushed and brushed, one of the rare luxuries I've ever permitted myself since I left the Cape. That wealth, that splendour of hair. Until one day, without any explanation, she cut it all off with my large sewing scissors. When out of shock I began to cry she simply watched in mild bemusement; it was one of the few times I punished her. But it was of course useless. Once again she'd asserted her independence from me; once again I was reminded that the solace I'd found in our relationship was my illusion only, no part of her reality.

At night I lay awake wondering what would become of her, disturbed by her intensity. After Piet had fallen asleep, breathing so deeply it seemed the very walls of the house distended and contracted, I often got up again to go barefoot to her mattress in the corner of our room. Even in sleep her narrow face appeared grave, yielding nothing to my gaze; sometimes she was still awake, her eyes meeting mine steadily in the light of the candle, imperturbable and wise.

"Why aren't you sleeping, Hester?"

"I'm just thinking." Or: "I was looking at the moon." Or: "I was listening to the jackals."

"Don't be afraid."

"I'm not afraid."

Once she asked: "What were you and that man doing in the dark?" She persisted in calling him "that man". Never "Oom Piet".

"It's very late," I said dumbly. "You should sleep now."

"He won't kill you too, will he?"

"He has never killed anybody, Hester."

"He killed my father."

I was less upset about the reference to her father than about the discovery that she had witnessed, albeit in the dark, Piet's laborious nocturnal assault on my unresisting but negative body; and the next day I told the slave women to move her mattress to the front room.

It was after that night, possibly because her remark had awakened me to it, that I made more disquieting discoveries about the fascination matters of the flesh held for her. One day I happened to hurry inside disgusted by the performance of the dogs in front of the house, to find her, unaware of my entrance, standing at the window staring out at them in such intense enthralment that I caught my breath. Her mouth was half opened and she was breathing deeply, almost panting, the tips of her fingers pressed to her cheeks, her dark eyes—when she finally turned to face me—glittering like liquid fire.

"What are you doing there, Hester?"

"Nothing." She absently, with the back of her hand, wiped a trace of spittle from her lip. On the tan of her cheek—there has always been a beautiful half-submerged darkness in her skin—I could still see the imprint of her fingers.

"You mustn't look at those dogs."

"Why not, Tant Alida?"

The gravity of her innocence unnerved me. I preferred not to discuss the matter. But I lay awake again that night beside Piet, his vitality overwhelming even in sleep, worrying about Hester. How would she ever adapt to our decencies? She had in her the same ferocious pride that had driven her abject father not to the shame but the courage of suicide. But if she would not submit, what other way was there open to her? How incurable would be the wounds inflicted on her by the men of this land? I thought of Piet; I imagined him and his sons walking across the farm: and after the merest tinge of pride—those are my men, I have fashioned them—I was left in awe not of what they were but of what, for women, they could never be. One of such would take her and presume to tame her as a dog would, a ram, a stallion, a bull. Or had she always been aware of it like a fever of the blood? Was that the root of her solemnity, ungraspable even to herself, my virgin almost-daughter?

That it would be one of my own sons I could not guess, although looking back it now appears unavoidable, if still uneasily tinged with incest. They roamed the farm together, the three of them and, yes, the slave boy Galant.

80

I find it difficult to recall him as a child. He was always there, in the background, a shadow to the others. I thought of him as Rose's child and might have disliked him for it; but he had an obedient, winning way. One could send him out with the boys, and of course with Hester, and be sure there would not be mischief, at least nothing serious. He used I think to know his place. Of course he did not have the terrible experience of my sons in being wrested from a mother to become a man in a father's demanding world. He never as far as I can remember caused any trouble. Now he has murdered my son. I am shaken by it, how can I not be?, yet I cannot grieve because it all seems so remote now. I have grown old, not so much perhaps in years, but inside. There is a sense of peace in this ultimate closeness to my speechless husband, but there is weariness too. Our graves are waiting up there in the small enclosure on the hillside above the house. It will be good to rest at last. I am reconciled to the earth. But I doubt that I shall ever understand. Nicolaas, my son.

NICOLAAS

Slaughtering days were busy days on the farm. Every Monday Pa had a sheep slaughtered for the week, but that was unremarkable. The real slaughtering day came in early autumn, just after the first frost, when the beans had been harvested and most of the outdoor work was drawing to a close and life on the farm was beginning to bend inward. Then there was slaughtering on a grand scale—ox and sheep and pig alike—to make sausages and brawn and *biltong* and salted ribs, to smoke hams and legs of mutton for the winter months. For Barend and Galant those were great days, but Ma tried to keep me away from the bloody business for as long as possible; until curiosity got the better of me and I insisted on going with the rest. "You sure you can face it?" asked Pa, in the way he had of making me feel useless. "I want to go," I whined. "I want to. I want to." Ma still felt reluctant but Pa was adamant: "If he thinks he's up to it, he'd better come with us. We'll soon find out if he's a man."

With a great show of bravery I went down to the large flat slaughtering-stone with them. But when Achilles cut the throat of the first sheep and the blood spurted all over his trousers and bare feet, I got sick. I turned away my burning eyes, hoping they wouldn't notice, for then I would never hear the end of it. But Pa never missed anything. "Well, Nicolaas?" he jeered, "why you suddenly looking so pale?"

Without wanting to I stammered, on the verge of tears: "I didn't want to be here." And that was the way it always was. I never wanted to be there.

There may have been a time when all was well. I should like to believe it, but what would be the use? What has

82

remained of it all? Odd names and memories presenting themselves at random: like when the fog closes in over these highlands swathing everything in its blankness—only the occasional rock or hump or shrub protruding: you know very well they must be connected in some way; hidden in the fog must be a continuous and significant landscape, yet it remains invisible. All sense relinquished long ago, leaving only a meaningless opacity. Once upon a time the sun was shining. Once upon a time there were two boys and a girl—three with Barend—once there were two boys — once a boy and a girl—once a child who got sick at a slaughtering-stone and was mocked by the others. Once upon a time there was a woman who was nobody's mother but whom we all called Ma, Ma-Rose, who dried our tears and laughed with us, and who used to tell stories better than anyone else in the world. Once upon a time there was a dam. Once there was a mountain. Once upon a time, long long ago. The ponderous world is smothered in a fog.

Ma-Rose. Hester. Galant. The few durable names from that past. And yet they all abandoned me. Or did the flaw lurk in myself?

They never approved of Ma-Rose. Pa didn't mind much, but Ma was suspicious and annoyed. "For Heaven's sake stop calling her 'Ma-Rose'. She isn't your mother. She's a Hottentot woman. And all this visiting with her must stop too. I won't have my children growing up in huts like slaves."

"But she tells us stories, Ma."

"Heathen nonsense. She'll land you all in hell."

As I grew older and came to understand more about these matters I tried my best to convert Ma-Rose. It was of great importance to me that she become a Christian. But even the great brown State Bible failed to impress her.

"I know that book backwards, Nicolaas. Every night of my life I got to listen to your father reading from it and praying."

"But it's the word of God, Ma-Rose!"

"Then you better listen to it, he's your God. Got nothing to do with me."

83

"He's master of the whole world. He made everything."

"Tsui-Goab, the Red Dawn, made everything. Even Gaunab couldn't kill him. Didn't I tell you his story many times?"

"There's nothing about that in this Book."

She spat on the ground, barely missing me. "Tsui-Goab doesn't live in no book. He's everywhere. Up there in the sun. In the growing wheat. In the trees sprouting new leaves after the winter. In the swallows coming and going. In the living stone. In everything."

"Ma-Rose, if you don't listen, God will send fire from heaven to destroy you."

"Let him send it then. Let him try."

"My Ma says—"

"Let her say what she wants. You listen to her. But there's nothing no one can say to me. My heart is my own. I'm the only free person on this farm."

Invariably it was she who got in the last word. Like: "You watch out, Nicolaas: this morning I saw a swallow flying into you-and-Barend's bedroom."

My Book was Pa's; hers was the whole world. And in it she could read whatever was required to deal with any conceivable occasion. Watch out if you hear a grasshopper chirping in the thatch, it's a sign of imminent disaster. Or a shooting star, someone stepping on a grave, a hen that crows, the hoot of an owl, a hammerhead bird. The hammerhead was the most dire omen of all, whether you saw it peering into the water of the marsh and calling up the spirits of the dead, or flying past the setting sun, or uttering its three mournful cries over hut or house.

Her warnings both scared and angered me. I could find no retort to them in Pa's Book, no means of exorcising them. And gradually she receded from my life, however much I felt I still needed her: something as large and safe as a mountain was moving away from me, leaving me exposed to sun and wind.

Galant seemed more amenable to our Book, although I suspected that he was mainly putting on in order to avoid quarrelling; I doubt whether he really felt convinced. With

84

great urgency I would plead with him to persuade him it was now or never: suppose God came to take away his soul that very night he might be damned for ever, which was worse than being struck by lightning.

"When I'm dead one day," he would reply lightheartedly, "there'll be more than enough time to lie in the earth and think of God."

Ma-Rose's hold on him, I presume, was too strong, And to preserve the peace and avoid losing him too, I held back with the Bible. For I needed Galant. He was the only one around who was prepared implicitly to accept me as an equal. To all the others I was either superior—*Baas* or *Kleinbaas*, "Master" or "Little Master" to the slaves—or inferior: to Pa and Ma, and Ma-Rose, and to Barend who'd always bullied me and whose main gratification seemed to exist in taking from me whatever I was really attached to. The little wagon Ontong had made me; the foal I'd marked for myself; the knucklebones I kept in the bag of musk-cat skin Ma-Rose had sewn for me; my clay oxen; my snake-skin; and the hoard of skulls I'd collected over a long time—birds and meerkats, baboon, jackal, warthog—; and eventually he took Hester too. But Galant was my mate. Of course we often fought, and competed, and quarrelled: but always as equals. Even in that, I suspect, Ma-Rose's hand was visible.

Hester came later. And in the beginning she kept very much to herself. Only gradually, almost unnoticed, did she begin to follow us about, staying well behind and without saying a word, but with that quiet persistence that came to characterize her every move. The first time I made her a clay ox, she held it awkwardly and demurely in her hands as if unsure about what to do with it; but afterwards I heard from Ma that she'd taken it to bed with her. And one of the few times she ever cried was when she woke up the next morning to find it in pieces.

"Don't worry, I'll make you another."

She followed us to the dam and sat watching with her big black eyes while I fashioned the new ox from the yellowish clay near the outlet in the dam-wall. A strange feeling it gives

85

one to see a child handle a mere plaything like that, holding it almost reverently against her breast as she carries it about from morning till night. From that day she was inseparable from us. It was something of a nuisance when we went swimming. In the beginning we tried to drive her off with stones or handfuls of clay, but she would retreat only far enough to be out of reach, and return the moment we were defenceless, in the water; sitting pertly beside our bundles of clothes as if to keep watch. It was a bit unnerving to see her poised like that, in her long dress and pinafore and small veldskoens and frilly bonnet while we were cavorting naked; but soon we overcame the initial embarrassment and simply ignored her presence.

The dam was our place above all others. Much later, after I'd got married, returning to the farm one day to borrow a plough and not finding Pa at home, I strolled up to the dam again. To my grownup eyes it looked curiously unimpressive, even drab, muddy, and dishearteningly small. But when we were children it was a world in itself. No grownups ever went there. It belonged exclusively to the children. Grown-ups, work, slaughtering days, beatings, trouble, fear—all that formed part of the other world beyond the willowtrees, where we were forever aliens in the adult world. But this was splendidly ours, timeless in its tranquillity, inviolable. And unobtrusively Hester became part of it.

One afternoon, insisting as usual to assert his authority as the eldest, Barend once again tried to chase her away; and when she refused he unexpectedly grabbed her where she was standing on the upper wall, and pushed her into the water. It came so suddenly that none of us could prevent it. He was obviously scared when he realized what he'd done; but since there was no way of satisfactorily undoing it we all stood petrified, looking on in dismay and defiance. She shouted a few times, swallowing mouthfuls of water, as she thrashed about and spluttered; then began laboriously to make her way to the edge. It couldn't have been easy in those heavy, clinging clothes and as far as we knew she'd never swum before; on the other hand it probably wasn't very far, and certainly not very deep. Drenched and streaked with mud and slime she crawled out on the far side at last, coughing up water as she stood on all fours, and shaking her head like a wet dog.

"Ma'll kill us dead if she hears about this," I said in awe. "We'd better find a way to dry her clothes."

Even before we could reach her she'd matter-of-factly stripped off the soggy clothes and spread them out on the bushes. As if it were the most natural thing in the world—and wasn't it?—she joined us on the grass to dry herself and frolic in the baking sun. The clothes still looked a crumpled mess by the time we went home, but she must have told Ma some wild convincing story—she always could turn Ma round her little finger—for no one referred to that afternoon again and since then she regularly went swimming with us. I doubt whether any one of us ever gave it a second thought. But even that didn't last. It happened just after one of the longest and most severe winters of my youth, which had kept us from the dam for much longer than usual. On the first warm day after the last frost had cleared up we returned to the dam. But as we reached the quince hedge leading up to it, Barend stopped and looked round. Hester was following us, but at a distance.

"Look here," said Barend, "Galant, you can't come swimming when Hester is with us." His manner of talking reminded me so much of Pa's that I started.

"Why not?" asked Galant.

"Because she's a girl, of course."

"What about you then?"

"She's one of us. You're not."

I looked back to where I could see Hester's blue and white dress among the trees. In a few minutes she would be stripping it off to swim with us, as always. But what change had the winter months brought unexpectedly to make me feel breathless at the thought? For the first time, after our interminable quarrels in the past, I felt myself more in sympathy with Barend than with Galant. Except that I would have preferred to send Barend away as well. At the same time I didn't want to insult Galant: he was still my friend. It was all very confusing.

For a while I didn't know what to do. Then, looking down and drawing circles on the hard ground with my big toe, I mumbled: "Galant, I forgot to tell you. Pa wanted you to go down to the horses to look at the brown mare. She's lame."

He must have known it was a lie. But his only reaction was to screw up his eyes and ask bitterly: "Who wants to swim anyway? The ducks have messed up the whole place."

We stared after him as he went away from us, kicking at small stones with his tough bare feet.

"Why'd you lie to him?" asked Barend.

"I couldn't just chase him off like that."

He muttered irritably. But before we could start a proper quarrel Hester reached us.

"What's the matter with Galant?" she asked.

"He doesn't feel like swimming." Barend looked away. "Today it's just the three of us." He seemed in a hurry. "Well, come on. Can't dawdle here all day."

We went through the last tangle of trees and bushes, inexplicably self-conscious, as if we'd never been there before; as if something might happen we were not prepared for; as if in fact we were being watched by the grownup eyes we'd always escaped by coming here. I couldn't look at Hester.

At the dam we found all sorts of pretexts to postpone the swimming: throwing pebbles into the water, chasing after the ducks, making footprints in the mud, gazing at the tattered remains of last year's nests as if there was something very special about them.

"Well?" Barend asked at last. "Aren't you going to swim today, Hester?"

"What's that to you?" she said. "What's the matter with the two of you today?"

Resentful at being linked to him in her remark, I tried to cut the knot. "See who's in the water first," I challenged them. But no one moved.

"Take off your clothes," Barend abruptly told her.

"Why?"

"You can't swim with your clothes on, can you?"

88

"What about you?"

"Come on, you're not afraid, are you?"

She glowered at him for a while, then calmly moved her hands to her back to undo the ribbon of her dress. We stared as if we'd never seen her before. My throat was so dry I couldn't even gulp.

"No," she suddenly said, dropping her hands. "I don't feel like swimming today."

"Take off your clothes!" he shouted, once again assuming Pa's tone of command.

A brief obstinate twitch of her lips; then she turned her back on us. Barend made a quick move as if to stop her; I was ready to grab him. But there was something half-hearted about his gesture anyway. Changing his voice he started pleading with her in a tone I'd never heard him use before:

"If you take off your clothes I'll give you all the sugar lumps you want."

She turned back, raising an eyebrow, but whether in amusement or premeditation I couldn't tell. "And your new wagon?" she said.

"Anything you want."

I drew in my breath, stunned by this show of generosity so wholly unlike him.

"And the snake-skin?" she persevered.

"I told you. Anything you want."

"Will you let me have a shot with your gun when you go hunting again?"

He wavered briefly. Then he nodded.

She stood considering the matter in silence. The ducks were trampling and diving in the water. I allowed myself to become fascinated by the transparency of a dragon-fly. Far away in the yard the hens were cackling.

"Please!" said Barend.

"Oh stop it, will you?" I suddenly flew at him, unable to bear it any longer. "Hester, don't let him!"

"Shut up!" he said. "Hester, I promise you—"

"No," she said calmly. "I don't think I'll have a swim after

89

all." With that she turned and walked away.

I was expecting Barend to vent his frustration on me, but he wandered aimlessly to the far side of the dam where he squatted and began energetically to knead a lump of clay. My eyes were burning.

After a while he hurled the lump into the water, angrily wiping his hands on his trousers. "You think I care about a stupid girl?" he asked.

Long after we'd put out the candle that night I was still lying on my back staring at the ceiling, as if I would pierce the darkness with my eyes. Something inside me felt like crying, I didn't know why. At the same time I was immensely relieved that he hadn't been able to have his way with her. No, it wasn't that either. He had very little to do with my feelings at all. They concerned only Hester, exclusively Hester. I didn't want her ever to swim with us again. In an exhilarating and subversive way the afternoon had confirmed my possessiveness towards her. Not that it had given me any claim on her; but it had induced me, quite unasked, to assume responsibility for her, demanding from me much more than at that age I could really dare to undertake.

"I'll see to it that they never bother you again if you want to have a swim," I assured her the following day, adding, without either reason or logic: "Promise?"

How could she have had even the slightest inkling of what I meant? I doubt whether I was fully conscious of it myself. She briefly looked at me in her penetrating way, then said with the slightest of shrugs: "All right." And from that day, whenever she went to the dam to swim, I would take up position out of sight among the lower trees to protect her from the outside world. There I would crouch trying to imagine her as I'd seen her so often in the past, the tawny body diving and turning in the water, smooth as an otter, her long dark hair all wet, drops glistening on her as she came out, her mysterious and miraculous girlishness. Never, not once, did I cheat by trying to spy on her while she swam, not even when she would innocently call to me to join her in the water. Against myself too, especially against myself, she had to be protected. For we are created flesh, inclined to evil.

Did she care about it one way or the other? Was whatever I might do or say of any concern to her? I made small furniture for her rough-hewn wooden doll; I blew out birds' eggs for her and shaped her a fragile necklace; I collected knucklebones for her. And she accepted it all with graveness and with grace, but remaining always aloof, as if having or not having didn't matter in the least.

Even at that early age one decision had already shaped itself in my mind: I would marry her. In that lay the hidden significance of God's ordinance that she should have come to live with us. Most of my other frail certainties had already been eroded. Hester made it bearable to go on.

To her I dared reveal thoughts I could never utter to anyone else, not even Ma: how I feared and resented the farm; how I'd never wanted to be there. I told her of my resolve to leave it as soon as I could do so with impunity, to go as far away as possible, perhaps to Cape Town, or even farther, to God knows where. Perhaps I could become a preacher. Or a transport-rider, at the very least. Anything, provided I need not remain imprisoned in an existence where others seemed to be at home but where I could never belong. She listened in silence, and nodded when reaction was required. I don't know what she really thought about it. But she appeared to trust me: at least she appeared not to distrust me: and that in itself was encouragement enough.

With spike-thorns we scratched the skin of our wrists to draw small specks of blood which we mingled to seal our covenant. With cool, dry lips she pressed a kiss on my mouth.

She remained remote; that she would never cease to be. And whenever she ran away to the grave on Houd-den-Bek not even I could restrain her. Until she discovered how much I loved to stroke or touch her long dark hair she would absently resign herself to my caressing; but once she'd discovered my addiction she cut it all off. There was always something hard and shy about her. Yet I was content. It was all provisional:

91

one day we would be together for good, and she would allow herself to share more generously.

"I'll ask Pa to let me farm on Houd-den-Bek when we're married," I told her. "Then you can always be where you most want to be."

She stared at me strangely and for a long time. "I thought you said you weren't going to be a farmer?"

"I'll do it for you: if you wish."

"There's lots of time still."

But there was less time than we'd thought. We waited until she turned fifteen. In this part of the world it's old enough. On the eve of her birthday—the day we'd agreed I would talk to Pa about it—I was too excited to go to sleep. My heart felt like exploding in my chest.

"What's the matter with you?" Barend complained after a while. "You're tossing and turning like anything."

"Barend, I'm going to get married."

His voice sounded stunnned: "You mad? With whom?"

"With Hester, of course. She'll be fifteen tomorrow. We're going to talk to Pa."

"Have you asked her?"

"Of course. Years ago."

He was silent for so long that I thought he'd fallen asleep.

"Barend?" I asked, unable to control my excitement. "Don't you say anything?"

"I never expected that from you."

Whatever that might mean.

At noon the next day, when we were all at table for our meal of bread and meat and milk, Pa looked up after saying grace, and said: "It seems Hester is old enough to get married now."

"What's that?" said Ma, putting down the plate she had just picked up.

Hester was staring straight down at the table, blushing lightly. It surprised me that she should have approached Pa before I had; but one never knew with her.

"Barend told me about their plans this morning," Pa said as he began to carve the blesbuck joint.

It was like being kicked in the balls. I couldn't see straight for a while; all the voices sounded distant. Across the table from me I saw her raise her head to look at Pa, at Barend, then at me; I'd never seen her quite so pale.

My own voice had a distant sound when I protested: "But that's impossible. It's Hester and I—"

"Barend is the elder," Pa said sharply. "It's for him to choose. Although I must say I would have preferred my sons to marry tall, large women. I'd like to see the Van der Merwes breed a strong and durable race. But if that's what Barend wants—"

"Has Hester no say in it?" asked Ma, with a sharpness I didn't expect from her.

"I believe Barend has already spoken to her," said Pa.

"That's right," Barend said. "Not so, Hester?"

"But my God—!" I burst out.

"In this house we do not take the name of the Lord in vain," Pa said very sternly. "In any case it has nothing to do with you, Nicolaas, so shut up. Well, what do you say, Hester?"

She looked up again, at nobody in particular, quite blankly; she moved her lips as if to say something, but then she dropped her head again. Through the duskiness of her skin she was as pale as a wall. If only she'd say something, explain something. To think that she could turn against me and deny me like all the others. God must have willed it like that. But if so, He must have discerned some unspeakable evil in me to punish me in such an outrageous manner.

—And yet there must have been a time when the world had been whole. Early mornings, hunched against the cold, squatting beside the black iron pot with Galant and Ma-Rose, scooping our porridge with our hands, our eyes watery with smoke. Prayers at night, the five of us round the long dining table in the light of the oil lamp, the slaves a dark bundle on the dung-floor near the kitchen door, Pa's voice droning on and on, shaping each word separately like mouthfuls of food chewed well. And bedtime, huddling under the blankets, the wind tearing at the thatch overhead, Ma entering with the

93

candle to tuck us in and briefly sit with us and hold us in her arms. Sunrise in the veld, Galant and I following the sheep in the joyful assurance of a whole day undisturbed ahead of us. Barend and Galant and I and Hester at the dam, robbing the weaver-birds' nests of their pale blue eggs. Hester pressing her wrist against mine to mingle our small smears of blood. The rare but precious occasions on the wagon to the Cape, with Pa.—

Pa. Always Pa. No one but him. The others seemed like the small branches and twigs one has to clear away to reach the trunk of the great, solid tree you wish to climb. He had always eluded me. That hard safe fork I never reached. And on that fifteenth birthday of Hester's the deepest hurt, I think, lay not in her, or in what Barend had done, but in Pa, who appeared finally to have turned away from me in that one withering remark: *It has nothing to do with you, Nicolaas, so shut up.* I'd always tried, God knows. When I was very small I had done whatever I could to help Ma, yet she forced me from the nest like a bird. To Barend I'd always given whatever he'd demanded, and more, in the hope that it would persuade him to like me and approve of me. Everything I'd done on the farm I'd shared with Galant, because I'd needed to have him there beside me. And for Hester I'd sacrificed everything in order to ensure that she would always remain with me. But behind all of them there had always been Pa, that single towering figure.

No one was as strong as he was. No one could walk up the ladder to the loft as easily as he, carrying the full bag of wheat on his shoulders. No one could match the ease with which he could hold down a bull-calf to castrate him. "A farmer isn't worth his salt unless he can outwork all his slaves," he used to say. And no man on his farm or any other in the neighbourhood could keep up with him, ploughing or reaping or digging or building. I wanted him to be proud of me. Or, if that was impossible, at least to acknowledge me. But in his eyes I never was good enough. "Got to be a *man*, my boy. A real man. Marrow in your bones. You're too much of a fancy turd."

"But what do you expect of me, Pa? Tell me. What is 'a man'?"

"A man's got hair on his chest and he farts like a horse." Followed by his guffaw, like the bellowing of a bull.

Barend sprouted hair on his chest. Not a rough mat of hair like Pa had, but impressive enough. I remained smooth, to my eternal shame. To me it was a sign that I would never live up to Pa's expectations. But I swear I tried. I swear to God. I toiled on the threshing-floor until I staggered and fell down. I kept up with the reapers until I got sunstroke and had to be carried home in a high fever, my mind rambling for days. When we went to Cape Town I would take my turn at driving the wagon, putting everything I could into it so he could see how good I was: but all he did was to smile indulgently as if he was at most amused. Not once did he really acknowledge me. And on that day, when he said: "It has nothing to do with you, Nicolaas, so shut up", it was a final confirmation of my worthlessness in his eyes: a man without hair on his chest.

And yet I tried again; once. Hope is an indestructible weed. (Was even my marriage, later, to Oom Jan du Plessis's daughter Cecilia another attempt to prove to Pa my manliness? I'm not sure. It had more to do, I should think, quite simply with saving face; with proving not to others but to myself my chances of survival.) What happened was the coming of the lion, and perhaps because it followed so soon after Hester's birthday it offered itself as a last opportunity to win his favour. At the time of her birthday the animal had already made its presence known in the neighbourhood: we'd heard of damage done on this farm or that, of sheep caught and dragged from the kraals at night, of tracks much too large for a leopard or other common predator. And then a slave child was caught at one of Pa's grazing places: dragged right out of the hut where it had been sleeping among the other people. And in that same night we heard its roar in our mountains, a sound that set one's whole body atremble, one's very skull and guts and marrow. Even though one had never heard that sound before, the moment it came there was a dark instinct that recognized it and reacted to it, as if one had been

95

expecting it since birth. A single roar, followed by a series of deep rumbling sounds as if the mountain itself was heaving; and then a rhythmic sighing, almost too deep to hear, a subterranean presence sucking one in and out as it breathed, in and out. In that sound one discovered how untamed the land still was, and how untameable. There hadn't been a lion in these parts for God knows how long: but suddenly, behold, it was there.

There was no need to send out messages or confer with neighbours: the next morning, unbidden, the whole of the Bokkeveld turned up for the hunt. And just as sure as our recognition of the sound the night before was the resolve not to return before the intruder had been killed. It was a simple imperative, an appointment with death. Not just the lion: but death itself, which always prowls among us even though we may not always recognize its sound so readily.

This, I knew, was the chance I had of proving to Pa that I should not so lightly be dismissed or disregarded.

In that morning's hunt all our earlier hunts seemed to be revived. We'd always hunted in single file whenever we'd gone in search of leopard or hyena or lynx: Pa in front, then Barend, then I, and Galant bringing up the rear. When it was dangerous, we stuck closely together, each hard on the heels of the man before him—with the result, inevitably, that when Pa stopped in his tracks the rest would bump into him, one after the other. One day, stalking a wounded leopard that had eluded us more than once, Pa had warned us several times not to tread on his heels like that, but we'd been too scared to pay attention. Until he properly lost his temper.

"Barend," he shouted, "if you bump into me again I'll thump you!"

Numb with fright, Barend could only mumble: "If you thump me I'll thump Nicolaas."

(And if you thump me, I'll thump Galant.)

Yes, in spite of the frayed tempers, there had been a closeness among us on the hunt, a togetherness in the invisible presence of that threatening leopard (which we later found,

96

harmlessly dead, in a thicket). I felt an intimation of that same closeness on the morning we set out to hunt the lion, Galant and I with a handful of unarmed helpers going off on our own. For those few hours everything that had recently happened seemed to recede and become irrelevant; it was as if even Hester's birthday had never occurred at all. I was so wrapped in thought that the lion came charging at us before I properly realized it. Quite instinctively I jerked the gun up against my shoulder; but the cock got stuck. Running blindly, I'd already resigned myself to what seemed inevitable, when I heard the shot behind me and the lion came tumbling down on me, throwing me to the ground. Even then I couldn't believe I was alive; I was, in fact, still amazed by the ordinariness of death when Galant grabbed me by the arms to pull me to my feet. I was covered in dust. My eyes were burning. But worst of all was the horror of knowing I'd proved myself a coward in front of everybody. It was so damned unfair: it had been the gun's fault, not mine. When I saw Pa and the others approaching I couldn't face them with the truth.

"He nearly got Galant," I panted, breathless, as Barend came up to me. "I got him just in time." But I was really talking to Pa who stood behind him, his broad-brimmed hat between me and the sun.

What difference could it make to Galant? It was immaterial to him whether he or I had shot the lion. To him it was nothing but a hunt, an animal tracked down and dispensed with. To me it was a last attempt to grab back something of what I should have known was irrevocably lost.

"Well I never," Pa muttered briefly, glancing at me before he turned away to round up his hunters. He must have read the truth in my eyes. No doubt of that. And the contempt of his silence was worse than any blatant accusation of having lied.

The others were all thronging around us in excitement, shouting, laughing, jostling, prodding the dead animal with their feet or their guns. But at last, after they had all gone off, the two of us remained to skin the carcass. Always the two of

97

us. Galant and I. If only he would say something. But his considerateness in keeping silent branded me with a deeper guilt than could be expiated with words. I hated that dead lion as we squatted beside it to skin the body: how could it lie there so wretchedly, allowing us to go about our degrading business? Only minutes ago it had been awfully, terrifyingly alive. Now it was a dusty old carcass, its mane tangled with dirt and thorns and dried grass, its teeth worn and broken, its head disproportionately large for its bony body, its eyes blueish in the blindness of death, its claws blunted. I didn't want to have anything to do with it: it was unworthy of a lion to be like that.

A giant, a great roar in the night, a creature that could inhale and exhale one in the deep living sound of its breathing, had turned into the miserable victim of everything that had gone wrong between us. Its death was the death of something I would have wished to be, something that desperately needed to remain inviolate, something no man should be allowed to relinquish. Like losers we tramped back home in the dust, carrying its skin as the trophy of our defeat; I in front, Galant far behind. If I were to stop unexpectedly, there wouldn't be anyone near enough to bump into me. And all I was conscious of was that I didn't want to be there; that I wasn't meant to be there: as on that distant day with Achilles at the slaughtering-stone.

ACHILLES

I have nothing to say about those days. What happened happened afterwards. It's their business, not mine. It's their land, not mine. My land is where the ship brought me from, where the 'mtili trees grow, and that is very far away. They came with the long guns to hunt us the way one hunts hares. The old ones they shot or clubbed off into the bush. It was only the young ones they wanted. They examined us very carefully—eyes, teeth, muscles, legs; they felt our balls; they broke into the girls to test their depth, and bruised their teats. And then they drove us from one slave pit to the next, on the long road that runs from Zim-ba-ué to the sea, where the palm trees grow and the sun rises from the water. Those who'd grown too feeble were left behind for dead. The rest of us were loaded into the ship in row upon row, bound in long chains. Impossible to stand up or turn over on your side. Those who died died in their chains. Those who didn't, survived. Salted meat and pork and sour beer. We arrived in the Cape, skeletons with loose teeth, sick with the smell of vinegar. Food and arrack for a month in the lodge to revive us; then into the stone quarry below the Lion's Rump to strengthen us. At last there was the auction, and the gong beating.

I ran away from the first farm. They brought me back and flogged me. I ran away again. They brought me back and flogged me. And again. Then I was sold to a more distant farmer. I ran away, but he too had me brought back and flogged. After I'd been sold another time, and had run away again, they branded me with irons and kept me in the Dark Hole of the Castle for a long time. In the end one gives up trying to run away. You know it's no use. You know you won't ever find your way back to your own country again, the land with the baobabs and the *'mtili* trees with their bare white trunks and dark crowns; where you had a name that was your own, Gwambe; where you had your place beside your mother, and where your father sat with the headmen of the Bakonde. Here you are called by another name: Achilles. It means slave.

The big man brought me on his wagon from the Cape to this place beyond the mountains. As soon as we arrived on the farm he had all the slaves flogged, me too, so that we would heed him. I never tried to run away again. One gets old before one's time. But one never forgets. When I sleep I can still see the moon rising from the dark sea moving against the shore. There is a wound that never heals, like the scar from the hot iron, except this one cannot be seen although you never stop feeling it.

What did they know about it? They were children. Barend and Nicolaas, who used to tease me or shout at me as if I were their size. Galant, whom I'd taught to drive the wagon: I could see that he was clever with his hands, but I never thought he'd learn to kill too. And the little girl Hester who would often come very quietly to watch us work; and who sometimes smuggled a biscuit from the kitchen in the pocket of her pinafore. She was different. But she too was no more than a child and couldn't be expected to understand.

HESTER

The feel of things. Textures. The hairy skin, gently pliant to the touch, of Dad's jacket. The worn head of a clay pipe and the jagged edges where the stem had broken when he fell. The cold metallic shock of a gun-barrel. The large coarse hand enfolding mine; and then the silk and bristle of the horse against my legs.

The surfaces of kitchen and living-room and bedroom, confining me. The fine hard top of the yellowwood table at mealtime, yielding easily to a nail, uniformly even to the open hand. The blandness of a water-candle tapering smoothly to the coarse wick. Copper, iron, wood. (Smells too: cinnamon, cloves, onion, wood-fire smoke.) A mattress stuffed with chaff, pleasantly prickling to bare skin, adjusting slowly to the insistence of a body.

Above all the things outside. The wooden farmyard gate, worn away and oiled by hands. The jaggedness of rock grating the skin, ridges and crevices, the weight of a stone in the hollow of a palm. The dried grass of a weaver's nest and the perfect fragile shell of the small egg; the rough bark of a willow-branch scratching the skin of inner thighs. The squelchiness of mud worming through fingers or toes. The feel of water: droplets running from a cupped hand down to the elbow; splashing icily against a face immersed in a mountain stream; laving and enclosing lasciviously the swimming body. (Keeping watch, out of sight, as I lolled and swam, was he warding off others as he'd promised, or himself secretly spying? Rather hoping he was, I offered him in his absence more of me—here is my body: look; see what I can do, what I am—than when he was near, servile and attentive.)

101

But this is not enough. Not only to feel but to know what it feels like to be feeling. Not to feel the surface of the rock against your skin but to know how from inside it feels you. Its weight in the earth, its stillness, its silence. And how it feels the rain. The first drops, their smell, and how they bring to life the smells of grass, heather, lichen, earth. Soaking you to the skin; the feel of clothes clinging in cold lust, sucking at your flesh as he sucked that other day, after the snake; the smell and feel of your own body, separate limbs, an aching ecstasy inwards. I would sit in the rain, if they let me, head down, arms and legs drawn in, the shape of a stone, to feel it wash over me, permeate me entirely. Thunder. Not coming from clouds above but reverberating in the earth. The wish to be bare then, the nakedness of desire. Skies aflame, a sound of mountains falling, crashing about me; a dissolution into pure liquid existence, shaping me, running and beautiful. Once when I went back to Houd-den-Bek there was such a storm, the first I'd ever been part of; and when they found me—why in such a frenzy? why so nearly desperate?—it didn't matter that I hadn't reached home. I had been cleansed and that was enough.

It was in search of him that I went back every time. They wouldn't take me to his funeral: perhaps there had been no funeral—even though, afterwards, there was the grave. Once I even tried to dig it up to make sure, but I tore my nails on the hard soil and had to abandon it. It would have been no use anyway. What I needed of him was more than the touch of his jacket, his crusted boots, his father-smell: I needed his memory of me which they'd taken away. That man had come and flogged him like a runaway slave, tossing me this way and that as I clung to his thrashing arm screaming in terror and rage; then took me away on the horse. And afterwards, when I went home, Dad had gone. The memory had gone. There was so much about myself of which I knew nothing: the beginning, the early years, Mother. But he'd been there, he'd witnessed it, he'd become the custodian of my wholeness and when he died it could not be retrieved. Everything about me

102

which he'd known had been buried with him. Driving my father to his death that man had obliterated part of myself: there had been Mother, then Tant Nan, then Dad: in losing him I lost my grasp on them all.

To grow attached to anyone means running the risk of forfeiting that part of oneself entrusted to the other. Never again. No one would possess me again. Yielding would mean giving up my only chance of survival among them. I had to live with them; I knew I would have to marry one of them. But I would never belong to them. That I owed to myself and to that of my father which lived on in me: to belong only to myself, separate and intact. Memory; rain. To be washed away entirely, oblivion: and so to be reunited with memory lost.

Nicolaas came close. His gentleness and patience were dangerous, threatening me with the generosity of his small gifts. It would have been so easy to succumb. But he couldn't understand the panic inside me: *For Heaven's sake, don't give me things. Don't hold me. Don't stifle me.* He was so obtuse in his meekness, his persistence. I did not mean to be perverse— enticing him only to reject him later—but I lacked the strength to repulse him altogether. I needed that gentleness too. If only he could have offered it without demanding my life in return. In a way I almost preferred Barend's bullying, his overt viciousness: pinning an arm behind me to see if I would wince; tearing my dress to force me to tears (in vain). His favourite act of petty torture was pulling my hair. It was the one form of pain I found difficult to bear: more than pain: it touched what meagre pride I dared allow myself. And the only way to thwart him was to hack it off. Fingering the stubble in the dark I cried; but I knew the act had repulsed him and had confirmed my own integrity. In comparison with him, Nicolaas was too limp, an obedient dog at my heels, wagging his tail, eager to please. And still I might have married him, I saw no other way. In a place like this, what hope for a girl like me? *All right, on my fifteenth birthday.* It seemed a long way off.

I couldn't believe my ears when Barend spoke. It would

103

have been so easy to contradict him, to reduce him to shame. I waited for Nicolaas to intervene. The immediate shock subsided: I was amazingly detached, looking on at a scene the reality of which I couldn't believe. Even a sense of wry pride, who knows, at being fought over. But there was no fight at all. Nicolaas half-rose from his chair, then fell back lamely, crushed by that man's single command and by Barend's audacity.

It was the worst insult he'd ever inflicted on me: to lack the courage even to try. Simply to let me go like that, pitying himself. And there was in Barend's presumption, his boldness in brutally taking possession of my life like that—even though it would never really be his, but how could he know?—an excitement so fierce that it burnt in my womb, kindling a desire I'd sometimes felt in watching animals copulate, watching that stiff erect red thing plunging into the depths of cow or mare or placid sow, frenziedly pumping away, arrogance asserted, life assured. I stared at him, stared at that man his father, at his dispirited mother, at Nicolaas crumpled in humiliation, and in pride and anger I felt my womb burning, felt the wetness forming in me, so that I had to bow my head to hide the fever on my cheeks, to gulp away the lump in my throat. The fight ahead, I knew, would be the surest way to make me survive.

I had felt it once before, dare I admit it?, just as suddenly, as impossible to justify or explain. On my way to Houd-den-Bek, one of the many times, I'd passed Galant in the veld, who was tending the sheep (I knew there was no danger: he was the only one who would neither stop me nor betray my secret afterwards): we'd spoken for a while, he'd shared a crust of bread with me, and then I went on. Hurrying to be home before dark, relishing in advance the rare night on my own (my small fire burning, jackals and hyenas howling, the silent mountain louring against the stars; the mound where Dad, according to them, lay buried), I never noticed the puffadder, until, as I nearly stepped on it, it sank its fangs into my leg. I kicked at it and screamed for help. By the time Galant reached me I'd

104

already crushed the flat triangular head but the bloated beautiful body was still wriggling in the dust. *Oh my God, I'm going to die, I'm going to die.* He pushed me down and tore open the ruffled pantalette to get to the neat double incision on my thigh. Bright blood. And then he was sucking—sucking and spitting, sucking away voraciously, spitting, sucking madly. He seemed like a young animal gorging itself (the leathery feel of a cow's bare teat; the thick-veined udder): and, even knowing for sure that I would die, oh certainly, I felt that burning of the womb, dissolving as in rain, but warm rain, not coming down but welling up inside; as if it was my breast he was at, which had recently begun to form, the merest swelling, aching nipples both tender and tough to the inquisitive touch.

He pressed a blackish stone to the small angry wound, applied herbs he had in his knapsack, prepared by Ma-Rose I should imagine; I barely noticed. There was just that disarming, sudden emptiness after he'd stopped sucking. I'd never before felt shy of him, but now had to avoid his straight contented stare. Was he too thinking of a distant late afternoon when, coming from the mountain in a thunderstorm—how I'd wished to stay up there and never come down again, but he'd tugged at me and picked me up and carried me home—Ma-Rose had stripped our clothes from us and bundled us into a kaross to dry and warm us up? I don't know for how long we were there in that warm kaross in the dark, only the dung-fire burning, its acrid smoke causing one's eyes to water and one's nose to burn. Perhaps it wasn't even for very long, but it felt like many nights merging one into another, and we merged in the coarse kaross, huddled together. Because it was so dark and safe I risked to caress him: it wasn't him, it wasn't me, only two small bodies anonymously touching with no threat or responsibility implied. The two of us, both orphans—the only ones on the farm who didn't belong at all; the only ones perhaps who really cared. A tentative touch, a shifting of weight, a head adjusting itself on a shoulder, a hand straying. He didn't react. I knew he wouldn't dare, so I pretended to fall asleep, and in my sleep I think he dared.

105

An innocence now lost. But the touch, oh God, remains. Is it utterly inevitable then to go on without, always, losing something on the way, relinquishing possibilities, forfeiting hope? And only the memory of a touch remains: even that is precarious and may be taken from one. Rain: beating down, beating down, wearing away all grit and rock, washing remorselessly clean. Naked anatomy. Roots clawing at eroded earth. The roughness of stone grazing the guileless palm. The harshness of reed, a thin rough blade of leaf. A petal brushing the cheek. A hand, the intricate course of veins, knuckles, sensitive fingertips probing, exploring, venturing, bruised.

The shape and rough folds of an empty jacket hanging on a hook. Dried mud, once slithering through toes. Saliva from a mouth. Another secret wetness. A young animal tugging at a teat. Acrid smoke.

The sharp sweet smell of buchu: the smell of solitude.

The jackals will be howling again tonight.

BAREND

There was always a distance between them and me. I was several years older of course, but that was not the reason. When I was very small the whole farm was mine to roam on and explore. And wherever Pa went I was carried along on his broad back. There was no one else to claim his attention. At night I slept between them in the big bed. Nothing was as comforting and secure as that deep mattress stuffed with down and their bodies on either side of me, like large soft loaves protecting me. But when Nicolaas was born it changed. I was jubilant when Pa told me I had a brother; but the helpless and hideous little creature in Ma's arms was a disappointment, if not a downright betrayal. Still, I tried to be friends, carrying to his cradle whatever I thought might interest or amuse him: lizards, frogs, grasshoppers, a tortoise. But that set him howling and Ma would come rushing in to box my ears and bundle me out. What could I do but resent the little miscreant? A few times when no one was around I tried to smother his yells with a pillow, but invariably somebody would come to the rescue. For most of the day he and Galant would lie side by side on a kaross beside the house, and often I saw Ma-Rose suckling them, one to each breast. Always the two of them together and I apart. A deep bitterness settled heavily in me.

As they grew up they never gave me any peace, tagging along wherever I went, whining for attention, crowding the solitude that had become my refuge, nagging me with their constant and unreasonable demands. I tried to scare them off by leading them on footpaths thick with thorns or along mountain trails where they would fall and graze themselves

107

(once an arm was broken); I would push them into the dam, or dare them to climb trees I knew were dangerous for them. They remained undaunted. At times, I must admit, it was not unenjoyable—swimming, riding the young bullocks, chasing baboons, hunting hares or porcupines or buck; and it was useful when they could lend a hand with the work. But when I wanted to be alone they were impossible. More than once I felt like strangling them.

Because I was the oldest I was held responsible for whatever went wrong, and Pa could be hasty with sjambok or strap. Otherwise, again because I was older, I had to join the men in the heavy work while the two of them were either fooling around or given undemanding little tasks. Slaving away with the farmhands, sowing, ploughing, hoeing or building, I couldn't bear to hear them splashing and squealing in the distance. Impossible to escape from Pa's blunt admonishment: "Come on, Barend. One day you'll be taking over from me and you've got lots to learn."

There never was time for me to be free like them. The work was never-ending. If I were to be master one day I had to prove my worth. And I did: I wouldn't allow either freeman or slave to outdo me, whether with spade or plough or sickle or axe. And Pa's obvious satisfaction came as balsam to me. Especially when I could please him as a hunter; it was the one thing I could do almost without effort; handling a gun was natural to me. But even that could not completely stifle the urge I sometimes felt to break out and simply enjoy myself or muck about. Just once in a while. But it was denied me. "Come on, Barend. You're my first-born. You must set an example on the farm."

I remained wary of Nicolaas. He could be difficult to handle, moody and secretive, often eager to ingratiate himself, but always ready, the moment one's back was turned, to turn against one or split to Pa or Ma. With Galant, at least, one knew where one stood. He would never split. But he always was a cheeky little shit. Even in those days I felt Pa was treating him much too leniently, more amused it seemed than

108

annoyed by Galant's mischief. Admittedly, he was impressed by Galant's alertness, his adroitness at almost anything he applied himself to: but at the same time he was getting out of hand. A slave should be kept on a short leash right from the beginning, otherwise there's trouble. I especially disapproved of his thickness with Nicolaas. That was taking things too far. Playmates, all right; but one should keep one's distance and they wouldn't. I tried to keep it in check, believing that in the long run it would be to Galant's own benefit, but I was thwarted all the time and Pa turned a deaf ear and a blind eye. So I had to resign myself to it; one couldn't risk provoking Pa too much.

Why dwell on these days at all? What use to dig into a dry anthill? Looking back now I have the impression of being wholly absent from our childhood. They were there: not I. In later years, on family visits on Sundays, Nicolaas would often say: *Do you remember this?—Do you remember that?* But it was theirs, not mine. Why flaunt such memories anyway? Perhaps for them there was pleasure in it. But I: I was never allowed to be a child; there was never time for that. And it is too late for regrets now. Life has always kept something from me, but why kick against the pricks? It's long past. One learns to seal up one's heart and carry on.

Only Hester was, in a sense, different. She didn't bother me in the same way as Nicolaas or Galant. Yet from the beginning I found her difficult to understand. She was like a small animal, a lovely furry creature one wanted to cuddle or protect, but which snarled and bit when one came too close. In the first spring after she'd come to live with us I brought her a castaway lamb from the veld. "What do you expect me to do with it?" she asked disdainfully. Her reaction unsettled me. She pretended to ignore the lamb; but I soon discovered that when she thought she was alone she would delightedly frisk and play with it or cuddle it against her. Once I stood behind the baking oven watching her for a long time. There was no one else in the yard, so there was no reason for her to be ashamed or shy. But when at last I came out and called her,

109

she jumped up and angrily pushed the lamb away from her. "What are you spying on me for?" she hissed at me. "I saw you playing with it," I said as soothingly as I could: "So you do like it after all?" She stamped her foot: "No, I don't. I can't stand it." "But I saw you cuddling it," I said. "You even kissed it." "That's a lie!" she shouted, attacking me with her angry little fists. "Why, it's nothing to be ashamed of," I said. "Everybody likes little lambs." "I don't want the damn thing!" she cried.

I decided to test her. "All right," I said. "Then I suppose you won't mind if we slaughter it?" I hadn't for a moment meant to do it. I only wanted her to admit that she liked the lamb I'd given her. But I'd never seen anyone so stubborn.

"Slaughter it if you will," she said. Her face was as white as death, but that was what she said.

"Won't you understand reason?" I was almost pleading.

"There's nothing to understand. Kill it if you want to. I don't care."

I took out my pocket-knife, hoping that would intimidate her. But she stood her ground, her whole body rigid.

"You won't really," she said defiantly.

"You like the lamb, don't you?"

"I don't. You're just trying to scare me."

I honestly expected her to change her mind at the last moment. By that time I was already kneeling beside the lamb, holding it down on the ground, forcing back its thin white neck, the knife in my hand. "Well?" I said, "say you're sorry. Say you want me to let it go."

She was trembling as she stood there, but obstinately refused to say a word. I felt close to tears. But there was nothing else I could do without losing face; she would forever remember me as a coward. I had no choice but to kill the lamb.

Ma was furious when she found out. But I told her it was Hester who'd asked me to slaughter it.

"Hester?" she asked. "Is that true?"

"If he says so."

"I want to hear it from you."

"Why should I care about a lamb?" she cried, then suddenly turned round and fled. I found her in the quince hedge afterwards, sobbing; but she didn't see me and I made a detour to avoid her. There was something in her I would never come to grips with, something that both scared and challenged me.

Since then I would often find her alone somewhere and try to speak to her, but her only reaction would be to pull faces at me or put out her tongue, or even to spit at me. And if I grabbed her and wrenched her arm up behind her back, or pulled her hair, she would remain absolutely rigid and quiet, staring at me with those large black eyes as if to dare me, to see how far I would be prepared to go, just like that afternoon with the lamb. "Say *Please!*" I would demand. Or: "Say *Baas!*" But not once could she be forced into submission. Tears would spring into her eyes, her whole narrow face would be contorted with pain, but those lips would remain pressed very tightly together. She might utter a moan, but she would never cry or plead. And in the end, invariably, it was I who had to let go and turn away. And honest to God, I never wanted to hurt her. She was a small, wild, vicious, beautiful little animal I wanted to possess. But her teeth were as sharp as the spikes of a thornbush.

Didn't she understand? I never meant to bully her. I loved her. She is the only person I've ever loved or wanted. When I wanted something from Nicolaas or Galant I would ask for it and take it, with or without force, to show them who was *baas*. But with her it was altogether different. I didn't want something from her: I wanted *her*. And when Nicolaas told me, that night, that she was going to marry him, it felt like life itself being taken away from me. There was only one desperate remedy. I couldn't talk to her: she would simply laugh at me. The only possibility was to tell Pa the matter was settled, and to take it from there. I knew only too well I was putting everything at stake. A single word from Hester would destroy all and leave me shamefully exposed. And then I swear I would have hanged myself.

She looked up when I spoke. I shall never forget the

111

expression in her eyes across the table. She didn't say a word. Nicolaas wouldn't dare to; I knew I had nothing to fear from him. (He wasn't even much upset. His only concern I think was to get a wife. Any woman would do. What other explanation could there possibly be for his marriage, less than a year later, to Cecilia du Plessis from Buffelsfontein, a girl so severely plain that no one would have looked at her twice, however considerable might have been her other qualities?) But I was waiting for her to protest. And when nothing happened it was the most devastating and exhilarating feeling I'd ever had.

Afterwards, I asked her: "Hester, do you mean you'll really marry me?"

"I didn't say anything."

"But you didn't protest either."

"You've already arranged everything the way you want it."

"It's because I—" How could I say those words to her: *Because I love you?* That was what, more than anything else, I longed to say. But if I did it would be a repetition of the day with the lamb. Except this time she would be holding the knife.

"Hester, I want you." I found it difficult to speak.

"You've always got what you wanted."

"But with you—" I took her by the arms. She didn't resist.

It wasn't necessary either. She must have known already—the still, dark arrogance of her eyes—that for the rest of my life I would pay the price for that one outrageous and irremediable decision.

PART TWO

CECILIA

It was raining the day Nicolaas and I got married. Father —Mother had died long ago; few women survive in these parts—Father and the other menfolk were foolishly happy. They saw the hand of the Lord in the rain, after so many months of drought; and to Piet van der Merwe it was a sign of fertility. But I was worried. It was the wrong season for rain, drought or no drought; and when something misses its appointed time and place it usually spells misfortune. It was no ordinary rain either. Not the kind that brings relief and soaks the earth and causes growth, but an excessive flood that washed away the soil and tore rocks tumbling from the mountains and broke gashes into the earth and drowned cattle and sheep. It was almost impossible to ride up the Witzenberg after the ceremony in the Drostdy. From up there the whole mountainside seemed to be streaming down to the valley below, there was nothing solid left, only one vast flood. One of the oxen slipped and fell up the last stretch of road and broke a leg. It had to be shot. The carcass was brought home on the wagon, staining my wedding dress with blood, which was no good omen either. But the men were in exuberant mood. They roasted the ox on a spit in the shed and almost burned the building down.

"Why not?" shouted my father-in-law. "What's the use of a wedding if it doesn't set the world alight? You should have seen the place the day I got married."

He always gave me an uncomfortable feeling. That boisterous laugh reverberating throughout the house. Those large hands with their hairy backsides. The patches of perspiration on his shirt. His smell. His way of staring at one: as if one were

115

a heifer brought to auction. And the things he said at the wedding feast, gesturing with a chunk of meat in one hand and his brandy in the other: "Cecilia is a daughter-in-law after my own heart. I've always told my sons to choose their women with care. Tall ones, large ones. They breed well. And we Van der Merwes will tame the land for our descendants. It's not that I have anything against Hester"—she stood apart from the rest in the shadows, thin and dark, smouldering in her angry way like a fire burning without giving off light—"but Cecilia is the sort of woman I'd have chosen for my son myself. Eat and drink up, my friends. The blessing of the Lord is on us."

I didn't see Hester again that day. She had this habit of disappearing unnoticed from a group. I know she bore me a grudge for moving into the house at Houd-den-Bek, which she somehow regarded as her own since the time her father had been Oom Piet's foreman. But what concern was it of mine? It was their decision; and it was the Van der Merwes who prepared the house for us; Father gave the furniture and lent us his wagon to transport our things. And the dowry; the hundred sheep, the five milking cows, the two horses, the slave woman Lydia, and the twenty bags of wheat ready for the mill. That, I guessed, was what I was worth to him. (And Lydia was thrown in only because he found her unmanageable on his farm, a useless creature, soft in the head, always ransacking the yard for feathers and odds and ends. What for?)

I had nothing against Father, but it was a relief to move from Buffelshoek to Houd-den-Bek. He'd always tolerated me—he was a God-fearing man and had no choice—but he could never forgive me for not being the son who'd been the purpose of his marriage. Mother had given birth to two boys before me, but both had been stillborn; and since my own birth she remained bedridden. He had little use for me on the farm. Although I tried to prove both to him and myself that I could fill the place of a son, he never seemed impressed. I did much of the outside work, looking after the poultry and tending the kitchen garden, even taking the sheep out to graze when no one else was available; I would drive the wagon to

116

Tulbagh when he was unable to go, and shoot game when we wanted venison; often I rode out on horseback to inspect the grazing places, especially Elandskloof which would have been my farm had I been a boy. After Mother's death I once asked him directly: "Why can't I take over Elandskloof? You can't manage two farms on your own."

"How can you handle a farm?" he asked, sighing. "If only you were a boy. You're my punishment for some sin I must have committed unwittingly. God's ways are inscrutable."

"I can do anything a boy can."

"I know you're trying hard, Cecilia. But you were born a girl and the best we can do now is to find you a good man. A Lubbe perhaps, or one of the Van der Merwes. We can approach them when you're ripe."

"We'll do nothing of the kind!" I objected. "I won't be put up for auction."

"You don't want to sit around until a man like Frans du Toit asks you, do you? You know he doesn't skip anything in his way."

It pained me to think of that unfortunate man with the hideous birthmark on his face, conjured up by all the mothers in the neighbourhood whenever they wanted to strike the fear of God into their nubile daughters. But I refused to budge: I would not be auctioned off like that.

"But you can't stay unmarried forever!" Pa retorted. "What will become of you when I'm no longer there to look after you?"

"Then God will provide, if it's necessary."

"Cecilia, you're not too old for a thrashing yet."

"That won't change my mind, Father."

On another occasion he would not have taken such recalcitrance lightly, but that afternoon he was too dismayed to speak. He trembled, not with anger I think but with incomprehension. And all he finally said was: "You've set yourself against your own father. God will punish you for it in His own good time. And when He does, you mustn't complain."

Instead of pursuing the argument he went out to the shed

117

where he kept his kegs of brandy. From that day he retreated to the shed much more regularly than before, while his solemn curse continued to burn in my mind like a live coal. I went on my knees to humble myself before God; but not before Father. What had been ordained would happen, and I would accept it. My obstinacy to him had not been prompted by any resistance against the idea of marriage—that was my destiny, and I would submit—but God forbid that I would offer myself to anyone. Since childhood I had accepted Father's word on good and evil. But this once his right was my wrong.

God must have approved, for when His time was right Nicolaas turned up. I was already much older than the age regarded as suitable in these parts: in fact, I was twenty, and Nicolaas only eighteen. But if that was God's will I would not question it. Suppose it had been Frans du Toit? So Nicolaas put the question and I gave him my word, and Father seemed content as well. It happened very much out of the blue. We'd just heard the news that Barend was going to marry Hester; and all of a sudden Nicolaas turned up on his horse. Without beating about the bush, that same evening, he asked: "Well, shall we get married?"

"I thought she was never going to be asked," Father said before I could answer. "It meets with my approval, Nicolaas. Sit down, I'll fetch the *sopies*."

There was a curious reticence about Nicolaas in those days. Sometimes he became moody, almost as if to blame me for having said yes; but men are hard to fathom, and I knew my place. If it is not a shameful thing to confess I must admit that I felt motherly towards him. As if I were much older than my age, and he much younger than his; as if he were more in need of my protection than I of his. Some nights I lay awake in doubt and wonder, and not without a feeling of resentment; but in the end I overcame this pride in myself. I'd been brought up to accept that one day I would marry in order to be a help to my husband; and I felt ashamed at the signs of resistance I'd discovered in myself against the will of God. If only I could be entirely sure that this were the only way to do

118

His will; but it would be sinful to ask for a sign. It was a question of faith. And so we were married in the torrential rain. Was that perhaps the sign I'd prayed for? But God reveals Himself in ways inscrutable to us. Humility. That is what is required. So that the wife can glorify the Lord through submission to her husband.

The boisterous nature of the wedding feast also irked me, but I accepted it as another ordeal to be endured in order to strengthen the spirit. The strange thing was that after everybody had finally left in the rain, leaving the two of us behind in disconcerting silence, I suddenly missed the noise. Even that small house seemed too big for us. In the bedroom the shadows of the candle were dancing on the walls, while the rain came dripping through the leaking roof. Nicolaas and I alone: it was the very first time. He stood by the window looking out, although there was nothing to be seen, only blackness.

My throat felt taut. But I went to him and stopped behind him.

"I suppose we should go to bed now." I almost added: "My child." He was looking like a small bewildered boy.

"I—well—," he stammered. "The roof is leaking."

"We can fix it in the morning."

"I'd better have a look right now."

"It's raining so hard. Why don't you send the slave Galant?"

But he was already on his way. The candle was nearly blown out when he opened the back door. Black water came streaming in and formed a puddle on the floor. I didn't want him to leave me behind alone. Suppose the foundations were washed away and the house fell in? I pulled open the door to call him back. In a moment I was drenched.

"Go back!" he shouted out of the night, with such vehemence that I obeyed.

In the corner of the half-dark kitchen there were bodies under a blanket on the floor. The slaves Galant and Ontong, sent by Father Piet; and Father's slave woman Lydia. I found it repulsive to see them so brutishly lying together under the

119

coarse blanket, the kitchen pervaded by their smell. Indignant, I pushed against the bundle with my foot: "Lydia, get up. Make me some coffee."

"Yes, Nooi." Meekly, and dazed with sleep, she stumbled out, naked. I couldn't make out the others in the gloom, but their eyes were an invisible presence, an intrusion in my own home.

"For God's sake, Lydia, put on your clothes!" I ordered. "You can't go about like that. It's indecent."

"Yes, Nooi."

Still vexed, I went to the bedroom to take off the wedding gown and put on my new night-dress. I sat down on the bed. Outside it was still raining heavily. I felt myself abandoned by Nicolaas. And when he came back? I shuddered lightly at the thought, remembering the bundle of dark bodies on the kitchen floor; the smell. When Lydia brought in the coffee my eyes penetrated her dirty shapeless dress, resentfully discovering the body and the breasts. *My God, we aren't animals.* Yet soon, as meek as she, I should have to submit and be dominated myself.

Without moving, without bothering to pour the coffee Lydia had made, I remained sitting long after she'd gone away on her soundless bare soles. Steeled against predestined humiliation, I wanted Nicolaas to hurry up now and get it over with.

When he returned he was drenched, his blond hair dark and plastered wetly against the skull.

"I thought you'd be asleep by now," he said, sounding almost reproachful.

"I was waiting up for you. Come, you're shivering." I got up to pour him lukewarm coffee. He was still standing in his dripping clothes.

"You must undress now and come to bed," I said.

His eyes seemed unnaturally large in his wet face. The oblong shape of his skull. Who was this stranger, my husband? An unexpected, shaming desire for him began to glow inside me. Breathing deeply, I slid into the bed and turned my back so that he might undress.

120

After a very long time he crawled in, wearing his night-shirt, shivering with cold. He blew out the candle and remained rigid on his side of the bed. It suddenly struck me that he was scared of me; much more scared than I'd been a little while ago; and again there was the feeling that he was more son than husband to me.

"We're married now, Nicolaas," I said, my voice sounding hoarser than I'd meant it to be. "Now you must take me as your wife."

"I'm sure you're exhausted," he said. "It's been a long day for you. Sleep now."

"There's a right way and a wrong way of doing things, Nicolaas," I insisted softly. "Do not let us provoke the wrath of the Lord."

He bent over me, still shivering lightly. "Good-night, Cecilia." His lips felt cold and damp, like raw flesh. Then he turned away to sleep. I lay in the dark listening to his breathing and to the rain beating down outside. The roof was still leaking; I could hear it dripping. I felt sympathy for the unknown man beside me, but it was mixed with—what? Fear. Anguish. A sense of inadequacy, of having failed, of being at fault. What had happened—what had been avoided—was incomprehensible to me. Was I so repulsive then? In the flood in which we seemed to be drifting, drifting like a dilapidated little ark, there was neither reply nor hope.

A week later I told him resolutely: "Nicolaas, if you don't do it now I shall have to speak to your mother."

"There's a time for everything."

"Our time was a week ago. Or do you have something against me?"

"I wanted to make it easy for you," he said wretchedly.

"I'm your wife."

He lay stiffly beside me in the big bed, much too big for us; paralysed it seemed by anxiety or resentment or both. I realized that it was up to me now. A disconcerting feeling for one who had always had to bow to the will of men. From it I seemed to draw a form of determination I hadn't been aware of

121

in myself before; a strength previously denied me. But it seemed shameful as well, for this was presumption and beyond the province of what could rightfully be expected of me. Still, I knew that if I were to shirk from it our marriage would become a mockery. And if this arrogance were the punishment brought upon me by Father's curse years ago, then it was only proper to yield to it. *God*, I prayed by myself, *if this be sin, then let me through this smaller sin ward off a larger.* I turned to his body, soothing him at first the way one comforts a dog. He tried to resist; then yielded to my more insistent caresses. In the end a wildness seemed to take hold of him and he crushed down on me in a frenzy. It did not frighten me; it was as I'd anticipated it and for the sake of his pride I was prepared to undergo the shame. How could he know that long after he'd gone to sleep I remained wide awake: not because of the humiliation of my torn flesh, but because of a discovery so momentous that even then it was too much for me to grasp. Only in the years to follow did it define itself for me: that through his use and abuse of my body a peculiar power of my own over him had been asserted.

In due course the child was born. The girl. Salt in the wound I'd borne since childhood, as daughters could bring only shame and sorrow.

"Forgive me, Nicolaas," I said. "I prayed the Lord for a son. But He thought differently."

His reaction was not what I'd expected: neither disappointment nor resignation, but almost relief. "There is enough time for sons," he said, looking down at the baby and touching her small head with what seemed like awe. "We must call her Hester."

I looked him in the face but without seeing him; long after he'd gone out I was still lying with the knuckle of my forefinger held between my teeth, biting myself to contain the deeper pain. For the first time I began to understand something about his reticence.

The child was christened Helena. It had been my mother's name and I insisted on it as the proper thing to do. The second could be Hester if he really wished; and so she was. The third was also a girl, Katrien. Nicolaas still showed no resentment at all. From the first day he was fond of them and loved to take them with him wherever he went on the farm; especially little Hester who was his favourite. Sometimes I even had the impression that he preferred them to sons, unless it was to spare my feelings. Father was the only one who refused to resign himself to the fact that even a grandson was denied him.

"What was the use of working my hands to the bone to build up those two farms?" he asked after Helena was born. "There's Elandskloof. There's Buffelshoek. Where can you find a better site than up there on the Wagenbooms River? It's the most fertile soil in the Bokkeveld. And all I have is a daughter and a granddaughter."

His disappointment lay heavily on me. Surely he deserved some reward for all his toil in his old age. But it was out of my hands; basically it was no longer my concern. In marrying Nicolaas I had shifted my weight from Father's farm to Houdden-Bek. This was my new responsibility. And here, in a sense, I was in charge. Through patience and submission I had achieved this: I would not easily let go again. I had acquired a hold on my husband. In this house I was mistress. In this yard I had the final say. I had alterations made to the house to suit my own needs, especially after the first child. Not for the sake of more space, but to have it adapted to myself, cancelling its past connection with Hester. I had the walls raised so that a proper attic could be fitted in under the thatch, with a broad stone staircase running up the side of the house. On the right a bedroom was added for the children. Outside the kitchen I wanted, and got, a dairy; and the shed that later became the schoolroom. In the hearth I had a baking oven built so that I could work more comfortably indoors. The kitchen garden I changed to my own taste and way of cooking.

Galant did most of the building; he knew better than Nicolaas what to do. A thorough and skilful worker. And yet I never felt at ease when he was around. From that first rainy night: his way of staring silently at one. Not that he was

123

impudent. That would be something one could punish and overcome. It was that singular expression, as if his eyes were free. There was also his refusal to address Nicolaas as *baas*. Had it been me I would have had him flogged. But to me he was subservient. *Yes, Nooi. No, Nooi. Right, Nooi. If you say so, Nooi.* When I spoke to Nicolaas about it he would only laugh and shrug: "That's unimportant, Cecilia. We understand one another. We grew up together."

They should have abolished slavery long ago. I cannot stand slaves. They cringe.

And there were those frightful dreams I used to have about them.

In Father's house they hadn't bothered me much—except in the form of that one recurrent nightmare—probably because I, too, was an underling. But in my own house and in my own farmyard it became annoying, an aggravating circumstance. Wherever one came or turned or went they would be hovering in the background or shuffling past soundlessly on their bare feet, eyes gleaming in the half-light. Like shadows, like cats; everywhere. Looking down as one came past—except for that Galant—or suddenly busying themselves very conspicuously; but as soon as you'd passed you could feel the eyes following you again. One wasn't free to be mistress in one's own home while they were around. In their meekness and ubiquitousness they ruled over hearth and home. Because they knew, and I knew, that they were indispensable. Like something soft and pliable that gives way to a prodding finger: but the moment you let go it returns to its original shape. Or like water. Unlike the solidity of stone: this is fluid, it chooses circuitous ways, it recedes and returns; it erodes.

Granted: we built and farmed and prospered. Side by side Nicolaas and I continued on our separate ways. I began to resign myself to the fact that his secretiveness was inevitable, part of our condition. Leaving in the early morning, returning for lunch and an afternoon nap; then out to the veld again. Sometimes he went to Tulbagh—more often I think than was strictly necessary—leaving Galant behind to keep an eye on

124

the farm. He also developed the habit of getting up from the supper table at night and walking out into the dark without a word, sometimes staying away for hours. To that, too, I resigned myself. I had to allow him his way of life without questioning him about it. But below the surface the process of erosion had already started.

My first discovery of it had come one evening when he'd gone out on his own as usual. I'd gone to bed, but it was a warm night and after a while, feeling thirsty, I got up. In the familiar darkness of the house I went to the water-barrel in the kitchen. The dung-floor was seductively cool under my bare feet. I pushed open the top half of the back door to let in some air, and stood there looking out into the peaceful night for a long time. There was no wind. The high serrated outline of the mountains opposite. The imperturbable moon. Then I saw him coming back towards the house: not from the gate he would have used to visit the kraals, but from the opposite side, through the old cherry orchard, from the direction of the huts. Those were all in darkness. Only one door stood open, revealing the flickering light of a fire inside. It was the hut where Ontong and Lydia lived. But Ontong, I knew, wasn't there. He'd left early that morning to go to a grazing place where jackals had caught a lamb.

GALANT

It's different. No matter how, but it's different. Houd-den-Bek is not Lagenvlei. Nicolaas can never be master like the Oubaas. "Galant," Oubaas Piet says, "Nicolaas is going to marry Nooi Cecilia from Buffelshoek. He'll be needing a pair of good hands to get Houd-den-Bek going. I'm giving you to him as a present. From now on you're his slave."

Ontong comes with us, only on loan as I have it, but in the end he stays on. And after a while Achilles also joins us: in exchange the Oubaas will get part of the harvest for seven years, they tell me. At Lagenvlei it's Ontong and Achilles who keep an eye on me, but here on Houd-den-Bek I'm made *mantoor* over them. Doesn't matter. "You treat a man who's older than you with respect," Ma-Rose warns me. "Specially if he could have been your father. If you don't I'll put the night-walkers on you so they can suck you dry. You heard me?"

"I heard you, Ma-Rose. But I'm not sure about Nicolaas yet."

"You're going to Houd-den-Bek with him, that's all. It's not for you to ask."

I keep my eyes open and already on the day of the wedding I can see Nicolaas hasn't got it in him to rule his wife. And I see Hester keeping to herself, away from the other guests, ready to snarl at anyone; even at me, when she hurries through the kitchen into the rain, as if it's my fault that she will now be cut off from Houd-den-Bek and the grave of her father. In her eyes, too, it seems, I'm only a slave now. That sets me wondering about Nicolaas again.

Soon after the wedding he takes me up the Sandberg with him. It rises right out of the marshy *vlei* behind the house,

126

layer upon layer, red and grey. From up there one can see very far. Down below is the marsh, now swollen from the rains into a dam so long and wide among the hills that coming from Lagenvlei you have to make a great detour to get to the yard. Newly whitewashed, severely white, the narrow house with its thatched roof stands in the middle of the bare yard, with the orchards and beanfields below, and the strips of wheatland, as far as the first stony outcrops of the Skurweberge opposite. An unusual mountain range, this. Down towards sunset it stretches all the way from the Rear-Witzenberg, past Elands-sfontein, to the elbow of Wagendrift where it disappears, only to reappear opposite Houd-den-Bek, like a river that runs underground part of the way. In the direction of sunrise the veld swerves round the marshland and the Sandberg towards Lagenvlei. Everywhere, as far as the eye can see, it's Houd-den-Bek.

"I'm no longer under my father, Galant," Nicolaas says, looking out over what is now his. "I'm a married man now and you and I are going to turn this place into a proper farm. It's not what I wanted but it's what God has ordained for me."

"Why you talking about you and me?" I ask him. "The farm is yours."

"You're my right hand, Galant. Without you I'm stuck." He points to the far side of the narrow valley where the rocky foothills come out of the earth. "You can have a field of your own over there, for pumpkins and beans and vegetables, and some wheat. I'll give you all the seed and manure you need. And if you work well I'll set a heifer and two lambs aside for you every year."

"You'll be a good farmer," I say without looking at him.

It is not what I have in my mind to say, but I say it nevertheless. For from his way of talking I know it is different now. We're not boys any more. It's different. There's a harness holding me; there's a rein. Sometimes it's short and sometimes slack, but it's there for good.

"Is that all you can say?" he asks, and his voice has the sound of disappointment in it.

127

I do not reply to that. How can I know what he really wants me to say? It is his farm; I am his slave. In silence we go down the steep slope again, separate and together. It starts drizzling again, which makes it easier to keep one's thoughts to oneself.

In the house, too, each goes his own way although we all live together. These first weeks, until the rain lets up, we have to sleep in the kitchen; the old huts have not yet been rebuilt. It's Ontong and I in the corner by the hearth, and the woman Lydia from Buffelsfontein between us. A good woman, a generous body; but she's not right in the head. At times she suddenly starts running about like a chicken stung by a bee; then she must be subdued and brought back, her mouth foaming and her eyes turned up so you can see the whites; and whenever she's not working, and even sometimes when she's supposed to be working, she's picking up things, feathers and twigs and leaves, which she stuffs into the mattress. All because of a blow with a kierie on the head when she was a child, Ontong says. But Ma-Rose believes she must have stood in someone's shadow at sunrise, for that is supposed to bring a darkness into one which only very special medicine rubbed into an incision in the skin can cure. Still, Ontong is Malay, and even he can do nothing for the woman: Lydia remains what she is.

It makes a man ill at ease to be with someone like that, but if she's the only woman around, you have to accept it: and in the dark it's not so difficult. She may be strange, but it's better than nothing. So Ontong and I take turns with her. Until her moods get the better of me: "You keep her, Ontong," I tell him. "You got more patience."

As soon as the rain is over Nicolaas takes me out into the messy yard. "The Nooi is getting fidgety with the lot of you under her roof," he says. "I want you to cut wood in the kloof and build yourself a hut. There's clay and reeds in the marsh. Ontong can also build one."

"A hut just for myself?"

"You need a place to live."

That's why I'm saying Houd-den-Bek is a different sort of

128

place. All my life I've been living with others. Now I'm allowed a place of my own, like a weaver-bird building its nest in the first warmth after the frost. All those nests overhanging the dam. But keep the dam out of it. Its time is past.

It's hard work, chopping branches and carrying armloads of rushes and reeds; but in the late afternoons when she finds the time Lydia gives a hand to cover the reeds with clay. Before the first bean harvest the huts are finished, mine well apart from the one shared by Ontong and Lydia. Look at me: master of my own hut, its dung-floor hard and smooth, my kaross rolled open in the middle, *kist* against the far wall, all my things from Lagenvlei. Good enough even for Ma-Rose to move in: I can see her heart is bent on following me to Houdden-Bek. But when at last she decides to make the move it's to a hut of her own, at half an hour's distance from us, all by herself. "I won't be tied to another man's yard, Galant," she tells me while I finish off her hut in the first frost of winter. "I don't ask favours from any man. I'm free."

"The lightning will strike you up here on the hill," I warn her. "It's too exposed."

"I'm not scared of no lightning."

And I know why. I've seen her in storms before: if the lightning grows too wild or comes too close to her liking she goes out in the rain and bends over with her backside to the storm, and raises the back flap of her kaross. Nothing scares off the Lightning Bird so effectively as the sight of Ma-Rose's bare behind.

In the end I stop complaining about her independence. For it is the time of Bet's arrival on the farm, the young woman from the distant Eastern Border who turns my limbs to water. An easy woman, Bet. Difficult when she's difficult, but easy with her body. Usually, when there's a new woman in the neighbourhood we all go to her like horses to a trough, for a woman's cunt is a precious thing in these parts and a man is in need of wetness. So when Bet arrives, and before the moon is full again, I ask her: "What do you say, Bet? Look at this hut, it's mine. Are you moving in?" Like a weaver-bird she inspects

129

the nest, plucking out bits of straw here and there, looking inside and out, ordering me to move the door so it faces the sunrise, the way the Khoin people want it, telling me to change this and that; and in the end it is to her liking.

I go to Nicolaas to tell him: "I'm taking a woman to be with me. It's Bet." And he generously marks an extra two lambs for us to celebrate.

The work of course goes on as usual, for the place is neglected and gone to waste and the hands are few. From time to time Nicolaas takes on Hottentots who happen to come past; or Frans du Toit or some other farmer in the neighbourhood sends over the hands they can spare; but the permanent hands are few, mine and Ontong's and later Achilles's too. In the beginning we do everything together. But gradually the work gets sorted out. The horses are mine. Nicolaas doesn't like horses; same as with dogs. He never trusts them properly and so they're wary of him too. But I'm a horseman. I can spend a whole afternoon brushing them or leading them or feeding them or whatever. True, I'm the *mantoor*, I got to keep an eye on everything on the farm: but it's the horses that are mine above all. And then the building. Nicolaas wants walls all over the place. Kraals. Stables. Sties. A stone wall round the farmyard and the kitchen garden. Another round the small graveyard of Hester's father. A new mudwall to dam up the sunrise side of the marsh. And new furrows everywhere to take water to the beans and the wheat and the orchards and the small patch of tobacco. Digging, paving, then plastering with mud. All this stonework is mine. Ontong is the one for the tools and implements. He cures the hides and cuts the thongs, he works in the smithy in the back shed, he mends ploughs and wheels and wagons; and if there's time, which isn't often, he can make tables and chairs and *kists* better than any other man I know. When Achilles comes over to Houd-den-Bek he is given the sheep and goats and the small herd of cattle to look after.

This is our regular work, each man to the shape of his hands. But there's other work we have to share, the work of the

130

seasons. On Houd-den-Bek something of everything is sown and planted, and that keeps us busy. The old lands, overgrown and gone to seed, must be weeded and ploughed again. Wheat and barley down in the bottom of the valley. And that means laying out a threshing-floor and smoothing it and spreading dung and hardening it. Closer to the house are the beanfields and the orchards. The old cherry orchard. The young peaches in front of the house. The apricots and apples.

On the far side of the marsh, the *vlei*, where the Sandberg begins, Nicolaas tries to get a small vineyard going too, but it never works. Unlike Lagenvlei, where the Oubaas picks enough grapes for his few half aums of husk brandy every season, Houd-den-Bek's brandy all comes from Tulbagh or Cape Town, a few barrels kept in the shed; and I am in charge of the key.

Just as in my childhood the work runs with the seasons. When the swallows fly away after the beans have been harvested Achilles takes the sheep to the winter grazing of the Karoo; those of us who stay behind must weed the bushes from the veld and burn dry grass and prepare the lands for ploughing, come frost or snow. By the time Achilles and the swallows come back the lands are ready for sowing. And then it's hoeing and weeding and watering till midsummer when the wheat turns yellow, when it's reaping and stacking and threshing and carting away to the loft. And almost before that is done it's time for the beans again and the fruit, picking and drying, as the days grow shorter and cooler round the edges. Before the first frost settles in, tea must be harvested in the mountains, and there's curing of hides to be done, and hunting, and slaughtering for winter; and the wagons are prepared and loaded for Nicolaas to take the year's produce to the Cape. The same coming and going as at Lagenvlei, always beginning again and drawing to a close like the sun rising and setting; and then beginning anew.

I'm appointed over the others and Nicolaas stands over me. And still I don't know about him; about my place. Right hand or slave? We're not children now. These days he always wears

131

shoes; I go barefoot as before. What does it mean then, to say: *You and I will farm together?* I try him out with a plough, one afternoon in the last frost of winter. It's a bad day for ploughing, drizzling, and the North-wester blowing right through one, but Nicolaas insists the work must be done. Today we'll find out, I think. And I see to it that the plough gets broken on an outcrop of stone. At sunset the work is still undone and Nicolaas comes down to have a look.

"What's this?"

"Broken."

"Why didn't you come up to the house to tell me?"

"I tried to mend it myself."

"How did it get broken?"

"I broke it," I say. "I told you this was no day for ploughing."

He grins, but nervously. His eyes are searching me; I stare back; he looks away. "Oh well," he says at last, "anyone can have an accident."

"I pushed it over the stones."

"These banks can be treacherous," he says. "One never sees them before it's too late."

I can see he knows it's not like that. But he wants to believe what he believes. He must avoid what has really happened; he must avoid me. What will he do on Houd-den-Bek without me? But what will I do if he refuses to let me find out what I am here?

Whistling, I walk through the unevenly ploughed lands, back home to Bet. But I know the matter is not in the open yet. This horse has not been broken in. He's been knee-haltered, but not for long. Nicolaas is still scared to jump on his back and ride him as he should. But it has to happen, sooner or later. We can't avoid it for good.

And all the time, day after day, the work goes on. It pays no heed to weariness or pain: back-ache, tooth-ache, coughing, a runny stomach: Ma-Rose gives medicine and the work goes on. Like a worn-out nag tied to a millpole one goes on, round and round, winter and summer.

Still, there's merrymaking too. When Nicolaas is off to

132

Cape Town and Nooi Cecilia spends some time with her father who is ill, we rule the roost. In the evenings the men arrive on horseback, Abel and others, and it's music and dancing and cavorting and showing off. No one can play the violin like Abel; no one can keep up with him when he dances his wild reels. And when one gets tired there's husk brandy stolen from barrels on many different farms; and when we run out of that there's always old Achilles's honey-beer with a kick worse than any stallion's. It takes a full year to mature before it's properly ripe for drinking, and then it's pure firewater. It's a dozen eggs or more in a clay pot, and vinegar on top, or lemons if they're available which isn't often; and when the eggs have disappeared, shells and all, it's honeycomb in abundance, and milk, and stolen brandy; and some of Ma-Rose's nameless herbs if it's to be something really special; and after months in a dark corner of the hut, it goes into calabashes sealed with clay, until the following winter. Achilles's honey-beer is the fiery heart of all our wildest merriment. It's dancing and drinking and joking and quarrelling from darkness to dawn. Lots of fights over the few women among us many men. Over Bet too. I won't allow another man to touch her now that she's moved in with me. One night old Adonis from Buffelsfontein rides home with my axe still stuck in his skull. There's one who won't try to fool around with Bet again. Afterwards I lay into Bet with a kierie just to make sure she won't make eyes at other men; and then I lay her down and ride her so she won't forget she's been ridden. And outside in the yard the merriment goes on, filling the night with its shouting and music.

But in the last spasms of the dying night, when the coals begin to turn from red to grey and the jackals cavort like the spirits of the dead, when the baboons start barking on the highest cliffs and the night-walkers creep into the huts of sleeping men, the merriment subsides; and I steal away from the others to take Nicolaas's stallion from the stable and ride off into the dark on my own, everywhere and nowhere. It feels as if death is hard on my heels, and sooner or later it will track

133

me down. There's a loneliness in such a night, lonelier than anything I've ever known; as in the distance I hear Abel and the others ride off, back to the farms of their masters where soon, in the clanging of the slave bells, they will have to get up, without ever having been down, for a new day's work. So brief is our merriment: and then the runaway horse is returned to its harness.

I get off from Nicolaas's stallion and I pick up a stone which I hurl against another, striking up sparks in the dark. I go to one of the stone walls we've built and I begin to break it down, heaving off stone after stone to hurl into the night like pebbles thrown into a dam, except this time there is no water and one sees no rings. I shut my eyes very tightly as I throw the stones, trying to shatter the images of children swimming in that black dam, all of them with their smooth otter bodies. *You can't go with us today, Galant. You're not allowed to look at Hester. You're a slave.*

But I hit nothing.

Panting and shivering from the effort, I go back to the horse and steer it towards Ma-Rose's hut. She never minds being woken up.

"What you gnawing at your heart like this?" she asks.

"I'm fed-up with myself, Ma-Rose."

"What do you want of me?"

How do I know? Would it help to be a child again and crawl in beside her under that heavy kaross, yielding to the caresses of her skilful hand, stroking and stroking my little thing until I fall asleep? It's not so easy any more.

She brews bush-tea on her smoky *tkoin*-wood fire. Her eyes are watery. She's as old as the mountains.

"Tell me a story, Ma-Rose."

"You mad? You grown-up now. It's no time for stories any more."

"Tell me about the Great Hunter Heitsi-Eibib. Tell me about the Water Woman. Tell me about the Lightning Bird that lays its eggs in the ground."

I go back to the hut built with my own hands and to the woman who is mine.

134

She moans sleepily and sits up rubbing her eyes. The warmth of her woman-smell. "Where you been all night, Galant?"

"Just riding."

"Cocky at night, limp in the morning," she says, her teasing voice lazy and low with sleep. "Come to me."

It helps. She understands. She knows the needs of my body. She looks after me night and day. Now that she's cook in Nicolaas's house she brings me meat and other food apart from what has been set aside for us. "Eat," she says. "Meat is what you need." She also brings me morsels of news and gossip she's heard in the house. Another slave run away from Barend: it happens all the time: he has a heavy hand. Other news too. This master or that has gone away for a day or a week or a month, there's a new place for making merry at night. But it's especially on the days the newspaper is brought that Bet keeps her ears open to bring me news. A new law about slaves in the Cape, she says. Man and wife can no longer be sold separately. There's been another meeting in the Cape. They want slave children to be set free at birth. But the Government is against it. There's always news, and mostly it has to do with slaves.

"You sure it's true?" I ask her eagerly, anxiously. "You sure you heard right?"

"I heard. And I read it too."

"You can read?" I ask in amazement.

"They taught me at Bruintjieshoogte where I lived."

"Then you must bring the newspaper to the hut so you can show me."

"They won't ever let a newspaper out of their hands. You know how it is."

"But you working in the house. It's easy for you. You can always put it back afterwards."

"I already told you everything it says."

"Why you backing out now?"

"I'm not backing out. I just telling you."

"Bet, you want another hiding?"

135

Even beating her is useless; she's a stubborn woman. So I have to do it on my own without her knowing. In the afternoon I see her going out to the hut. I know Nicolaas is at a distant grazing place and the Nooi in the kitchen garden. I hide among the young peach-trees at the front door, carrying a bundle of wood so I can explain if someone sees me. When I'm quite sure there's no one around I slip through the door. The newspaper is in the *kist* in the front room, the *voorhuis*; that much I know from Bet.

Hearing the squeak of the back door hinges, I hide the paper in my bundle of wood and I hurry out in front, ducking behind the trees.

"Here it is," I say to Bet in the hut. "This must be the one you saw yesterday. It was right on top."

"Galant, this is trouble."

"Read." I push it under her nose. "Read to me. I want to hear."

"I already told you everything."

"Read, woman!"

"It's about the Government."

"Show me the Government's mark. I want to see it with my own eyes."

"Here." She presses her finger on a row of tracks in the middle of the paper. I study it closely.

"And what does it say here?"

"About the meeting. The things they said."

I grab the newspaper from her hands, crumpling it.

"Don't!" she cries. "The Baas will—"

"His name is Nicolaas."

"He's our *baas*."

I push her aside and thrust the crumpled paper back into her hands. "Show me that mark of the Government again."

"I already showed you, Galant."

"I want to see it again."

She's frightened now, I can see that. Hesitating, she presses her finger on one of the small rows of tracks.

"That's not the mark you showed me just now!" I shout.

136

She trembles and tries to crawl out of reach. "The Government has many marks."

"You lied to me, Bet. You can't read, no more than I can!"

"I tried to make it easier for you, Galant. Now please—"

"You cheated me. I don't take that from anybody."

I pick up the axe I used to chop my bundle of wood.

"No, Galant, please!"

"Bet!" the Nooi calls from the kitchen. "Where are you?"

I have to let her go. But I remain in the hut until I hear the horse coming through the gate: then I go out, the newspaper openly in my hands.

"I want to know what it says about the slaves," I tell Nicolaas as he pulls the reins over the horse's head.

Surprised, he takes the newspaper from me. "What are you doing with things you don't understand?"

The world is trembling before my eyes, but I restrain myself. "Nicolaas, I want to know what this thing says."

He laughs, but uneasily, keeping the horse between us. "It says all sorts of things," he answers, smirking. "It talks about a white hen that hatched a black cat in another country."

I have the reins in my hands. The knuckles of my fingers show up pale through the skin.

"Now unsaddle the horse and rub it down," says Nicolaas. "The sun is already setting."

I know I cannot touch him. He knows it too. It's different between us. I see it in the way he walks back to his house. All I can do, that night, is to ride Bet bareback, to ride her hard.

I ride her well, and now she is with child.

This is something different again, and it makes me resentful. What am I to do with a child? What will become of him? Every new foal born on this farm is broken in; and I don't want that for him.

"I don't want it, Ma-Rose," I storm at the old woman. "This is no place for a new child."

"But he won't be a slave like you," she reminds me. "He'll be Bet's child and she's a free woman, she's of the Khoin like me."

137

It trickles through my body like a draught of old Achilles's honey-beer. A terrible lightning. I feel like crying; but I also feel like laughing. Under the stars I ride home on Nicolaas's horse, looking up. This child will come and go as he likes. He can go as far as the Cape if he wishes. Here I am, riding in the night: but that child will trot off into the sunrise. Tomorrow has never been any concern of mine. All I've ever had is my bit of today. But this child: his tracks will run all the way to the daybreak.

It is such a dizzying thought that when the horse stumbles over a stone I lose my grip and roll over the ground, grazing knees and elbows. I feel like cursing; but I'm laughing too. All you bloody white hens, I think, you can breed as many bloody black cats as you wish. What do I care? Tether me if you want to; keep me on as short a rein as you can find. But this child of mine will run off into the rising sun.

HESTER

There was no need for Barend to choose this place. He is the eldest, he had freedom of choice. And Houd-den-Bek is the better farm. Water in abundance, wheatlands on the plains, veld for grazing. The soil is rocky but fertile and deep. It is an open farm, even the graveyard lies exposed. But to keep me from the grave of my father and the house in which I'd been born he chose Elandsfontein, in this narrow valley between two steep ridges of mountains, remote and austere, here to confine and possess me.

It is a fight of animals, nightly resumed, and as he claws and thrusts to subdue me, hoping no doubt to break me in like a mare, I resist in the savage knowledge that he is more vulnerable than I, that even as he rides me there can only be abjection in his triumph when, limp and ludicrous, he withdraws, having bruised and torn no more than my body. This is the true struggle: to keep desire and the dream intact. The body must survive. Our limits are circumscribed by its contours and urges. But the body is a moveable asset and there is earth below, and the liquid insistence of water. These he cannot possess by using me; yet I, in my own body, have access to them.

Our children are the result of this unremitting war. I did not wish them, yet in having them, boys both, I have acquired a new invulnerability. They are not of me, yet strangely shaped by my body they assert my independence from him. In the beginning it was fruitless. There must be a bitterness in my womb, I thought, poisoning his seed and killing it; and I relished it. Children I believed would but confirm his hold on me, and in my monthly flow I asserted a fierce virginity which had nothing to do with the first stained sheet he had hung from the window for only the swallows and the mountain eagles to see. My barrenness was exemplary and proud. I thrived on the anxious staring of his mother and the annoyed whispers of that man who is now my father-in-law: "I told you to pick a tall strong woman, Barend. For God's sake, man, what is to become of the Van der Merwes?"

When I first fell pregnant I was numb with revulsion. I refused to accept it. It must be some growth inside me, a sickness. Everything in me denied a child. He was the last to whom I would admit it, yet he must have suspected it. Whenever he thought I was unaware of it he would stare at me, not in lust or anger but with what seemed like awe. A new gentleness became apparent. Perhaps that was what revolted me more than arrogance or assault. It reminded me too much of what Nicolaas had been like before. Against violence I could arm myself; mildness was more insidious. When I was alone I would fold my arms across my stomach and try forcibly to expel this growing thing from my body, this alien presence threatening my solitude from within. Then came the first tentative stirrings, the merest flutter of minute limbs, an eyelid-flickering of tiny fist or foot. And something changed. I fought it as if my last freedom was at stake; but I knew I'd lost. The child was inside me and I wanted it. More desperately than I'd ever dared to want anything since the death of my father I wanted this living moving child within me. When I lost it—and it was so unnecessary, so stupid—I wanted to die. I knew that whas why I'd lost it: because I'd desired it too much, the way it had happened with other things before. But this time it was worse. The aching emptiness inside was not a return to what had been my normal state but a confirmation of loss. Losing what one has never had is more searing than physical pain; it is the death of the possible. It is a retraction of the horizon, a revised and ruder definition of the body itself. Earth eroding; a subterranean spring drying up.

As I lay in the bed in pain after losing the child, Barend came in. Something welled up in me: a desire for him to come

140

to me, to hold me. I needed to tell him I was sorry. I needed forgiveness and closeness. But I saw the hard anger in his eyes and realized again how much he hated me for what had happened. So I remained silent and he left. It was the last chance, I think, we had of reaching out to touch. Pregnancy had made me vulnerable; I knew I had to be doubly careful lest I be invaded.

There was no repetition of the first elation when it happened again, and if there was no acquiescence there was no resistance either. It was no marvel; it was only inevitable. "Normal." Not an act of extension but of simple and necessary fortification against the future. The dream did not die but only, by entrenching itself, sealed itself off more effectively from the world, allowing less than before of private hope or tenderness.

I was forbidden to return to Houd-den-Bek again, except on the occasional obligatory family visit with Barend. The first time had been, of course, for Nicolaas's wedding. I'd known it would be torture: Barend flaunting me; that man his father expounding on the virtues of large fertile wives; the old woman going out of her way to make me feel "wanted"; neighbours peering to detect the first signs of pregnancy even though we'd then been married for barely two months; Cecilia parading in anxious pride through what had been my home, baring her large teeth in a fixed, uneasy smile as if desperately to prove that her stays were not too tight for that strong ungainly body; and Nicolaas staring with vulnerable eyes like an antelope wounded and waiting, uncomprehending, for the shot that will put it out of its misery. And torture it was, even though mitigated by the rain which limited the crowd and inhibited their merriment—unlike the outrageous throng that had mobbed us here at Elandsfontein and driven me to seek refuge behind a barricaded bedroom door, later broken down forcibly by Barend for the first pitched battle in our interminable war. Even so their feast became too much for me and I slipped from the *voorhuis* as soon as I could. In the kitchen at that moment there was only Galant; the other slaves were in front, serving meat and brandy.

141

It was a strange pocket of silence: the crowd inside; outside the streaming rain—and in the kitchen none but the two of us.

"You looking for something?" he asked.

"I'm going."

"Shall I bring your carriage?"

"No, I'll walk." I hadn't planned it at all; but as I said it I realized the full extent of my need to be alone, even in that rain. No: because of the rain.

"You can't go in this weather," he said.

"I've always liked the rain." And suddenly I added: "Don't you remember?"

He remained impassive. He'd probably forgotten. In a sense it was a relief, I suppose; yet there was a curious feeling of rejection in his attitude as if he were denying not only his own memory but part of what, who knows, might have been important to me.

As I opened the door the rain threw me back into the kitchen and I had to gasp for breath.

"I told you it was bad," he said.

If he hadn't I might have stayed. Now he'd turned it into a challenge and I said: "I'm going."

"I can walk with you to show you the way."

"I'll find the way."

"You'll need a lantern."

"Don't be silly. In this rain?"

He watched me sullenly as I stood with my weight against the door.

"Galant," I said, in a surge of urgency—unable to take him by the shoulders and shake him, with only my voice to persuade him—"you'll be living here now. For God's sake, look after the place for me."

"I will, Miss Hester."

It stung me. He'd never called me that before. I turned round and hurled myself into the rain, leaving him to shut the door. The storm was worse than I'd thought. Much worse. Once I'd staggered out of the yard there was total blackness. It felt as if the whole world was being washed away. Within

142

moments I was drenched. I found my way back to the outbuildings and stumbled into the stable, a steaming darkness with softly neighing animals and the piercing smell of urine. I knew them well and as I spoke to them they recognized me. Shivering, weighed down by the wet heavy clothes, I sought and found heat against their large bodies until I felt I could brave the rain again. No need to grope for reins and saddle in the dark. Choosing the horse I knew best I led it outside and scrambled on its back, lying forward to steady myself, feeling along the entire extent of my body the reassuring power and warmth of the great animal moving through night and rain, a contraction and motion of muscles, the deceptive obedience of so much savage strength. More than once I nearly fell asleep on his back from exhaustion, waking up only as I started slipping or when he would suddenly stop or swerve to avoid some invisible obstacle.

The new grey uninspiring day had already lightened up considerably by the time I reached Elandsfontein. I was numb all over and I could feel a dangerous fever mounting; and Barend, galloping home frantically from wherever he'd been scouring the veld for me, was in such a rage that he hit me. I offered no resistance. Not only because of the numbness, the strange euphoria of exhaustion, but because of an inexplicable contentment in me: the way I imagined one would feel after making love all night long with a man one truly desired.

In spite of his explicit interdict I often returned to Houd-den-Bek in those early days. Not on foot, alas—it was much too far, two hours at least on a fast horse—and always taking the precaution of carrying with me a basket with newly baked bread, or jam, or a joint of meat as a pretext: but if no one saw me as I sat at the grave or simply roamed about, I would not seek them out to deliver the *karmenaadjie*. There were angry scenes with Barend every time he found out, but in the end he resigned himself to it. He had trouble enough with slaves running away. His wife, at least, came home again: if not willingly, at least from a sense of obligation.

When I was with child I became absent-minded, I suppose.

I'd always loved riding as fast as possible. Speed shook loose my thoughts; it set them free to take off on their own. On that day the horse suddenly took fright—a snake, a tortoise or a meerkat in the way—and swerving at full gallop to avoid it, trod in an aardvark hole and threw me. That was when I lost the baby. Afterwards I found the urgency to return to the grave abated.

In the beginning, in the delusion of adolescence, one believes in savage rebellion. Ensnared in your condition—woman, wife, underling—only two escapes offer themselves as alternatives to violence: madness, or suicide. But survival as such takes precedence, even over dignity. It is not surrender, but an ultimate patient readiness in the body and the mind.

Domesticity. Becoming more and more like Tant Alida? No. Mine is not acquiescence but abeyance. Knowing that life is more than this. Looking at a barren land one may not suspect the hidden water courses running below. It is a subdued existence; what battle there is has become submerged, with only the occasional eruption to shake and revitalize one. There is a wildness and a violence lurking somewhere, ready at the right moment to lunge like a horse running dangerously in the night.

BET

It was a long road I had behind me and I'd hoped finally to find peace at Houd-den-Bek, but what happened? We were only a handful of Khoin, trekking this way and that through the years, from Outeniqua to the Camdeboo, round the Snow Mountain and up to the snake-bends of the Fish River; from the dry scrubland of the Karoo to the *gnap*-trees of the Suurveld. But life was growing ever more troublesome; the Law was following in our footsteps wherever we went. One could no longer come and go without a pass; before you were allowed to do any work you had to be booked in with a master; you could be shot before you even knew you were trespassing. And so we decided to settle in Bruintjieshoogte with what remained of our goats and fat-tailed sheep. We found work with several Boer families—Prinsloos, Labuschagnes—and for a long time we had no complaints. Then life became difficult again. The Boers were pushing from one side; and from across the river Hintsa's people, the Red Blanket Men, were pushing back. One would wake up in the morning to find all the cattle kraals deserted. Then the commandos would set out on horseback, law or no law; and at night the Xhosa fires would be burning on the hilltops: and soon there would be a new raid.

I tried to stay out of it, listening to the talk from both sides. We've opened up the land, said the Boers, this belongs to us. No, said Hintsa's people, Tixo made the world for everybody so that a man's cattle may graze wherever they find good land. And so it was one word after another, and soon it was war. We just happened to be in Grahamstown for the Baas's Christmas shopping, and we were surrounded right there in the small

145

white town among the green hills. The Xhosa warriors came streaming down the slopes like black water from a broken dam. Oxtails swinging, ox-hide shields shaking, assegais sailing through the air like swarms of locusts. I thought we'd never come out alive again.

But it wasn't from fear that our group made a getaway as soon as the worst was over. If your time is up you'll die, no matter where you try to hide. What sent us fleeing was knowing that it wasn't our war. What concern was it of ours? If Boers and Xhosas wanted to kill one another, let them, as long as we of the Khoin weren't crushed between their two millstones. No one can stand that. And so the handful of us made our escape while the gunpowder was still covering the town like a cloud.

I left with my baby on my back, but it died on the way to the Cape. There were few of us when we set out; but we were even fewer by the time we crossed the mountains from the Karoo. There we split up into twos and threes, each going his own way; the tribe was no more. I worked on the farms I passed, sometimes in a kitchen, otherwise in the fields; and in the time of the bean-harvest Baas Nicolaas found me in Tulbagh and hired me. Said the Nooi needed someone in the kitchen. She had one slave woman but it seemed the two of them didn't get on well; and what they really needed was a cook.

"Then it's just the work for me," I said. "In Bruintjieshoogte I learned to run a household from kitchen to *voorhuis.*"

And I had no reason for complaint. They were easy people to be with and I soon took a liking in Galant. Old Ontong was living with the slave woman Lydia. Achilles was a bit of a washout; and the others were just casual workers hired for piecework. I'd been without a man for a long time then, not counting the few encounters on the other farms where I'd been doing odd jobs on the way, and that makes one ruttish and moody. If the root isn't planted the furrow goes to waste. So I was relieved when Galant took me. He wasn't a man of many words and he could be very brooding and apart at times. But he had lightning in his hands. And I'll say this for him, that he

146

was a rider second to none, of horses and women alike.

I soon learned to fit in with the Nooi's way of working. She had a quick temper and couldn't stand bungling or skimping, but that suited me. She never did me short in anything. It was only with Lydia she couldn't control herself, and we often discussed it round the fire of an evening. We all knew about the Baas's weak spot for Lydia of course, and his visits in the dark of the night; but that was his right and none of us complained about it. But the Nooi simply couldn't stand Lydia; and the Baas must have given her cause for that, for every time after he'd taken his evening walk to the woman's hut there would be trouble the next day. Then Galant or one of the others would be called to tie Lydia up in the stable. It usually happened as soon as the Baas had gone off to the veld; and the Nooi would take the strap herself. Now there's flogging and flogging and I've had some of both in my life; and that's why I say it wasn't proper the way she did it. Once she'd started she couldn't control herself. Only after Lydia's screams had changed from the sound of a woman in labour to the whimpering of a dying puppy the beating would stop. Then the Nooi would come out, shoving Lydia ahead of her, and Lydia wouldn't have a stitch of clothing on her body. Sometimes the clothes were beaten to shreds; mostly they were just torn from her in rage. And that was a bad thing to my mind for Lydia isn't a child any more, she's older than me, she's got children of her own. But as naked as my finger she would be driven out to the veld to collect wood or dung-cakes, even in winter. Sometimes the ground would be covered in snow, white-grey as cinders and crackling underfoot, but no matter: Lydia would be naked. Then we usually sent someone with a kaross after her when the Nooi wasn't looking, to cover her up until it was time to come home.

The first time I saw it, it made me feel sick. I was expecting Galant's child then and I suppose one has less resistance in a time like that. It wasn't just the beating: it was the Nooi's way of talking while she went on flogging the woman. A strange moaning tone of voice, almost sobbing. Once I listened at the stable door but I couldn't make out anything she was saying, except that it sounded like the Bible, which I knew from being called in for prayers every Wednesday and Sunday night. Galant found me there and angrily took me away; I was shivering, not only with cold.

"Come away," he said. "You got nothing to do here."

"The Nooi will kill Lydia yet."

"You stay out of it."

"Why don't you talk to the Baas about it?" I asked.

"It may make it worse."

He took me to our hut. But after he'd gone out to give Achilles a hand with the cattle I returned to the stable. That was when I saw Lydia coming out naked. But it was the Nooi herself I couldn't help staring at. Her face flushed a deep red, her hair all dishevelled and damp with sweat, her cheeks streaked with tears; and she was panting. It might have been of tiredness, it was enough to wear anyone out, even a woman as strong as the Nooi. But it was something else that upset me, unless I just imagined it because of the child in me: but my first thought when I saw her was that she looked like a woman who'd been with a man all night.

If Galant didn't want to interfere, I thought, perhaps I should speak to the Baas myself. But then something happened that really shook me. After one of the beatings, just as Lydia was on her way home in the late afternoon with her load of dung-cakes, naked, and black-and-blue, the Baas came round the corner of the shed from the orchard. He stopped in his tracks when he saw her and he grew pale. There was still light enough to see by, and I'd just come from the kitchen with the water barrel.

"What's the matter, Lydia?" he asked.

Her face was smeared with tears and snot. She was covered in bruises, not only her back but everywhere, even her belly and her breasts. Yet she held herself straight, tall and gaunt as the aloes of Bruintjieshoogte, with the load of dung on her head, staring at the Baas without saying a word.

At that moment the Nooi came from the kitchen, impa-

148

tiently pushing me out of the way. "Have you ever seen such shamelessness, Nicolaas?" she said. "She's been impossible all day. And no matter what I say to her she cheeks me back. I've spoken to you about her often enough: today you must do something."

He still seemed very pale, but he said: "Lydia, lie down there." And then he gave her a flogging with his sjambok.

All the time the Nooi was standing behind me on the doorstep, breathing open-mouthed. When I couldn't stand it any longer I went away to fill my barrel and came back round the house to enter through the front door. I'd seen enough. At least, I thought, this would be the end of his nightly visits. That would be something. But the very same night, I swear to God, he came out to Lydia again. And the following evening we were all called to prayers as usual, as if nothing had happened at all, and the Baas and the Nooi sat at the table with the brass lamp on it, and he opened the clasps of his big brown book and started reading to us, slowly and deliberately, savouring every word.

That was when something inside me turned against them. I'm an easy-going person by nature and I usually get along well with others; but in the kitchen I began to shut myself off from the woman. I would do the work I was given to do; but I kept my heart out of it. And to my mind the Baas was worse than the Nooi. What she'd done was bad enough; but in her own way she might have had a reason for it. White people are strange in their ways. But what the Baas had done was a shame and I didn't want to have anything to do with it.

I was tired of trekking about; and I had Galant's child in me. Had it not been for that I think I would have packed up and left. As it was, I stayed on, but only with much resentment, and trying to keep out of the Baas's way as well as I could. I would say good morning or good night to him because that was my duty; but no more. I wouldn't forgive him for not having had the guts to stop his wife in her bad ways.

And that was why the thing with the child was such a shock to me. I just couldn't understand myself at all. Why should

149

one wish to do what repulses one most? It turned me into a stranger to myself. Truly, one is an abyss; worse than any in the cliffs of the Skurweberg.

We were delighted with the child. I'd never seen a man so ridiculously happy as Galant. I felt my breasts aching with an uncontrollable flow of milk out of sheer joy to see him like that. And just as well, for Galant became as addicted to my milk as the baby. Said it was the sweetest drink he'd ever tasted. There were times when I had both of them at my breasts at the same time, father and son together, pumping and drinking greedily and noisily; and as I looked down on their faces, their eyes closed with contentment, I could properly feel my stomach turn with happiness.

"You mustn't fuss over the child like this," I warned him sometimes. "It's tempting the evil spirits. Suppose something happens to him?"

"Whatever can happen to him? You're here and I'm here too."

We called him David. One night the Baas read about David, it was a Wednesday, because the prayers were shorter than on Sundays; and he read about David and King Saul, and how the king had thrown his assegai at him and how David had got away into the mountains, knowing the time would come when he would be king himself. And when he went back to the hut Galant said: "We'll call him David. Because his day will come too. He isn't a slave like me."

"What's so bad about being a slave?" I asked him. "There's not much difference between my life and yours on the farm. They're good to you. The Baas made you *mantoor*. You're in charge of everything. You can sow and reap, and you got heifers and lambs of your own. They give you food and clothes for nothing."

"I'm still a slave."

And that was all he said. I left it at that, for it was no use arguing with him when he was in that mood; he always was a deep one.

The child was about a year old, just over, I was weaning

150

him, when the Baas sent Galant to the Karoo to fetch some cattle he'd bought. Fifty-eight cattle, I remember well; it was just after the winter, in the time of the big housecleaning and the replastering of the walls. Galant was away for twenty-six days. I counted them off, for when a woman is weaning one gets bothered by one's swollen breasts and the only thing that helps is the root of a man.

David was difficult to manage, for he was used to drinking whenever he felt like it; and he was teething too, and snotty. I was tempted to take him back to my breast again, but that would be even more bothersome. For the child was becoming a nuisance in the house and in the yard, and the Nooi had already complained a couple of times. She was not the sort of woman I would like to give reason for complaining. I had more work than I could handle, not only in the house: in the absence of Galant and Achilles I had to give a hand with the sheep too. So it was a bad time and one had to be sharp to stay out of trouble.

It had already happened once or twice that when I'd left the child at home—when it was possible, Ma-Rose would come over to keep an eye; but she was also helping out with the farmwork—he would come crawling to the house after me. Clever little bastard. But difficult. Then the Baas gave me a warning: "The child is getting troublesome," he said. "You better see to it that he doesn't get under the Nooi's feet."

"Yes, Baas," I said. But what I thought in my heart was: *You better watch out. Don't start ordering me about. I'm not Lydia.*

I spoke to Ma-Rose and she promised to do what she could, but it wasn't going to be easy. And just the following day as I brought the sheep in to the kraal I saw that there was something wrong. David was lying beside the hut, tied to the bitter-almond tree, and making little sobbing sounds in his sleep as he jerked and twitched his legs. My insides went numb. When I came to him and untied him I noticed the black bruises all over his body.

"What happened here?" I asked Ma-Rose, struggling to keep calm.

151

She was preparing skins in the backyard, turning up the heavy *brey*-stone that stretched them and made them supple for Ontong to cut his thongs. She seemed composed, but I could see she was working much faster than usual. Once she was nearly hit by the stone as she let go of the skin and the weight came whizzing down to the ground.

"Ma-Rose, what the hell happened here today?"

"I had to tie the child to the tree. He came crawling to the house again and Nicolaas told me to take him back. Then I had to take the washing down to the *vlei*."

"What about these marks?"

She wound up the skins with the stone again. It came down spinning like a whirlwind.

"I know nothing about that," she said at last, not looking at me. "Why don't you ask them at the house?"

First I suckled the child. No matter that I'd been weaning him; he was in need of mother's milk. Still holding him to my breast, his small body shaken by violent double-sobs, I went to the house, scattering the chickens in my way.

"Yes, Bet?" asked the Nooi when I came into the kitchen.

"I came to ask what happened to my child," I said. Thinking: *Just tell me I'm cheeky. Then I'll pick up one of these pieces of firewood.*

I suppose the Nooi could see I was in no mood for nonsense.

"There was trouble in the yard, Bet," she said. "The Baas got very angry. I told you to keep the child away from the house."

As she said it he came through to the kitchen from the *voorhuis*, stopping in the middle door. He said nothing, just stared at me with his smoky blue eyes. His shirt-sleeves were rolled down, but loose. I stared back at him. I thought: *If only I didn't have this child at my breast right now.* But I couldn't say a word. I remembered Lydia, and the day he'd said to her: "Lydia, lie down there," and how she'd lain down on the ground in front of him, offering dumbly her bruised body to his lash. Something inside me contracted in fear. My man was

152

not there; he was far away in the Karoo with the cattle and I was alone.

Without a word I turned round and went out. I couldn't see properly and it was just luck that I didn't stumble over anything.

It must have been about a week later. David was all right again. Amazing how quickly a child recovers. I had to prepare the meat that morning; it was a Monday, slaughtering day, and the meat had to be washed. It's a long way from the yard to the washing place and I couldn't manage the child at the same time. So I let him drink his fill and closed him up in the hut.

How could I have known that such a small child would manage to open the door?

Ma-Rose had left early with the sheep as Ontong had to water the orchards that day; so there was no one near.

After I'd finished with the meat I took the barrel back to the kitchen. Just as I came out again the Baas said behind me:

"Bet."

I looked round. He was as pale as the day with Lydia.

"Bet, didn't I warn you about the child before?"

That was all he said. But I knew immediately; from his face.

The child was lying outside the hut on his side. He was still breathing, but only with difficulty, a rattling sound. I saw his body. But I couldn't cry. I picked him up and carried him down to the water where I'd washed the meat. I bathed him and brought him back. On the way I saw Ma-Rose in the distance with the sheep. She waved. I didn't reply. Just before sunset the child died.

Ma-Rose was with me then; she went over to the house to tell them.

It was full moon. In the rising of the moon the Baas came to the hut. I was sitting on the bare dung-floor, my breasts heavy and painful with milk. He stooped in the doorway, as large as the night.

"Bet, you've got to forgive me," he said. His voice was rasping in his throat. "I quarrelled with my wife. I lost my

153

head. I never meant to do such a thing. You know I'm not like that."

"Yes, Baas," I said.

"My God, Bet, tell me what you need. Anything. I'll give you anything."

I sat looking down, and swallowed a lump. I wasn't crying. There were no tears at all in me. How was it possible?

The next day they buried David, wrapped in his small grey blanket. No one was sent for, no one came to look at him. He was buried just like that. I didn't want to see.

The Baas came to the hut again. "Bet, you must forgive me."

I pressed my head against his hard knees and grabbed him by the legs. I couldn't let go again. I felt I was drowning. I was thinking of Lydia. *Lie down there.* The way he went back to her the same night to abuse her torn body. I understood nothing about it all, and I still don't. I knew I'd lost Galant. He would never forgive me or anyone else. But that wasn't what shook me as I knelt there holding his legs and groaning like an animal, the sound Lydia made when she was beaten, like a dog, a bitch in heat. That was it: an emptiness growing and expanding inside me all night so that I felt like crawling out to the yard to howl under his window like a dog.

That was it: and from that day I couldn't let him be. I lusted after him day and night. I followed him wherever he went, begging with my body to be taken. He paid no attention. But I followed him. He had me in his hands as if I were a slave. I wanted him to order me: *Lie down there.* I silently pleaded with him. I followed him. I felt that was the only way ever to fill up the emptiness inside me again.

Did I really believe that, somehow, it would bring my child back to me if I turned my body into carrion and threw it to this man so he could tear me apart like a vulture? Surely that was madness. But one doesn't think straight at a time like that. You only feel it burning. You're thirsty. You're thirsty. Take me, I wanted to tell the Baas. Break me. Galant will never touch me again. I've lost my man. I've lost everything. I'm

154

rejected by everybody because my child is dead. It's lonesome.
It's night. Take me. Break me apart.

But he wouldn't. Mad Lydia was good enough for him; not
I. To him I was sinful. In my womb I carried death.

LYDIA

But my feathers. The beatings, the shouting, the voices around my ears. What are they saying? The men with the cocks. The big featherless cocks. Pinning me down. The pain. Break me like a lump of earth. Why won't you let me be, why not for a single night? But I got my feathers. Stuffed into my mattress in the hut. Goose feathers, chicken feathers, swallows, weaver-birds, cranes, vultures, even the mountain-eagle. The feathers of years and years, picked up and carried home. The men are hurting me. Day and night. The woman with the sjambok. What are they saying? Voices, voices. But my feathers. I speak to the birds. Those with feathers, in trees. I speak to swallow and wild-goose. All feathered things. They tell me to wait. One day I'll fly away like the swallows.

BAREND

After much thought I have come to the conclusion that our troubles started the day the English arrived in the Cape. We had problems with the Government before that: Pa often told me about Great-grandpa's quarrel with the Landdrost in Tulbagh; and over the years there would be the occasional agent or bailiff turning up to collect taxes or bring news of new laws. But for us the Cape was always remote, and the land is big. If there was trouble in one place one could load one's wagon and move off to where no man had left his footprints before and where no neighbour's smoke smudged the horizon. But since the English arrived—in the beginning it wasn't too bad, they probably felt uneasy to venture far from the Cape; but since 1806 or thereabouts they became more intrepid and troublesome—since then we've had problems.

Take the droughts to start with. We'd always known droughts in this land; it was drought, among other things, that had sent Great-grandpa trekking again after having staked out his part of paradise at Houd-den-Bek. Still, drought came and went, and if one humbled oneself before the Lord one could always count on survival. But the English, who did not have the true faith—they couldn't even speak the language of the State Bible, how did they expect God to understand them?— brought the wrath of God upon the land. And nowadays, when there's drought it remains dry; and the rains only come when the earth has been devastated, and then it's a flood. Then there's locusts. We'd never known them in the Bok-keveld before, Pa assured me. There had been rumours from elsewhere, but our highlands were safe. Suddenly, these last few years they arrived three times to lay waste the veld and the

157

wheatfields. Not to speak of the inspectors and commissioners and other pests who began to wear out the wagon-road over the Witzenberg to plague us here. All of a sudden there's levies to be paid, and taxes, and quitrent, and God knows what; and forms have to be filled in listing everything one possesses or doesn't possess. Wheat, fruit, sheep, goats, cattle, pigs, slaves, poultry; the lot. And if you dare raise voice or hand against them you can be sure there will be a bailiff on your doorstep in no time—perhaps even a platoon of Hottentot *pandoers*—to drag you to the Drostdy.

It was a detachment of *pandoers* that started the whole business at Slagtersnek. We'd heard enough about that, all right; and when the Hottentot woman Bet came to work for Nicolaas, he questioned her very carefully about the whole matter, knowing she'd come from those parts near the Border. I'm not saying anything about the right or wrong of it, because I've heard those Border Boers can get troublesome—not that one can really blame them. But when it came to hanging, after Freek Bezuidenhout had been shot by the *pandoers* and his brother and the rest had taken up arms against the English, God intervened with His own hand to break four of the five ropes on the gallows. Any Christian would have let the condemned men go after that. That's what the Scriptures say. But to me it was the surest sign of all that the English were godless, when they simply called for new ropes to hang the four men again, finishing them off this time.

"I swear a holy oath," I told Pa the day we first heard about Slagtersnek—it was shortly after our wedding, on a Sunday; we'd all gone to Lagenvlei for the service; only Hester had stayed at home—"if an Englishman ever sets foot on my farm to force his law on me I'll shoot him on the spot."

Nicolaas, I remember, reproached me in his holier-than-thou manner: "Render unto Caesar what is Caesar's, Barend."

"No Englishman is my Caesar," I said curtly.

"A Roman was Caesar to the Jews," he said. Nicolaas mellowed considerably in his views afterwards, once I think he discovered the Bible could not be applied literally to the ways and laws of the English; but in those early days he could be infuriating at times. If there had been Englishmen in Biblical times, I told him, God would have said something different. And if we didn't look out they'd be taking this land from under our feet.

The day we got married Pa gave us a word from Joshua to cherish. I don't have much time for reading, I'm a farmer and I have work to do; but when I do have some time to spare I enjoy rereading those words in the twenty-third chapter, from the fourth verse:

Behold, I have divided unto you by lot these nations that remain, to be an inheritance for your tribes, from Jordan, with all the nations that I have cut off, even unto the great sea westward.

And the Lord your God, he shall expel them from before you, and drive them from out of your sight; and ye shall possess their land, as the Lord your God hath promised unto you.

Be ye therefore very courageous to keep and to do all that is written in the book of the law of Moses, that ye turn not aside therefrom to the right hand or to the left; that ye come not among these nations, these that remain among you; neither make mention of the name of their gods, nor cause to swear by them, neither serve them, nor bow yourselves unto them; but cleave unto the Lord your God, as ye have done unto this day.

This word was always honoured on my farm, on Elandsfontein; we never turned right or left. What trouble we had came from outside. Unless Hester be termed trouble. One thing that weighed upon me from the beginning was the extent of my addiction to Hester. The Bible says nothing about coveting one's own wife. And yet I often felt that the extreme nature of my desire must be sinful, ever since my eyes had been opened for her the first time, a bare girl in a dam. I thought marrying her would assuage the fever, but it made no difference except possibly for worse. Through the years it steadily increased, as before my eyes she matured into a woman, even though she

159

retained that hard thin negative body. And her resistance against me, her efforts to fight me off with tooth and nail so that in every encounter I had to tame her anew without ever really succeeding, were enough to drive me to distraction. She would throw me like the grey horse Pa had given me when we were small and who'd refused to allow anyone on his back until in the end Galant had broken him in. Not that I would have liked to see Hester docile. Her very wildness increased my desire.

From the first day I seemed unable to do anything right in her eyes. I could have chosen Houd-den-Bek as my farm, a fertile place I'd set my heart on for years, but I brought her to Elandsfontein to spare her the constant memory of her father—but even that failed to please her.

I knew there was something godless in it. The way she resisted the idea of having children, for instance. I wanted to fertilize her and see my child grow inside her; I believed that would finally break her in. Pa had always said: "The only way to manage an impudent woman is to put her up the pole." But it didn't work with her; she seemed to reject my very seed. And when at last it happened, when I'd almost begun to give up hope, after more than three years of barrenness, when she was already eighteen, she deliberately mounted the wildest horse on the farm, spurring it on with her sjambok until it threw her and she brought down the baby. I thought: If ever I raise my hand against a woman it must be today. A man cannot be mocked like that; it is an outrage before God. But when I saw her lying in the big bed all the rage left me: her dusky skin terribly pale, the big black eyes glowing in the narrow face, the dark hair tousled on the pillow Ma had embroidered, the high cheekbones, the wide mouth drawn into a narrow line of hate against me; and her hands on the white sheet, the long fingers, the bitten nails; the upper arm and the roundness of her shoulder. My body turned to water; I was a tree growing in water, and I could feel my roots losing their hold. What I desired above all else was to go to her and kneel beside the bed and say: "Forgive me." But why and for what? What had I

160

done that required forgiveness? And I knew only too well that stooping to such unseemliness would earn me her contempt forever. As on the day with the lamb I felt close to tears. But I had to restrain myself. She would despise the slightest sign of weakness in me. So I turned round and went out again. Outside I had to wipe my eyes with the back of my hand. I tried to convince myself it was only because of the fierce sunlight, but I knew it was really because of this woman who was my wife and whom I desired so much that I felt like the burning thornbush which just burned and burned without ever turning to ashes.

Even after the children had been born it made no perceptible difference to her. She would remain my adversary until the day of my death; and the only way in which to remain worthy of her was to be as strong as she, never to give in, never to show a tender spot on which she might get a hold, for then she would destroy me.

That, too, in a way, had been predestined by the interference of the English. For the day we'd gone to Tulbagh to get married it turned out the Dutch *predikant* had made a mistake with the date and had left for Cape Town; and unless we were prepared to go home and come back the whole way the following week we had to make do with the English clergyman. What could we do but resign ourselves to the inevitable, even while knowing it could lead to no good? And in due course God proved me right: but at what cost.

Still, most of our troubles came from outside, from the Landdrosts and their underlings. In the early days they'd all been people of our own stock. In the time of Landdrost Fischer we never had any problems about slaves and other business when we took the matter to Tulbagh; but the Englishman Trappes was a bastard. And it was clear for all to see that God disapproved of the man too, because he'd barely been in Tulbagh six months when the Drostdy was practically washed away by a flood. After that we had to travel all the way to Worcester for legal business. And what with all the new laws and regulations the English were making in the Cape

161

there hardly ever came a newspaper without more problems. How the slaves got wind of such events and speculations I couldn't tell. They must have been blown about secretly like a plague; and the moment you put a foot wrong they knew all about the new laws and ran off to the Drostdy to complain. The only choice left us was whether to follow in pursuit immediately or to wait until the summons came. We had no proper say on our own farms, and that was asking for trouble.

I'd always had problems with runaways. They said I ruled them with too hard a hand. Even Pa once remonstrated with me. But it was easy for him to talk: he'd had his slaves for years, they'd all been broken in long ago and each one knew his place. It was different for me, starting with a new lot. And times had changed too. They knew it only too well. All the more reason to break them in harshly so they would be sure who had the last word on the farm. I was *baas*, and they'd better accept it right from the beginning. Otherwise they'd bruise my heel the moment I turned my back. One could take no chances with them: they might look servile enough, but deep down they would always remain savages. Perhaps I should have followed Nicolaas's example and taken over some of Pa's old trusted hands. But the idea didn't appeal to me: slaves are like dogs that don't take readily to a new master. Above all I wanted a fresh start on my own farm, all ties with the depressing past broken.

Whoever didn't do his work properly had his backside tanned without any more ado. The problem was that they knew my hands were really tied by the Government; so whenever they felt my punishment had been excessive they'd run off to Tulbagh. A few times I managed to overtake them on the way and bring them back for another, more severe flogging: if after that they still felt like complaining at least they'd have sufficient reason. And once old Landdrost Fischer had branded a runaway's back with his irons he would think twice before deserting again. Even so I lost two for good (and several Hottentots as well—but these had always been a worthless lot anyway) and that was quite a loss, for they were

162

damned expensive. And when Trappes took over I soon found out that with the English even a runaway slave's word sometimes counted for more than his master's. That time with Klaas I was fined fifty rix dollars. But at least I had my revenge when Klaas came back.

"Let's see what my fine is worth to you," I said as I tied his wrists and ankles in the shed and flung him across the barrel.

For once I was prepared to go all the way: and whatever the consequences it would be an unforgettable warning to the rest. But Klaas was tough, he kept us busy all afternoon. And in the end it was Hester who came to put an end to it. Which was quite a shock, because she'd never previously interfered with my management of the farm. Her place was indoors, I'd given the house into her hands to run; the rest was my responsibility. Except for that once. At sunset she opened the door of the shed where we were working on Klaas, and came inside. At first I thought she'd brought me some coffee, for a flogging makes one thirsty. But she stood there empty-handed, trembling.

"Will you stop this immediately?" she said. Right in front of the slaves.

"Hester, you stay out of this. It's none of your business."

"I tell you it's going to stop."

I couldn't allow myself to be humiliated in front of my inferiors. Once again I raised the sjambok and brought it down on Klaas's shoulders. Suddenly she was beside me, grabbing the frayed end of the sjambok.

"Don't you understand how this bastard insulted me?" I said, shaking, but trying to be calm. "Cost me fifty rix dollars. I lost four days in the process, and it's sowing time. And when he came back he cheeked me again."

"As long as I'm on this farm you're going to behave yourself with the slaves."

"Hester, watch your tongue!"

She was still pulling at the sjambok, trying to wrench it away from me. If I hadn't been so angry it might have amused me: I could have pulled her off her feet in one jerk had I wanted to.

163

But to start a disgraceful tug of war with my own wife, with all the slaves looking on, was unthinkable.

"Untie him," I ordered my helpers. "I hope he's learned his lesson."

Hester looked on in silence while they untied Klaas. After they'd dragged him out she said, without deigning to look at me: "Is this the only way you can be master to them?"

"Hester, you're looking for trouble."

"Are you threatening to beat me too?" she said.

I grabbed her by the arm. It was like the occasions in our childhood when I would try to hurt her and she would refuse to cry. She didn't even groan. Suddenly I let go, turning on my heel to stride out of that shameful shed smelling of straw and hides, and of Klaas who'd pissed and shat all over the place. Didn't she realize it was for her own good too that I was forced to act like this? I had to turn this farm into a paradise for her so that we could rule over it together. How could I risk to let her live among half-wild creatures unless they'd been thoroughly broken in? I had to make the world a safe place for her to live in, so that she would be proud of me. Yet every time she wounded me.

That night I subdued her in another way. But once again she uttered no sound, no groan, no whimper of pain or delight. She was dry. Unyielding and dry, sterile as hate.

The next morning I found that all the casual labourers, all of them Hottentots, had absconded in the night. But Klaas was still there. Partly I suppose because he couldn't walk; but I don't think that was the only reason. He'd learned his lesson, and from that day he was as docile as any dog. Just goes to show. Later I acquired Abel too. A difficult fellow, and not the most dependable of workers; but he was a good influence on the farm. A man who could laugh at anything, a real rascal who'd never outgrown his boyish pranks; and with music in his fingertips. I've never known anyone who could play the violin like Abel. He brought a new spirit of co-operation to my slaves; and even the ones I bought much later he taught to pull together, like a good team of oxen.

If only the English had left us in peace we would have prospered on Elandsfontein. But all the time they were there, like a boil that wouldn't clear up properly, reappearing in different spots, now here, now there, making you unhealthy and irritable; but scratching doesn't help. At first there was the *opgaaf*, the tax on slaves. Then, in quick succession, a flood of new regulations, each causing more trouble than the others: slaves were no longer allowed to work on Sundays; working hours were fixed at ridiculous times which paid no heed to the requirements of farming: did they expect one to stop harvesting or threshing at appointed times even when a storm was brewing? Punishment was prescribed: so many lashes, administered with such an instrument, under such circumstances. Slaves had to be taught religion. Man and wife could no longer be sold separately. With a lot of it I had no quarrel: I knew for myself that a man worked harder when his wife and children were at hand, and that was to the master's advantage too; we'd always read the Bible to our slaves and prayed with them. What got me was that these regulations were made in the Cape as if we were a lot of heathens. What need had I of them? On Elandsfontein I was the *baas*, it was my right to decide what was good for me and mine. All right, argued the newspaper, but in the West-Indies or some other godforsaken place slaves were treated poorly and the English law had to apply to everyone, everywhere. Even so I felt that the Bokkeveld was no concern of the English. They knew nothing about us and had better keep out. It wasn't England who'd cleared this land of wild animals and Bushmen and vagabonds and other pests. It wasn't the English who'd suffered here from drought and floods and snow and jackals and leopards and vagrants. And it certainly wasn't England who would be separating the sheep from the goats on the Day of Judgement. Whatever the Bible said I would try to do; what the papers said England could stick up its arse.

The Bokkeveld had become a worried and anxious place. Wherever one went the farmers were cursing and complaining. Some of the older men like old Jan du Plessis, Nicolaas's father-in-law, tried to keep out of it, but the rest were grumbling. "I got no complaints," old Jan would say when the matter was brought up. "It depends on the master. If you treat your slaves properly

165

nothing will set them against you."

"But they're plotting in the dark, Oom Jan."

"My slaves respect me. Ask old Adonis."

Many of my arguments were with Frans du Toit who'd recently been appointed Field-cornet in our part of the world—a post I would have been much better equipped for; but he knew with whom to ingratiate himself. "It would be much better for all of us if we could learn to make do without slaves," was his line. "The only problem is that the Colony is too big to be cultivated without their labour. We're only a handful and the land is enormous. So it's a necessary evil."

One of the others, Hans Lubbe, was in favour of going it alone anyway, before the situation got completely out of hand. "If we free all the slave children at birth no one will get hurt," he proposed.

"But the work on the farms is increasing all the time," I said. "Do you expect white men to start doing slave work?"

"We'd better get used to it while there's still time," he said. "I know we've been getting a bit soft, but—"

"It's not a question of getting soft at all!" I interrupted angrily. "It's just that there's a difference between slave work and white man's work. Why did God give us slaves if not to make things easier for us? Do you want to set yourself against the Bible?"

More often than not Nicolaas would enter the conversation at this point: "Who will suffer most if the slaves were to be freed? They've got more to lose than we have. How will they ever subsist on their own? They can't do without us."

Once Hester also butted into one of our discussions. Usually I tried to keep her out of it—there are things a woman simply cannot understand—but it was impossible always to avoid such topics when she was around. On that particular day, if I remember well, the conversation had been going on for a considerable time and was getting quite heated when she suddenly asked in her calm but provocative way:

"Would any one of you like to be a slave?"

"Why must womenfolk always be so difficult?" I said, trying to be patient so that she wouldn't turn vicious in front of the others.

166

"It's not a question of liking or not liking. It's quite simply the way things *are*. And the land's got to be cultivated."

Then Cecilia also decided to make a contribution. Normally she was very restrained and commendably silent in our presence, but I suppose Hester's comment had provoked her; the two of them were always at each other's throats. "One thing I can tell you," she said to Hester, and a pretty withering response it was, "I don't know of a single slave in this country who has to lie awake at night for fear a white man would come and murder him in his sleep or carry off his belongings."

"I shouldn't think they have anything one could carry off," Hester said tartly.

But the brief exchange had given me new respect for Cecilia. She was not what anyone would call an attractive woman: she was much too big and clumsy for that; and then that unnaturally pale freckled skin and red hair and almost colourless eyes; but a formidable woman nonetheless, her feet planted firmly on the ground; and she knew her place.

When Hester asked: "But don't you read the newspapers? Can't you see what's happening in the Colony?" Cecilia answered very firmly.: "I read the Bible and that's enough for me. The newspapers only confuse one with all their reports, and what you don't know cannot hurt you."

These conversations were taking place wherever one went, all the way from the lower reaches of the Warm Bokkeveld, up our narrow valley and spilling into the Karoo; and then back again, across the mountains to Tulbagh and from there to Worcester or seaward to the plains of the Four-and-Twenty Rivers. Everybody talking, talking all the time. And whenever a new *Gazette* was delivered by someone who'd paid a visit to a town beyond the mountains, or whenever a new messenger or agent from the Government showed up in our part of the world, the beehive would be stirred into action again. Worst of all was the feeling of angry impotence created by those papers—English papers and almost unintelligible to start with. Who was this Government they constantly spoke about? It wasn't something one could touch or grab by the throat to throttle it. Far away in the Cape

167

anonymous gentlemen gathered in closed offices to decide our destinies; or worse still, in strange cities across the sea, sending their messages by ship while remaining well out of our reach. And all we could do was to bow and say *Yes, Baas*, no longer allowed to decide or arrange our own affairs. We couldn't even properly take it out on those under us: we needed them too much; and they were only too well aware of it, and exploited it at every turn. Something in the world had become unjust and unmanageable; and it was obvious that only evil could come of it.

There was the business with the slave Goliath. I'd acquired him a few years before in Worcester, for four oxen, from a man who'd run into problems on a trek to the Karoo. A well-trained youngster of fifteen or sixteen. Never gave me any trouble until the harvest before last, when we were working day and night to bring the wheat in. Then, one Sunday morning, he didn't turn up for work; and when I went to look for him I found him sitting in front of his hut in the shade. Why, he said when I spoke to him, it was against the law now for a slave to work on Sunday; I couldn't force him.

"Then it's time I explained a few things to you, Goliath," I said. "What the law in the Cape says is one thing. What I do on my own farm where I'm the master is something else again."

After I'd flogged him he was quite willing to follow me to the lands where he worked very diligently until well after dark. But when the morning star came out the next day and I rounded up the farmhands to resume the reaping Goliath turned up carrying a skin bag over his shoulder.

"Where do you think you're going?" I asked him.

"I just come to tell you, Baas. I going to Worcester to complain about yesterday, Baas." Very restrained in his manner, almost obsequious.

I realized immediately that the others must have egged him on; Abel most likely. But in his servile way he could obviously be stubborn enough.

I didn't have time to waste; the wheat was waiting to be harvested. "I'm giving you one more chance, Goliath. Are you

168

coming down to the lands with us or not?"

"I'm sorry, Baas, but I got to go to Worcester first, Baas."

"Then listen very carefully, Goliath. By all means go to Worcester if your soles are itching. But God is my witness: the moment you set foot on the farm again I'm going to give you a thrashing you won't forget for as long as you live. Do you understand?"

He gulped; I saw his adam's apple move up and down. But he was adamant. I went down to the wheatfield and he set out for Worcester. It was a bloody difficult time of the year to do without a pair of hands, but I refused to be made a fool of. Every day he stayed away I added something in my mind to the punishment I owed him; waiting for him to come back. We'd just brought in the last wagon of wheat, eight days later, when a messenger arrived with a note from Landdrost Trappes summoning me to appear before him on such and such a date etcetera.

Hadn't Hester nagged me so much I would have deliberately ignored the matter to await the consequences. But she insisted she needed groceries and dress material, and that the hides and pelts on the loft were taking up the space we would be needing for the wheat; and so I left for Worcester after all. Two days down, and another half-day taken up by the hearing. A good thing the Landdrost didn't fine me like the previous time with Klaas, for I may not have been able to restrain myself; he was content to let me go with a stern warning and a long explanation of the latest regulations. What upset me most was to be told by the turd Trappes that in future he would regularly send out commissioners to make sure I and the other farmers in the Bokkeveld were abiding by the law. Just because Goliath had had the cheek to tell him about the arrangement we'd made before his departure.

"Now you go home on foot," I told Goliath the moment we got outside the Drostdy. "And you better hurry for I'm not allowing you more than two days." Then I trekked on ahead with the wagon.

Hester was in one of her intractable moods when I arrived

169

home—"I hope you've finally learned your lesson, Barend"
—which made me so mad that I saddled my horse and rode
over to Houd-den-Bek just to find someone to talk to.

Cecilia, exemplary woman that she was, served coffee and I
gave vent to all the pent-up frustration in me. Initially Nicolaas
seemed his usual cautious self, but Cecilia immediately sided
with me. She was also growing fed-up with the slaves, she said;
especially Galant who was getting more and more out of hand.
Later Nicolaas and I went out to the stables where he wanted to
inspect the harnesses of the threshing horses.

"Did you have Goliath flogged at the Drostdy?" he asked.

"When did you go down to the Drostdy last?" I said, flaring
up. "Nowadays any black man's word weighs heavier with the
Landdrost than a Christian's." I took a thong from the hook and
tested it against the bottom of my trousers. "But just wait till he
gets home. He'll get the thrashing he deserves. Can't wait to lay
my hands on him." Thinking of Goliath made me angry all over
again. "And if they do send a commissioner to inspect my slaves
I'll teach the man a lesson he won't ever forget."

"Ai." He sighed. "I wish the first commissioner who stepped
ashore in the Cape broke his neck right there. Then we would
have had some peace of mind."

It comforted me to hear him agree with me, although I
couldn't be sure that he really was sincere about it: Nicolaas
never wanted anything so much as to be liked, and he might say
anything merely to win approval: like a dog begging to have his
head stroked so he can wag his tail.

"If it goes on like this," I told him, "it won't be long before
they get it into their heads to free the slaves altogether. And what
will become of us then, I ask you?"

"That would really be a mess," he agreed, still sorting out the
harnesses for the following day.

"Let them try. The first Englishman who sets foot on my farm
to free the slaves I'll blast right into the mountains with my gun."

"What frightens me," said Nicolaas, "is the thought that if we
start fighting against the Government the slaves may stab us in
the back."

"Don't worry," I said. "If ever they seriously start talking about setting them free I'll first shoot all my slaves in a heap and then face the English."

"We're living in difficult times, Barend. It's getting very confusing. I've had no end of trouble myself these last months."

"It's because you're too lenient with them," I said. "I'm not saying one must be unreasonable with them. But if you're too lenient they shit on your head. A slave needs his food on time and the sjambok on time, the way it used to be on Pa's farm. That's the only language they understand. Especially now that the English are prompting them."

"We're all in this together," he said bravely, but then resumed his old cautious attitude: "Provided we don't deliberately provoke trouble."

"You think I'm to blame for what's happened to me?" I said. "You want my wheat to rot on the lands just because Goliath prefers to spend his Sundays on his arse in the shade?"

"I didn't mean to criticize you, Barend. I was just saying."

"Well, I'll let you know when a commissioner turns up on my farm. I'll send messages to all the neighbours, then we can all get together to blast them into hell."

The commission arrived sooner than I'd expected, barely a week later, when Goliath was still recovering in his hut from the flogging I'd given him. My first thought was to grab my gun and shoot the impostor. But one had to be careful; I didn't want to provoke the Government into sending a whole army into the Bokkeveld. So I invited the man to sit down in the *voorhuis* and have tea with Hester while I went out at the back and gave Abel instructions to set out for the neighbouring farms and round up the farmers. Then I walked up to the huts and looked in at Goliath's. "Listen," I told him, "if you want to get out of this alive then you better do as I tell you."

And when, an hour later, the commissioner insisted on personally inspecting all my slaves, Goliath demurely told him that he'd been thrown by a horse, which accounted for the state he was in; and that he had no complaint, thank you very much. The visitor didn't appear too satisfied, but there was nothing

171

more he could do. And after the afternoon coffee, just as he prepared to go, the neighbours started arriving in response to the message Abel had carried, each man with his gun. Didn't say a word. Uttered no threats. Simply formed two rows so he could pass between them on his nervous little horse. We rode with him.

"What's the matter then?" he asked after a while, obviously uncomfortable in our presence.

"Just riding with you to make sure you don't get lost," I said. "And who knows, we may find something for the pot on the way."

As luck would have it we spotted a small herd of eland in a kloof not far from the farm. And when the shooting broke out, by an amazing coincidence the fidgety little man kept on finding himself between us and the eland, so that a hail of bullets would come whizzing past him, once even chipping a bit off the rim of his hat. The horse got such a fright that it started neighing and rearing, and in no time the man was thrown. At that stage he was so scared that he started scampering off on all fours, while the bullets struck up dust left and right. In the end, of course, we stopped shooting and fetched him back and put him on his horse again, and offered him brandy from our hip-flasks, begging his pardon for what had happened: how unfortunate that he should have landed in the way of the eland. He didn't say anything. He only glowered at us from under the torn brim of his hat; and he had the look and the smell of a man who'd learned his lesson thoroughly. We knew we would not have to fear any more trouble from English commissioners for quite some time.

But back at Elandsfontein, after the neighbours had ridden off, a very disturbing thing happened. As I came round the stable leading my horse, I saw the slave Abel coming from Goliath's hut. Behind him in the semi-darkness I could make out the shapes of other men, but I couldn't see who they were.

"Abel!" I called. "Come and take my horse."

He quickly stood up from his stooping position as if he'd been caught in some mischief.

172

I waited, the reins held loosely in my hand.

Suddenly he swung back towards the hut he'd just left and picked up a spade that had been leaning against the wall: I didn't know how it got there, as everybody had strict instructions always to put away the tools after use. Holding the spade casually balanced on both hands he turned to me. There was a long silence between us; neither of us moved or uttered a word. Perhaps he didn't mean anything by it; but there was something in his attitude which hit me in the stomach with a numbness of fear I'd never known before.

"Abel?" I said at last.

He still stared at me silently, the heavy spade in his hands. Behind him were the shadows of the others in the darkness of the hut.

I suddenly remembered the gun still stuck into one of the saddle-bags. Reaching behind me I gripped the muzzle and slowly pulled it out. It must have caught Abel by surprise. For a moment he still glared at me; then he dropped one end of the spade and came towards me to take the horse, casually swinging the spade in one hand.

Had it all been my imagination only? Or had I really been saved by the gun? Worst of all was the sick feeling with which, afterwards, I realized that if he had come at me with the spade I would not have been able to shoot after all. The shock had too much dazed me. I'd, quite simply, been too scared to move. It was like walking in the dark and suddenly becoming aware of something moving: you can't see anything and you're not quite sure that you actually heard it: perhaps there is no real danger at all: it is only an intimation, a disturbing suspicion that the night is no longer as safe as you've always thought.

Had I been truly convinced that Abel had deliberately threatened me I would have flogged him as severely as I had Goliath. But what perturbed me was the uncertainty of it all, a vagueness infinitely more dangerous than any predator or enemy I could recognize and kill. In one brief illumination I'd caught a glimpse of how precarious our peace really was, how exposed our lives: how easily the earth could be washed away from under our feet.

173

If the gun hadn't been at hand that afternoon, what would have happened?

But if it had really been only the gun that had saved me: what about the moment, imminent or remote, when one might be surprised without it?

MA-ROSE

In the beginning there was nothing but stone. And from the stones Tsui-Goab made us. But then He saw that we couldn't live without water, since it's water that makes the grass sprout and the trees grow and which is drink for man and beast. The inside of a woman is water; her children swim from her into the world. And whenever the earth gets dry and threatens to return to stone, it's rain we pray for, in the prayer my people have said since the beginning of the world:

You Tsui-Goab
Father of our fathers
Our Father!
Let the thundercloud stream
Give life to the herds
Give us life too, we beg you.
I am so weak
Of hunger
Of thirst
Let me eat juicy veld-fruit.
For are you not our Father
Father of our fathers
You, Tsui-Goab?
That we may praise you
That we may bless you
You, Father of our fathers
You, our Lord,
You, Tsui-Goab!

These are not words lightly to take on one's lips. Not for any ordinary little drought. For it's something I've noticed long ago: the same water that turns the veld green with life and provides drink for man and beast also floods the earth and drowns flocks and levels mountains. These Skurweberge of ours, these Rough Mountains, have always been here and they're always the same—and yet they're always changing. What changes them is water. Sometimes patiently, wearing away its courses through many years; sometimes in a wild and sudden flood. Which is why one should be very sure of what one wants from Tsui-Goab before saying the Rain Prayer. For He gives life, but that life may bring destruction too. Only through water can the world be changed; but one cannot force it to do one's bidding. Once you've prayed for water and it is sent you cannot predict the changes it may bring about. You got to take it as it comes, even if it washes you away with the soil in which you're rooted.

That was why I kept telling the people not to be impatient. It was better to learn to endure and to wait. But men don't know patience; they don't know what it means to wait for the breaking of the water. "Just don't give up," I told them when they came to me for advice. "Don't press anything. You yourself don't know what water you're asking for."

I could feel it coming. An impatience, a restlessness in the earth itself. And each was worried by it in his own way.

There was Nicolaas who'd started coming to me for help since the early days of his marriage. He didn't want the others to see him at my hut, so he would wait till late at night, pretending to stroll about in the veld. When there were others with me he stayed away; I could hear his shadow passing in the night. But if I was alone he would come in to my fire like the days when he and Galant would come to me for stories. It was some time before he came out with it, only after many visits when he'd do nothing but say good-night and sit in silence for a while.

"Ma-Rose," he said at long last, "you've got to help me."

"What's the matter then, Nicolaas? I been watching you for a long time and I can see you got a deep thorn in your heart."

"I'm married now, Ma-Rose. But I'm having problems with my wife."

176

I had eyes in my head to see; but I pretended not to understand. "She looks a fine woman to me. She'll make a good mother. She's broad-hipped."

"The fault doesn't lie with her, Ma-Rose. It's with me. I can't do it properly."

"What?" I tried to drag it from him.

It was quite a while before at last he blurted out: "It's what a man does with his wife, Ma-Rose. It won't work for us. She's too impatient."

"What makes you think she's impatient? You know what to do, don't you?"

"I have no desire to do it."

"Is it because of Hester?"

"Why do you ask that?" he said angrily.

"I know you had your heart set on Hester long ago. But that's an egg you won't hatch just by brooding on it."

His voice became shaky. "But what can I *do*, Ma-Rose?"

"You got to be a proper husband to your wife."

"I know. I've tried. But it doesn't work. I think she despises me. She treats me like a child, not like a man."

"Then you got to show her you're different. Ride her like a man."

"I—" Even in the firelight I could see him blush. "That's what's wrong, Ma-Rose. Is there no medicine you could give me to cure it? I can't go on living with Cecilia in this humiliation."

"Pretend she's Hester."

That stung him. "I don't think such things about Hester!"

"I thought you wanted to marry her?"

"Of course. But not to—not to do that to her."

"I don't understand you, Nicolaas. You white people make unnecessary problems for yourselves."

"I need your help, Ma-Rose! What will Pa and Ma say if they must find out I can't do it?"

"There's nothing wrong with you, Nicolaas. I watched you and Galant often enough when you were small. You had a horn as good as his. You think I don't know what you used to do behind the dam-wall?"

177

"But what's gone wrong then?"

I tried to comfort him with medicine—the herbs we give to old men—and told him to take it with a stiff *sopie* of brandy at night. What the herbs couldn't do the brandy might. And for a while I believe things improved for them. But soon he was back again.

"Only one remedy I can think of," I told him at last. "It's a sort of blight some white men suffer from. Perhaps your women aren't deep enough. A man's root needs the water she has inside her; and some white women don't seem to have it."

"What must I do then?"

"Soak your root in a black woman. That'll let it grow and give it life."

"I won't! It's sinful."

I shrugged. "If you won't you won't. But don't keep on coming back to me then, complaining you can't make it spurt."

"It's against the Bible."

"You want to tell me your own Pa did what was against the Bible?"

"What's that?!" He stared at me as if a horse had kicked him.

"Who do you think made your Pa the man he is?"

Perhaps it was wrong of me to tell him. But he had to know. "I didn't always look the way I look now," I said. "Today I'm an old dried fig. But when I was young I had a body. And your Pa knew me."

He left in a hurry, as if I carried some evil disease; stumbling in his haste to get away from me. And he didn't come back after that. But I kept my eyes open. And my ears too. When he began to visit Lydia at night I couldn't help smiling by myself. And when the first child was born I thought he was on the way to recovery. What I hadn't expected and what disturbed me was the way his wife started treating Lydia. What did that poor madwoman know about right or wrong? It was a bad thing. But I had to watch my step with Nooi Cecilia; she could be very short-tempered with us.

And I was worried about Nicolaas too. It soon became clear

178

that his problem lay deeper than just in the root. With his father it had been simple. He could be treated with the wetness of women. But the moisture Nicolaas needed was different, deeper and darker and more dangerous. It was the flood I felt swelling below the surface of our farms long before the storm broke out. An invisible flood, and all the more ominous for that. And what could *I* do to avert it?

Galant didn't make it any easier either. One night I found him in the veld where he was throwing stones in the dark. It was a long way from the farmyard, in the rocky spot where in the beginning of the world the stones had come tumbling down the mountain. For a long time I stood watching him without being seen. Picking up stones and throwing them, picking up and throwing, each one hurled with all his might, until I could hear his breath rasping in his throat.

"What you doing?" I asked, going towards him in the dark.

He swung round as if in fright; and wiped the sweat from his face. "Just throwing stones," he said sullenly. "Why shouldn't I?"

"You mad at someone?" I asked. "Who is it?"

I knew, of course; but I thought it was better for him to tell me and get it out of his blood.

He picked up another stone and shattered it against a larger rock, striking sparks in the dark.

"You better watch out," I told him. "If one of those stones fly back and hit you in the face, you're dead as dead."

"What do I care?" He threw another stone.

"Why don't you come with me, Galant? I'll give you some bush-tea. That'll calm you down."

"I don't want to be calmed down."

So I sat down a little way from him, out of reach of his angry stones, so that he could get it out of his blood. He went on throwing and throwing until he couldn't lift his arm any more, which is saying a lot, for Galant might be thin but he was tough as leather.

All the time he was throwing the stones he was talking too, shouting and cursing so that one could almost smell the

179

sulphur, as if the place had been struck by lightning; and in his voice I could hear he was crying. When at last he stopped, panting with exhaustion, he was sobbing too.

At last I said again: "Come home with me, Galant."

This time he came, breathless, his shoulders drooping, all his fight gone. He picked up something from a wagon-tree, and draping it over one shoulder like an empty bag he came back to me and we went on to the hut. It was only when we reached the fire that I saw it was a brand-new corduroy jacket he was carrying.

"Where you got that?" I asked him. "Did old D'Alree make it for you?" For that was just about the time the wizened old tailor and shoemaker had come to live on Nicolaas's farm. Having been with Galant ever since I'd suckled him as a baby I knew that this was the first new thing he'd ever had in his life: usually he got all Nicolaas's cast-offs as they were much the same size.

"Got it from Nicolaas," he mumbled, throwing it down in the far corner before he sat down. "Suppose it's to buy me off." He took a length of chewing-tobacco from his trouser pocket—I wondered where he'd found it, but I was careful not to ask—and put it in his cheek while I warmed the black kettle of bush-tea on the fire.

"Is it for the child?" I asked at last, not looking at him.

"Yes." He spat. "Gave it to me this afternoon. Didn't say anything, but of course I know it's for the child."

I kept myself very busy with the kettle, adding new bits of wood and blowing on the coals and stirring the tea. "Galant," I said, knowing that I had to be very careful now. "What's the use of going about with a thunderstorm in your heart? It's a bad thing that happened, but it's over."

"Nothing is over," he said in the darkness heavy with smoke. "Let me tell you something, Ma-Rose. Nothing ever goes away. It stays about you like stones lying on the ground. Some you stumble over. Others you can pick up to throw. They're lying there. All the time."

"It's a hard thing you saying there, Galant." I poured the tea, strong, the way I liked it and he needed it.

180

"I can take whatever happens, Ma-Rose," he said, as gloomily as before. "We're grownup. Our time is passing. But there's always the children. And where is my child today? When I left Bet to go to the Karoo to fetch the cattle, David was still here and there was nothing wrong with him. When I came back he was buried. Bet said he got ill. She said the reason he died was the illness, it had nothing to do with the beating. Now I'm asking you, Ma-Rose: I got to know."

"Bet is your wife. If that is what she says you better believe it."

"It's you I'm asking."

"I wasn't near the house the day it happened."

"No one wants to tell me. They all afraid."

"Have you spoken to Nicolaas?"

"Bet said he came to ask forgiveness. She said he never meant to kill the child. It died of illness."

"Nicolaas is *baas* on the farm, Galant. His hand is on us in life and death. It's the way it is."

"But David was my child."

"It's a terrible thing that happened," I said, blowing my tea cold, watching him over the rim of my mug. His eyes were glowing through the smoke. I thought of the day he and Hester had sheltered in my hut in the storm, huddled under the big kaross, so many years ago. "It's a terrible thing," I said again. "But you're a young man still and there's nothing wrong with Bet. You can have a whole hut full of children."

"I'm through with Bet."

"You got along well with her."

"She didn't look after the child."

"You can't blame her."

"She didn't stop him."

"Who can stop him? He's the *baas*. Galant, you got to get this into your head. No matter what he does, he got the right to do it because he's *baas*. Stop asking questions or you'll land in big trouble. Nicolaas is *baas* on Houd-den-Bek."

"Houd-den-Bek, yes," he repeated quietly, bitterly. "Shut-Your-Trap." That was all he said.

181

In silence we finished our tea; and when the mugs were empty we remained sitting. It was like the old days. And the night grew heavy over us, a darkness that lay on us with its full weight. In the deepest blackness of the night we suddenly heard it, both of us at the same time: a strange dark sound: *Tha-tha-tha.* It was impossible to tell which side it came from; impossible to tell whether it was coming or going. But we heard it all right. *Tha-tha-tha.* I grabbed my kaross and crouched beside Galant and covered our heads with it. We didn't even breathe, I think. He was trembling as if he felt cold, but it was a warm night. It was the *thas*-jackal. I recognized it immediately. No one has ever seen it, but it's out there; and it wanders about when somebody has trodden on a fresh grave. It's the spirit of the dead that turns into a jackal to haunt the living. *Tha-tha-tha.* Through the thick hairy skin of the kaross we heard it; and we remained like that until at last it was beginning to sound as if it was moving away, deeper into the night, perhaps in the direction of the farmyard.

"I'll strew buchu leaves on the grave in the morning," I promised him when the night grew silent again and we crawled from under the kaross. "That will set him to rest. Now it's time to sleep."

"I'm not going home in the dark."

"No. You can sleep here."

He curled up in a corner. I sat beside the smoking coals staring at the small bundle he formed in the dark, the new jacket covering his head. I remembered his childhood, the way he'd always slept beside me, snuggled against me; and how, when he was restless, I would stroke his little thing until he'd drop off to sleep. This night, I sensed, he was in need of a woman again. Not me; but a woman who could be a wife to him in his need. He'd turned against Bet, and that was a bad thing. A man like him couldn't do without a woman.

I remembered how he and Nicolaas had both tugged at my teats when they'd been babies. My two lambs, black and white. And as I sat there watching over him in his fitful sleep I thought: *Tonight I'm split in two, like an old stone falling*

182

apart. For I love them both. And I pity them both.

I thought and thought. So many things had been stirred up by that *thas*-jackal. The child who'd died. All the dead filling up the world. Soon I would be dead too. And Galant. All of us. One by one we were dying as we lived. And one day, when the last of my race had died and we would remain only as a memory, a tale told by the Honkhoikwa to their children at night, all the innumerable dead of my tribe would wander about desolate in the dark. At night, when their homes grew silent and everything seemed deserted, the dead would wander in countless numbers, all those who'd died in this beautiful, violent land where my people had once roamed free. Only the dead would remain. Like a vast black flood they would fill up the hollows, rising higher and higher, soundlessly, until everything was smooth and even, black and shimmering in Tsui-Goab's moonlight. *Tha-tha-tha.*

NICOLAAS

A river rising. I was still holding blindly on to something, branch or tree; but my grip was loosening. When had it started? Even about that I had no certainty. There was the death of the child of course, but that in itself only brought awareness of a flood already swelling. Still, in a way it was decisive.

If only I could have explained it to Galant. But how could I do that when even in my explanations to myself something remained beyond my grasp? Was it enough to blame Cecilia for driving me to the deed? I'd married her, I'd tried to be a dutiful husband to her, I'd even tried to desire her. But in her aggressive insistence to be used, to be degraded in order to vindicate her womanhood, she intimidated me. That sturdy milk-white freckled body had become a nightmare, so daunting in its health, so strenuous in its demands, sucking me into her as if to devour me entirely in order the more passionately to condemn the baseness of the act when kneeling beside the bed as soon as it was over she would ask for a cleansing of the accursed flesh.

Was it made easier or worse by the terrible remedy first suggested by Ma-Rose? I still hesitate to find an answer. Did I proceed in desperate obedience to her or in helplessness against the evil fascination of the deed she'd conjured up? *When I was young I had a body. And your Pa knew me.* Was it revenge against him or an effort finally to be worthy of him even if it meant damning my soul? Surely this was the ultimate blasphemy: would I yet burn for it, or did God's punishment reside in the very beastliness of the act? Those laborious hours with Lydia in the stench of her dark hut: her

184

passivity driving me to ludicrous inventions and excesses of lust and cruelty, knowing in advance that she would unquestioningly submit to whatever I desired. Whether I flogged her to placate Cecilia for some imagined wrong done to her, or caressed her, would be the same to Lydia, a submission to the whims and idiosyncrasies of the master. She would neither question nor seek to comprehend whatever I did to her, or why. My desire would mean as little to her as my rage, my need as little as my abhorrence of myself or her. I was the master, she the slave, she would do what I wished; that was all. Whether I fondled her or kicked her in the crotch or derisively strewed feathers from a torn mattress all over her sticky body, was entirely immaterial to her. And if I felt driven, some nights, almost to strangle her in order at least to force some reaction from her, I finally held back in the knowledge that even that would be part of what she considered my "right". Perhaps the only absolution lay in the disgust it awakened in me, and in the consequent ferocity with which I might then return to my own wife, so starkly clean and civilized, and waiting so piously and eagerly to be abused.

Wouldn't it have been easier, less despicable, to make use of Bet rather than of the poor imbecile Lydia? I must admit to a peculiar fascination Bet had for me after the death of her child: the way she almost flaunted herself. Yet that was what restrained me in the end. Not guilt alone—and God knows there was enough of that—but fear. For why, if not in search of revenge, had she taken to following me about wherever I went? And what would be easier than for her to get at me when in the spasms of lust I was most vulnerable? The temptation was there, but I was too scared. And the abhorrence I felt for Lydia in a way neutralized the sinfulness of what we did together: in the deed itself lay its punishment. With Bet there might be a real and less complicated pleasure, and that would be damnable. If only Cecilia would say something, accuse me, curse me, attack me, ask God to forgive or punish me: but piously and without a word she would subject herself to me, in her own way as submissive as Lydia in hers. And even when I failed with her, if in the middle of our loveless coupling my mind would wander and I would fall asleep, she would gently persuade me that it did not matter: using her, whether aggressively or through inaction, was all that was required.

Yet she did become more restless as time went on, more assertive; there came a keener edge to her voice as she became more accustomed to the paradox of her strength. And gradually the taunts began. Why could we have no sons? All other respectable people had sons. Unless it was punishment for some dark, unspeakable sin on my part? (There she would pause, looking pointedly at me, but without ever taking Lydia's name, or Bet's for that matter, on her lips.)

"It will happen in time," I insisted. "If it is God's will."

"Even Hester has a son. Who would have thought that flat body could ever give birth to a child? But there she is, with a son, and a second on the way. I'm sure it will be a boy too."

"Why do you blame me?" I once flared up. "If you're so eager to have sons, why don't you have them? It's your body that shapes them."

"Even slaves have sons!" she retorted. It was the first time she'd gone so far and I think she too realized how outrageous it was; but having said it, she persisted: "Even Galant has a son."

Perhaps that was why she'd been against his child from the beginning, complaining of the nuisance when it cried about the house, tied in a bundle on Bet's back, or "messing about" once it had begun to crawl.

"But I don't really care about sons, Cecilia," I said. "I'm happy with the daughters God has given me. I love them."

"There must be something wrong with a man who doesn't want a son." There was a tone of bitter glee in her voice. "That's what it is. You're not a real man. Why else do you grow limp when you're doing what a man is supposed to do?"

I could strike her then; but Ma-Rose was standing in the kitchen, listening. In helpless anger I stormed out, and as I went round the house I stumbled over Galant's child who came crawling towards the kitchen in search of its mother. I could not control myself. But I swear to God I never meant it

186

to die; on another day I would not have laid a hand on it.

What was this strange, mad, blinding rage that came upon me almost without warning at times? I could not remember having experienced it as a child. It was as if in such moments I suddenly became a stranger to myself: as if I was looking down, from somewhere high up, upon myself raging and ranting; it seemed like madness, so unnecessary, so foolish. I wanted to reach down and touch that raging man and whoever was his victim, and ask them not to pay too much attention, it wasn't meant to be like that at all, it was a dreadful mistake: but there was nothing I could do to stop it. I wanted to cry out to God: Why was He doing this to me? Why could I no longer understand Him? I had always tried to live according to His commands. As a child, listening to the deep drone of Pa's voice, I'd found everything so clear, so reassuring, so self-evident. Why this confusion now, this feeling that the Word itself had become inadequate to cope with my grownup life, this inability to control the world of which I was supposed to be master? *For the good that I would I do not: but the evil which I would not, that I do.*

But even that confused me. In my utterance it became powerless, another evasion. If only I could break through to someone; to Galant. But between us lay a dead child. And what terrified me was the apprehension that this need not be the worst: that this, in fact, might be only the beginning.

ONTONG

"How can you look on without ever raising a finger or say a word in protest?" they often asked me.

But it wasn't for me to interfere. I'd seen what happens to those who do.

I have nothing to say about myself, it concerns no one. My body was in their hands but my thoughts were my own. I wish I could say that Allah knew my heart, but He'd abandoned me long ago, and I Him.

"How can you look on when they do these things to Lydia?" they asked. "You live with her. You got to stop them."

Yes, I lived with her. But what we shared was ours; in everything else that happened we were apart. If the Baas had the right to sleep with her it was also his right to do other things with her body. Bodies are public. When we closed the door of the hut to shut out the world I would hold and comfort her, and put ointment on her wounds: that was ours. But when the sun rose and the slave-bell rang we would return into the world, each on his separate way. What must be will be.

"How long can one resist before one breaks?" Galant sometimes asked.

There was no reason or need to break, I told him. If a man broke it was his own fault. There was Achilles: a broken man. Because he'd been a turbulent creature in his youth who'd not recognized the difference between what can be changed and what cannot. And now, on Sundays or when the Baas was away, he would get drunk on his own honey-beer and break down, sobbing in a dark corner or pestering others with snotty tales about the distant land he'd come from, and the trees of that place, and the people, and the tits of the girl who was to have been his. Then it took a lot of persuasion to talk him out

188

of his mood; or even a blow to the head or a kick under his arse. What was the use, I would ask him, behaving like that? A man was made to endure, to carry on. The one most patient, most resilient, most prepared to wait, I told him, would survive. A stone can be picked up and thrown away, or split with a crowbar. But water cannot be held in a hand, no man has power over it. So one should be like water.

He annoyed me no end. I too could, if I wished, recite names that would bring a shiver of pleasure to the spine, musical names that would help me forget the aches of the body. I could say: Jogjakarta, or Madura, or Rembang, or Tjirebon, or Tjilatjap. I could say Surabaya, and Ranjuwangi, and Kediri, and Melang. And these would ring in my mind and bring back a view of palm-trees and flying pigeons and the sea, and lumbering buffaloes blowing bubbles in the water; and the taste of coconut milk on the tongue; and the sound of boys calling in the *padis*; and the smell of cloves and coriander and saffron and pepper, and the sweet curled bark of cinnamon. But these I kept to myself; they concerned only me.

And the dreams. I would dream of moonflowers and birds, and of a woman like a palm-tree, a woman as lovely as the young girl Lys who'd been Galant's mother; and I would wake up, sad and stiff, and only Lydia would be there beside me. But how could I blame her for not being the woman of the dream? I would gratefully take her, and share with her what the night had to offer us, knowing it would soon be day again and the days were hard. The dreams made it possible to endure: but I knew it would be no use packing up to go in search of that impossible woman. One had to accept responsibility both for the dream and for the waking, otherwise there could be no survival.

"Do you understand that?" I asked Galant.

"I'm trying to," he said. "But it's not easy."

"I know. But at least it's easier for you than for me: you've always been where you are now. You were born here, it's your place. Mine was taken from me before I was ten years old."

"I'm not so sure," he said. "Perhaps it's easier for you after

189

all. When things get bad here you can dream of your own place. Whether you're there or not you know it's somewhere. But I can go nowhere. And I don't belong here either. So what do I do?"

"It's just because you're young that you say such things," I said. "Wait till you're an old man like me."

"You think I *want* to become an old man like you?"

"It'll happen, whether you want to or not."

Of course that didn't satisfy him. And I kept on wondering and worrying about him. Could he really be my child? How often, in the evenings or at work, I would stare at him when he wasn't aware of it, looking for an expression, an attitude of the head, a fold of the ear, a posture of the body I could recognize as my own. But can one ever be sure? Or doesn't it really matter? He was there and I was there, harnessed to the same carriage.

In the beginning, when we first moved from Lagenvlei to Houd-den-Bek, we used to take turns with Lydia at night and shared our work in the daytime. I had the impression that he was going to settle down all right. He remained and would always be a loner, of course, preferring to keep his own company—something he might have got from me—but I wasn't aware of anything ominous or wrong. It was obvious that things between him and Nicolaas had changed, but that was to be expected: they weren't children any more. And they were trying to adapt, each to the other; like two young dogs sniffing and circling each other before making friends. When Bet came to the farm it was even better. For the first time Galant really seemed to relax. And I was confident that everything would work out well after all.

It was only after the death of the child that I began to feel worried. I know he went to Ma-Rose to talk things over with her and she must have straightened him out for there was no immediate storm. But he went on brooding. Nothing had really been settled. He seemed to be waiting for something to happen, almost deliberately looking for trouble. Sometimes when we went to the kitchen to wait for the food which Bet

190

dished out, Galant would go to the doorstep, making sure he could be heard from the front room, and pick a quarrel with her:

"I say, Bet. Aren't we getting anything to eat today? Or do they want to keep us waiting so we can be fed with the dogs?"

"Looking for trouble, are you?" she would answer, glancing nervously over her shoulder towards the middle door.

When the food was brought he would look at it and sneer: "What's this mess again? Do they think they can feed a man soup only? They waiting for an animal to die before we can get some meat again?"

"I'm just doing what I'm told."

Once Nicolaas came through to the kitchen while they were arguing like that. I drew back and busied myself with my pipe, not wanting to get involved in any of their trouble: but I could still hear what was being said.

"Don't you like the food then, Galant?" he asked.

Galant mumbled something I couldn't make out.

"You never complained at Lagenvlei."

"The Oubaas never gave us reason to. But meat seems to be scarce here at Houd-den-Bek."

I could see that Nicolaas was growing tense. He raised his hand towards the back of the door where the sjambok usually hung, but he didn't take it from the hook. It would take much more provocation than that for him to strike Galant. We all knew that. And that, I suspected, was why Galant went on defying him: he wanted to find out how far he could go. He must have known that after the death of his child he would have even more scope than before, because it was clear for all to see how heavily the event lay on Nicolaas's mind. But someone like Galant would never be satisfied with that. He couldn't have any peace of mind before he'd established beyond all doubt how far the bough could be bent before it would break: testing it—forcing it a bit more—easing up for a moment—pushing some more—listening for the inevitable splintering sound. And that was what I couldn't accept. It was unnecessary; one could get by comfortably without such

191

constant strain. But it was useless even to try to make him see reason.

He was always at it, in all sorts of ways. What really surprised me was the business of the horses. Galant had always had an extraordinary way with them. I used to eavesdrop as he tended them in the stable, treating each horse as if it were human, as if it were a woman: stroking and caressing it, nudging it, talking to it with endless patience and understanding. He would regularly, without any permission from the Baas, go up to the loft to fetch them wheat or barley for a treat. Even sugar, stolen from the kitchen—especially after the slave woman Pamela had been borrowed from Nooi Cecilia's father's farm when the Nooi couldn't get along with Bet any more; for Pamela took a liking in Galant from the beginning. Not that he seemed to respond to her, not at first, although she was not a bad-looking woman. A bit on the thin side perhaps, but with fine features, quiet, almost shy; and a hint of embers smouldering deep inside her. She possessed in fact that rare mixture of fire and water that does something to a man. And so whenever Galant needed something from the house—an extra bit of meat, a *sopie* from the brandy jar, sugar for the horses—Pamela would get it for him. And she even took the punishment for it if it was discovered; without ever revealing that she'd been instigated by Galant.

But in those days Galant started taking his frustration out on the horses. Not every day, he was much too fond of them for that; and not on all of them either: he would single out Nicolaas's own horse, the liveliest animal on the farm, a beautiful black with a star on his forehead. And I began to notice that whenever there had been trouble between Nicolaas and Galant—not even open trouble, just that silent testing and measuring and weighing that went on between them—Galant would take it out on the horse. I knew he adored the animal. Apart from Nicolaas he was the only one ever allowed near the stallion; and he used to spend more time with it than with the rest of them combined. But now he deliberately started maltreating the stallion. When he led it down to the *vlei* he would tug fiercely at the reins to hurt the tender inside of the horse's mouth. He seemed deliberately to provoke the horse into whinnying and rearing up in fear or pain; and that would give him reason for another angry tug. Once he'd managed to work the animal into such a state that it would start bucking and running, hurling Galant this way and that, he would take the sjambok and lay into it, beating the horse until it was trembling over its whole body.

The first time I came upon him doing it I ran to him to stop the beating. "What you doing?" I shouted at him. "You got mad or something?"

He stopped beating the horse, breathing heavily, a wildness in his eyes as if he didn't recognize me properly. Then he threw away the sjambok and stalked off, leaving me to lead the stallion back to its stable.

"Don't you ever do this again," I told him after he'd calmed down. "How can you do that to a horse?"

He said nothing. He didn't even look up; too ashamed to face me.

And yet he did it again. And then Nicolaas discovered it, one evening when Galant provoked the horse into another frenzy. I was close by, working on a wooden fence for the chicken-run, and watching them askance, pretending not to notice.

"Galant!" Nicolaas shouted, hurrying towards him. "What the hell are you doing?"

Galant stopped, as he'd done the first time when I'd interrupted him, hanging his head. But after a while he looked up to stare straight at Nicolaas, although he still said nothing.

"How dare you beat my horse like that?"

"He broke the gate."

"He's never done a thing like that before." There was a long pause before Nicolaas added in a low, angry voice: "If I ever catch you doing that again—"

"What will you do then?" asked Galant.

"Galant, you've been trying me for a long time. One of these days you'll be going too far."

"How can I go too far? I'm just a slave and the son of a slave."

"I'm warning you."

I couldn't hear Galant's answer.

"It's the last time, I'm telling you. Your work is going from bad to worse. You're looking for trouble. Do you understand me?"

"No, I don't understand you at all. If I don't do my work well I must be punished. You're the *baas*, or aren't you?"

"Galant." I could hear the strain in his voice; he was still struggling not to lose his temper altogether. "We've always got along well."

"That's for you to say."

"If it happens again, only one more time—"

Galant gave no reply to that. I collected my tools and went off to the shed. They must have gone on arguing for quite a while yet for it was quite dark before I saw Nicolaas coming home, leading the horse. Galant went off into the veld on his own. I felt annoyed at both of them that evening. They were changing an unnecessary thing into something neither could avoid. And there was nothing I could do to stop them.

We others often discussed it, usually in the evenings after the day's work had been done—lands tended, sheep put in the kraal, cows milked, wood chopped, the farmyard tidied up—and we all agreed that it had been caused by the death of the child. But when Bet was there she would get furious at such talk.

"It's no use talking about what's past."

"We're not talking about what's past, Bet, but about what's coming."

"And what is that? The Baas asked forgiveness, didn't he? He said he never meant it to happen. So what can still be coming?"

"You're very quick to defend the Baas," Pamela said once, when she was also with us.

"You stay out of it," Bet flew at her. "What do you know about it?"

They could never stand one another, those two. Bet was annoyed because Pamela had been brought in to do the housework after the Nooi had turned against her; and Pamela seemed to blame Bet for Galant's moodiness. She never quarrelled openly: she had a way of just looking at one in silence, and that would be enough to wither you. And even though Galant was still keeping to himself one could see that Pamela was already siding with him against Bet.

There were two other new hands on the farm by then, two youngsters, both Hottentots, Rooy and Thys, whom the Baas hired from the Swartberg region. Since they weren't slaves like us, and much younger, they usually kept out of our conversations; but when Galant wasn't present they sometimes joined in cautiously and one could see that they, too, were worried about the whole thing.

People from other farms in the neighbourhood also took part. Usually over weekends or when one of the masters had gone elsewhere. There was a lot of riding to and fro at night, and the visits often lasted until the morning-star came out. The top dancer and talker of them all was Abel, from Barend's farm. A handsome man, tall as a tree and strong as a bull, a great lover of women. He had a go at Pamela too in the beginning, but she soon put an end to it. From time to time he had a ride with Lydia, who never seemed to mind who it was or when. Otherwise Abel rode to more distant farms in search of female flesh. And he was the only one who didn't seem to worry too much about Galant. "Let him be," he would say when we discussed the matter: "It'll soon sort itself out. It's like a sickness in the stomach." Then he would take a large swig from the calabash or pick up his music or give us another show of reel-dancing in the firelight.

The others from Barend's place were more apprehensive. Klaas, the old sourpuss, mostly agreed with whoever had spoken before him; and we were careful about what we said in his presence, for one never knew what tales he might carry back to his master. Goliath was very cautious. He was still a young man and preferred to stay out of trouble, which was why Galant's ways worried him. That was long before Goliath himself ran into trouble with Barend, of course; and a bad business that was.

One man who used to talk a lot was Dollie. He'd come to work for the old tailor-shoemaker D'Alree who was farming on a part of Houd-den-Bek, not far from our place. A large Mozambiquan was Dollie. And a bad influence, I think, on Galant. "Just you wait," he would say, obviously enjoying the thought. "One of these days we'll get a proper chance. I'm just biding my time to run away, then no one will ever find me again."

"Where will you run to?" sneered Achilles. "They always find you and bring you back. I tried."

"It's a big land," said Dollie.

"Big enough to get lost in, true. And if the masters don't find you the wild animals will get you. Otherwise you'll just die of hunger."

And if old Adonis from Buffelshoek was there he would say: "Talking's easy. Lot of big mouths you are. How d'you think we'll manage if the masters aren't there to look after us? They give us food and drink and clothes and everything. And I tell you, my Baas Jan is the best *baas* in the land." Then a strange session of bragging and swaggering would start, usually involving the older ones, each trying to outdo the rest in praising the strength or skill or goodness of his own master. Among the biggest talkers were Oubaas Piet's men, old Moses and Wildschut and Slinger and the others; and inevitably quarrels would break out, ending often in noisy and spectacular fights.

Through all our nights Galant went his way as if he couldn't care less about our opinions. No one could persuade him to turn back before things had gone too far. And so the inevitable happened.

Just after we'd harvested the beans, after the first frost. Nicolaas took the wagons to Cape Town; and the Nooi went too. Galant had wanted to go with them but Nicolaas wouldn't let him: said he had to stay behind to run the farm; that was what he was *mantoor* for. It was a time of nightly parties on Houd-den-Bek, uproarious festivities the likes of which I'm sure these parts had never seen before or since. Almost nightly a sheep would be slaughtered and roasted on the coals. Galant

196

arranged for everybody to take turns providing meat and drink. The farmers in the neighbourhood couldn't make out what predator had got in among the sheep; while we had a roaring time of nightly blow-outs leaving us reeling and bleary-eyed in the mornings.

Bet was against it from the start—Pamela had gone to the Cape with the family—but Galant reined her in very quickly: "I'm *mantoor* on the farm," he told her. "And if I say a thing can be done it is done. You just open your mouth to Nicolaas when he comes back and see what happens."

When the others heard it they closed in round the two; and I suppose that intimidated Bet. Resigning herself, from then on she sulkily took part in all the eating and drinking.

It came to a very sudden end when Nicolaas arrived home almost a week earlier than he'd been expected. One afternoon—one of the still, colourless days of early winter before the snow sets in—we saw in a state of numb shock the wagon approaching along the narrow strip of veld between the mountain ranges. Galant was at the slaughtering stone, skinning and cutting up the sheep for the night's festivities. When he recognized the wagon he stood up to watch, very calmly, the blood still on his hands. He didn't seem scared at all. In fact, he almost appeared content at having been caught in the act.

Nicolaas didn't immediately grasp what was going on.

"It's late in the week for slaughtering," he said in mild surprise. "Did you skip Monday?"

"We slaughtered on Monday too," said Galant.

That was when I realized there was going to be trouble.

"Oh?" said Nicolaas, still incredulous.

Galant started washing the blood from his hands in the barrel beside the stone, working very meticulously, rinsing each finger separately and cleaning the nails. Then he put on his jacket. The smart corduroy jacket Nicolaas had given him after the death of the child.

"We worked up an appetite for meat," he said calmly.

The Nooi and the womenfolk were unloading in the

197

distance. Galant and Nicolaas were alone at the slaughtering stone; and I was standing at the stable corner, watching and listening.

"Didn't I leave you in charge to keep an eye on everything?" said Nicolaas.

Galant shrugged.

"Where are the sheep?" asked Nicolaas, coming a step closer.

"In the veld where they belong."

"Bring them to the kraal. I want to count them."

Galant gave a curious little smile. Without saying anything more he sauntered off in the direction of the grazing veld, leaving Nicolaas to take care of the carcass. I made a wide detour and followed Galant, in case he should need a hand. Together with Achilles, who'd taken the sheep out that morning, we brought the flock home to the kraal where Nicolaas stood waiting at the gate, one foot resting on the lower beam, his pipe between his locked teeth. He didn't say anything as we approached. In silence he counted the sheep.

Five short.

"Ontong?" said Nicolaas. "Do you know anything about those five sheep?"

That was a nasty question, I thought; and I was reluctant to give a straight answer. "You think something caught them?" I asked.

"I'm not thinking anything. I'm asking you."

"It's difficult to say, Kleinbaas."

"Achilles? What do you know about them?"

"I just brought the flock home, Kleinbaas."

I stood looking at Nicolaas. His eyes were on Galant; but Galant was staring away into the distance, half-whistling through his teeth, although it didn't sound very convincing.

"Did you find any leopard tracks?" asked Nicolaas, going out of his way it seemed to make it easy for us.

At last Galant stopped whistling and turned to Nicolaas. "It wasn't a leopard," he said. "It wasn't the jackals either."

"What happened then, Galant?"

198

"I slaughtered them myself."

"You had permission to slaughter one a week. Wasn't that enough for you?"

"We wanted more."

Nicolaas pressed his thumb into the head of his pipe and put it away in his shirt pocket.

"The two of us had a lot of trouble before I left, Galant," he said. "I hoped to see an improvement when I came back. I warned you, didn't I?"

"That's so."

"Ontong. Achilles." He was speaking slowly to control his voice. "Go and tie him up over the empty barrel in the stable."

I tried to stall him. "Kleinbaas—," I said.

But it was clear that he'd finally made up his mind.

"Come on," Galant said to us. "Take me." And as we took him away he still looked at Nicolaas over his shoulder as if to make sure he would follow us.

He took up position over the barrel by himself, offering his wrists and ankles to be strapped down. We stood there sheepishly, avoiding each other's eyes, until after what seemed like hours Nicolaas came in with a sjambok and a leather thong. The thong he gave to Achilles, the hippo sjambok to me. It wasn't to my liking at all. If a *baas* feels like beating his slave he must do it himself. It's no work for slaves.

"I've had enough from you, Galant," Nicolaas said. "Come on, Ontong. What are you waiting for?"

Straining to raise his head Galant looked round at Nicolaas. "Why you asking them to do it?" he said. "You scared to do it yourself?"

"Ontong!" said Nicolaas.

I brought down the sjambok on Galant's back. Dust came swirling up from the smart jacket.

"You scared?" Galant taunted Nicolaas again.

That seemed to make him mad. He grabbed the heavy sjambok from my hand and started laying into Galant like a whirlwind, without paying much attention to where and how the blows landed. He went on and on until that outlandish

199

jacket was torn to shreds and the hippo hide started cutting into the bare flesh. Not a sound came from Galant's lips. Only a dull groan from time to time, barely audible.

"Kleinbaas," I said at last. I didn't want to go against the man, but I was afraid something bad might happen if Nicolaas weren't stopped in time. He paid no attention, almost sobbing with rage with every blow. When I could stand it no more I touched him lightly on the arm. "I think that's enough, Kleinbaas. You killing him."

Nicolaas stopped as suddenly as he'd begun. He swung round to me, a savage gaze in his eyes. Then he threw down the sjambok and strode out.

In the deepening dusk Achilles and I untied Galant and carried him to his hut where we brought him round with cold water.

If only he'd learned his lesson now, I thought. This thing had been coming for a long time, but now the storm had broken. Perhaps it was just as well; perhaps the air would now be cleared and peace be restored on Houd-den-Bek.

But I'd underestimated him. And what must be will be.

GALANT

A young horse in a walled-in field. *Watch that wall,* they tell
you. *Stay inside. If you dare jump over*—You never know for
sure what will happen if you really do. Impossible to know
unless you jump. And that's not easy. This side everything is
familiar. You know where to run and where to graze. But the
stone wall is always there. You may pretend not to see it, or
turn your head away, but the wall remains and within it the
field seems to be growing smaller every day. Unless you are
prepared to jump it may crush you in the end. Now I've made
the jump. I'm over. And I have survived.

Useless to go on threatening and bobbing and ducking like
two bantam roosters: like the fighting cocks of the Cape
Achilles talks about. "Watch out, Galant," says Nicolaas. And:
"I'm warning you." And: "For the last time." But it's never
really the last time, and there can be no peace before it has
been proved. Where is that wall? And can I make it? The
flogging of the horse makes my own flesh tremble. Damn you!
I want to shout at him. Why do you stand there and let me flog
you? You're so much bigger and stronger than I am. Why
don't you rear up and trample me with your great hooves?
Why don't you break loose and run into the mountains and
never come back? But he doesn't. He allows me to beat him
and abuse him and break him. He accepts whatever happens
to him. I can't stand it. I can't stand it.

"Don't challenge the man like that, Galant," says Ontong.
What does he understand about it? It's not Nicolaas
I'm challenging. His wall is nothing to me. It's my own wall I
got to face. Otherwise you may as well dig me a grave and
cover me up with earth: and don't bother about buchu,

let the *thas*-jackal roam as it wishes.

I can see right through it now. To be children at Lagenvlei is one thing; to adapt to Houd-den-Bek is another. Often, when we face each other in anger or despair, Nicolaas cries: "For God's sake, Galant, what's the matter with you? I don't know you any more. We always got along so well."

How can I explain it to him? It's that stone wall both of us are facing. Both must make the jump.

It has nothing to do with the beating. The blows smart; they tear into the skin and expose the flesh. One's legs are unsteady when they untie you and there's a blackness from which they have to bring you back with water; you don't even recognize their hands. Yet the beating itself is not the wall; it only brings awareness of the wall. And there's joy in knowing you've made the jump. You can hardly move for the pain, but it's worth it for now you're on the other side. Now at last you know.

Then, in the darkest hours of the night when everybody else is asleep and you're the only one awake, in pain but relieved too, there is another discovery to make. You've crossed the wall. But now there is another. Before the jump your only thought is: *I must get over. I must get over.* Now you're over and there's another. There will always be another. Wall after wall. There is terror in the thought; a weariness that over-whelms you even before you've tried the next jump. But then you fall asleep and it brings a new sense of peace.

In the early dawn you crawl from the hut. The morning star is still shining; the frost forms grey mouldy patches on the ground, not yet hard enough to crackle when you step on it, but the cold seeps through the soles. The slave bell hasn't gone yet. You're stiff and numb from lying curled up in the cold and as you move about the pain creeps back into your body. It feels as if you'll never be able to straighten your back again or walk upright, but you clench your teeth for there's a long journey ahead. Before the bell goes you must be gone from Houd-den-Bek.

It takes an effort to stir new life into the coals to warm up some bush-tea on the smoky fire; above all, Bet must not be wakened. The warmth eases the worst stiffness; the fragrance of the tea briefly soothes the pain. You cover yourself with the tattered remains of the new jacket and tiptoe away from the fire. A single person emerges from a hut as you pass by. The woman Pamela. Is she watching you even at night then? Something in her look says: *Come to me.* And you know it will be good with her. You've tried her once or twice, the way things happen on the farm. But because you have that slight experience of her you deliberately keep off. You've had one bad encounter with Bet. Now you got to mind your step. You can see it in Pamela's eyes. There's women you can go into and pull out again, and that's that. But there's others, and you can see Pamela is one of them, who are different: you get in between her legs and you're in for good. It's like climbing in the mountains, when the world is shut off behind one and only the cliffs and rocks remain: and unless you go all the way to the far side you'll die there and leave only a skeleton for others to find long afterwards; not even a footprint in the stone.

"Where you going then, Galant?" says Pamela, and her voice still has the heaviness of sleep, all the stillness of woman and night.

"Over the mountains." I am reluctant to answer; begrudging her the question.

"You going to complain?"

Those eyes seem to peer so deeply into me that I feel like covering up, but it's useless.

"Yes." Suddenly I feel a need for her to understand. "It's not about the beating."

"Because of the jacket then?"

"Why you asking?"

"Because I care."

It makes me blind with anger. She has no right to say this. She has no right to interfere with me. I swear to the Blue God: all my life no one has ever cared a damn. Not even Ma-Rose: not really. And that's saying a lot.

In the dull dawn light I stare at her sternly. She shows no fear. There is something about her that reminds me of a gazelle. The

203

eyes. The attitude. As if she may dart off at the slightest move.

"What you looking at me like that?" I ask her.

"I don't understand you."

"So?"

"You must come back, Galant."

"Of course I'll come back. Where else could I go?"

Inside me something seems to be saying: *Here is another wall.*

"If they ask you about me," I say, "will you tell them I've gone to Tulbagh to complain or will you be silent?"

"Do you want me to tell or do you want me to be silent?"

"You can tell them."

"Then I'll tell them."

The light is turning to grey. Soon it will be time for the bell. But it's not the bell I carry with me in my thoughts as I limp along. It's the woman. This Pamela. All the way, and it's a long way, it's Pamela who keeps me going when weariness and pain threaten to overcome me. Her eyes are with me. And her attitude, a young gazelle ready to dart off, thin and wild.

The pain is so bad that the usual day's journey stretches to two and a half. There's an ache in every step. My footprints strain at my feet, pulling me back to Houd-den-Bek. To this woman. To Nicolaas. Pain. In every brief movement I'm reminded of back and shoulders, buttocks, legs. My chest is aching as I breathe. In my feet I drag along my whole world. Impossible to shake it off.

Nicolaas, I think: if you'd taken me to the Cape with you I may not have been struggling through these mountains today. I begged you. You know very well I've always wanted to go. When we were boys you were the one who told me about the Cape and its tall white houses and its people, about the flat-topped mountain and the hill from which the cannon is fired when the ships come in from the sea; about the horse races and the markets, the streets and gardens and the castle, and the soldiers with their red jackets and shiny buttons, and the slaves dancing to their own music on Sundays. You told me. And I begged you to take me along. But all you could say was: "I want you to stay here. Who will look after the farm if you're not here? I trust you, Galant. There's no one else I can rely on."

You have Ontong and Achilles to rely on. You have a brother living on a farm barely two hours away. No need to deceive me with kind lies. What you really mean is: "I'm the boss and you'll do as I say." Don't try to bribe me with smart new jackets. Jacket today, tatters tomorrow. And my child lies buried in the earth. Don't ever forget that.

Step by step I drag my torn body through the mountains. Far overhead I can see the last remaining swallows coming and going, diving suddenly, changing course, careering in the wind, as my feet keep feeling their way across earth and stone, daunted by the demands of the journey.

"I come here to complain," I tell the gentleman of the Drostdy. One feels out of place in such a place. The high white walls and the arches and the beams of the ceiling and the tall stoep. Everything seems tall here; only I am shrunken in my tattered jacket and stained floppy hat. "One gets flogged at Houd-den-Bek. The food is bad too. And when one is given a new jacket it's beaten to shreds by their sjamboks. Look at me."

"Where's the letter from your master?" asks the Landdrost.

"What letter?"

"Didn't you ask his permission to come here?"

"If I ask his permission he'll just beat me again."

"So you deserted? Do you realize that is a serious offence?"

"I didn't desert. I came here to complain."

"Who do you think you're talking to?"

So I'm put away in a cell down in the cellar. Not much light there and the straw is heavy with the stench of old piss. A small bowl of rice water, a chunk of bread, a piece of rancid pork fat. Somewhere high above the small window, under the awning of the tall roof, a family of swallows must have built their nest. What are they still doing here in winter, not gone with all the others? I cannot understand them. They are free to go, yet they stay. All day long one can hear them twittering. Only after sunset they grow silent and an awful loneliness settles in

205

the cell. How long will I have to wait before somebody comes for me?

Just as well I told Pamela about it, so it turns out to be only one night before Nicolaas arrives. But it's a night that changes the look of my world, the way an unexpected rainstorm rips open a new course for a mountain stream, milling and turning the pebbles below, scouring off all ridges and edges so that round and smooth they form a dependable new bed for the water running above.

It is a night of endless talking. There are three of us in the cell, but one is very old and broken, whimpering by himself in a corner and paying no attention to us; so it's only the other man and I. A giant of a man who'll have no trouble lifting a loaded wagon with one huge shoulder. When he bends those great arms his muscles bulge as if to shatter the heavy chains that bind him. I am unbound, but his arms are in chains and his legs are shackled; in some places the flesh is visible where the iron has worn away the skin. From time to time, when he moves to change position he utters a groan, for he's been flogged. I'm there in my tattered clothes but he is quite naked and in the dim light one can see that no part of his body has been spared. The red of flesh. And in places the white of bone and of gristle. When he groans it's the great deep sound of a lion. How can I ever forget the sound of the lion that faraway night, and its roar, as if the very earth is trembling?

"What you doing here?" he asks me when they first throw me in and I slide on hands and knees through the rotten straw.

"I came to complain. Now they keeping me until the Baas comes."

"You still bother to complain?" He laughs harshly, but it is more like a groan, and I hear the chains clinking. With a great effort he pushes himself up against the wall and grabbing the bars in front of the window pulls his broken body up so he can look out; but outside there's nothing but the untimely swallows, and only from time to time. The light touches his broad shoulders and the muscles of his arms, his knotted bloody back, his buttocks, the legs as thick as logs.

206

"You still bother to complain," he says again, holding on to the bars with one hand so that he can turn painfully to look at me. "You'll learn it's no use. I'm past complaining."

"What did you do then?" I ask.

"The worst."

"Killed your master?"

He grimaces. "You think that's the worst a man can do?" Letting go of the bar he sinks back to the ground. Once again I hear him utter the low growl of a lion; then he's silent for such a long time that I'm wondering whether he's given up talking. But at last I hear the chain again and he starts to speak; but he doesn't seem to be speaking to me, it's to himself. He tells me about a hunt. I don't know when. Perhaps it's not even a real hunt, only a dream, but what does it matter? He's trekking with his *baas* and with a host of other masters and slaves, with sunrise on his right and sunset on the left, laying waste the land as they go on. Buffalo. Eland. Zebra. Rhino. Elephant. Whatever crosses their way. Until the wagons are groaning under the weight of the ivory and horns and hides. On the trail of the carcasses packs of hyenas follow the trek, and jackals, and vultures. From the circles of the vultures in the sky one can follow their progress from afar, for weeks on end, all the way to the Great River. And there they find people, a whole colony of them: bastards, runaways, all sorts of people who have escaped over the years to settle there and be free.

"I don't believe it," I say.

"Saw them with my own eyes," answers the big man. "Spoke to them myself. They used to be slaves like you and me. Now they living there in their own place."

"What did you do when you got there?"

"The masters wanted to shoot them, but the people brought us milk and vegetables and all we needed. In the night they all disappeared as if they'd never been there; only the tracks of their cattle were left, and the empty huts."

"And then?"

"The masters burnt down the huts and laid waste the fields, but it was no use anyway. The people had all gone. They're free."

207

"Slaves like you and me?"

"Yes, like us." The chains grate on the stone floor. It's almost too dark to see him, but his deep lion's voice goes on talking.

"On our farm there's a big rock some distance from the house, with a piece of rusted chain still fixed to it. I heard the people say that in the old days there was a slave woman who used to run away from the farm ever since she was a young girl. A Malay, I think. Every time she was brought back and punished. But no matter what punishment they gave her, inside or out, she always ran away again. At last they tied her up there in the chain fitted to the rock, far enough from the house so no one would hear her screams. Once a day a child was sent with some food and water; and they even put up a small shelter on poles to keep away the worst rain or sun. There she stayed all her life, and the people say she lived to a very old age. Chained to the rock she remained, and never spoke another word to anyone. At last she died, and the beasts of the veld and the vultures devoured the carcass and scattered the remains. In my time there was no one left who'd known her. But the rock was still there, and the piece of chain. And whenever a slave got it into his head to run away he would be taken there for his flogging to be reminded of the woman. So no one ever dared to follow her example. But after we came back from the big hunt I would often go into the veld after the day's work was done, to sit on that rock and think about those people of the Great River. Couldn't ever get them out of my mind again. Free men, like real people. And that was when I first ran away too."

"That's not the worst a man can do!"

"Running away was just the beginning."

"What did you do then?"

Another of those long silences. When he speaks again his voice has a sullen sound as if he blames me for asking. "It was the Nooi's fault," he says. "Kept on nagging me. She'd wait until the day's work was done, then she'd give me something else to do. And if I complained she went to the Baas. So he

208

would flog me. And the next day she would be back nagging me over this or that. A small thin woman, but a real bitch. Always trying to provoke one until you said something back, and then she'd slap you in the face and run off to the Baas to tell on you. She was there with the floggings too. Egging him on. More. More. And if I tried to run away, day or night, back to the free people of the Great River, they'd follow my trail and bring me back and everything would start all over. Until I couldn't take it no more. We were reaping on the lands all day in the baking sun, prickling and burning with chaff. I was down at the fountain washing myself when she came to me. Ordered me to go and cut fodder for the cattle. That wasn't my work but the man who used to do it had botched it up somehow. 'I'm tired,' I said. 'Who are you to talk to me like that?' she said and she slapped my face. Sometimes there's a blindness that gets into a man. I grabbed her hand to stop her. Suddenly she started screaming like a pig. I just wanted her to shut up. The screaming gave me a scare; it made me mad. As she struggled to get away her dress got torn, right here in front, all the way down. She gasped. And suddenly, her mouth still wide open, she stopped screaming and just gaped at me, clutching the torn bits of her dress. 'Look here,' she said. 'Let me go. Please let me go. I promise you I won't tell anyone. Just let me go. Don't touch me.' She was no longer the Nooi to me. It made me sick to see that creature pleading so sloppily with me. And in my anger I pushed her. She fell. She made no effort to get up or to move away. Just went on sobbing and pleading and slobbering. I don't know what got into me. I just started tearing at her until she had no more clothes on, lying there like a bony white chicken plucked of its feathers, squawking and clucking and kicking its thin legs. 'Do what you want,' she said. 'Do anything you want. But please don't kill me. I'll give you anything you ask.'"

"And so you took her?"

A fierce clattering of the heavy chains. "Of course not. I don't fuck chickens."

"But you said—"

209

"I kicked her, that's all. Looking down at her, lying there like a bloody slaughtered chicken, I kicked her in the crotch and walked away."

"That all you did?"

In the dark I hear his angry laugh again, that rumbling lion-sound. "That all? Don't you know that's the worst you can do in this world? The honour of a white woman: there's nothing can match that."

"And what's going to happen to you now?"

"They finished with me here. Now it's off to the Cape, they said. The horses will be here in the morning to take me."

"What they going to do to you?"

"If I'm lucky I'll die on the road. Otherwise, again if I'm lucky, it's the gallows."

"And if you're not?"

"Then it's the island."

"The island?"

"Robben Island. With chains on your legs. Where you break stones till you die."

"It must be better than the gallows. You're still alive."

"A man is not alive there. It's the irons. And every day you can see the Mountain across the water. Don't you understand? It's like that woman they chained to the rock till she died. You're tied up there, chained for life; and behind your eyes you still see those people of the Great River. The free people with their own goats and gardens. You don't think that's worse than death?"

"You said the masters burnt the huts and destroyed the gardens of those people. So what's the use anyway?"

"Makes no difference. They're free."

All through the night there's his voice talking in the dark. At times he stops, and I doze off; but when I wake up I hear him talking again.

"You better have some sleep," I tell him.

"Perhaps it's the last chance I'll ever have to talk to another man," he says. "You hear me? On that island you're not allowed to talk. Tonight I got to talk."

"I don't know what to say."

210

"Don't say anything. Just listen. Don't fall asleep. I got to talk."

Later he begins to ramble. It is quite impossible to follow his thoughts any longer. Bits about his childhood, about this woman or that; his master and the Nooi; the people across the Great River; all mixed up. He starts giving me long complicated messages. *Tell Siena this. Don't forget about Thomas. And if Katrina asks you—*

"Who's Katrina?"

He doesn't even seem to hear me.

"Where do you come from? What's the name of your farm so I can send them a message?"

"Don't talk," he says. "Just listen."

His talk gets more and more confused, the groans in between grow deeper and heavier. The sound of the chains becomes a steady rattle and I realize that he is shivering from cold fever. But whenever I try to say something he starts talking again, on and on. Sometimes I stretch my legs and try to peer through the barred window. A small slice of sky is visible. Stars. It's like those childhood nights when the Oubaas came to Ma-Rose and I had to sleep outside. Except this cell is small and dark and the smell is bad; and the man never stops talking. He doesn't even notice when I drop off to sleep, plagued by bad dreams. There's a lion charging at me and I can't move for I'm chained to a rock. A woman offers me water. "I care," she says. But I know it's useless, the vultures are already circling; and somewhere there are people like you and me, only they're free. Then the lion groans again and I wake up to the deep voice of the man in chains. It drones on and on, broken by what now sounds like moaning sobs; until in the first light of day the swallows start chirping outside again, flitting from their nest and back; then he sinks into a sleep of exhaustion, sighing and mumbling.

In glaring daylight they come for me because Nicolaas has arrived; he goes with me to the high big room I know from the first time, except now the Landdrost isn't there, only his assistant.

"What would you like me to do to him?" the man asks Nicolaas.

"I thought a good flogging might bring him to his senses."

In the courtyard there's a tall post they tie one's hands to. Post and ground are stained as with rust. Overhead the rare swallows come and go undisturbed even by the sound of the blows falling.

"Will you go back with your master now and do as he says?" the man asks me after the flogging. "If not, we'll have to put rings on your legs."

"I shall bear what I deserve from you and my master."

"All right. Then you can go. But if it happens again you won't get off so lightly."

"Thank you, Baas."

As we go out the man calls Nicolaas back to him; and standing outside the door I can hear them talking.

"Mr Van der Merwe," says the man, "I've done this to satisfy you. But in future you should be more careful when you flog your slaves. A thong or a strap or a cane is in order but a sjambok can cause trouble. If this should come to the notice of my superiors you may lose the slave. The Court in Cape Town is very strict on procedure nowadays."

Nicolaas has brought a spare horse for me; and together we ride off from the Drostdy. My body is torn. From time to time the pain makes my head reel. But I'm hardly conscious of it as I sit thinking about the man with the lion's voice, wondering whether he's on his way to the Cape now and whether he'll be lucky or not. And I think about the Great River which must be very far away indeed.

The man remains in my thoughts all the time, even in the night while we shelter against the fog in the mountains. Nicolaas tries to talk to me, rambling on and on like the man in chains; otherwise he drifts off into sleep; but I stay awake. Not because of the pain, but through thinking about the stranger. Here I'm on my way back to Houd-den-Bek, even more bruised than when I came to Tulbagh to complain. Yet I hardly care about it: in a way meeting that man has made it worth my while. But do not ask me why.

212

GOLIATH

It was not worthwhile going all the way to Worcester to complain. It was Abel who insisted I should go. "You just ask Galant," he said. "I've often talked to him about it. If the law says something the Baas got to listen. And if the law says no work on Sundays and the Baas makes you work in spite of it, then you got a case for the gentlemen." If you let the Baas have his way, said Abel, you are giving him the boot to kick your arse.

That's the only reason why in the end I went to complain. True, in a way I suppose I won my case; but I know I really lost. The day in Worcester, when the Landdrost told me to go back to Elandsfontein, I knew I'd lost. No matter that he promised to send the commissioner to make sure everything would be all right. For days and weeks and months in between there would be only Baas Barend and us; where would the commissioner be then?

And when the commissioner came, a fat flabby breathless man who never looked anyone in the face, I knew that my complaining had just made everything worse. "Does your master treat you well?" he asked me. What could I say, with Baas Barend standing there next to him listening? He'd already told me what to say. And the commissioner was in a hurry; I could see he was in no frame of mind really to pay attention to me. "Come on, speak up," he said. "I haven't got all day, you know."

"The Baas treats us well," I said.

Why should he pretend to be so powerful? I could see he *wanted* to believe the story the Baas had told me to tell, that a horse had thrown me. For if he couldn't believe that it would

213

cause him trouble and I know he didn't want that. He'd been sent to check on us; but if it really came to a choice he was one of the masters and they would always stand together. We're on one side. They're on the other. And it can never be different.

"I'm never going to complain again," I told Abel after the man had left. "I'm in the Baas's hands and I'm not going to go against him."

"You going to let him do just what he wants from now on?" he said.

"He got the right to do what he wants. My right is to suffer whatever he does, and no more."

"I'll be waiting for him with a spade in my hands when he comes home tonight," he said, choking. "Then we'll see."

I wanted to stop him but I was still feeling weak after the flogging of the week before; and I knew Abel wouldn't let anyone interfere with him anyway. And to tell the truth, there was a last desperate rush of hope in me that whatever wild thing he might attempt he would succeed. But when the Baas came home from the hunt and called Abel to take his horse I saw him obeying very meekly. And I thought: If even Abel is too cowed to do anything there is no hope at all.

From that day I did whatever work was given me to do without complaining. It was the only way to survive. If one isn't alive one is dead. And of life I know a little bit, but of death I know nothing at all.

NICOLAAS

What perversity decreed that my survival should depend on him?

We were delayed in Tulbagh—there were traders and messengers from the Cape and men from distant farms had come to town—so it was past noon before we steered the horses from the cluster of whitewashed black-thatched houses towards the wagon-road up the slope of the Witzenberg. How I abhorred those tracks ground into the very stone, on which I moved to and fro, forced always back to the farm, allowed no will of my own, predestined on my course by the wish of a father with no concern for private urge or aberration. Before we were half-way through the mountains, soon after we had dismounted to lead the horses where the track became too steep, the fog came down; one of the silent, swirling mountain fogs descending so swiftly that the world is obliterated before you have become aware of cloud. Vision shrank to three yards, two, a foot. Occasionally an unexpected whorl would still open up a dizzying, brief glance of slopes below, a precipice, a tangle of protea or erica; but soon there was only a blinding whiteness.

"I think we'd better turn back while we still can," I proposed. "We can stay over in town and try again tomorrow."

"You scared?" he snarled.

"Of course not. But it may get dark."

"So?"

I looked at him, but there was only the challenge of his obdurate stare. We went on for a while. The horses were getting restless, snorting noisily. I stopped again.

"Galant, we're looking for trouble. This fog is not going to let up."

He shrugged.

"Let's turn back," I said, reining in my horse.

"If you insist," he replied. "You're the master."

There was a defiance in his voice, which stirred up new anger in me. After all that had happened there was still no sign of subservience in the way he carried his battered body; there was pride in the very tatters he wore and through which I could see the arrogant accusation of black and bleeding welts and bruises. He said nothing, but already he had made it impossible for me to turn back without acknowledging defeat. The anger subsided. I felt weary. I had hoped—for what? Anything but this. Had it become impossible then to conduct a simple relationship without a constant sense of having to measure my will against his? But if he refused to yield, then neither would I. Stumbling blindly through the wet fog, we went on, dragging the horses whose hooves sent loose stones rattling down slopes and cliffs, the sharp separate sounds of their falling soon muffled in that gentle but insidious whiteness that enveloped us, obscuring the solidity of the mountain, altering geography, mocking both memory and sense of direction.

"Where you going?" he asked once.

"Up the wagon road, of course," I said. "Can't you see?"

"Oh." There was a dull smile on his face, his eyes brooding but mocking.

Regardless, I went on, following what I grimly forced myself to believe was the well-worn track through the mountains; but my confidence was eroded by his silence; certainty ebbed. From time to time I stopped, but it was useless to look for landmarks in that uniform mist. Bent double, both to keep my eyes as close to the ground as possible and to counter the resistance of the horse with my full weight, I led us on, satisfied in the simple knowledge of plodding upward, not down. From the fog sudden shapes would present themselves, swimming towards one like obtuse fishes in muddy water: a gnarled wagon-tree, an eroded rock, a wet green shrub. And even as one looked at them their stark outlines would fade into

216

a blob, a blur, and disappear again. My only reassurance lay in the animal presence of the two horses and in Galant.

"I wonder whether he got away," he said unexpectedly. "In this fog they won't easily find him."

"Who?"

He looked at me sharply as if my voice had surprised him; perhaps he'd been muttering to himself.

"The man in chains," he said.

"I don't know what you're talking about."

"No, you don't." He offered no further explanation, and again I stumbled on, driven by the urge to keep moving as if that in itself was our only hope.

"You can't go up there," he said behind me.

"I know the way. Just follow me."

There was a track visible in the fog, running horizontally to the right; thirty or forty yards further on, if I remembered correctly, it would swing sharply to the left again for the next steep climb. Without waiting for him, I plunged into the fog which was darkening rapidly now; the sun was probably setting. But if my hunch was right we didn't have very far to go to the last ridge. And from there, even if the fog persisted, I would have no trouble to find my way. Soon we would be riding over the farmyard at Elandsfontein, where we might stop for a cup of tea with Barend and Hester—yes, certainly with Hester—and then up the narrow valley that runs between Duiwelsberg and the Skurweberg, round the forbidding heights of Vaalbokskloofberg, to the gentler plains of Houd-den-Bek.

He grabbed me so suddenly from behind that I cried out.

"What the hell are you doing?" I shouted in rage, raising the sjambok to strike him.

"Look," he said.

I stared, but could see nothing except the fog and the dull dark shapes of rocks looming at a few yards' distance. Then there was a momentary thinning of the mist as it swirled and folded in the wet wind, and I saw the earth breaking away from me, no more than a step or two ahead, a sheer drop to an

217

invisible bottom, a hundred or a thousand feet below. The next moment the fog closed in again.

Galant was still holding me by the arm to steady my sudden fit of trembling. It took a while before I could pull away, pushing the horse back so that I could get past him along the ledge I'd mistaken for the wagon road. Avoiding his eyes, I stood peering into the mist; but I no longer expected to see anything familiar. For a long time, trying to recompose myself, I couldn't speak at all.

"What are we going to do now?" I asked at last.

"We can shelter under some rocks not far from here," he said.

"How do you know?"

"It's near the wagon-road. To the left. I've sheltered there against the rain before."

"But how in God's name—?" I drew in my breath slowly. "Do you mean to tell me you knew where we were all the time? And you let me—"

"I tried to tell you, but you wouldn't listen."

"Stupid baboon!" I growled at him. It was not what I had meant to say; but I was still weak with shock.

At first sight there didn't seem to be much shelter under the tall pile of rocks that must have tumbled from the cliffs countless years ago. But Galant knew his way through them. Slipping over and under them, quick and sure as a lizard in spite of his tortured body, he led me to a small hollow in their midst, its sandy floor still dry. We tied up the horses outside, ignoring their meekly protesting whinnies; inside, he told me to light a fire—there was dried bracken and driftwood among the rocks, damp from the mist but not unmanageable—as he scuttled off without explanation, returning some time later with an armload of bushes: heather and protea and buchu, their sweet and acrid smells prickling to the nose. These he arranged in two rough piles to serve as bedding for the night. There was hardly enough space for both of us beside the fire, but leaning back against the uneven rocks, we managed to dig ourselves in without too much discomfort. The fire gave off more smoke than heat, causing one's eyes to smart unmercifully; and from time to time we clambered out, ostensibly to check the horses but really to gasp some fresh air. The fog persisted; there were no stars.

There was a disarming closeness in that small hollow, as we sat with shoulders pressed together and legs drawn up to share what heat there was. At last, after the months and years in which we'd lived our separate lives, each carefully avoiding the other, we could no longer pretend to be untouchable. For a long time we both remained rigid, straining with our minds to deny the contact of our bodies; but as one yielded to sleepiness and fatigue, as the night wore on and lay more heavily on our limbs, the tightness relaxed. While my body slackened I could still feel him resisting in the glowing, smoky darkness next to me, but in the end he, too, succumbed.

"You saved my life," I said at last, grateful for the protection of the dark.

"I just stopped you. It was nothing."

"Do you remember the day we dug into the sandbank and it collapsed on us?"

"That was long ago."

"We had good times together."

He said nothing. His resistance was maddening; yet I went on prodding, trying to force some response from him, some sign at least of repentance or remorse, an acknowledgement that the past was not entirely irrevocable, that redemption was still conceivable. It was ridiculous, of course, and in any other situation I would have recognized it as such; but it seemed particularly necessary, in that small hollow, forced so closely together, to go beyond the obvious. He refused to co-operate and if I hadn't been so tired I might have given up, or lost my temper. But one draws a strange persistence from weariness. In the new vulnerable state of my dependence on him, that night, I realized that this had been at the root of my outbursts against him: this urge to force a response from him, to move him, to prise him out of that passivity in which he was untouchable, a smooth intractable surface of rock which one

219

could scale or explore without finding any fissure. The very wounds I'd torn into his body might have been efforts to get inside him, to break through that surface; and indeed the skin had broken, but there were membranes of the mind which kept him forever inaccessible. But surely there was no need for it: this was the fierce conviction that urged me on. There was no need. Yet his patient silence in itself confirmed how wrong I was. Our innocence was irrecoverable: but why did it mean so much to prove the contrary? Between us, indeed, lay the death of the child; and my increasing gnawing guilt; and perhaps the body of a black woman. But there was more to it than that. Those were only the obvious symptoms of a more insidious evil at which I could only guess and towards which I could only grope. It seemed a night made for it. But what was the use if Galant refused to respond? After trying in vain several times to prod him I withdrew from his sullen antagonism and immersed myself in my own thoughts.

All right, he was undoubtedly in pain, and blaming me for it. But that in itself had only been the result of that other evil I could sense but not explain. That we were no longer heedless boys but master and slave: could either really blame that on the other? It was something neither could avoid or even wish undone: the very condition of our mutual survival.

I must have fallen asleep at some stage. I remember confused snatches of dreams before the image settled: Galant and I were boys again, playing in the sandy bank below the dam, tunnelling into the mud left soft and sodden by the rain, crawling inside, huddled together, whispering and giggling; and then it subsided. Only, in my dream it was not the wall that caved in but the dam itself that burst, and a great black flood of water came washing over us, drowning us.

"Hey!" A voice called through the flood, and it was Galant shaking me by the shoulder to wake me up.

"What happened?" I stammered.

"You shouted. I think you were dreaming."

"I was. I dreamt about the dam breaking. You and I were in the tunnel together."

"Why can't you forget about it?"

"I don't know." Suddenly I said: "You know, when I married Cecilia and my father gave you to me—it was because I'd asked him to."

"Why?"

"I knew we'd get along on the farm." No, it wasn't that. I tried again. "I felt I—well, I thought I couldn't handle the farm without you. I wouldn't know what to do. Do you understand what I mean?"

"You said it before. And what is it to me? You learned to farm when you were small."

"I know. But Pa was always there. He was always in charge. Then I got married and suddenly—it was just I. Suddenly everybody was expecting me to be a man and a farmer like the rest. I had a wife, I had a farm. And I—all I wanted to do was run away. But I knew I would never be able to look Pa in the eye again, and that would be the worst of all. He'd always looked down on me. It had always been Barend, Barend, Barend. I wanted to make a success of it. I damned well had to, I had no choice. But I didn't know how to begin. And all I could think of was to ask him to let me have you so you could help me."

"You doing all right." After a brief pause he added, with a small bitter touch in his voice: "You're a good master."

"That's not what I meant." He didn't answer. And I couldn't stop; in the vulnerable aftermath of sleep, in that dark hollow in the heart of the mountains, the coals burning so low that Galant was no more than a shadow outlined against dull red glow, I felt more acutely than ever before a need to unburden myself. "You know I never wanted to be a farmer," I said. "Barend could never wait to be his own boss and run his own farm. To me it was worse than a prison."

"What did you want to do then?"

"That's the worst of it. I don't know. I've never been given a chance to find out. But somewhere in the world there must have been something else for me to do. I would have become a man in my own right. Now I'm chained to the farm."

221

"Why didn't you go away?"

"I couldn't let Pa down. I was scared of him. And afterwards —well, then I got married. Now I have a family. I have responsibilities. It's impossible to give up everything and go away. Sometimes I try to persuade myself that I have a good life, that I'm free. But the land itself holds me captive. I have to obey the seasons. What I do depends on rain or heat or the soil or the grazing. Sometimes I wake up at night and it's like the day the sand caved in; I can't breathe. I want to cry out, and I want to get up and shout curses that will wake up the whole house. But all I can do is get up and go out, and walk down to the kraal to look at the cattle or sheep lying there, all those dumb sheep, chewing their cuds, stirring when they see me, too stupid to do anything about it; and then I think I'm just as dumb as they are, locked up in my kraal for the night, driven out in the morning to graze, and brought back at dark. And sometimes I wish a bloody leopard or a lion would jump into the kraal and kill me and drag me out for good."

"You're stupid," he said in quiet contempt. "You got everything you want. You don't need a lion to kill you."

"For God's sake, try to understand." Unreasonably, irrationally, I was now pleading with him. "You've got to understand."

And he asked: "Why?"

For a long time I didn't speak again. His question was burning more surely into me than any hot coal. Why indeed? Why the need to humiliate myself in this vast night, prostrating myself in front of a slave, begging him to understand me? But there was no other who might, and that must have been the answer. In all the world there was no one to whom I could go to beg for this understanding I now required of him. This was an agony for which Ma-Rose would have no remedy. Hester? She could only make it worse by quickening the need. There was no one but Galant, and he denied me the single word of comfort I required.

I fell asleep again, and this time dreamed of Hester. Her dark solemn eyes set so far apart in the narrow face, the

222

beautiful lines of cheekbones and stubborn chin, the small straight nose and wide mouth, the vulnerable throat; I remembered the candid grace of her body when we were children, the sultry tone of her limbs, the fascination of the bluntness in which she differed from us; and I woke with a smothered cry, swollen and erect and achingly without her.

"You dreamed again," Galant said, a sound of accusation in his voice.

"I was dreaming of Hester."

"Hester?"

But I didn't answer. This time I was possessive of my dream and I leaned forward, drawing my arms tightly round my knees as if to hold on to what I'd already lost, trying to retain the exquisite hardness even as I felt it, throbbingly, subside.

"Once when we were small," he said, "she and I came home in a storm and Ma-Rose covered us in a kaross and dried us in front of her fire."

I glared at him in the dark, resentful of his memories, yet at the same time feeling a new warmth in me moving out towards him, in the awareness of sharing something of her in this night, even though his memory could never be as intimate as mine. If this were, absurdly, all we had to share it still lent meaning to the darkness in which we sat huddled somewhere in those godforsaken mountains far from home. In this fitful sharing there was an aching, exhilarating awareness of a freedom I'd never known. For once, for those few brief dark hours, we could share an experience because neither had to look up or down to the other. And yet, what mockery in that momentary freedom. I knew I was sitting beside a man whose body had been torn and broken at my own bidding.

"What did you dream?" he asked again.

"It's gone already," I lied, reaching in my mind for the remembrance of that forbidden desire. "You know how it is. Don't you ever dream?"

He shrugged.

"What do you dream of?"

He remained silent. After a long time—and one was

223

conscious of time then, because the wind had risen and was tearing and wailing round the rocks; and occasionally the horses stamped or snorted outside—he suddenly said: "Tell me about the Great River."

"What about it? You know I've never been there."

"The Cape then."

"What do you want to know about the Cape?"

"Anything you can tell."

"You should have gone with us."

"I asked you to take me. You said no."

"You had to keep an eye on the farm. There was no one else I could trust."

"When we were children you promised to take me one day."

"Next time you can go with me." I thought: *If I'd taken you, all this may have been avoided. Was this your way of taking revenge?*

"You promise?"

"I promise."

Again he said: "Tell me about it."

Like many years before, when Pa had taken Barend and me to the Cape for the first time, I told him whatever I could recall, whatever I thought he might like to hear. The bustle in the squares and cobbled streets, the military parades, the wagons arriving from the interior loaded with produce, the boisterous sports meetings at Green Point, the open-air concerts, the congregation in the Groote Kerk on Sundays round the pulpit with its carved lions in dark gleaming wood; we'd even done the fashionable thing and climbed Table Mountain (the slopes strewn with the soles and heels of flimsy shoes discarded by our predecessors), and I told him of the stupendous view from up there, the blue and green of two great oceans mingling, the patterns of white breakers changing lazily, almost imperceptible to the eye; I told him about the fleet of ships sailing into the Bay like a flock of sea birds approaching with wings outstretched and white plumes fluttering, and the throng in the harbour as the rowing boats docked, sailors and soldiers and passengers mobbed by townsfolk and

224

slaves fighting and jostling to offer their trays laden with wares for sale; I told him about the changed fashions—the dull colours of years ago yielding to the brighter hues of lilac and blue, mulberry and rose and green; women's waists growing smaller, waistlines dropping, the wide skirts fuller and more graceful than ever; the men in tall tophats and tailcoats. All the time he interrupted me, too eager to wait, anxious to hear everything simultaneously, plying me with questions about the cannon on Signal Hill—ships arriving and leaving—the clothes worn by slaves—the gatherings at the town fountain and the mill—clandestine cock-fights in the quarry below the Lion's Head—music in the Gardens—the shops and stalls run by slaves—the markets—the mountain—the sea. I was surprised by what he already seemed to know; but when I prodded him he grew evasive, mumbling something about remembering what he'd been told by me before, or by Ontong and others: and then he'd start a flurry of new questions. What I knew I told him; what I didn't know I invented. What did it matter? He wasn't concerned with truth or falsity, only with an image as outlandish as possible of that distant place, the gaudiest colours, the wildest adventures. In our improbable night everything seemed plausible; and as I went on I entered more and more into the spirit of his imaginings, feeding him on the fantasies he so obviously craved. Some of my inventions were so marvellous that we would both burst out laughing, and like a child at play he would urge me on: more! more! It made the time pass more rapidly, it diminished our awareness of discomfort and cold (for the last wood had been burnt and the embers were dying); above all it reinforced the amazing closeness developing between us as we sat in our hollow remote from our everyday lives, close to the bright possibilities of childhood. But perhaps it was informed by anguish: perhaps our talk was compulsive: for below the territory of memories and dreams and wishful thinking we explored ran a dark slow current which I tried to deny but which was there and which, whenever we fell silent, obtruded like the night. It became as necessary for myself as for him to

225

keep talking, pretending, laughing, and weaving fantasies. But that subterranean course was there, welling up below, forcing its way up ever more closely to the surface where sooner or later, I knew, it had to break out and flood the forced gaiety of our make-believe.

"There was one terrible thing I'll never forget for as long as I live," I said; and in saying it I knew I shouldn't, for this was the dark current running below and for the first time I recognized it; but of course, having acknowledged it, it was too late to stop. I faltered for a moment.

"What happened?" he prodded.

"We were walking away from Greenmarket Square, up towards the Lion's Head. A slave came past us, on his way from the mountain; a young Malay in a red turban, carrying a huge bundle of firewood and an axe. I'm not quite sure how it started, but I believe he was jostled by someone, a soldier, and the bundle of wood fell on the pavement. The thong holding it together slipped loose and the sticks were scattered on the ground. A few people laughed. Someone jeered. When we looked round it was just in time to see him suddenly going into a frenzy, and raising the axe. The soldier tried to ward off the blow but it hit him on the shoulder, almost severing his arm. People started screaming. The slave was swinging the axe in all directions, beating them off. I could see the whites of his eyes as he hit out this way and that, bellowing like a bull. And then he ran right into the crowd, dispersing them like a bucket of peas, throwing over the tables and stalls of the vendors, kicking out of his way their buckets and barrels, as his arms went on flailing and striking out. Everybody was shouting: 'Amok! Amok!' A young girl stumbled as she tried to get away from him. The daughter of a colonel in the regiment, I was later told. She was wearing a pale yellow dress. The blunt side of the axe caught her on the side of the head. Suddenly there was blood everywhere. Then he axed down a small slave child who must have thought it was all great fun for he was just standing there laughing and jumping up and down."

I wanted to stop but I couldn't.

226

"And then?" asked Galant.

"Then a detachment of soldiers came. They surrounded him but he wouldn't give up. He was still bellowing. Everybody else on the cobbled square was dead silent after the child had been hit. Hundreds of people, but not a sound. Not a movement. All the fruit and vegetables and eggs and hides and other produce littering the square like a battlefield. One single small bright butterfly fluttering over a bucket of flowers. You could almost hear its wings in that silence. As if everybody was holding their breath. Only the soldiers in their scarlet coats advancing in a ring, very slowly, very cautiously. And then the mad Malay made another rush towards them, his head down, axe raised, bellowing. He hit the first soldier who tried to stop him. The axe came down. It made a strange sound. The man's skull was split open like a pumpkin. The curious thing was that, because of the silence, everything seemed to be happening very slowly, you could see each individual movement as if it were isolated from all the others. That's what it was. Everything was separate. Nothing made sense. But as his axe struck the soldier the square came to life again and it was pandemonium. They opened fire. Because the place was so crowded several people were grazed by shot. The slave went down, his arms still churning, his body tossing and squirming on the ground like a snake."

"What happened to him?"

"They dragged him off. We didn't stay. I felt sick. There was no point in remaining there, gawking like vultures."

"But afterwards," he insisted. "What happened?"

"How must I know? We left the next morning. I suppose they hanged him. Perhaps they first flogged him and cut off his ears. I don't know what they do to them nowadays."

"Where did they hang him?"

"The gallows stands outside the town just below the Lion's Rump. Three tall pillars with three crossbeams."

"Do many people go there?"

"I suppose so. I believe it's one of the great spectacles of the Cape."

227

"And afterwards?"

"What do you mean, afterwards?"

"After they hanged him."

"How must I know? I guess a murderer's body is quartered afterwards and his head is stuck on a pole in the place where he used to live so that people can see it and be warned."

"And it stays like that?"

"Perhaps the vultures come."

He was silent for a long time. Then he said: "At least he got the soldier."

"What do you mean?" I asked, shocked.

"You said he killed the soldier."

"Yes, of course."

"The others: were they also killed?"

"I don't know. I think the child died later, from what I heard." I shuddered beside him, feeling again the nausea I'd felt in town that day. "Can you imagine such a thing?" I asked. "The man must have been mad."

"They threw down his firewood," he said.

"For God's sake, what's a bundle of firewood?"

He didn't answer; and I didn't feel like talking any more. It had been a mistake. The hidden current had emerged from what had seemed such solid earth and now we were in it, struggling in silence not to be drowned in its darkness.

All the other memories came back to me, the many things I'd been battling with ever since that unfortunate visit to the Cape. For indeed, this time it had not been the fun-fair of earlier visits as I'd tried to persuade both Galant and myself. That dark undercurrent had been there all along. The visiting fleet, for all the colour and exuberance it had brought to town, had borne disturbing rumours, all the more worrying since no one seemed sure how much of it had been based on fact, how much on conjecture. The town was rife with speculation. And at least this much was clear, corroborated by hints in the *Gazette*: that, perturbed more and more by the flow of ominous reports from missionaries at the Cape—undoubtedly the misguided dangerous fools from the London Missionary

228

Society—philanthropists in England were increasing the pressure on the Government to take away all our slaves. And one of these days, I heard people say, Hottentots would no longer be required by law to work or to live in a fixed place: they would be free, just imagine, to come and go as they wished. Some people had gone to talk to the Governor about it. But what reply did they get? "The matter is being investigated." No attempt to deny anything, only covering up for as long as possible, knowing no doubt they had us at their mercy. But others said no, the Governor himself wasn't free to do as he wished, he had to wait for orders from across the sea. No one could say for sure what was going to happen, or when. Any day a ship might come from that distant place none of us had ever seen and where all laws, it seems, are made, to confirm the worst rumours. And what would become of us then? It was one thing to resent the farm as I had always done, and to wish for a different life; but to be driven from it by the laws of strangers, with nowhere to go and nothing to do, that was something else. And that was precisely what would happen if they suddenly came to take away our slaves. How could we possibly till this rude land on our own? It was so vast, there were so few of us.

But even that bleak prospect was not, in itself, the worst. What really made me numb, as if I'd been bludgeoned, was the impotent rage that came from the rediscovery that our lives were held hostage by the whims and wishes of a distant adversary we didn't know and had no hope of influencing. Whatever we planned or decided was quite simply irrelevant: invisible forces might intervene at any moment to ridicule and destroy our cautious schemes.

In the past I'd often argued with Barend about the English and what had seemed to be his blind hatred of them; I could not reconcile this rebelliousness with God's injunction to obey the authorities set over us. But on this visit to the Cape I'd finally been persuaded that he was right after all. Not the fact that they were English made them evil, but that they were foreigners, aliens in our land; that they ruled from a distance;

229

and that they removed from us the control over our own lives and well-being. For as long as I could remember we'd handled our own affairs and made our own decisions and scrupulously planned our own future. This, I think, was the heart of it: to be denied that control which gave one a stake in the future. Take away a man's grasp on the future and you take away his dignity: the one cannot exist without the other. Some of the townsmen jeered at us. "You're just too lazy to do your own bloody work." "How can you complain of threats to your freedom if that freedom is built on slavery?" "All you people are concerned with is lording it over others. Freedom is not at stake at all, it's only the lust for power." They did not understand about that dignity without which existence is a mockery. Cushioned and comfortable, what did they know about our lives out there beyond the mountains, a sprinkling of people devoted to taming a wild land so that others might live in safety? Did we choose to be there? If God had not willed it, how would we have survived? Even I who resent my bondage to the farm must submit to that Will. And how was that conceivable without at least believing in a purpose beyond our daily toil and the sweat of one's brow? And what purpose if not to tame and civilize? The past was a mess, the present perplexed me; all I had to hold on to was the future, and that lay embedded in the very land that oppressed me. It was the paradox of my condition; and submission to the land meant submission to God. That was what made it tolerable. But to accept this destiny, this tenuous grasp on the future I had to make the farm prosper with the help of those God had given me. *Servants, be obedient to them that are your masters according to the flesh, with fear and trembling, in singleness of your heart, as unto Christ.* Why else did God in His infinite wisdom cause Ham to err if not to make his masters flourish in the land given unto them? *Cursed be Canaan; a servant of servants shall he be unto his brethren.* How could these men from Cape Town know that a man's need of slaves has nothing to do with oppression or wealth but with one's responsibility to the future?

Even among those I'd seen in Tulbagh the day before there had been weak-minded men softened by the curse of the Cape. There was old Karel Theron, puffing away at his pipe, surrounded by his nine sons, announcing with great conviction: "Only one way to outwit the bastards. Do what I've done; sell all your slaves while you can still get a good price. Then the Government can't touch you. It's the only way to be a free man."

"Not all of us have nine sons," I reminded him.

He glowered at me. "Then go home and start making some. You're a young man, damn you. What's wrong with you then?" As if Cecilia had prompted him.

"While you're waiting for them to grow up," said one of his sons, "ask your neighbours to give you a hand. What else are neighbours for?"

"It's easy for you to talk," I said. "Here in Waveren you all live close together. But what about us in the Bokkeveld and elsewhere?"

"You should have thought of that before you staked out your farm."

"There were no problems with slaves then."

"Then hire Hottentots."

"You don't know what you're talking about," said a farmer from Piquetberg. "Even as it is they come and go as they wish. What do you think will happen if they're no longer forced by law to work? Haven't you heard all the rumours? One of these days we won't have a single labourer to depend on, and whatever we still manage to produce will most likely be stolen by the vagrants."

"There's still time to think about it," said old Karel Theron. "Change your way of farming or move to another neighbourhood. Nothing forces you to stay in the Bokkeveld."

"You call that being a free man?" I asked. "Changing your whole way of life to suit the Government in the Cape?"

"The law's the law."

"There's no such law yet."

"But change is in the air. Can't you smell it? Better do

231

something about it now than cry over spilt milk later."

"What about the slaves themselves?" I asked, as in so many earlier arguments with Barend. "What will happen to them if we just let them go? They have nowhere to turn to. They'll die of hunger. They need us even more than we need them."

"If you don't have slaves you don't have to worry about them," said the old man, rounding up his sons.

In the Cape, before returning home, my final argument had always been: "Let them try to set free the slaves and they'll soon see for themselves. If you treat your slaves properly they'll never abandon you, not even if the law says they're free."

"How can you ever be sure?" The retort had come from Cecilia's cousin, a foreman on a wine farm near the Eerste River.

"I know my slaves," I'd answered confidently. "I know they're loyal to a man."

Then, returning to Houd-den-Bek, the first thing I'd witnessed was Galant killing my sheep: the one slave I'd trusted above all others. How could I not lose my temper? So much more than a lamb had been at stake: not just my trust in him, but what had remained of my faith in the future.

And now we were thrown together in a small hollow in the mountains, the direct outcome of all that had gone before; and in me were the turbulent recollections of all those interminable arguments, the heated discussions, the rising tempers, the sudden explosions among people who'd always been friends: in Cape Town, in Tulbagh, wherever one went, as if the Devil himself had been let loose among us to help us destroy ourselves even before the Government could. All that lay heavily on my mind as I sat beside Galant in the silence that followed my description of the Malay who'd run amok.

It was an oppressive silence and he was again very rigid next to me. It occurred to me that the reason why he wouldn't lean against the rock like me might be that his scourged back hurt too much. I would have liked to ask him, but it seemed indecent; anyway there was nothing I could do about it, not now. And he'd brought it on himself, hadn't he? Rather teach

232

him a painful lesson now, and painful not only to him but to me as well, than allow this thing to get out of hand. We'd come a long way; we had a long way to go together. I sat there wishing fervently I could convey this to him. *For God's sake, I wanted to say, we understand each other, don't we? We need each other! We're companions. The past is not important. It's the future. I need you on the farm, damn you.*

But all I could say was: "Galant, in spite of what happened I want you to remain *mantoor* on the farm."

"That's for you to say."

"I want to give you another chance. We'll make a new start."

He made no reply. Perhaps the story of the Malay was still weighing on his mind, as on mine. Yet it had been necessary to tell it to him, for his own sake and mine. Neither of us was allowed the precarious comfort of ignorance any longer. We too had eaten of the fruit—somewhere, sometime between that innocent day our tunnel had caved in and this night in our hollow in the mountains.

When I could no longer bear his silence I crawled outside. The wind threw me off balance; I had to gasp for breath in the shockingly cold moist air. The fog was still swirling. Overhead patches of sky would suddenly be revealed, blacker than the dull opaqueness of the mist, with incredibly bright pinpoints of stars and once a sliver of moon like a cut-off finger nail. Then the swift fog would cover it once again and I would have trouble to keep my balance where I stood, legs far apart, braced against the wind, trying to pee and spilling it on my trousers. An awareness of something physically closing in from all sides. I knew now that the feeling of oppression in our hollow had been caused neither by the proximity of Galant nor by our cramped quarters but by the sombre knowledge of the Bokkeveld itself closing in, a frontier world shrinking around me, a natural freedom contracting. And I wondered achingly how, and for how long, we would still be able to cope and to hold our own, how long we would be able to reconcile our awareness of the need for justice with the imperatives of

233

the moment. To survive, to survive: but at what price? A Malay drawn and quartered on the square below the Lion's Rump in the Cape. Galant in the hollow below the pile of rocks somewhere in the fog behind me, scourged and wounded in order for both of us to be reminded that I was his master, he my slave: and that in this land neither could survive without this subtle and subjugating bond approved by God. It had become too complicated to understand. Braced against the wind, I blindly exposed my face to the wet lashes of fog, trembling in a terrible ecstasy as if I required that exposure, that punishment, not to feel vindicated but to survive. That word again. And I knew that from now on it would never leave me.

I was so cold that it took some time before I realized that Galant was with me, grabbing me from behind.

"What you doing here?" he shouted. "You got lost again?"

"No," I stammered back with numb lips. "Of course not." But perhaps he was right. And in a strange humility I allowed him to lead me by the hand, back to the shelter where all signs of the fire had disappeared and where the only warmth that could keep us alive came from our shivering bodies pressed together as in childhood.

Sleep seemed unthinkable; and yet from exhaustion we both drifted off into a stupor from which we woke, first I, then he, when the hard colourless light of day struck into our hollow. We could hardly move but forced ourselves outside. The wind had died down. The fog had cleared somewhat, although it soon settled in again. He obviously had more difficulty than I; he was in pain. I avoided looking at him. Neither of us spoke: the night was both too remote and too intimate to be discovered in words. Stamping our feet to drive out the numbness, blowing into cupped hands to restore some warmth, we halfheartedly revived ourselves, and untied the horses, and set out to complete the rest of the tedious journey home, back to the light drizzle and the sharp-edged North-western wind of a Bokkeveld winter. At Elandsfontein I stopped for tea while Galant spent some time with Abel tending the horses. Barend was out in the fields, but Hester was home: more distant and silent than ever, and pregnant with what later turned out to be her second son.

ABEL

"Look at Tatters." It was Baas Barend who first called Galant by that name. And in the end we all used the nickname, but only behind his back and when he was safely out of earshot, for Galant had a quick temper. Only Goliath once risked to call him that to his face, quite playfully—"Hey, Tatters, I say!"—but that was the last time, and we had to carry Goliath down to the fountain to bring him round again.

It was on account of the jacket of course, the one he flaunted so much when he first got it. One would have expected him to throw the useless rag away after it got so tattered, but he insisted on wearing it. And not shamefully either, but proudly, as if he wanted all the world to see it. "This is my child's jacket," he told me, for we were close friends and he would confide in me what he would say to no one else. "I got this for David. I'll never part from it." A very stubborn man Galant was, once he'd got his mind set on something.

I was working in the backyard, Klaas and I both, sawing wood, when they arrived from Tulbagh that day, a cold drizzly morning with the first fog of winter. It was an old habit of Klaas's to make me saw wood whenever he really wanted to take it out on me, for he knew how much I loathed it. And no use complaining either, because he'd just been made *mantoor* over me and he couldn't wait for me to do something wrong so he could split on me. I used to be *mantoor* at Elandsfontein, ever since Baas Barend first bought me at the auction on Wagendrift, together with the bed and the two rams and the chest of crockery; and I remained *mantoor* until the time Galant ran into trouble while Baas Nicolaas was away to the

236

Cape with the wagons. The most roaring time we'd ever had in the neighbourhood and I know what I'm talking about for I grew up right there with the Du Toits. Wagendrift lies in the elbow of the narrow valley running up from Elandsfontein, where the mountains swing to the right towards Houd-den-Bek. It's a farm Oubaas Piet Lagenvlei had always wanted on account of the way it cuts into his family's property; but the Du Toits held on to it even after their old man's death when the Madam quarrelled with her sons and sold the lot. So I knew everybody in these parts. As a child, whenever I had to lead the oxen on the annual winter trek to the Karoo, I became friends with Galant. We saw a lot of each other through the years, a bit here, a bit there. But in all that time we never knew another month like the one Baas Nicolaas spent in the Cape, especially because it coincided with a fortnight Baas Barend was away hunting, for it was the time of year when Elandsfontein comes alive preparing biltong and dried sausage and salted ribs for the winter months ahead. I'd always been the huntsman on the farm, but that year there was some bad blood between Baas Barend and me because of a gun he said I'd broken and so out of spite he didn't take me along. Now that had already annoyed me; and what with the nightly parties I suppose we overdid things a bit. Afterwards we all suffered the consequences. All right, I know my work wasn't quite what it should have been in Baas Barend's absence, but the main reason was that I'd talked back to Nooi Hester. All because I'd had another of those nights. And I'd really meant well: I'd planned to stay home all night because I knew the Baas was due back from his hunting the next morning and I wanted to look him in the eye when he came; but in the deep of the night I had visitors, Galant and all the others on horseback, looking for something to drink. "Sorry," I said. "I got nothing either, but I'll help you look." And so we all set out for the nearest farms, Nooitgedagt and Koelefontein and Modderrivierskloof and such like. It was past sunrise before I got home, by which time Klaas, of course, was already at work; and the Nooi wanted to know where I'd been. My head was splitting and I

237

could hardly see straight, so I suppose I gave her a rather gruff answer which Klaas of course reported to the Baas the moment he set foot on the farm. "And when you speak to Abel," Klaas told him, "ask him where he spent his nights while you were away." As if the bastard hadn't been drinking with us all along. I tried my best to explain, but I'm afraid anyone could see that very little work had been done during Baas Barend's absence, so that was that. And I didn't feel so bad about the flogging I got either: it was my due and I took it as it came, the way one takes sun and rain in the Bokkeveld. But what I couldn't take was that the Baas put an end to my *mantoor* job, which was one thing I'd always cared for. To make it worse he appointed Klaas over us, that old cunt-face.

And not two weeks later, when the thorn was still smarting in my heart, Galant and Baas Nicolaas arrived at Elandsfontein out of the fog.

"Why you looking such a sight?" I asked him, although I'd already been told about the beating by Ontong when he'd come over a few days earlier with a smoked ham for Nooi Hester.

"Gone to Tulbagh," Galant said glumly. "I went to complain but all I got was another flogging."

"Then things must be really bad," I said. "Baas Nicolaas always favoured you above the others."

"Look how he tore my jacket."

"Why do you care about a jacket?"

"You know it's my child's jacket. I got it for David. No one got the right to lay a hand on it."

"Come and have some tea," I said, trying to calm him down.

"Keep your bloody tea," he said, sulking.

"Sarie will pour for you."

"I don't care who pours it."

"You come with me, man."

After all, there are few things in life so bitter that the sweetness of a woman and of tea cannot cure them. Take bush-tea: it's got all the sun and rain of the mountains in it, drawing its taste from under the earth and from the mountain mist; and then it's plucked. It is spread out and warmed in the oven to sweat it out, and it's beaten and trodden, and in exchange it gives you the sweetest of sweetness. Just like a woman.

In a sense it was Sarie who brought me to Elandsfontein. I learned about her the day she set foot there, although at that time I was still living at Wagendrift with the Du Toits. It was something like the smell the bees catch when the wagon-trees come into flower. In a land where women are scarce all the men immediately know when a new one makes her appearance. It's something you feel swelling inside you; and it makes you stiff like strung wire; there's a new smell in the air. Sarie was generous from the start, and when she was with me she held back nothing. In those early days, whenever Oubaas Du Toit gave me a Sunday free I'd see to it that I arrived at Elandsfontein before the Saturday sun had properly set; and if the weather was good the two of us would slip away from all the other men and spend the night among the tea-bushes in the mountains. At a time like that a man's rod keeps poking till daybreak; and all day Sunday. In between I reach for my fiddle to play for Sarie. I tune the strings and turn the mountains into water for her. And then I roll over on Sarie again and I tune her and I put my fiddlestick to her and I play her as if she were a violin herself, till she sobs and cries for joy, music in my years. It goes more and more slowly as the Sunday wears on until in the end there's barely any kick left inside you, yet nothing can stop you. That's the way it was with me and Sarie. And when at last the night filled up the hollows among the hills like a winter *vlei* swelling and spilling over its banks, we would have our fill and I would be drained to the last drop in my body: then I'd put my fingers into her and draw the sticky sweetness from her to last me the bitter week ahead. Back at Wagendrift I would bind up one of my fingers with a piece of rag and then fall asleep like a dead man. On Monday I would stagger through my work in a sort of daze. By Tuesday life would be slowly coming back, encouraged by Sarie's whiff on

239

my fingers. By Wednesday the sniffing would grow ever more vigorous as the smell began to fade. The next day, as the drought inside grew worse, I would undo the bandage on my finger to draw new courage from Sarie's preserved memory. Even that used to be gone away by Friday; and when Saturday came around I would be biting the nail to the quick in search of Sarie.

Small wonder that, by the time Ounooi Du Toit quarrelled with her sons and decided to sell out, my mind was made up about the woman I needed. There was a big crowd at the auction and several of them seemed to have an eye on me, including Frans du Toit himself; but I had no wish to be his slave. Not that he was particularly hard on his slaves—in these parts there's no man could match Barend Van der Merwe for strictness—but because one never knew how things stood with him: one way today, another tomorrow. So I checked Sarie's finger—it was a Friday: by that time I could already tell the days of the week from the state of my finger—and I cornered Baas Barend: "Baas," I told him, "if you buy me I promise you you'll never regret it."

That the man had a good heart in spite of his reputation was proved when he not only bought me but the fiddle as well to keep me happy. For himself he bought the bed and the rams and the crockery; but the fiddle was for me. And that night there was wailing and singing and sobbing among the tea-bushes again.

Which was why I knew what I was about when I told Galant that morning: "You come with me. Sarie will pour you some tea." For by that time she was living with me; and I never begrudged another man some of my pleasure: nor Sarie neither.

And it worked out well, as I'd thought it would. The tea cleared up his heavy mood; in its sweetness he found comfort.

"Now tell me what happened," I said when Sarie handed him the second mug; and I took him by the arm to lead him round the house where we would be sheltered from the drizzle and where I could keep an eye on the gate so that Baas Barend wouldn't catch us by surprise. "How's things in Tulbagh?"

He made himself as comfortable as he could on the wood-pile next to the baking oven, keeping his raw back away from the wall. "Did you know," he said, staring past me into the mist as if he could see right through the mountains, "did you know there was a place where slaves can run away to, where nobody ever finds them again?"

"Where's that place?"

"Across the Great River. There's a whole lot of them there."

"I've seen what happens to slaves who run away."

He paid no attention: only sat there staring at things I couldn't see, making me feel quite uncomfortable; and when he spoke he seemed to be talking to himself. About a man in irons he'd met in the jail at the Drostdy, and who'd got away in the fog. About a slave who'd run amok in the Cape and whose head had been put up on a spike for the vultures to pick clean.

"Just forget about it, will you," I said. "You back home again now."

"Yes, I'm back," he said. "But my heart isn't back."

I'd seen other slaves before him with that expression in their eyes, as if they couldn't see what was happening right there in front of them; and it worried me because I'd always been fond of Galant. "Pull yourself together, man," I said. "We've all been flogged before. It's not so bad."

"It's not the flogging." Once again he stared right through me. "Abel," he said, "you call this a life?"

I laughed, but there was an uneasy feeling in me. "What else do you expect? I'm not saying it's easy or it's all right. But we got our bit of fun, don't we? You can still drink your mug of tea. You can have your honey-beer, or even your brandy if you're sharp. You can puff a bit of *dagga* when the world looks bad. And there's women too."

"You think it's enough?"

"I don't think anything. But it's the same for everybody. You get born, you live a while, and then you die. Me, you, the lot of us. What's so bad about it?"

He was staring into the drizzle again, his eyes screwed up

241

against the thin wind. "We're stuck in it."

"It's just because you got a raw back on you that you talking like this," I said. "Why don't you ask Ma-Rose for some herbs and stuff when you ride by her place just now, then it'll be all over in a couple of days."

"You still think I care about my back!" He stood up as if he had an itch in his arse. "There's something I don't understand at all, Abel. When they untied me from that post in Tulbagh I could kill Nicolaas with my bare hands, I tell you. But as I'm standing here right now—you know what's the worst of it?—that I even feel sorry for him." Shaking with anger he spat, almost hitting me. "I don't understand it, Abel. I don't understand nothing no more."

"I'll fetch you some more tea."

"I don't want no bloody tea!" He pushed past me; but then he came back. "Abel, you think that man in the irons managed to get away?"

"How must I know?"

"I'm asking you. I got to know. He was sitting beside me all night. He was like a lion in the dark. And last night, when the fog came down, I kept on thinking: 'If only he can get away in this fog they'll never find him again. He'll reach the Great River.' Now how do you explain that? I'm asking you. I want him to get away. Not just for his own sake. For mine too. And if he can't—"

"You can't go on eating out your head like this, Galant."

He didn't even hear me. "As I was sitting there beside him I kept wishing the whole damn building would fall in so the man could get away. I never wished anything so hard in my life."

Strange that he should have spoken about the building, I thought afterwards. For only a couple of days later we got the news from over the mountains that there had been a terrible storm at Tulbagh: and as far as I could make out it must have happened the very night after Galant had left. The whole front gable of the Drostdy, we were told, had cracked, all the way from the foundations upward, so that the rain fell right

242

through to the cellar. Almost all the windows were blown in. The pillars of the back stoep had been washed away, as well as some outbuildings.

In a way the news seemed to comfort Galant when we next spoke about it. But that wasn't the end of it. Nothing is ever over when it's done. It's like water running, and then the stream dries up: but below the ground it continues on its way, invisible to the eye, and in the most unexpected places it comes out again. In the late winter, when the North-wester was at its worst, Frans du Toit who'd just been made Field-cornet brought a report that because of the bad damage to the buildings in Tulbagh the Drostdy was being closed and the Landdrost was to be moved to Worcester. Imagine: almost a whole day's journey further. I suppose, I said to Galant, they did it just to make it more difficult for him to complain next time. But he didn't find it funny. Anyway, the move hit the masters as badly, for in order to pay for the rain damage a new tax was levied on the slaves, all the way from Worcester and Tulbagh, through the Warm Bokkeveld and the Cold Bok-keveld, to the most distant mountains: two rix dollars on every one of us, man and woman; and a couple of shillings on every child. Right, I thought, let the bloody Dutchmen pay. But Baas Barend was so mad we all had to stay out of his way. Fortunately it was just about that time when the Nooi had her second child, another boy, which caused the Baas to forget about his anger as he strutted about the farm as if he was the only man who'd ever had a son. We were all given a double *sopie* of brandy, and a special sheep was slaughtered, and that night the fiddle sang and cried again like a woman in rut.

It gave me the feeling again. I don't understand this itch in a man, but that's the way it is: in the early days when I had to come all the way from Wagendrift to Elandsfontein to be with Sarie a week was almost too long to be without her. Joy is but a finger's length and I could think of nothing else than to get back to her and ride her again. But now that I had her to myself, nightly available, a desire for other women returned to me. It was Pamela's wetness I lusted for. Just after she'd come

243

to Houd-den-Bek I'd been with her a few times: not much, she wasn't easy to tame. But of course that only added to my heat. But unlike other women whose no could turn to yes just like that Pamela kept the men at bay, including me. That fig wasn't there just for the picking. I'd soon discovered that she was really eyeing Galant, but after his break with Bet he was still keeping away from women, fool that he was. And so I got it in me to pay Pamela another visit that night.

"Where you going?" said Klaas as I led the horse from the stable.

"Riding."

"You looking for trouble again."

"I'm looking for fun. Stay out of my way."

For a while I rode very slowly so as not to be heard from the house. But once I was out of earshot I kicked the horse to a gallop. Even so, the fires were already down by the time I reached Houd-den-Bek. But I woke up the people and gave them a tune on my fiddle. Old Achilles brought out his oldest honey-beer and soon most of them were dancing. Only Galant didn't join in. No matter: my aim was Pamela, sitting there opposite me, the light of the new fire dancing on her pale brown skin, the cheekbones, the shoulders, the round nippled breasts that trembled when she moved, a trembling like that of water barely touched by wind; enough to make a man's spine grow rigid.

But Pamela did not feel that way inclined, and when I pressed the matter Galant interfered angrily: "Let the woman be, can't you see she's otherwise?" So I had to unload on Lydia who was always available; except she would just lie there like a joint of meat on her feather mattress, waiting for a man to get it over and depart. It left one with an insipid taste in the mouth; and I felt very gloomy on the way home, plodding through the night, fiddle over my shoulder. The lust had gone; only weariness remained. I thought: What's the use? A night is short, and then it's day again.

The day turned out even worse than usual, for Klaas had split on me as I might have expected; so there was another fallout with Baas Barend. And for the first time I remembered what Galant had said the day he'd come back from Tulbagh: "It's not the flogging." Now I began to understand. Indeed, it was not the flogging. Yet what it was I couldn't tell. Except that it had something to do with the fun of the previous night, the drinking and dancing and music; and then the dark road home. Not Pamela's stand-offishness. Not at all. Something else, something much more complicated. The Baas had had a son, so he'd encouraged us to break out and enjoy ourselves. For one night we were free to indulge, to abandon ourselves to music and joy, wilder than wild hemp and sweeter than bush-tea, its taste lingering on the tip of the tongue. But once it was over one had to turn back to the yoke. Always back. Always the same. At the end of every joyous road: the Baas and his sjambok.

Perhaps I was beginning to understand a bit more, then, about Galant and his torn jacket. And I was more prepared than before to discuss things with him. It certainly was a time when a lot of talking went on all over the place. For the newspapers were stirring up trouble again in our parts; and whenever one of them made its way through the Bokkeveld you might know in advance that Galant would be in a black mood. Something was building up again, as I gathered from old Ontong and the others. And when the next harvest came there was another quarrel between him and Baas Nicolaas. Soon after the fruit had been brought in, just before the beans, he went all the way to Worcester to complain. It was Pamela who told me, when I went to Houd-den-Bek one night to have another go at her; and this time she told me outright: "No. I'm lying with Galant now." Of course I left her alone after that. It was a bad time for me anyway, for that was when Baas Barend took me to Cape Town with him.

The Nooi was supposed to go with, but she was obstinate. Sarie told me about the quarrel, she'd heard it all. "You've got to come with me," Baas Barend said to the Nooi. "There's nowhere else you can go while I'm away." "I'm not going anywhere," the Nooi replied. "I'm staying right here with my children." And that was that, for the Nooi never took orders from anyone; and rather than keep on nagging her the Baas loaded the wagon and the two of us rode off, leaving Klaas behind to run the farm. For once I was happy not to be *mantoor*. A second wagon came from Houd-den-Bek, driven by the two youngsters Thys and Rooy: Baas Nicolaas didn't go with us as he'd been to the Cape the year before and there was an arrangement between the brothers to take turns so there would always be one of them to keep an eye on the farms.

Away from home, all alone with the wagons, Baas Barend and I got along very well. And in the evenings by the fire, after Thys and Rooy had done their chores, I used to play my fiddle for them. The Baas enjoyed that. He seemed to loosen up on the trip, not only towards me but in his hold on himself too. And the music, I think, helped. One night, I remember, when the Baas got properly drunk, he told me: "Abel, you really know how to tickle a man's insides. We'll be going a long road together, the two of us, I can see that. We belong together." Then I brought the bow back to the strings and in that music we sat together till the morning star came out.

All the way to the Cape life was fine; and even better once we got there. Drinking and cavorting night after night; splendid blow-ups with other slaves at the water pump, and throwing dice and fights with knives and kieries, the lot. But best of all was the cock-fights every afternoon in the stone quarry below the Lion's Rump. Especially Sundays. All the slaves of the Cape crowding round the cocks in the hollow while a few men kept watch, as the constables could make life difficult if they came upon one unawares. Some of the cock-men had been running their business for generations, handing down their tricks from father to son. Once the cocks were let loose, wings flapping and spurs flying, it was blood and feathers everywhere. The crowd roaring and shouting and screaming and jumping up and down. For those cocks were big business. There were men in that quarry, I was told, who'd risked flogging and prison sentences to steal a few shillings they could bet on the fighters. And with my own eyes, one Sunday

246

afternoon, I saw a man from Constantia, his name was Josua, betting and losing his wife and three children on the cocks. Just like that.

It's with sadness I remember it, for that was how I lost my fiddle, the very same Sunday.

"Why you coming here day after day just looking?" they asked me. "It's not a show, it's money business."

"What can I put up then?" I asked them.

"Whatever you got," they said.

I started with the handful of rix dollars I'd got for my jackal and lynx pelts. But the other man's fighter, a fierce little red fellow, tore mine to a messy little bundle of feathers. By that time the urge was already in my blood and when the last two cocks of the day were brought out I put up my fiddle.

At first I didn't feel so bad about losing it, for the winner, a thin stick of a man called Achmat, assured me I could try to win it back the next afternoon; if not, he'd be prepared to sell it back to me for five rix dollars. All I could dream about that night was the fighting cocks. Couldn't wait to get back to that quarry. But when I told Baas Barend about it he got so angry he refused to let me go, let alone lend me five rix dollars for the fiddle. And when I kept on pleading with him—for it gave me a terrible shock when I thought about really losing my music—he gave me a clout in the face, and that in front of Thys and Rooy. Back home, on our own farm, it was different: there he could do what he wished. But in that town square in front of two youngsters still wet behind the ears I took it badly. A proper blow with the fist might have been all right too; but not a slap. That was the way one dealt with women and children, not grown men. To make it worse, Baas Barend appointed Thys and Rooy to keep an eye on me so I wouldn't slink off to get my fiddle back. And purely out of spite he ordered us to make ready for the return journey two days sooner than we'd planned.

"My God, Baas," I pleaded with him. "I can't leave that fiddle behind."

"Serves you right for gambling it away."

247

"Baas!"

I wondered whether he regretted his own hastiness on the way back, those quiet sullen evenings around the fire with not the slightest sound of music to cheer us up; but he never mentioned it. It must have been the first time in my life I kept silent for a full week, saying not a single word apart from yes or no in reply to a direct question.

All right, so it was my own fault. I'd gambled and lost, just like that poor fool Josua who'd put up his wife and children. So what? I could have won that damn fiddle back. Achmat had said so. I'd had the chance. But the Baas had stopped me.

As we got back to the farm Sarie and the others came running out to meet the wagons. "Hell, Abel," they said. "We been missing you, man. This place is quiet without you. Tonight you going to play the fiddle for us again, hey?"

"Fuck off," I said. And I sent them away and rode Sarie. It was all I could do. But my heart was crying for that fiddle that had been my friend for so many years.

Looking back now it seems to me that the trip to Cape Town and our return to the farm marked the end of a term of my life. Not that we had any lack of fun afterwards: I even made a new fiddle and although it wasn't the same sound it was better than silence; and we still had drink and women. But something had been shut off as if a gate had been closed behind me.

The newspapers were coming thick and fast; and every time a new one had gone the rounds in the Bokkeveld we could see a difference in the masters: in the looks they gave us; the unexpected rebuffs; the way they bunched together talking and gesticulating, and falling silent the moment one of us drew near. It hit Galant badly, I could see that: worse than most of the others, for he'd always had a thing about newspapers. In the earlier days one could ignore the papers: what did they really matter?—one could still have all the fun one needed, there was no need to cut out the music or the drinking or the boisterous riding of women. But something had changed and a shadow was moving across our veld, something you couldn't lay your hand

248

on. It was like water oozing into the ground; reappearing when you least expected it.

There were funny moments too, admittedly. I could kill myself laughing about Frans du Toit and the newspaper: but Galant saw nothing ticklish in it and so he never told me the full story. But as far as I could make out, Baas Nicolaas had gone to Lagenvlei that day, his mother being ill or something; and Frans du Toit arrived in his absence with the latest newspaper. He must have been pissed, he'd always been fond of his *sopie* and over the years it had grown worse, which is what happens to a man without a wife. What woman would have him, with the birthmark on his face? No wonder he started behaving like that. His weakness was well known all over the Bokkeveld, and mothers usually made sure their daughters were out of the way when the poor man was around. And it was just because he was so thick with the English in Worcester, they said, that he'd been made Field-cornet: nobody in our part of the world would have chosen him if they'd had a say in it. So there he was, arriving at Houd-den-Bek, dead drunk and finding nobody at home; and as he stumbled about in search of someone to leave the paper with he came round the pigsty: so it was he and the sow. It was Frans du Toit and the sow and a hell of a mess in the dung and the mud; and when Galant came upon it, he was promptly ordered to hold down the pig. I wouldn't have cared a damn if it had been me, I'd known about his weakness all along, we'd grown up together; but Galant was the hell in, especially when Nicolaas turned up unexpectedly and chased the man off his farm, trousers round the ankles, leaving the newspaper hopelessly fouled up in the mud, with all its new tidings about the slaves and the Government. I laughed fit to kill myself when I heard about it, but Galant just sulked. And it was only after we'd discussed it that I started seeing it his way and thought that maybe it wasn't so funny after all; maybe a man should rather cry. For a white man is supposed to be master, and to see him galloping off like that with his bare white arse bobbing up and down on the saddle and the scared sow squealing in the mud, must have been a sight to set a man thinking about things. If it went on like that we might soon have to say Baas and Nooi to the pigs.

When harvesting time came round again there was the business with Goliath, for by that time we'd heard the rumours about slaves no longer being required to work on Sundays and a lot of other things: working time fixed at ten hours a day from April to September and twelve from October to March, with extra food for overtime during harvesting and threshing and so on; floggings limited to twenty-five lashes at a time; enough food and drink to be given to us; and a *dominee* instructed to make the rounds once a year to marry slave couples and baptize their children; that sort of thing. Which was why I told Goliath, and I'm still not ashamed of it, to put in a complaint. "It's the only way we can find out if it's true or not," I said. "Perhaps it's just a lot of lies. But perhaps it's true and then we got a right to know." He was very obstreperous about it all, shit-scared of what might happen to him. But the moment Klaas was out of sight I belaboured him properly. "It's not just for yourself you got to go," I explained to him. "It's for the whole lot of us, man. How else will we find out what it says in the newspapers?"

After all, one can feel it in one's guts when there's something rising and swelling and pushing from below like a flood; and you got to find out in time if you don't want to get drowned. That was how I saw it when Galant and I discussed it, and that was how I put it to Goliath.

And so in the end he went, and it turned out a bad thing. The commissioner came round and questioned Goliath, and then rode off again, accompanied by all the jolly farmers of the Bokkeveld. It was difficult to restrain myself that day. I had murderous thoughts in my heart. But what could I do? I couldn't take on Baas Barend and his gun all by myself. The worst of it all was that he didn't even realize I was mad. Just called me to take his horse, and took off his gun and went home; and that was that. Wiping his arse on the lot of us. I stood there, in that dying day, looking after the Baas and thinking by myself: Now it's no longer fun: now it's serious. No matter what the newspapers say, they're white men's things and they lie. We got nothing more to hope for from over the mountains. We're on our own here, in this lonely place, and it's a scary feeling it gives one. Now it's up to us.

HESTER

New day; old familiar ache. It never recedes into oblivion, it is always there, even though its intensity may vary from a mere dull presence to the stab that amazes the flesh.

For one strange month, while Barend was away to the Cape, it was different. Not freedom but a suspended existence, a wholeness I'd known only in pregnancy before. But different too: this time there was a feeling of being more intact, there was no disquieting intrusion of another life in my body; at the same time I missed the experience of existing round the kernel of a child, enclosing it, securing in the process a new self-containment, an independence from the world. This time the children were there to be cared for, there was a household and a farm to run; even Klaas's obsequious competence was obtrusive. I was lonely, not alone; but if that were the price of a brief respite I would pay it.

Barend had wanted me to go with him, of course. He'd even insisted. And not quite sure in my own mind whether the enchantment of the Cape might alleviate the daily ache, I might yet have yielded. But then in one of our fierce quarrels he'd struck me. It hadn't been the first time, but in the past it had been in the rage of his efforts to gain entry into my body. This time it had been more calculated, in contempt, and in the arrogance of his superior strength. And this made it easier to hold my own and disobey. The boy Carel was there too, howling in terror at seeing me struck, and that immediately set the baby crying too; but a cold detachment ruled me, as I thought: *Look sharp, Carel, you'll need this recollection later. This is what I'm bringing you up for. To do the same to your women one day. It is the only revenge accorded me.* Leaving

252

Barend to comfort and explain, I went outside and saddled my horse. And when that night, for the first time in our married life, he asked forgiveness and begged me to go to Cape Town with him, it was easy to refuse.

"I don't know what got into me this morning," he said. "For God's sake, listen to me, Hester. I promise you it won't ever happen again."

I smiled and turned away. What would be the point of telling him: *Of course you will do it again. There are always new thresholds to cross. How else shall we survive?* Already I could see us in our old age, two dry bodies clawing and fighting each other to delve ever more deeply in search of whatever rare moisture remained in the hideous bone-dry carcasses.

And it did happen again, just after his return, on the first Sunday when he insisted on going to visit Nicolaas and Cecilia. Still unused to his new presence after a month on my own, refusal came naturally. I might have justified it as resisting another exposure to Cecilia's immaculate household and her pious Sunday face, or to the quizzical dog's eyes Nicolaas would turn towards me; but essentially it was rebellion against being forced into renewed obedience. Once again it became a violent and unnecessary argument; once again he struck me.

In fury I hit back, but he caught my arms and held me out of reach.

"I swear to God," I hissed, choking in frustration, "if I were a man I'd break your neck."

"Well, you're not and you're going to do as I tell you."

"If my father had been alive you wouldn't have dared."

"Your father was a drunken good-for-nothing."

I cried out in rage, trying in vain to wrench myself free, kicking him. The baby was crying on the bed and attracted by the noise little Carel also came in.

"Go on," I told Barend. "Show your children how bravely their father can fight a woman."

"Get out!" he shouted at Carel, who began to scream.

253

In shame and anger, like the previous time, he let me go.

"One day your sons will be strong enough to avenge their mother," I said, still panting, and pulling together the flaps of my nightdress that had been torn in our struggle. That was always the first he would go for in our fights: tearing my dress to expose my breasts.

"It's your own fault," he said. "You drive me to it. You know I don't want to."

"I told you before you'd do it again," I said, and picked up the baby to comfort it. Looking at him over the small head I said: "All right, we can go to Houd-den-Bek. I'd like to see my father's grave again. Now please go out. I want to get dressed."

We left early. It was more than two hours by carriage to Houd-den-Bek. We rode in silence, as usual, Barend holding the reins and Carel sitting between us, his back very erect, his frail shoulders squared in the innocent independence of his three years. I was holding the baby but from time to time, as the cart swayed and rattled over the uneven tracks across the ochre veld, I tried to support Carel with my arm, relishing in secret his small fierce shrugs of refusal. My boy. My little man. Would it not have been normal to be pained by his amusing self-assertions? Through what perversity did I take pride in seeing him emerge as the boyish copy of the man with whom I was locked in unceasing battle? And yet in his very independence he was mine, formed and shaped by myself; in him I had a hold on the man he would be one day. I'd never wanted girl-children. If there had to be children at all, let them be men. The mere idea of a girl repulsed me: her pathetic challenge to others to prove themselves through her, her ultimate vulnerability. In a girl-child I would finally have to acknowledge my own defeat. Were boys, then, simply a means of getting my own back? Had vengeance become the only conceivable course and utterance of love? No, no. I did love them, I do; perhaps in their frailty I even discovered the possibility of gentleness concealed in the man who himself had no choice but to dominate me in his blind struggle to survive in his stern man-world. In my sons something of

254

myself lay invested for future freedom. For the first time I was beginning to understand my mother-in-law and the sources of her strength. She, too, could exist only for the future through her sons. Even though that might be illusion too: for what freedom was there in store for them if it lay exclusively in the possibility of subjugating others? But that awareness came later, I think. All awareness came later, in that terrible night. On that bright Sunday morning, so serene in its essential Aprilness, in the first intimation of autumn, leaves yellowing, grass turning brittle and white, a hint of brown creeping into the reeds and rushes of the marshy *vleis*, all I did was thoughtlessly, bluntly to resist the unpredictable motion of the carriage, shaking and jolting on its way between the rude and unselfconscious ridges of mountains towards the more exposed openness of what had been my home.

The first time Barend spoke was when we drove past the small cottage the old tailor D'Alree had built on a corner of Houd-den-Bek. "Just look at it," he remarked, striking the horses in annoyance. "That bloody man doesn't know a thing about farming."

"He's not harming anyone," I said. "Why shouldn't Nicolaas allow him to stay?"

"The place is a mess." And indeed it was, with the remains of a few old broken wagons strewn across the yard, chickens scratching all over the place, a sow with her litter grunting and wallowing near the back door, half-built outbuildings abandoned before they'd been finished. There was a wretchedness about the place that depressed one; and yet I felt a spontaneous warmth towards the old man whenever I met him as he busily stumbled about on his spiky legs, wild white mane unkempt, myopic eyes squinting against the light. He must have been a failure wherever he'd been and whatever he'd been doing; but here he could live in peace with his handful of undisciplined labourers. And there was something in his gentle inefficiency that reminded me of my father, which was why I always spoke up for him whenever one of the periodic family quarrels would erupt around his continued presence.

"I'll speak to Nicolaas again," said Barend, and I knew it was only because he had to reassert himself after we'd spoken of my father in the morning. "It's not only that D'Alree is wasting a useful part of the farm, but he's attracting all sorts of vagabonds to the place. If he stays on he should get a good foreman to run the place for him."

I hardly paid attention. Barend was always planning other people's lives for them. And as it turned out he never, as far as I know, got round to broaching the subject of old D'Alree with Nicolaas that Sunday, for instead of the peaceful Sabbath on the farm we'd expected the visit turned out a deeply disturbing experience.

The baby was crying as we drew up at the front door, and all I wanted to do was to take him inside to change and feed him, which was probably the reason why I was unaware of any commotion at the back. Cecilia came out to greet us, her red hair as always drawn back in a severe knot, a flush on her very white freckled face, her lips negative like cold porridge; and the three little girls followed in tow, blonde, red, blonde.

"We haven't seen you for months," she said. "Come inside. Shall I take the baby?"

Although I knew he would probably fall silent the moment he was pressed against that soft, luxurious bosom I declined. But once inside, after I'd changed him and while I was fussing with the bottle, she swept him up, unbuttoned her dress and started suckling him; her own youngest daughter, at fifteen months, had not yet been weaned. Offended and spare in the face of her overwhelming motherhood, I had to restrain myself from snatching my child from her; but I knew she would satisfy him better than the bottle. At home he was nursed by the maid Sarie but there had been no room for her on the carriage with us, which was another reason for my reluctance to go out.

"Where's Nicolaas?" Barend asked after a while.

"He'll be here soon," she said, offering a finger to the baby's small fist. "He's correcting a slave in the stable. There's been some trouble again." She sighed. "These people don't even leave you in peace on a Sunday."

"I'll go to him," said Barend. "Perhaps I can give him a hand."

"Why don't you stay out of it?" I asked angrily.

He grinned. "Haven't exercised my arm for a long time." Ignoring my attempt to stop him he went out.

"Shall we have some tea?" asked Cecilia; and without waiting for an answer she shouted: "Pamela! Tea!" The baby, already half asleep against her breast, started, choked, then went on gorging himself, a thin line of milk running from the corner of his mouth.

"I told Barend we shouldn't come today," I said resentfully.

"Nonsense. Sit down." Again she shouted: "Pamela!"

For an hour we sat in the *voorhuis* having tea, trying to make conversation, my child sleeping blissfully against her crude body, the two elder girls perched on the edge of their chairs like little ground squirrels, the youngest pursuing a kitten on the floor; in the harsh light coming through the open door I occasionally caught glimpses of Carel running about, riding on a broomstick. If only I could be there with him; or in the veld; or back at home—anywhere but in that oppressive room with its severe furniture and stark symmetry. Chairs, stinkwood bench, *kists*, large dining-table, chest of drawers, cupboard; on the dark floor the skins of springbok, a leopard, and the lion. From time to time she went out to keep an eye on whatever the slave women were preparing in the kitchen. (Once, as she rose, I managed to take back my child from her.) Our desultory talk was an ineffectual battle against the silence weighing on us from all sides. I'd always been made to feel an intruder in their house but never as much as on that Sunday. Almost nothing was recognizable from the time it had been mine. This woman had rebuilt and refurbished it entirely, enlarging it, smartening it; its very smell was different—soap, linseed oil, homemade starch. All the intimacy of my earliest years had disappeared. And there she was, this large ungainly red-haired female, bolstered by a bland confidence in her own salvation as she ruled over the domain that had been my father's and mine—with a sudden pang I remembered the

257

smell of his pipe, the feel of his jacket—in preparation no doubt for Heaven where, with a host of lesser angels at her beck and call, she would immediately set about cleaning up and rearranging the furniture.

The men came back, and the ground squirrel girls rushed with excited little shrieks to welcome their father. Nicolaas seemed nervous, his face flushed; and he was breathing deeply.

"Don't touch me," I said as he came towards me to kiss me.

He stopped, obviously perplexed. "What's the matter then?"

"She's in one of her moods again," said Barend, watching from the door, absently wiping his hands on his hips.

"I didn't mean to keep you waiting," said Nicolaas. "I was just—"

"You men make me sick," I interrupted.

"I hope you taught him a proper lesson this time," said Cecilia in a tone of satisfaction. "I'm sure you would like some tea." The customary shout followed: "Pamela!"

"I'll take the tray back." Laying down the baby on the bench where I'd been sitting I began to collect the cups.

"For Heaven's sake, leave it to Pamela," Cecilia said disapprovingly. "They've got little enough to do."

But I paid no attention. I knew that if I didn't get out of that room soon I'd scream.

"Really, Hester," said Nicolaas, trying to hold me back, his voice openly pleading, "if only you knew how much trouble he's already given me. And this morning I caught him—"

"I'm really not interested, Nicolaas," I said, holding my breath. "Now please let me go so that I can bring you the tea you so richly deserve."

"He nearly flogged my horse to death. If I hadn't stopped him just in time—"

I went through to the kitchen. It was empty. In the hearth hung several pots, some iron, some copper, one or two of them hissing energetically. I took the tea things to the tub on the scrubbed table near the back door and started rinsing the cups vigorously.

"You really shouldn't get upset so easily," said Cecilia behind me. "Where's everybody? Isn't it typical? Turn your back for a minute and off they go." She went to the back door and raised her strong voice in a shout to waken the dead: "Pamela! Bet! Lydia! For Heaven's sake, where are you?" She sighed, moving over to the hearth. "These people. You give them everything and this is what you get in return. Suppose they're all sulking now because at last Nicolaas has got round to teaching one of them a lesson again. He's too soft with them, that's what. I keep telling him." Then, turning to me, without a pause or a change of voice: "Bad time of the month for you?"

"No," I said fiercely. "It's a wonderful time. It keeps Barend away from me."

"Tsk, tsk," she said behind me as I went back to the *voorkamer*, leaving her to pour the men's tea.

They were still discussing the slaves when I came in. Trying not to pay attention I made sure that the baby was comfortable, then went to the front door to look out into the brilliant autumn light.

"It's the only way to keep them in check," Barend was saying. "They're all being poisoned by these rumours from the Cape. It's the bloody English."

"At the moment it's just rumours," said Nicolaas. "But one morning we'll wake up to find that they've all been freed overnight."

"You needn't be afraid of that," I suddenly said, trying in vain to control myself. "The English are men just like you."

"What do you mean?" asked Barend gruffly.

"It's obvious, isn't it?" I sneered. "No one will think of liberating an ox or a horse. You can only bother about liberating a slave if you think of him as human. So how do you expect men to think of slaves in that way if they haven't even discovered that women are human yet?"

"What you need is a proper lesson!" said Barend.

I went out into the dazzling light.

"Where are you going?" Nicolaas called after me.

259

I turned to look back at them. "To my father's grave," I said. "Oh for God's sake, Hester—!"

I walked on blindly, down to the left, into the narrow valley. Just as well no one followed me; I might have done something irresponsible. For a long time I simply went on walking, through the gate in the farmyard wall and across the veld. It wasn't the right direction, but it didn't matter. It was no use going to the grave in that frame of mind anyway. Heading for the rough foothills opposite, I felt drained of thought, reduced to simple motion; and when at last, high among the foothills, I became conscious of fatigue I sat down on a stone, raising my face to the uncomplicated forgiveness of the sun and the breath of the wind. Once again, as in those distant years when I was a child, there were the familiar textures: smoothness and roughness of rock, brittleness of grass, the resilience of skin on my upper arms as I held them tightly to contain myself, the reassurance of bone in knees, the gentle hardness of thighs. This was I: yet who was I?

A recognition of the body. Twitches of hunger affording a particular satisfaction in the stubborn knowledge that it would not be stilled; numbness from sitting; a familiar pressure in the bladder. What strange sense of defiance in simply drawing up my skirts and squatting there, not hidden behind stone or bush but openly in animal simplicity, heels apart, the small irregular jet hissing from my invisible self, fine droplets spraying my ankles, the dark stain on the ground spreading unevenly, seeping reluctantly into the dry crust, oozing away, leaving a momentary frothiness, then gone; a miracle as of birth; a most fleeting part of me forever secured by the abiding soil. Only through the water of one's body can one commune with solid earth. Not past or future was freedom, but this insignificant, tremendous moment. One always thinks of freedom as of something "out there", remote and separate, a territory to be reached by climbing a mountain or swimming a river or crossing some frontier. But is there, ever, anything "out there": freedom? truth? Can it ever be anywhere, or otherwise, than here, in here, inseparable from who you are,

260

what you are, what you were, what you alone allow yourself to become? Curiously content, I walked back at last, making a detour to avoid the front of the house, then cutting across the backyard in the direction of the small stone enclosure of the graveyard.

Passing behind the stable I heard a moaning sound, but so dubious, more sigh than sound, that it might have been my imagination. Suddenly the anxiety returned, flooding me. I went round the stone building. Ontong and Achilles were squatting on either side of the wide door, staring sullenly ahead.

"Good afternoon," I said, hesitant in their presence.

"Good day, Nooi Hester." Old Ontong's face was as inscrutable as always.

"What are you doing here?"

"The Kleinbaas told us to stay here, Nooi."

"Why?"

Again I heard the sigh, the moan, and this time it was unmistakable. Clenching my teeth, I stepped into the doorway. It was so dark in the stable, after the brilliance outside, that I was blinded for a while. Then a shape defined itself, black upon black. A man dangling from one of the crossbeams in the roof, his feet barely touching the ground, his arms stretched and tied above his head. He was naked. It was Galant.

It had never occurred to me that it might be he. My stomach contracted. My head was reeling. Supporting myself against one of the rough doorposts I turned back to Ontong:

"What's he doing here like this?"

He was still staring into space, refusing to look at me: "Baas Nicolaas said he must stay there until tonight."

"Cut him loose, Ontong."

"The Kleinbaas will kill us."

"Ontong, I order you to."

He didn't reply.

I moved a few steps inside again; then returned to the door. "You can go to your huts now," I said.

261

They refused to move.

"Ontong. Achilles." I had to restrain a sob of anger in my throat. "Go home. I'll tell Nicolaas myself."

They looked at me. Ontong shook his head slowly. But in the end they got to their feet, mumbling something I couldn't make out, and went off, obviously reluctant.

"Galant," I said.

"Go away," he hissed, his body shaking as if in rage.

"Why did he do this to you?"

"Go away." He was so obviously in pain that it was more a groan than a command.

"Let me help you," I pleaded.

"I don't want you here."

I looked round hopelessly. It was still difficult to distinguish objects in the dark and only after some time I discovered a heavy wooden box filled with straw which, with great difficulty, I managed to shove towards him so that he could take the weight off his arms. At first he refused even that relief.

"Please!" I said.

"I told you to go away."

Kneeling beside the heavy box I shoved again, trying to force it right under him. I looked up at him. It was still dark, but my eyes were growing accustomed to it. Until that instant I'd been concerned only about his agony. But kneeling there, looking up, it was the discovery of *him* hanging there, and naked, that shocked me. Clutching the grainy, splintered wood of the box I pressed my face against it, feeling it graze the skin of my cheek and almost relishing the cruelty of that harsh touch. It was the immediacy with which a remote past returned that shook me so. There was no sense of myself being there, in that dark stable smelling so piercingly of horses and urine and straw, and recollecting images from many years ago: those images were tangible in their urgent reality. For a few instants we *were* children again, clutching one another for warmth, sheltered under Ma-Rose's voluminous kaross, our bare skins conscious of its rude caress. For a few instants we were gliding smoothly through the muddy water of the dam, the weavers flitting and singing overhead. For a few instants I felt the warm insistent sucking of his mouth against my leg as he drained the snake's poison from the precise marks of the wound. But at the same time we were *not* children any more. It was a woman kneeling in the straw; and this was the body of a man.

Was he aware of it too or was it an inevitable reaction to shock that below his belly that dark shape should stir uneasily, and jerk, and grow monstrously before my eyes; that man-thing I had never seen, least of all in my husband whose violent couplings had always occurred in the dark and to whom I'd never shown myself in return? Now it was there, visible and aggressive, impossible to deny, and for the first time in years another submerged layer from my youth returned—that fascination, that luxurious terror with which I'd furtively stared at bull and cow, at horses, dogs and goats. Pure animal experience and for that very reason innocent and fierce.

"Go away," he groaned again.

That made it easier for me to get up, turning away from him briefly, aware of practicalities again.

Then there was a sound at the door, and a dark figure appeared.

"Hester? What are you doing here?" It was Nicolaas.

I didn't move, still trying to control my breathing.

"Hester?"

"Untie him," I said.

"But—"

"I told Ontong and Achilles to go. Now untie him."

"You don't understand. He nearly killed my horse."

I struck him in the face. "You disgust me, Nicolaas," I said. "It's the sort of thing I'd have expected of Barend, not of you. I'm ashamed of you."

He stared at me. His face was contorted as if he wanted to cry. In rage I snatched a sickle from the wall and thrust it in his hand.

"Now will you cut him loose?" I shouted.

He climbed on the box and started sawing at the thongs that held Galant's wrists. Galant must have lost consciousness for he slumped the moment his arms were loose, and fell.

Tie up a man, I thought then, and he is no longer a man. There is no limit to what you can permit yourself to do to him. Untie his hands, I know now, and there is no limit to the responsibilities you may have to assume for that simple act.

"He'll be all right," Nicolaas stammered. "They're tougher than you think."

I didn't look at him. He went to the door.

"Hester," he said. "Honestly, I—"

"I'm not interested in what you have to say any more."

He went out into the blinding light.

There was a wooden bucket half filled with water in the corner near the door. Only afterwards did it occur to me that it might have been dirty, meant for the horses. It didn't matter then. There was no cloth of any kind, so—in that strange numbness, as if it were all happening in my sleep—I tore a piece off the hem of my dress, and soaked it, and started washing Galant's face. After a while he moaned again.

"Go away," he said.

Even if I'd wanted to obey I couldn't. There was neither will nor thought left in me. In mere mechanical movement I tried to contain myself, struggling obtusely against this dark flood threatening all understanding. I didn't even *want* to understand. Soaking the cloth at intervals I simply went on washing him, cleaning his body, the way I presume one cleanses a corpse. Only he wasn't a corpse, and he was in pain, for he winced and twitched at times; and occasionally, although he visibly tried to stifle them, there were muffled sobbing sounds coming from his throat. I washed the blood from him, but it was not because of the blood; it was the need to find atonement for everything I couldn't grasp in a violent world where neither he nor I belonged. I washed his body as if for the first time in my life I was discovering the shape and reason of limbs and their miraculous relationship. I even touched that

264

fierce club rising from his loins, accepting that in that half-dark hour nothing should be avoided or denied. He groaned again; again he murmured: "Go away," but he must have known by then that I had to continue. In a way I wasn't even concerned with him, this slave, this man, Galant. In having him cut free from the thongs that bound him it was myself I'd tried to liberate; in washing him I was praying for my own impossible salvation.

Someone entered. It was the slave woman Pamela who'd served tea that morning and whom I'd seen before.

"Baas Nicolaas told me to come," she said.

I resented the intrusion; at the same time it offered release—if only through postponement of what I couldn't comprehend anyway.

"You would have come even if he hadn't sent you," I said, not knowing why.

After a moment, meekly, I rose to my feet. Neither the woman nor I said a word; Galant, too, was silent. Staring at each other over his prostrate body we didn't move. There was an intensity in that wordless confrontation which, it seems to me, is possible only between woman and woman.

I wanted to say something, but I felt my voice struggling in my throat like a bird fluttering to escape. At last, mumbling incoherently the first words I could think of, I turned and left. I don't think she even heard me.

"Take him. Look after him. Don't let anyone ever do this to him again."

That was what the woman said. I wasn't sure I could trust her just like that; one cannot be too careful with these people. In the evenings they read to you from the Bible but the next day it's something quite different. Much safer to be wary and to keep one's own counsel. I stood at the stable door watching her as she walked through the yard past Baas Nicolaas who was still standing near the chicken-run; he tried to talk to her but she walked right past him, and that persuaded me that she'd been sincere. Even so I waited until he too had gone inside before I dared to return to Galant.

"Can you get up?" I asked him.

"What makes you think I can't?"

But it took quite an effort to help him to his feet and on the way to his hut we had to rest several times; just as well that Bet had already gone to the kitchen for I was in no mood to have her around. The others kept their distance when they saw us approaching, as if it embarrassed them to look at us openly. I preferred it that way as I felt even more exposed than Galant, as if it was I dragging myself naked through that yard; in any case he was my responsibility now, not theirs.

"The woman was kind to you," I said when we stopped outside his hut so he could catch his breath.

"What's she to me?"

"Come inside. You must lie down."

"I'm all right."

Obstinate. But he didn't even know what he was saying; and when I helped him down on the mattress he passed out again and I had to bring him to with water. After I'd made him comfortable again I sent one of the youngsters, I think it was Rooy, to fetch some medicine from Ma-Rose, for he was clearly in a bad way. Just before sunset she came down to see for herself, with a skin bag filled with ointments and medicine; soon the whole hut was filled with the smell of her camphor brandy, linseed oil and castor oil, Dutch drops, honey and herbs, and the many weird concoctions she'd brewed herself. Even that was not enough to her taste and after a while she went out again.

"Where you going, Ma-Rose?" I asked.

"Got to get some brandy from Nicolaas. I need it for Galant."

"You not going to ask them anything. I won't have it."

But she refused to listen and perhaps it was just as well for the brandy put him to sleep. Only then, with a grunt of relief, did she return to her own hut. Soon afterwards Bet came home from her evening work in the house—Nooi Cecilia wouldn't go to bed before everything was in its place—but I stopped her at the door:

"You better go to sleep somewhere else. I got to look after Galant."

She didn't object. It had been a bad day and I suppose she knew as well as anyone else that it would take only a small spark to set everything alight. After she'd gone, at long last, silence settled on the farmyard. From time to time one of the dogs would bark or yelp briefly, or start chewing something; or there would be an uneasy stirring in the kraal; for the rest it was silent. In the distance, once or twice, the call of jackals: the sort of sound that expands the night and hollows it out. Then nothing. A silence brooding heavily on the world. But I didn't mind at all. Hanging from its hook the lantern was burning steadily, turned very low. Galant was sleeping. I sat beside him, staring at him in the deep silence, still unable to believe that he was at last with me.

From the very first day Nooi Cecilia had brought me to the farm I'd noticed him, probably because he mostly kept away

267

from the rest and never forced himself on me. The others, every one of them from old Ontong and Achilles down to the young ones—the bragging Thys and little Rooy who couldn't even properly make a horn yet—were pestering me day and night; for a while I'd thought it might be useful to make them think I was keeping myself for Abel, knowing no one would dare interfere with his woman. But I could never really come round to accepting him: he was running after women too much, and anyway I didn't feel like taking a man just yet. Only to one man had I willingly given myself before, and that was Louis who'd worked with me at Oubaas Jan du Plessis's place: but then he'd been sold, leaving me behind with the child who later died of an inflammation. Pining for Louis had made me thin. And once I'd recovered I made up my mind that no other man would claim me for himself again. Which was why I almost felt relieved when at first Galant kept so much to himself. For I could see it wouldn't be easy to refuse him. I desired him, there's no shame in admitting it: but I was scared too, knowing that if ever something were to happen between us it would be like a river coming down and taking us with it, pulling out one's roots and breaking one's branches, and throwing one out on some forsaken bank one still dreaded to think about. I feared the possibility of that flood. At the same time I knew, even then, that nothing could keep it from coming down sooner or later. And when Nooi Hester looked at me that afternoon and told me: "Take him. Look after him," I knew the flood was ready to break. That brought a stillness into me. I still felt scared. But I was willing to give myself up to it. I was not only resigned, but ready. I wanted to have him and submit to him.

All night long I sat beside him, wiping his face when he perspired; and when he moaned in his sleep I would apply Ma-Rose's ointment to his wounds, very gently, cautiously, lightly, using only the very tips of my fingers, to soothe him and to cool the fire that burned him. When he shivered from cold fever I covered him with the kaross; and when he grew restless from heat I uncovered him again and sponged his naked body.

At last the restlessness seemed to leave him and he fell into a deeper and more peaceful sleep. Even then I kept watch beside him, gazing at him in silence, contented and amazed. Everything I'd ever known passed through my mind as I sat, as if it was imperative to sort it all out before I could go any further. The farm where I'd been born, beside the Breede River; and the people I'd known. The day in Worcester when my mother and I had been sold to pay for our master's debts; and the journey to Buffelsfontein on Baas Jan's big wagon, across the mountains and into the Bokkeveld. Nooi Cecilia who'd always been kind to me, passing on to me all her old clothes, teaching me to sew and crochet, to cook and to darn; and spending her afternoons reading to me from the Bible until, terrified at the thought of the eternal fire and brimstone of hell and the weeping and gnashing of teeth, I'd consented to be baptized at the very next *Nagmaal* in Tulbagh. Then came Louis. And soon afterwards the summons from Nooi Cecilia to join her at Houd-den-Bek as she couldn't see eye to eye with the other servants. Thinking back that night in Galant's hut everything seemed very far away indeed; as if the only sense in all those separate events had been to prepare me for this night. Round us lay the darkness without end; in the dim light inside we lurked together like children in the womb of a dark mother. And everything was still waiting to be born.

At last the cocks began to crow, although there was no sign of dawn yet. That was when Galant woke up, pushing himself up on his elbows and staring round him with a lost, bewildered look. Then he lay back again and gazed at me, gravely, with a small frown between his eyes, as if he neither understood nor wished to find out what was happening.

"Don't worry," I said at last. "It's only me. I'll look after you."

"I can look after myself."

"One can't go on like this."

Once again he stared at me in silence.

"You can't fight them on your own," I said.

"I'll be going to Worcester in the morning," he snapped.

269

"Not in this state."

"Then as soon as I can walk I'll be going. I got to complain."

"It will only make things worse. You can't start all over every time."

"I'm not. I'm pushing it further."

"That's what you think!" Anger choked my voice; I couldn't face the thought of it happening to him again. "Every time you come out of it the loser."

"No." He sat up, even though the effort caused him to wince in pain. "Nicolaas comes out the loser. It's he who got to follow me and bring me back. It's he who got to make them beat me. I can bear that."

"You think you can bear it?!" I touched his torn shoulders with my fingertips; he shuddered.

But he clenched his teeth. "Yes, I can! Don't you understand? In the past, when he wouldn't touch me, my hands were tied. Now that he beats me it gives me reason to fight back."

"No one can fight back."

"Pamela." When he said my name it became very quiet between us. "I thought *you* would understand me."

I bowed my head, leaning my forehead against him. "You must do what you know best," I whispered. "If you're really sure. I'll stand by you."

"You're right," he said after a while. "I can't go on alone any longer." He took my chin and raised it so that he could look at me; suddenly his voice had a smothered sound. "But I got no right!" he said. "Can't you see? I got no right to ask anyone to be with me. There may be a terrible thing coming."

"Then it's better to face it together than alone."

"You must leave me while you still can," he said.

"I'm here," I said in the half-dark. "Let me stay with you. Take me if you want to."

I had to help him. How he did it with that broken body I don't know; perhaps he felt, like I did, that no matter how much it hurt, and no matter what would come from it, this could no longer be avoided. Afterwards, with one hand, with the knuckles of his fingers, he stroked my face.

270

"Galant?" I said, as if his name was the most difficult question I'd ever asked. "Who are you?"

His eyes became troubled. For a long time he stared hard at me, before at last he began to talk, slowly at first and with long pauses in between; then more and more urgently as if he could no longer stop. He told me about Ma-Rose who'd suckled him, both him and Nicolaas, and of his childhood at Lagenvlei and all the things he and Nicolaas had done together; of a hole they'd dug and which had caved in on them; of swimming in a dam and of a lion they'd shot on the farm; of a man in irons he'd met in the jail at Tulbagh, and of the Cape, and of people living in freedom across the Great River. He told me about horses he'd broken in, and of long rides in the night no one knew about, off to nowhere, riding and riding blindly in the dark, rider and horse like one. In the wildness of that galloping, he said, one could forget about being a slave. All that mattered was the riding itself. Nothing could stop you. And all the world was yours. All these things came flooding out in his talk: and just because I'd asked him: "Galant, who are you?" But when at last he stopped talking I still didn't know the answer. He was sleepy, and his voice began to drift off into sleep as he spoke; and then we both slept, his body still a dead weight on mine; and I only woke up when I felt him throbbing back to life inside me, and by that time the light outside was already turning the depressing grey colour of an old mouldy loaf. But to us it didn't matter, not then, for we were together to comfort one another with the warmth of our bodies which was all we had. In such a night one aches with the awareness of death—not just because of what may have happened to one or the other, but because you discover it as part of yourself, marrow in your bones—and it brings suffering and soothing of suffering, and a tenderness, a willingness to share whatever is available of love and caring, to make the pain more bearable for one another, against the terrors of the coming day. So I opened myself to him, not just my body but myself, for him to flow into me and flood me and sweep me along with him like a tree uprooted by a swollen

271

river, wherever he might wish to take me, beyond all darkness.

Much later, when at last I dared to open my eyes again, I said: "You still haven't answered my question."

"What did you ask me then?"

"I can't remember."

We slept again until the bell rang. Galant stayed in bed; I told him not to move. Outside the hut, in the chilliness of the dawn, Baas Nicolaas found me as he came by, as always, on his way to the kraal. Obviously surprised to see me there he hesitated.

"What are you doing here?" he asked.

"I'm with Galant now."

He looked hard at me, a strange look that caused a fist to clench inside me, because he seemed to be looking into me at what he had no right to see. But I said nothing. Only, from that moment I knew that his eye was upon me.

He seemed to find it easier to speak to me than to Galant, and during the next few days he would often stop to tell me something meant for Galant: "Tell him he mustn't get me wrong on this thing." "Tell him to pull himself together." "Tell him it's for his own good."

But Galant wouldn't listen to anyone. He stayed in bed for three days. Then, still shaky and staggering like a drunken man, he got up to tell the Baas he was going to Worcester to lay a complaint. I tried my best to talk him out of it, knowing very well it would be useless: and even if I felt my heart contract for him I was proud too that he hadn't submitted— although I knew it could only lead to yet more suffering, first at the Drostdy and then, after his return, at Houd-den-Bek.

Bet blamed me for everything. "You're setting him on," she flew at me. "Can't you see what you doing to him?" But her heart wasn't in it; and perhaps she even felt relief finally to have him off her hands, for everybody on the farm could see that the man she really wanted was the Baas himself. And just after Galant had come back from Worcester he finally cut his candle with Bet and she moved to the new hut Ontong had made for her, while I stayed with Galant.

There was trouble with Nooi Cecilia too. She'd always been against Galant; in her eyes he could never do right. And I soon discovered that when there was trouble between Galant and Baas Nicolaas more often than not she was behind it. She could be very holy in front of others but when she thought they were alone she did her share of prodding—I could hear her from the kitchen. She also set to work on me in her nagging, persistent way. Sometimes while I was washing or brushing her hair, she'd say:

"Pamela, you'd better watch out for that Galant."

I would rinse the hair in warm water, pretending not to know what she was talking about.

"He's bad company. He'll lead you astray."

"I'll manage, Nooi." Then I'd start rubbing her scalp vigorously, which would make it difficult for her to go on talking. But I knew that at the first opportunity she would start nagging again. I tried to ignore it, but when our plan to get married became threatened by her attitude I began to feel cornered. After all, the Nooi herself had brought me up a Christian and I'd been told that slaves were now allowed to be married by a dominee. But when I mentioned it so she could talk it over with the Baas, she got angry.

"Why should you want to get married?"

"I want to live according to the Scriptures."

"Galant is a good-for-nothing."

"I want him for my husband. We want to have children and it's not good if one isn't married."

"I'll discuss it with the Baas."

But every time I brought it up she would avoid the issue, until I realized that she had no intention of ever mentioning it to Baas Nicolaas. And when in the end Galant went straight to him to ask his consent, Nooi Cecilia took it out on me:

"Didn't I promise you I'd discuss it with the Baas myself, Pamela? Why are the two of you scheming behind my back?"

"We just wanted to find out, Nooi."

"You're no longer the reliable girl I used to know."

I didn't answer. But I put the thought away with all the

273

others that had been boiling up inside me about the things that happened to me at Houd-den-Bek. In themselves perhaps they were not important; and taken separately, in fact, they were just a nuisance, no more. But not when it went on day after day, year after year. When we were making merry of a Saturday night, especially when Abel was there too, it was never long before the Baas would call from the house: "Will you stop that noise now? The lot of you drunk again?" When a couple of us sat in the shade in the heat of a summer afternoon, chatting and whiling away the time after lunch, it would be Nooi Cecilia's turn: "Don't you know I'm trying to rest a bit? Can't you people talk without raising your voices?" When one was in need of anything, flour or bread, lard, medicine or whatever, one had to go up to the house to ask for it. *Please, Nooi. Thank you, Nooi.* In the house everything was always kept locked up because we were suspected of carrying off whatever we could lay our hands on. And if something got lost, mislaid most likely by one of the children, either Lydia or Bet or I would first be accused: "Can't you keep your hands off other people's things?" And there would be neither apology nor explanation when the thing was later found, more often than not in the very place where it was supposed to be. Otherwise I might be working in the kitchen, the Nooi sewing in the *voorhuis*; then she would call: "Pamela, come and pick up the cotton, I've dropped it." I would pick it up from her feet and give it to her. Ten minutes later it would be the scissors. Or the needle. Or something else. After supper, when I was exhausted and in a hurry to get back to Galant, there would first be all the dishes to wash up, and then the house to be tidied from one end to another—in case the Lord decided to come in the night and found anything out of place. On and on it went. Until I had to admit that Galant had been right: violence was by no means the worst. But for his sake I gritted my teeth and took whatever came my way. I knew if I spoke to him about it he would just get mad at them again, and then he'd take it out on them one way or another: breaking a plough or a yoke, injuring a lamb, beating the Baas's horse, poking a

274

hole in the water barrel. He had many ways of getting at them without their ever suspecting it. And I didn't want to encourage him, since there was peace on the farm at the time, albeit a precarious peace in which one remained aware of something invisible brooding in silence, waiting for the right moment to break out. So I didn't do or say anything to provoke them, but tried to bear to whatever happened: accepting the remains of their food on my plate, their worn clothes on my body. And every night before supper I bowed my head and bent my back and contained the rage in my heart as I brought in the tub of warm water and knelt in front of them to take off their shoes and wash their feet with my soap and cloths, first the Baas, then the Nooi, then the children. Let Thy will be done. It was the thought of Galant that kept me going, knowing he was waiting for me in what was now our hut; and one day, when finally they'd made up their minds and given us their consent, we would be married, husband and wife in the eyes of the Lord. Or would it never happen? Since the day Galant had spoken to Baas Nicolaas about marriage I noticed that the Baas would use any ploy or pretext to keep Galant away from me, as if he begrudged us our time together: he would send Galant with a flock of sheep to a farmer in the Roggeveld; the following week he would be ordered to take a wagonload of produce to Tulbagh; and for days on end he would be sent to help old D'Alree on his little patch of land—that was before the foreman Campher was hired— and when he came back there would be something else again.

Most difficult of all to bear was the way the Baas had, ever since that early morning when he'd first seen me coming out of Galant's hut, of staring at me as if I was naked. Washing his feet was especially unsettling, for then I would feel his eyes on me from very close by. His leg pressing against me as I washed the foot, he would try with his sole to caress my body as he sat paging through the Bible in search of the passage he meant to read after the meal. Every night. And yet I never thought it would go beyond that.

How did it change then? There was a day just after the

275

winter, and the *vlei* was still swollen with water; the hens had already started brooding on their nests. Amid the preparations for the first big soap-making of the new season there was another quarrel between the Nooi and the Baas, what with her nagging about his not being enough of a man about the house, and unable to control his underlings, and allowing Galant to get out of hand. At the first opportunity I could find I slipped away to warn Galant:

"Watch your step with the Baas today. The devil is loose again on the farm."

But he was already in a black mood, scowling and snapping at everything in his way, because of something that had broken and for which he'd been given the blame. And when he went to chop wood later that afternoon he deliberately kicked to pieces a little wagon he'd made for the children a few days earlier. Strange that he should do that, he always had endless patience with the children; but he was difficult that day. And then Baas Nicolaas came upon him just as he was grinding the splintered remains of the little wagon into the ground with his heel. It so happened that I was on my way from the kitchen to feed the chickens, and from the tone of voice in which the Baas shouted: "Galant!" I immediately knew something was wrong.

I stopped in my tracks, the grain-box still under my arm. Oh God, I thought, not again.

"What are you doing there, Galant?"

"The thing got in my way."

The Baas walked towards him, slowly clenching and unclenching his fists, the knuckles showing white through the skin.

"You've been looking for trouble again lately, Galant."

Galant split a piece of wood with his axe, sending the two halves whirring through the air, narrowly missing the Baas.

"You trying to kill me now?" he asked.

"Get out of my way then. I got work to do."

Would there have been another ugly scrap if I hadn't been there? I don't know. As I stood there, trembling, I wasn't even

276

aware that I had any influence on the matter. I only saw the Baas turning away from Galant, trying I suppose to contain his anger; and then he noticed me, and stopped. After a moment he snapped at Galant:

"Well, hurry up and finish your work then."

"For God's sake don't provoke the man like that," I pleaded with Galant as soon as the Baas had gone.

"Mind your own business."

I went away to feed the chickens; afterwards I had to prepare supper in the kitchen. When the food was on the table, as I entered with the tub, I could see the Baas gazing at me again, but I avoided his eyes and lowered my head. Kneeling at his feet I untied the laces of his heavy boots and took them off. First one foot, then the other I put in the warm water, soaping and rinsing them. To dry them I had to lift them on my knees; and I could feel him resisting my hold in order to press his toes against my lap. It brought a sickness to my throat, but I kept it to myself, taking my time to finish with him before I moved on to the Nooi and the children. Then I carried the tub back to the kitchen. Every now and then they'd call me back for this or that: to pick up a spoon a child had dropped; to hand on the plates; to dish out more meat; to cut another slice of bread. After the meal I cleared the table and took my place with the other slaves on the floor near the door for prayers. There seemed to be no end to the Baas's reading and praying that night, the words washing over one like the lazy water of a broad river. But at last it was over and we rose to leave.

As I reached the kitchen door the Baas said behind me: "Pamela."

I stopped and looked round.

"You've been late with the tea these last few mornings," he said. "It will be much easier for you to sleep in the kitchen so that you can boil the water as soon as you get up."

"What's this, Nicolaas?" asked the Nooi, a sharp tone of suspicion in her voice.

"I'm master in my own house, Cecilia," he said without looking at her.

277

There was no thought in my mind. I tried not to feel anything. Numbly I turned round and went to the back door.

"Where are you going now?" he asked.

"I'm just going to the hut first, Baas. Galant is waiting for me."

"There's no need for you to go. I told you to stay."

"Yes, Baas." The words choked in my throat, but I managed to say them.

Behind him, sitting all alone by the long empty table, I saw the woman, large and straight-backed, her hand resting on the Bible; only her head was bowed.

That night, on the kitchen floor, in the dull warmth of the hearth, Nicolaas took me for the first time: with the violence of someone who's scared of what he's doing, but who feels himself provoked and will not let anyone stop him, for the very reason that he knows it to be wrong.

CECILIA

Not once did I speak a single word against his abominations. (Held back as much by a consideration of my state as by that recurrent dream that had plagued me since my youth and for which his conduct was in a sense the just punishment?) If he wished to bring a judgement upon himself it did not behove me as his wife to demean my indignation into presumption. I did what I regarded as my duty: humbling myself before God I assured the purity of my own flesh and that of my daughters. But when he began to take Pamela to him, and that within the sanctity of my own house, I called him to me and opened the Bible and admonished him in the words of Joshua:

Take good heed therefore unto yourselves, that ye love the Lord your God.

Else if ye do in any wise go back, and cleave unto the remnant of these nations, even these that remain among you, and shall make marriages with them, and go in unto them, and they to you:

Know for a certainty that the Lord your God will no more drive out any of these nations from before you; but they shall be snares and traps unto you, and scourges in your sides, and thorns in your eyes, until ye perish from off this good land which the Lord your God hath given you.

His face was flushed with anger. "What are you trying to tell me, Cecilia?"

I closed the Bible very slowly and fastened the clasps. "One day you came in here," I said, "and told me about a terrible thing Frans du Toit had done. You were shocked to think a man could sink so low. But today I'm asking you, Nicolaas: Is there any difference between what he did and what you're doing?"

279

"Cecilia, how dare you say such a thing?"

I refused to let him off. There was an extraordinary feeling of calm and reasonableness in me; I knew I had God on my side. "Last year when we went to Cape Town," I said, "I was amazed to see all the white children among the slaves. And it occurred to me that if it went on like that we would soon have no other choice but to set them all free. Can you imagine what that would mean? In this land which God has given us we will have become the equals of the beasts of the veld. In our madness we'll eat grass like Nebuchadnezzar."

"You're going too far!" he protested.

"Rather humble yourself before God," I told him. "Why don't you go down on your knees and ask Him to tell you who it is who's going too far?"

One thing I felt distressingly sure of: we were living in a house built upon the sand. And the rain would descend, and the floods would come, and the winds would blow, and beat upon that house; and it would fall; and great would be the fall of it.

NICOLAAS

So help me God. In that remote and impossible night on the mountain I had sworn that I'd never again raise my hand against Galant who'd saved my life. But the moment we descended into the Bokkeveld he shifted beyond my grasp again. In the enclave of that night it had been possible to talk to him; briefly, exhilaratingly, we'd been in touch as in childhood. Now we were back in our familiar positions, master and slave. I tried my best to honour the intention of that night, but it was almost impossible; and Galant made no attempt to make it easier. Even insolence, defiance, arrogance might have been manageable had they been the familiar refractory acts of a difficult slave; but it was the dark secret flood I could sense moving behind his actions that made me hesitate in uncertainty and anguish—all the more so since he too appeared to have no understanding of it. There was an increasing feeling of having irreparably lost my grasp, and the very effort to fight against the evil in myself had become feeble. It was such a simple discovery really: that revulsion diminishes; that only the first act of any series is important: the first time one forces oneself, in lust and loathing, upon a black woman; the first time one ties a man's hands to flog him; the first outrage to what had been one's "principles". After that, in spite of intentions or efforts to resist, there is no effective return. It is oneself one has diminished. All that remains is the agony of the silence surrounding every act—a silence no longer penetrable from inside or out.

It was hard enough, God knows, to live with Cecilia's pious reprimands and her contempt—making it more and more difficult for me to rule her as a husband; sending me with always greater urgency back to that dark replenishment of virility recommended by Ma-Rose, to which, while abhorring it, I'd become addicted; and which only made me more and more reprehensible in Cecilia's eyes. To punish her and assert myself; to punish myself and acknowledge her hold on me: how could I break out of this whirlpool dragging me ever inward? The sin in me; the sin in me.

And Pamela made it worse. She was altogether different from Lydia. Having learned to live with revulsion, I was shocked to find only lust when I contemplated Pamela. Perhaps not even lust for herself? But a lust derived from the agony of knowing her closeness to Galant. She was the only possible means for me still to touch him. God knows I did not mean to harm her or evoke his enmity: on the contrary. This woman, this body had known him; knew him. Through her I groped towards that terrible closeness to him I'd known in the one night of my life when I'd been wholly free.

It was, of course, in vain. She only added to the dark flood rising, rising, and over which I had long lost all control.

To whom could I turn in my distress? The mere idea of discussing it with Cecilia was outrageous. Pamela never spoke at all, except in direct reply to a question; her silence an accusation more eloquent than anger. Barend would simply laugh at me in scorn, and I'd long ago forfeited all hope of access to Hester. It was unthinkable, for different reasons, to face either Pa or Ma.

Ma-Rose? Perhaps. Yet the burning memory of how she'd been the first to encourage me on this road that had led me into the dark flood, inhibited me. In despair I thought of the old man who'd recently settled on a corner of Houd-den-Bek, the tailor and shoemaker D'Alree. He was a foreigner; he might not understand my urgency at all. Yet the very fact that he was a total stranger, disinterested, quite unconcerned with the motion of our lives, also commended him.

I hesitated for a long time, until I could really bear it no longer. On one of my customary night walks I stopped outside Ma-Rose's hut; in the smoky interior, glowing a dull orange in

282

the light of her small fire, I could see the old woman moving about, preparing her brews and concoctions. My stomach contracted in the ache of longing to go to her. But I knew I could no longer face her, and went on, stumbling over the uneven veld with its unexpected ditches and its outcrops of rock. There was still light in D'Alree's one-roomed thatched cottage. I made a detour to avoid the fire of the labourers— dark shapes swaying to music, laughing uproariously from time to time: the white foreman Campher sitting with the others. This fraternizing annoyed me; there was something improper about it. But it was none of my business. Through the open door of the cottage I could see the scraggy old man working at his rough table, his white mane tousled and shining in the lamp light.

"Oh, Mr Van der Merwe," he said, looking quite startled to see me, "What a surprise."

"I didn't mean to disturb you."

"Why don't you come in? Would you like a *sopie*?"

"No thank you," I said, but he was already pouring the brandy into two tin mugs, revolting stuff, burning up one's insides, leaving one quite light-headed.

"You must be very lonesome," I said, postponing the second sip of brandy for as long as possible.

He shrugged. "One gets used to everything." He drained his mug, smacking his long thin lips, and took up his awl to resume his work on a half-made boot.

"I've never understood why you should have chosen the Bokkeveld to settle in," I said. "You must have seen a lot more interesting places in the world in your time."

"Oh indeed." He slid a thong through his mouth, wetting it with spittle before he proceeded to sew up the back of the boot. "Come a long way I have. Born in Piedmont. You know where that is?"

"Never heard of it." Somehow, talking to him like this helped me to escape from the immediacy of my own anguish.

"Travelled all through Europe before coming here on my way to the East. Never got beyond the Cape." He suddenly

283

stopped and looked up, an eager smile on his ancient monkey-face. "Did your mother ever tell you I knew her in Cape Town, before she got married?"

With one casual remark he'd cancelled the only reason I'd had for confiding in him: the fact that he was an alien, and aloof from our lives. He'd known Ma. That explained why he'd come to live here. He was one of them. How could he be expected to understand?

"It's getting late," I said, putting down my mug without finishing his atrocious brandy. "I'd better be going."

"Why in such a hurry?" he asked in obvious disappointment. "We've hardly had time to talk."

"I just happened to be passing when I saw your light. Thought I'd look in to ask you—I'll be needing a new pair of boots soon."

"Let me take your measurements."

"I can come back another time."

"No, no," he insisted. "No time like the present, true?"

Impatient and irritable, I allowed him to go about his business, fussing and breathing in his asthmatic way. On my way home, later, I had the curious, uneasy feeling of having left something of myself behind. As if, in allowing him to take my measurements and draw the outline of my feet on his leather, I'd given him an unreasonable and insidious hold on myself.

Nothing had been resolved. Nothing could be resolved. In the dark kitchen Pamela would be asleep, passively at my disposal should I decide to wake her. And I knew I would. What else was there for me to do?

It was Galant I really needed to talk to and touch. But our sandy hollow had crumbled long ago and caved in on us. And the dark flood was rising.

D'ALREE

One is always alone. We talk and live past each other. After old Piet van der Merwe had first instructed Nicolaas to accommodate me on a corner of his farm I saw very little of my neighbours. From the beginning they resented the intrusion; I could feel it. They looked down on me as the foreigner, the stranger, the impostor. A Christian sense of duty obliged them to tolerate my presence, but I would never be allowed to belong. The Bokkeveld, I soon discovered, was reluctant to open its heart to outsiders. I would never be treated otherwise than with suspicion, as if I was not only a beggar living on their mercy but the carrier of God knows what evil diseases. The only one who occasionally deigned to come over for a chat was Frans du Toit, most likely because he felt as rejected as I did, if for quite different reasons. Rumour had it that the birth-mark covering the left side of his face was the imprint of the Devil. And yet I found him a pleasant enough young man, more knowledgeable than some of the others in the neighbourhood, and conscientious to a fault, although I'd heard it said, probably out of spite, that he'd been made Field-cornet only because he'd allied himself with the English against his own people. I don't judge anybody.

We had long arguments, Frans and I. "What's wrong about living alone?" I would say when he became rebellious about what seemed to be his destiny in life. "Keep your own counsel, then you won't ever have to depend on others. Once you get involved with others there's no telling where it may end. One gets drawn in before you know it. No matter what you do, heaven and hell are involved in every step you take."

"You should have become a preacher," he would say. "Not a shoemaker."

"The two are much the same. When one's hands are working with scissors or awl your thoughts are free to explore God and man."

"It's easy for you to talk. You're an old man; you can live without others." There would be a brief pause before he added: "You can live without a woman. But when a man is young he cannot deny the needs of his body."

Then, depending on the circumstances, I would smile or sigh; and pursue my own thoughts again. How could I attempt to explain my own life to them? To these people I must seem like a madman, an old confused dodderer neglecting his work and his fields and slowly going to pieces among chickens and pigs and junk while he works away in fits and starts at making clothes and shoes; and who wanders about talking to himself in a foreign language.

I found it difficult to explain it to myself: this heaven and hell I'd spoken to him about. For on the surface, admittedly, my life appeared so ordinary, even drab; and even what had seemed adventure in my youth now faded into irrelevance. It could all be summarized in so few words.—A young man bored with old Europe, and taking up his little bundle in Piedmont to set out and see the world; meeting a swaggerer in Texel who persuades him to join him on a voyage to Batavia; and landing three months later, after burying the big-mouthed acquaintance at sea, at the Cape where he is parted from his money in canteens and the female quarters of the slave lodge, so that he has no choice but to stay behind when the boat sails on; staying on temporarily as a shoemaker and a tailor, a sojourn that gradually lengthens into permanence, especially after meeting an affluent family, the De Villiers, and falling in love with their vivacious young daughter Alida, only to discover one morning that she has eloped with a wild man from the Bokkeveld; marrying another woman in due course, a decent good wife with whom he lives respectably and in mild prosperity until the day of her death, when he briefly returns to

286

the land of his birth where everything has however grown so strange that he soon returns to the Cape; and yielding one final time to the Mediterranean urge in his blood he loads his few remaining possessions on a wagon and treks into the interior in search of an impossible memory; finding at last, in joy and dismay, on a godforsaken farm in the Bokkeveld the lost Alida of his youth and accepting the invitation of her husband —now old and much subdued—to settle on a corner of his son's farm Houd-den-Bek where he can spend the few remaining years of his life in peace.—To me it was the closure of a circle long left incomplete. And all I wished was to be left in peace and not to become involved in the lives of others again.

I had but few needs; and apart from Frans du Toit I seldom saw people. Occasionally there might be an invitation to a Sunday meal at Lagenvlei where the whole family would gather in their prim old-fashioned best clothes. From time to time the old man would come round to my place to cast a disapproving eye on the untidy yard. The elder son, too, could be quite unpleasant, muttering dire threats when his father wasn't present. Nicolaas's wife I found a truly Christian woman, always ready to send over a bowl of soup, or a joint of venison, a basket of eggs, a pumpkin, some freshly ground flour; although she, too, had an unsparing tongue about what she regarded as laziness and laxity. Nicolaas himself seemed too much of a loner to spend time in conversation with me. Always friendly when one greeted him, and prepared to exchange a few pleasantries or comments on the weather, the harvest, or the unreliability of slaves; but that was the full extent of it. Only once he visited me of his own accord. It was very late one night and he seemed to have something weighty on his mind, but in the end it turned out to be no more than a pair of boots he wanted me to make for him. Strange, I thought, for a man to come over in the middle of the night for a thing like that. But another man's mind remains sealed in its own mystery.

And then, of course, Alida, who had been the aim and motive of my whole reckless journey across the mountains.

What could I possibly have expected before leaving the Cape? Yet one retains an image from a distant past and foolishly and fondly embroiders and embellishes it through the years. It was an acute shock to see her again. Not because of her age. Even then she was a handsome woman, although she'd become introverted and subdued, quite different from the sprightly young girl I'd known. Was that the real disappointment? To see such a light so dimmed?

A few times, after I'd settled on Houd-den-Bek, I drove over to Lagenvlei. Her husband was always present. We had so little to talk about that my visits were soon abandoned. Yet something refused to die inside me, an ardent memory, a hope, an unfulfilled and who knows unfulfillable wish that nourished me in my solitude. And in the end, after many months of absence, in the high summer of last year, I returned to Lagenvlei and found her alone. She remained remote, aloof, almost taciturn—which my experienced eye of course recognized immediately as but the obvious defence of a vulnerable woman. I suppose I should have made it easier for her by not pressing the matter; yet I felt that for once I had to be importunate, to make her admit what was already so clear to me: that she regretted the decision of years ago; that she still thought of me.

"Do you remember," I said, after the slave woman had served the tea and left us, "when we were—"

"There is nothing to remember," she said. "What is past is past. For ever. One has to resign oneself to the will of the Lord."

Her delicate head bent lightly as she leaned over to pour the tea, she sat against the white light of the bare window. No suffering worse than the remembrance of past happiness.

Through the open door I saw Piet coming towards the house. She was unaware of his approach. I half-rose to greet him, but even before he'd reached the door he turned on his heel and walked away again. I took the cup from Alida and sat down. The opportunity had passed.

Soon afterwards I heard that Piet had had a stroke on the

lands, undoubtedly shocked by what he'd guessed about Alida and me. How unnecessary. By that time I'd been living in the neighbourhood for two years; he must have known I could be trusted not to harm anyone. But they were a difficult lot, the Van der Merwes.

Not that I want to sound ungrateful. They were kind and even generous to me. It was Barend who hired labourers to help me out; even the slave Dollie was his choice—with the best of intentions no doubt, although Dollie gave me no end of trouble. I had a much better understanding with the slave Galant whom Nicolaas would sometimes send over to give a hand with repairs or with ploughing or sowing or reaping my small patch of land; during the last winter he would often stay for as much as a week at a time; and he was always quiet and obedient, a good worker. Strange how ungrateful a slave can be though. I still remember the jacket Nicolaas ordered me to make for Galant. Chose the corduroy himself, expensive stuff, the best I had. Now one would have expected Galant to treat such a piece of clothing with great care. It was much too good for a slave really. But barely a year later, when Galant came back here to give me a hand with some job or other, the jacket was torn to shreds, an insult to my handiwork. However, when he was working here that winter I felt sorry for him in the severe cold and gave him another jacket which I'd only worn for a couple of years: yet not once did I see him put it on. Went about in his old rags all the time. I'll never understand these people.

Still, he was a dependable worker. The only times he seemed to find it difficult to get started on a job was when I was making shoes. Then he would invariably think up some excuse to leave his own work so that he could watch me.

"What is it, Galant?" I once asked him directly. "Why aren't you getting on with the wall you're supposed to be building?"

"You must make me a pair of shoes too, Baas," he said, much to my amazement.

"But you're a slave. You're not allowed to wear shoes."

"You got to make me a pair, Baas. I'll hide them away so no one can see them."

"What do you want them for?"

"For walking."

"Your feet are tougher than any soles I can cut from my hides," I joked. "You can walk barefoot where I won't risk it with my shoes."

"I want shoes. I got to have them. And you must make them for me." The way he could persist!

"And how would you pay for them?" I joked, hoping to dissuade or dishearten him.

"I can pay you a whole sheep. Even more. Just tell me how much you want, Baas. I'll pay everything I got."

In the end he was nagging me so much that there seemed to be only one way out of it. "All right, Galant," I said. "I'll make you the shoes when I have time for it. But I'm a busy man and it may not be soon."

"I can wait."

I knew of course that it was entirely out of the question. The neighbours were already suspicious about me. What would they do if they found out that I'd made shoes for a slave? At the same time I didn't want to put him off altogether. Why should the trust of a slave have meant anything to me? Still, shunned as I was by most of the farmers because of my foreignness, and sneered at or ignored by the slaves, the simple fact that Galant accepted me—our only bond the possibility of a pair of shoes!—must have persuaded me to behave with such indulgence towards him. So I never gave him an outright No to his entreaties, while ensuring at the same time (considering my precarious situation in the neighbourhood) that I would always have a valid excuse for postponing the business of actually making the shoes. Once, when he was getting very excited and I began to fear the consequences of a refusal, I placated him by taking his measurements; on another occasion I went so far as to cut out the soles. Whenever he came over to work at my place after that he would first take out the soles and measure them on his feet and admire them and handle them as if they were infinitely precious. But that was as far as we got. I was hoping that in the end his enthusiasm would wane and he

290

would forget about the whole ridiculous business, but I'd never known such a persevering man. Patient, but persevering. Only once I really saw him in a temper. It was soon after Nicolaas had visited me in the night; and while I was working on his boots Galant came in, mistaking them for his.

"You making my shoes at last?" he asked eagerly.

"No, they're for your Baas."

"But I been waiting for a long time, much longer than he! Why you making his first?"

"Because he's your master, Galant," I said as soothingly as I could. "You must understand that."

He grabbed a hammer from the table I was working on; for a moment, fearing he might attack me with it, I cowered. But without looking at me he threw it down again and went out in such a rage that I didn't risk going near him again that day. And when I glanced through the window I saw him dismantling the stone-wall he'd been working on for days, lifting one stone after the other from the wall and throwing them away with such force that when they struck something I could see the sparks flying in broad daylight.

But the next day he was calm again and although we studiously avoided the topic of the shoes for some time after that our relationship resumed its even tenor. When he brought the matter up again it was without the urgency of before; perhaps he too had acquiesced in the knowledge that it would be no more than a game between us. At times he even waxed talkative, as if the shoes had lent me some special importance in his eyes. Perhaps my position as a foreigner, and the tales I could tell him of distant places, encouraged him to regard me in a light different from that in which he viewed those masters who had always inhabited his familiar world. I cannot deny that in a way I was moved by it. I certainly tried to use the opportunity to talk some sense into him; for the slaves seemed to be unusually excitable those days. On one occasion, especially, I was very frank with him. It must have been about April last year, just after the latest regulations about the punishment of slave women had been

291

promulgated, causing a wave of illogical reaction among the farmers.

"You know, Galant," I said—I remember it was a cool autumn day and he was wearing his jacket while he weeded the garden: not the presentable one I'd given him but the torn remains of the old one, as usual—"I really don't understand you people. If you consider everything the papers have been saying this last year—"

"What do they say?" he asked.

"You're treated much better than slaves in any other country I know of," I went on. "The Government has made sure that your circumstances are improved beyond all measure. You're given proper food and clothes. You're working for limited hours. There are restrictions on punishment. You have the right to get married. Husband and wife may no longer be sold separately. Provided you carry a pass from your *baas* you can move about with reasonable freedom. You can even have your own possessions. So for Heaven's sake tell me: what more do you want?"

And what did he reply to that? "Across the Great River," he said, "there are people who are wholly free."

I know I'm growing old; but truly I cannot understand such reasoning. One might have expected a hint of appreciation.

So in a way I was relieved when the foreman Campher arrived. Barend van der Merwe had hired him upon the recommendation I believe of a farmer near Graaff-Reinet for whom he had worked previously. A real Brabander, lots of hot air and very little hard work; and distressingly fond of spirits, especially over weekends. But at least he was a free man and a Christian, which was different from the mentality of a slave. He would be able to keep the labourers in check, I thought.

ALIDA

Such a little runt. Could this possibly be the man about whom I'd been wondering so often: *Suppose he'd asked me first?* Seeing him again after so many years was like a final renunciation. And what else could I do but bear him a grudge, not for being a runt but for diminishing me by exposing my dream as a mockery?

All I had left was what I had. That was the single bitter thought in my mind, the day they brought Piet back from the lands.

It had never really been otherwise; except that the dream had been intact. Now I'd been pruned like a tree. That was what his return had done to me. And here we all were, each woman left with the destiny of the man assigned to her. Hester with Barend. I with Piet. Cecilia with Nicolaas. Not even death could make a difference.

Another newspaper. I'm working on the farmyard wall repairing the damage where the wheels of the carriage dislodged a few stones, when Frans du Toit arrives with it in his saddle-bag and asks if the people are at home. "You can leave it with me," I say, "I'll give it to them." "No, I don't trust you with it," he says, "The news is much too important." As he eases the reins I jeer at him: "Why don't you go round to the pigsty first? It'll make the time pass more quickly." He aims a blow at me but I jump out of reach.

"Better keep your ears open," I warn Pamela. "If they say anything about the newspaper you must come and tell me."

"They never talk in front of me," she says. "The Nooi keeps me out of the *voorhuis* and the bedroom. Since the Baas began to use me she's brought Bet back into the house and I better stay out of her way."

"Keep your ears open when you working in the house," I tell Bet. "There's a newspaper come yesterday."

"Why should I tell you if I hear anything?" she says tartly.

"Because if you don't I'll bloody well break your neck."

But when I press her afterwards, all she can say is that the Nooi is keeping quiet about it: "If you ask me, the Nooi is just as scared of newspapers as you are. She says it can stay right where it is until the time comes to open it. We got enough trouble as it is, the Nooi says."

"Then there's only one thing to do," I tell Pamela, though it takes gritting my teeth to say it. "When he lies down with you again you must ask him straight."

Not even that draws anything out of them. All he says to her is: "There is a time for all things and this is not the time to talk about newspapers."

"You must bring me that newspaper," I tell Bet. "I got to know what it says, because I know it's about us."

"They'll kill me if I steal it."

"And I'll kill you if you don't."

For days on end they keep looking for that newspaper on the farm and all the while it's lying safely under my mattress. Next time I go to Oubaas D'Alree I take it with me and ask him to explain to me what it says. Why him? The others despise him. What respect, they ask, can one have for a master who doesn't behave like one? That is why I take to him, I tell them. Because he's not like them. He comes from a far place. He listens to me and talks to me as if he doesn't mind that I'm a slave. He doesn't laugh at me when I ask him to make me shoes. So I take him the newspaper. But this time he is different. He refuses to answer my questions and he has a scared look about him. "Why do you bother about such things, Galant?" he asks. "If you really want to know, go and discuss it with your Baas. I don't want to have anything to do with it." "But they won't tell me!" I cry. He keeps out of my way, pretending to be very busy with someone else's shoes. "If your Baas decides it's fit for you to know, he'll tell you himself."

I'm beginning to wonder about the man. What about those shoes he's supposed to make for me? Why can't he ever get them done? Is he lying to me? Are they really all the same?

The newspaper is burning my hand. By the Blue God, I think by myself, is there no one in the whole bloody world who can tell me what this damned thing says? I spread it open on an antheap and peer at all those weird small black ants running motionlessly across its pages. They are talking about me, that I know for sure, yet I can't make out a word they're saying. I press my ear so hard against the paper that it hurts, but I still hear nothing. Then something seems to burst inside me and I start tearing it to pieces; I thrust all the crumpled shreds into my mouth. If they won't talk to me I'll eat them up. Perhaps they'll start talking inside me. I chew them and eat them and swallow them until there's nothing left.

But it's the beginning of something awful. When I fall asleep at night beside the emptiness that used to be Pamela's place, those ants start swarming about in my guts. I can feel their tiny black feet moving about, this way and that, everywhere. I can feel them fidgeting, wriggling, burrowing. All through my body they're crawling, down to my toes, in my fingers, right inside my eyes, in my head. They're crawling and crawling, making dry rustling sounds, but I can't make out what they're saying. And then they start gnawing at my insides, and I realize they're going to chew me up until there's nothing left except a dry shell, like the shell of an old tortoise stripped clean by the ants. I start beating my own body, slapping wherever I can feel them crawling about and gnawing and chewing, but I cannot reach them. I bash my head against the walls to silence them, to stop them, but they go on gnawing at me, my tongue, my eyes, everything I got inside me. I start shouting, bellowing like a bullock that's being cut, and I jump up. And suddenly I'm awake, wet with sweat, and with the sound of my own bellowing still in my ears; and around me there's nothing, but I know very well the ants were there, they were eating me. I grasp at Pamela beside me but her place is empty, she's sleeping in the house, and it's Nicolaas who lies with her.

Just a dream, I keep telling myself. Have I become a child again then to have nightmares like this and scream myself awake? I should be ashamed of myself. It was only a dream! And perhaps everything is a dream: perhaps I never really ate the newspaper. Perhaps there never was a newspaper. Perhaps I never went to Tulbagh and never met a man with irons on his legs and chains on his arms. Perhaps I never had a child. How can I really be sure? All I have to prove that *something* happened is the tatters of my old jacket. But what does that amount to? I still know nothing about the newspaper, and now I'm too scared to ask. Suppose Pamela and Bet tell me they know nothing at all about it? All I can do is lie down again, and sleep. And then the ants return to gnaw and gnaw in my guts.

296

"You can't do this to me," I say to Nicolaas when at last I decide to talk to him. "Pamela is my woman, I chose her, and we want to get married. Now you expecting me to sleep alone, and the ants are eating me up."

"We need her in the house," he says, working on a new girth for his horse.

"You need her to clean up after supper," I say. "And then you need her again in the morning to make tea. In between she's mine. It's the only time we got to be together."

"There's nothing more to discuss," he says sharply, turning his back to me.

"Nicolaas!" I try to keep calm, but it's difficult. "I took Bet just because a man needs a woman. But Pamela I took because I want her to be mine. I never bothered much about women. She's the only one. Do you hear me?"

"Your work is waiting, Galant. Better get on with it before we have trouble again."

"If you don't let Pamela be you'll be the one looking for trouble."

He comes towards me with the newly cut girth in his hands. But at that moment Pamela comes from the kitchen, as if she's been standing inside listening to us; and she says: "Please keep out of this, Galant. I don't want to see another bad thing on the farm."

"You tell him that," I say, before I turn to walk off.

"Why are you wearing that torn jacket again?" Nicolaas calls after me. "How many times must I tell you I don't want to see the damned thing again?"

"It's my jacket."

"You're just wearing it to spite me."

"I'm wearing it because it is my child's."

Whistling, I go down to the kraal where we're raising the wall after a leopard managed to jump over the old one, barely a week ago. Straining to pick up and lift and settle the heavy stones I manage to contain the anger in me. Stone, stone, stone. But if he doesn't let Pamela be, I swear to the dark heart of the thunder, I can see a new storm coming. I've always

297

known it's better to keep out of women. It hurts you where you can't stop it. And with Pamela it's even worse. Trying to smother the thoughts I put everything I got into the lifting and stacking of the stones. But my mind stays out of it. It's Pamela I see before me. It's her voice I'm hearing. In the dark light of the lantern she asks: "Galant, who are you?" It's a word that tears me open, worse than any sjambok, ever. I'm lying on her, yet I cannot move, all because of that word. *Who are you?* Rooted deeply in her, I keep on talking and talking, telling her about Ma-Rose and Nicolaas and everybody; but I know it's not what I really want to say, it's not what I mean; it can't be what she wants to know. No one got the right to ask me: *Who are you?* I can try to tell her about my father—but who is he, what has become of him? About my mother—but where is she, what's happened to her? About Ma-Rose who brought me up; about Nicolaas who used to be my playmate. But those are other people, they're not I. To tell her what she wants to know: where do I begin, and how? In the dark of the night on which I'm drifting as on deep black water, I feel a blind knowledge welling up in me: I know something must happen, something must be done, somewhere I got to get to, so that she and I can know for sure: *This is me, I, Galant.* Now, in this moment, in this darkness, with her, inside her, I can feel myself although I cannot say it. This body with its bruises and cuts and scars, this body shaped from pain like a figure shaped from clay beside the dam of my childhood, this back and stomach and arms and legs, these balls heavy with life, this stiff root planted inside her. But can this be all? Surely there must be something more, something which can make others say long after I'm gone: *This is Galant.* And this is what I got to find: with her. Which is why no one in the world has the right to take her from me for in this night she has become a part of me without which I can never be Galant. Something in me is now forever chained to her, and willingly. Why does it not choke me then? Why this feeling that only with this chain on my body can I know the possibility of freedom? I try to find the sense of it but the thoughts lay too heavily in my mind.

When I fail to find relief in throwing stones I wait till nightfall to lead Nicolaas's big black stallion from the stable and ride bareback into the dark. The feeling of that great horse moving under me, the hooves thundering below, tears torn from my eyes by the wind. I'm like a stone picked up by an invisible hand and thrown into the air, never to touch the ground again. Perhaps death is like this.

But the moment I come back the ants return, gnawing and gnawing at me.

Pamela senses it. For what other reason would she slip from the house one night to come and soothe away those nightmare ants? She brings new light to my darkness, and once again her voice is in my ears in moans of joy: "Galant. Galant. Galant." In her voice I recognize myself. I know who I am. We are together.

On other nights she comes again, waiting for them to sleep before she unbolts the back door and slips out to me through the dark in her petticoat, soundless on her bare feet; and in her fertile furrow I plant my seed.

"What will they do if they find out?"

"They won't know. They all asleep."

I want to ask her: *Was he with you again? This wetness in you, is it his?* But I hold my tongue. It will bring a blight over everything and we have little enough.

"There's no need for them to know," she says. And just before daybreak she creeps out again; her place grows cold beside me.

But Nicolaas does find out. One morning, as I come into the kitchen with a bundle of wood, he is standing in front of the hearth where he has cornered her.

"Where were you last night?" he asks.

I put the wood down carefully, and the long-handled axe beside it.

"When I came to the kitchen last night you were gone," he says.

"She was with me," I tell him.

He pretends I'm not there. Still looking at Pamela he asks:

299

"Pamela, didn't I tell you I wanted you to stay in the house at night?"

"She was with me," I say again. "She is my wife and she comes to sleep with me."

"Let me be, Galant," she says quickly. "I'll have it out with the Baas myself."

"There's nothing to discuss," says Nicolaas. "Pamela, if you leave the house again at night I'll put the sjambok to you."

"You not allowed to beat a slave woman any more," I say. "Frans du Toit brought the newspaper that said so."

"What do you know about newspapers?"

Slowly I put out my hand and pick up the long axe, stroking the blade with my fingers. "We've spoken enough about Pamela," I tell him. "She's mine."

He stares hard at me; then at the axe.

"Galant," says Pamela.

"Look here," he interrupts her, speaking in sudden haste, "if I ever catch you coming in late in the morning there'll be trouble." Without another word he leaves the kitchen. At night she's mine again.

And now Pamela is with child. I can see her swelling. In the dark when she is with me, she puts my hand on her belly so that I can feel him stirring inside. Throughout the summer months, past harvesting and threshing, she carries the child, growing larger all the time; and I stride across the veld as if my feet no longer touch the earth. "There's a child coming," I tell Ontong. "Now everybody will know about Galant."

Usually it's she who brings our food to the lands—the wheatfields, the threshing-floor, the bean patch—whenever there's too much work for us to go home at midday. Sometimes it's Lydia or Bet; but mostly Pamela. Standing up to watch her as she comes towards us and walks away again, I feel something swimming and swelling inside me, fit to burst. There comes my woman. And it's our child she's carrying inside her. We are of today and yesterday; but he is tomorrow's dawn. "You wait. You'll all see him with your own eyes," I tell the others—Ontong and Achilles and the young ones, and the

300

hands from the Oubaas's farm, and Dollie and old Plaatjie Pas and also the white foreman Campher from Oubaas D'Alree's place, all working together to get the harvest home—"You'll see him. He'll be Galant just like me. And from where I stop walking he'll go on, all the way. With shoes on his feet."

But at night the anxiety returns; all sorts of different ants gnawing at me. For just about the time when I can feel the first stirrings of the child in Pamela's belly a bad thing takes place on Barend's farm. It's Goliath who's almost flogged to death after running off to Worcester to complain about working on Sunday or something. I'm in the stable feeding the horses when Nicolaas comes in with Barend who's just returned from the Drostdy. They are sorting the harnesses for tomorrow's threshing and when they start talking I keep out of sight behind the horses, for I can hear it's newspaper business they're discussing.

"There's a lot of new rumours about liberating the slaves," says Barend. "It's time we all join forces against the bloody English in the Cape."

"The slaves will stab us in the back," Nicolaas replies.

"We'll first shoot the slaves in a heap," says Barend. "I'd rather do that anyway than set them free. And then we can take on the English."

"You can count on me," says Nicolaas.

Barely a week afterwards we're told about an Englishman who's been shot off Elandsfontein and nearly killed.

"Now we got to watch out," I warn the others. "This is just what Barend and Nicolaas were talking about. So one of these days it's our turn."

"There are many more slaves than masters," says the foreman Campher, who is again with us. "If you all stand together they can't touch you."

An extraordinary man, Campher. Very thin, very blond, with a manner of speech different from ours, since he comes from another country. What amazes me is that he's as white as the masters, yet he's working with us like a slave. At Oubaas D'Alree's place he got a hut like Dollie and old Plaatjie Pas,

301

and when the slave bell is rung in the morning he has to fall in just like us. He's given his food and his daily *sopies* with us, although he's neither slave nor Hottentot and can come and go as he wishes.

"The way I see it," I tell him one day, "you must be a slave that ran away from your land."

He laughs loudly. "I've never been a slave in my life," he says. "Where I come from there are no slaves. Everybody is free."

"How can that be?" I ask. "Who does the work then?"

"Everyone does his own work."

"Don't believe you. They got slaves everywhere. Here and in Tulbagh and Worcester and in the Cape, everywhere. The only place there are no slaves is across the Great River, and those are runaways."

"The land I come from lies across the sea," says Campher. "There are many other countries too where there are no slaves."

"Must be true," says old Achilles. Usually he's very quiet, but for once he joins in our talk. "Where I was born, where the *'mtili*-trees grow, no one was a slave either. They came to catch us and made us slaves."

From that day I often catch myself staring at the man Campher, wondering what it must be like to sit behind his eyes and look at a land where there are no slaves.

"But if there's no slaves there," I ask him, "why must there be slaves in this place?"

"That's the way it is," he says. "But don't worry. It won't go on like this. One day everybody will be free here too."

At night when Pamela is with me I talk to her about the things Campher tells us on the lands. "Be quiet," she whispers, pressing her hand against my mouth. "The walls may hear you. These are dangerous stories."

"Campher says it's all true."

"How can you be sure that anything another man says is true?"

"When you tell me something I know it's true."

302

"Take me," she says. And this, I know, is true. Her body and mine, and the child between us; the child still to come but who is already inside her. It's true. No one can take him from us. Not even Nicolaas. There are some things even he cannot be *baas* over.

This is what I think when I am with Pamela, in the dark. But when the light returns and I find myself alone again, when she's slipped out quietly in my sleep to be back in the kitchen on time, I'm left wondering: Can I be sure that even this is true? Was she really here with me in the night, and I inside her, and the child moving between us? Or is it like the nightmare of the ants that never let me be? Truly, life is a mysterious and difficult thing.

All this is in my mind the day I ride out in search of the bullock. A Saturday. When we were cutting the young bulls the other day, his one hind leg got broken as we brought him down and so he was left with the young calves for the leg to mend; but at milking time that morning Achilles reports to me that the bullock has broken out. Knowing Nicolaas will be annoyed when he and the Nooi come back from Buffelsfontein where Nooi Cecilia's father has a birthday party, I decide to set out after it as soon as I'm through with the morning work.

"Where you going?" asks Ma-Rose when I pass her hut, all by itself on the low rise from where she can look out to all sides.

"That little bullock that broke its hind leg got away."

"I think I saw it grazing down there early this morning," she says, pointing. "What about some bush-tea before you go?"

"No, I'm in a hurry," I answer, for Ma-Rose is getting more and more talkative as she gets older.

At old D'Alree's place I dismount to enquire about the beast, but the little old man knows nothing about it: he's too short-sighted anyway, and all he's ever concerned with is cutting and sewing.

"Where's my shoes?" I ask him, not expecting much of an answer, for I have little trust in him left.

He only stares at me through his dusty round glasses and mumbles something about having to be more patient. So I

303

leave him and go to enquire from Dollie and old Plaatjie Pas who are cutting bushes on a new patch of land; and they point in the direction of the little stream that runs down from the next ridge.

But there's no sign of the bullock in the thickets on the banks of the stream; and as the chilly afternoon wears on I find myself moving further and further away from Houd-den-Bek, following the narrow valley between the mountains and round the bend of the Vaalbokskloofberg. From time to time when my hands grow too numb to hold the reins I stop to blow on them and rub some life back into them. In the late afternoon I reach Elandsfontein, where I go directly to the huts, as it's Saturday afternoon and I know everybody will be lying about.

"You're early," calls Abel from where he's sitting in the last patch of sun, holding his mug in both hands. "Have a drink."

"I'm just looking for a bullock that's run away, I'm not staying over. I got to get back to Pamela."

"Never let a woman tie you up too fast," says Abel.

Klaas comes towards us, suspicious and inquisitive as ever, looking hard at me. "I don't believe this bullock story," he grumbles. "Where's your pass?"

"Who're you to ask me for my pass?" I brush him off.

"Don't listen to that old cunt-face," jeers Abel.

It turns out that no one has seen the bullock; so I lead the horse to the water-barrel in the yard where he can drink before we set out for Houd-den-Bek again; the sun will be down soon.

"Good day, Galant," says Hester behind me.

It gives me a sudden wateriness in the legs to hear that voice; for it's the first time I see her again since that day in the stable, and it's a memory a man can get lost in.

"There's no need to look so nervous," she says. "Barend has gone to Lagenvlei."

"I didn't pass him on the way."

"He took the short cut through the mountain."

I tug at the reins to warn the horse. "I got to go back," I say, not looking at her. "I came to look for a bullock but Abel says he didn't come this way."

304

"You must be tired," she says. "Let me give you something to eat in the kitchen first."

"There's no need."

But without waiting for me to reply she goes towards the house ahead of me, her skirts swirling round her legs as she walks. The straightness of her body. It's always been like that. Suddenly, but why?, I remember the day with the snake. She's dying, I think, as I desperately tear open the ruffled leg of her pantalettes to reach the double marks of the fangs on her thigh. With clumsy fingers I open the little skin bag Ma-Rose has given me to carry with me wherever I go: and I press Ontong's snake-stone against the neat wound: the smooth round black stone with the grey spot in the centre, perforated with small holes: brought from his own land across the sea, and no poison can withstand its hidden powers. Holding her leg tightly against my chest I keep the stone pressed against it until all the poison is sucked out and she begins to feel better, although she's still pale and shaky. It takes an effort not to stare too openly at the thigh exposed by the tearing away of the lace. The smooth otter body of the dam. Keep away, Galant.

"Thank you, Galant. I'll never forget this."

Why shouldn't she? What is so special about pressing a snake-stone against a wound?

Forget it, I tell myself as I follow her across the great emptiness of the bare yard. From way back a man's voice speaks to me: *That's the worst you can do in this world.*

"Here's some meat for you. And bread."

"Thank you. I got to go now."

"There's some cold soup on the hearth. I'll warm it up for you."

"I've had enough. I'm not all that hungry."

"No, please stay. Come and wait in the kitchen. It's getting cold outside."

Somewhere in the front part of the house I can hear the children playing, but the middle door is closed and their sounds are muffled, making the house seem larger and emptier than it is. My throat feels tight. How close she is to me

305

as she bustles about stirring the coals, adding more wood, hanging the black pot on its chain. As if she is the slave and I the waiting master.

"How are things at Houd-den-Bek?" she asks, her back still towards me.

"No complaints."

"I hope Nicolaas hasn't—"

I don't answer. She turns round. A few strands of hair slide from behind her ears and shade her cheek. Her eyes are naked.

Naked I hang from a beam, my feet groping to touch the ground; the smell of horse-piss in my nostrils. Her hands. Quite shameless, her hands.

"He does things his own way," I say angrily, making an effort to counter the memories.

"You mustn't let him get you down."

"No one can do that."

"You know, I've always thought, even when we were children—" She pushes the hair away from her cheek and her voice closes up. "I suppose it's silly of me."

Outside the sun is down and the light is fading fast. But against the glow of the fire in the hearth I can see the gentle roundness of her cheek.

"What was it you were thinking?" I ask deliberately, finding in the falling dusk a reason to be more provocative than I would have dared to be in the light.

"You were the only one who really understood me."

"How can that be?"

"We were the only two who never belonged with them."

"The soup is burning."

She turns away hurriedly and resumes her stirring; after a while she ladles some out in a small bowl.

"Isn't it too cold for you to ride back now?" she says, watching me as I gulp down the soup.

"What else can I do?"

She is silent for a while. I finish the soup, still standing.

"That's true," she says, her voice shallow, like shallow water. "I suppose there really is nothing else you can do."

306

"Thank you for the soup."

"Let me give you a *sopie* for the road."

"I don't want to drink anything."

"Then take it with you."

She takes a small jug from the shelf and goes out to fill it in the *voorhuis*; coming back, she hands it to me.

"Thank you. I got to go now."

"Yes."

I go outside, stopping as the cold strikes me. Hesitating, I look back. She's standing on the threshold, her dark head leaned against the doorpost. But she says nothing.

On the far side of the farmyard I notice a shadow scampering past, stumbling over something in its way, mumbling a curse. It is Klaas.

Back home Pamela is still finishing her chores in the kitchen, and I give her the jug of brandy to put away on a shelf. Late in the night we hear the carriage returning from Buffelsfontein, and I have to get up again to help Nicolaas put away the horses.

"Where does this brandy come from?" he asks me the next morning.

"Hester gave it to me."

"What were you doing at Elandsfontein then?"

"I was looking for the lame bullock that got away."

"You should have known it could never go as far as that," he says, annoyed. "You stay away from Hester."

"She gave me something to eat."

He glares at me for a long time; but just when it seems to me that we're heading for trouble again, he swings round and walks away. That is the end of it, I think. But later the same morning, soon after the last frost has melted, Barend unexpectedly arrives on horseback, riding so hard that the animal is foaming at the mouth. For a while he and Nicolaas talk heatedly at the gate. Then, leading the horse behind them, they come towards me. Nicolaas is trembling with anger; his face as white as anything.

"Barend tells me he heard from Hester that you were

307

interfering with her last night," he says, his voice shaky.

I stare at them in amazement, my ears ringing with the sound of cicadas.

"Is that what Hester said?" I ask at last.

"Are you accusing me of lying?" shouts Barend.

Then it's back to the stable.

"Please don't go away to complain again, Galant," Pamela pleads with me, clinging to my legs. "You know it never works out."

"I'm not going to complain. This time I'm just running away. They won't ever find me again."

"You can't leave me behind like this. The child's time is coming close."

"I'm done with this place," I answer. "This is the end. One can take it for years. But one day you just know it's over."

"It is madness, Galant," she says, sobbing; and when I pay no heed to her she calls Ontong to talk to me. "Just give it time, man," he says. "Tomorrow things will look different again."

"It will never be different. I've had enough of this place and all its shit."

"Now don't make trouble again," says Achilles, sighing and shaking his grizzly head. "You'll bring a cloud over all of us."

"Then look after yourselves!" I shout. "I'm going off, this very night. I'm going all the way to Cape Town and I dare anyone to try and fetch me back."

They're all talking and shouting and threatening at the same time; and Pamela is crying. But I feel blind and deaf and numb; and the black ants are gnawing at my insides, crawling up in my throat and attacking the root of my tongue. I try to spit them out, but they won't let go. Tonight no one will stop me. Try anything you want to. Let the masters try too. Anyone. I'm going. Tonight I'm taking my freedom. I'm going to Cape Town. There I'll get on a boat and sail off to a land across the sea where there are no slaves. With my own eyes I shall see it. I'm taking my freedom. Let the ants do their damnedest.

KLAAS

If Baas Barend should get it into his head one rainy day to say: "It's dry," I'll answer without even looking up from my work: "Yes, Baas, it's dry." And if in the middle of the night he were to say: "The sun is shining," I'll answer without opening my eyes: "Yes, he's shining, Baas." One learns. In the early days I resisted. All it brought me was a raw back: worst of all that day the woman interfered to stop the flogging. Which was a bad thing. It was bad enough among us men; but when the woman came it turned bitter. Man is stone: you can see him clearly, you can walk round him and touch him, he's right there. But woman is water, you cannot stop it. That was what I couldn't bear.

Ever since then I did things his way and that made life easier. I was made *mantoor* and even Abel who used to be over me had to listen to me. By being a worm to the Baas I was given the right to shit on their heads. It made them so mad that sometimes I wondered whether I would wake up one morning with a knife between my shoulders. But what can one do? I had to survive.

I could have stayed in my hut the evening Galant was here. But I knew the woman was alone. I didn't mean anything bad, following them. It was just the feeling that, perhaps, this was my real chance. She'd come in among the men the day of the flogging; no insult to a man's pride could be worse than that. And now, perhaps, I could have my own back.

"Galant interfered with the Nooi tonight," I told Baas Barend when he came home. "And she didn't stop him either."

In a way that even gave me a hold on him. He would never look me in the eyes again; that gave me a power I'd never known, even though I remained a slave. And it had really been so easy.

309

DU TOIT

When they need me, in the face of danger or perplexity, it is with alacrity and enthusiasm that they call on me, addressing me as "Field-cornet" or "good old Frans"; but as soon as everything·has returned to normal they no longer feel the need to acknowledge me. The mothers hide their daughters when I turn up on their farms, and the men are invariably too busy to invite me in. When there are new proclamations on grazing licences or the *Opgaaf* or regulations on slaves I'm instructed by Landdrost Trappes to spread the news through the district: but the farmers blame me personally for it, as if I were responsible for promulgating the law. For the representatives of the Government I'm a wretched bumpkin they can order to fetch and carry as it pleases them; for the Boers I'm the darling of the English, a harbinger of evil with the Devil's own mark on my face. And when I feel driven beyond endurance by the need and the desire of my lonely flesh, I realize in my humiliation that God Himself must have rejected me. No curse is for them too terrible to brand me with. But the moment anything untoward occurs in the district it's once again the Field-cornet who must be solicited and courted to help them out.

Like the time the slave Galant absconded. I was rather suspicious when I heard about his desertion, knowing too well that there had been trouble between Nicolaas van der Merwe and his slave before: every now and then a complaint or a report of new conflict; and Landdrost Trappes had asked me to keep a special eye on the Van der Merwes who had proved themselves only too ready to take the law in their own hands.

The problem was that one couldn't simply arrive unannounced on a farm to make enquiries, for those farmers were fiercely possessive of their slaves. It was better not to get involved unnecessarily. On the other hand I knew Galant to be a difficult character; on one occasion he'd landed me personally in a most unfortunate position, but it is a matter that does not concern the present instance.

"Are you sure it's necessary to send out a search party?" I asked Nicolaas after he'd explained the case.

"Would I have come to ask you if it wasn't necessary?"

"For how long has he been gone?"

"Three days."

"What makes you think he didn't just go to Worcester again?"

"He told the labourers before he left that he was going to Cape Town."

"Give him another couple of days just to be on the safe side."

"You want to make quite sure he gets away?"

"I want to see justice done. To round up a commando only to find out afterwards that he'd done no more than exercise his right to lodge a complaint in Worcester seems rather extravagant to me."

"Frans, you're just as bad as the damned English with whom you are in league."

"I'm not in league with anyone." His irresponsible accusation cut me to the quick: how often had I heard it before? "In a civilized land there must be respect for law and order, otherwise everything will go to pieces."

"Look, if you're too scared to do something, then tell me, so that I can round up my neighbours myself to hunt the slave. But then we'll do it *our* way."

"But don't you understand?" I said, trying to be as reasonable as I could. "In the old days it was different. Every man had to fend for himself. But the world has changed, Nicolaas. There are more and more people around, the towns are getting more populated and they're moving closer to us. Now the law

311

must be enforced to make sure that one man's justice doesn't become another's injustice."

"You can be very glib about justice and injustice. To you it's something you read about in books or newspapers. To us it's a matter of life and death."

"But not each man for himself, Nicolaas. We're not animals."

"Who are you to talk? No pig can feel safe near you."

It took all the restraint I could muster not to strike him with my riding crop. The insults one has to learn to bear.

"A lot of people living together don't create a civilization just like that, Nicolaas," I pointed out. "One needs a law before which all men are equal."

"Not if it affects my right to decide for myself what is to happen on my own farm."

"It's a price we all have to pay. Each must give up a measure of his freedom to ensure justice for all. And even if it means that some individual has to bear the brunt of it from time to time, it is still worth while, for the sake of an ordered world that guarantees justice and room for everybody."

"It's always easier to talk than to do something," he said in bitter reproach.

"I believe in what I'm saying!" My voice sounded more shrill than I would have liked it to be; but it was terribly important to me to make him understand my urgency. What, if not justice, was there for me to believe in? What would become of us all unless we agreed to step in under a single legal yoke and pull together in one team? If we forfeited that it would mean negating the very meaning of our presence in the land: and all our forefathers would have lived in vain. Law. Law and order. This was the only passion permitted me. The only recourse in a miserable world.

"The law has become your God!" he said contemptuously.

"Certainly not. But we cannot survive without it."

"Let me tell you something," Nicolaas said. "No law can be good in itself. It depends on who applies it. Only a man whose hands are clean dare handle a law. Else it's smudged with his own dirty fingermarks."

312

"You're being personal again, just because you can't stand me."

"No." In his characteristic manner he pushed his right hand through his white hair so that it stood stiffly upright. "I'm only surprised that you should find it necessary to preach such a long sermon when the only thing I asked of you was to bring back Galant."

In the end I persuaded him to postpone action for one more day. I would have preferred a longer period, but the next morning old D'Alree's foreman Campher brought me a message that Galant had been to their place—in search of a pair of shoes, of all things!—and when he was turned away he went to a grazing place of old Piet van der Merwe where he stole a gun. That left me with no option but pursuit.

I called up a dozen men for commando duty—I, the two young Van der Merwes, Campher, old Jan du Plessis, D'Alree, and six Hottentots—all of us armed. We rode out from my farm, past Elandsfontein, and over the mountain to the grazing place where old Piet's slave Moses was in charge. However, he couldn't tell us anything about the robbery as it seems he'd gone to Lagenvlei for new provisions the previous day. The two Hottentots, Wildschut and Slinger, told us their story, which I took with a pinch of salt since their versions differed rather startlingly on several points. In broad outline it seemed that while they'd been asleep the previous night their gun had been stolen; and upon waking up in the morning they were confronted by Galant who threatened them with the gun and ordered them to slaughter and roast a lamb for him; after devouring a substantial part of it he packed the rest into a knapsack and went off into the mountains, waving his hat at them and announcing that he was now on his way to Cape Town.

These mountains make search or pursuit well-nigh impossible. Rocks, cliffs, boulders, precipices. Horses are useless and even on foot one makes difficult progress. Out of the question to look for tracks: the terrain is too rocky and uneven for that.

313

And Galant had been born in this neighbourhood: he knew it like the back of his hand.

"I'm still puzzled by something," I said to Nicolaas. "What on earth made him decide on such a drastic step? In the past he always came back on his own."

"He just ran away."

"After a flogging?"

"Does it make any difference?"

"But what did he do?"

"Well, if you really want to know." He posted himself directly in front of me. His nostrils were deadly white, and flaring. "He interfered with my sister-in-law."

"You mean he—?"

"What he did or didn't do is no concern of yours!" Barend interrupted, grabbing me by the lapels. "You just do your job and bring him back. Dead or alive."

But it was impossible in those mountains. After the first few hours we split up into several small groups in order to spread out across a wider area to prevent him from slipping past us in the direction of the Rear-Witzenberg, on the way to Cape Town. But he'd already disappeared without a trace. For five days we went on scouring the mountains, but then the farmers had to return to their work. The weather had worsened too: the real Bokkeveld winter that made one grit one's teeth with cold. A sudden spread of snow when we got up one morning. A sky murky in the howling North-wester. No hope at all to track him down.

"Well, I suppose that's that," Barend said grimly. "Let's hope the bastard froze to death."

After the snow had melted and the wind abated slightly, I sent out a few more search parties, giving the Hottentots a firm instruction: "If you find a spoor, then follow it wherever it leads, even if it means going all the way to the Salt River in the Cape." But after another fruitless week they, too, gave up. For all we knew Galant had either died in the mountains or reached Cape Town.

It must have been more than a month after his desertion

314

that I heard about his unexpected return to Houd-den-Bek. Quite voluntarily it seemed. The gun he'd stolen he handed over to Nicolaas, and he willingly accepted his due punishment. And that appeared to have settled the matter. The farmers were free to forget about me again.

THYS

It was a changed Galant who came back from the Cape, descending from the mountains after the last snow had melted. He was very thin and sinewy, his hands and feet cracked, his face ashen. But there was a gleam in his eyes, the way a man might look when he's seen something he has never seen before. I'm not sure how to put it, except that he looked new and different, as if he'd been washed inside and out.

Rooy and I were the first who saw him. We'd just come back with the sheep from the winter grazing in the Karoo, and we were mending a hole in the temporary kraal of logs and branches we'd put up for the new lambs, where the jackals had broken in the night before. Galant came down to us and sent me to the Baas to find out whether it would be all right for him to come back and give up his gun. If not, he would just be on his way again.

"Of course," the Baas said, looking terribly pleased with the news. "If he gives himself up I won't hold anything against him." One could see he really felt relieved, for things had been going badly on the farm without Galant to run it.

But the Baas did not behave properly towards Galant. After all he'd promised, and after Galant had given up his gun, when he came to the kitchen for food, the Baas suddenly lost his temper and started beating him with his *kierie*, until it broke. And when we thought it was all over, the next morning, the Baas called Ontong and Achilles to tie Galant up in the stable; and it was a bad thing, the way he was flogged then. We all expected him to run away again after that, as we'd known him to do in the past. But all he did was to keep away from all of us for a long time, without saying a word to anyone. Which is why I said he was a changed man. He stayed with Pamela until her child was born, for her time was near. And when, afterwards, we asked him about his plans he just shook his head and said his days for running away were over. Life was different now.

"I saw many things in the Cape when I was there," he said. "And I know my place is here. I got to be at my own place when the freedom comes."

"What freedom?"

"They all know about it in Cape Town. It won't be long now. They told me the things the newspapers spoke about is just the beginning. We won't be going about barefoot for much longer now."

And then he started telling us about the Cape. He'd seen the man of the Tulbagh jail again, the Man-without-a-name who'd been taken away in irons. The man had overpowered his guards on the way to Cape Town, said Galant; and he'd broken open his chains with a crowbar, and now he was going about as a free man, hiding in the bushes of the Table Mountain in the daytime and coming out to hunt at night, like a leopard. And it was this man who told Galant that the people were making preparations for the big day.

That was only the beginning of Galant's stories. He told us about the horse races in Green Point. Someone had lent him a horse and he'd won, which didn't surprise us for we all knew Galant's way with horses. With the money they gave him for winning he bought the horse for himself. A great grey stallion, he said, the best horse the Cape had ever seen. And from then on he just kept on winning, winning all the time. But the other men at the races were getting envious about all his wins, so they sent soldiers to catch him, saying he'd been causing a disturbance. There was a hell of a fight. They just kept on shooting and they even killed his horse and took all his money; so he and his friends had to hide in the Mountain. But in the night they came down and attacked the barracks, and the second battle was even worse than the first. The cannon was brought down from the Lion's Rump, and many people were

317

shot to pieces. At daybreak they nearly caught Galant, but he got away and hid himself on a ship in the harbour, a ship bigger than three houses. But just as it started to sail away a fire broke out and the ship went down and everybody drowned except Galant who swam ashore.

Another time there was a man who ran amok in the streets, attacking people with an axe as far as he went, chopping them to bits; in the end it was Galant who overpowered him and took away his axe. For that, everybody said, he deserved his freedom. So he was taken to the Governor's room deep in the heart of the Castle, but unfortunately the Governor wasn't there that day, so the whole plan had to be dropped. Afterwards, said Galant, he went right up the mountain to where one could see all the way to the Bokkeveld. And then he pissed from the highest cliff and it hit the Governor who just happened to be passing below. So Galant was caught and taken to the gentlemen of the court, and they said he had to be tied to four horses and torn apart; but on the appointed day, when they took him to the town square, he recognized his own grey stallion that he thought had been killed but wasn't, so he started speaking softly to it; and just as they prepared to tie him up he tore himself loose and jumped on the back of the big grey stallion and galloped off. From then on he had to keep out of the town, so he lived with his friend, the Man-without-a-name, in the bushes on the Mountain. When it got dark they came out and made merry in the streets. Once they broke into the Church and held a party; all the slaves from the Cape were there and they danced right through the night. They made friends with the slaves from the Castle and arranged for them to steal food from the Governor's own table, dishes and dishes the likes of which no one in the Bokkeveld had ever seen. And they discussed everything about taking their freedom. They wanted Galant to be their leader and promised him he could live in the Castle when the big day came; and Pamela too. But first they wanted him to go back to the Bokkeveld to prepare the people for the day of freedom. Which was why in the end he came back to the Bokkeveld and gave up his gun. And that was why he couldn't care less about the floggings, for he knew it wouldn't be long; it was just a matter of bearing it for a little while longer.

"I could have stayed there," he often said to us. "It's a good life in the Cape. But I came back so that we can all be together when our freedom comes." And then he would take us one by one to ask each in turn: "What do you say? Are you with me or against me?"

"If that day is really coming," Abel said, "I'll be right at your side. Dancing all the way to the Cape."

"You can count on me," Dollie also joined in. "If the Cape is such a good place why don't we go there right away?"

"Because this is our place," Galant answered. "We got to walk about right here with shoes on our feet."

"I think I'll stand by you," Goliath said, still rather cautiously. "But I got to be really sure it won't go wrong, for then we've had it."

The people from Oubaas Piet's place also had their say; as well as those from Buffelsfontein. Only Ontong and Achilles seemed careful not to take sides.

"Let's wait and see first," they said. "If the day comes we can make up our minds. We don't want unnecessary trouble, man."

So each man had his own opinion about it. And in the end Galant would come round to me and Rooy: "What about you two? Are you with us?"

I tried to keep out of it for as long as I could, but it wasn't easy. I was scared by all the talking. What was it to me? I had my work to do and it was about as much as I could manage. Minding the sheep, and preparing the clay when it was time for replastering the walls of the outbuildings and the farmyard wall, planting and harvesting beans, weeding and cleaning new lands and burning scrub, enough to keep one going all year round; and at the first sign of dawdling or skimping the Baas would be there with his strap. And there was Rooy to keep an eye on too. The day our mother died of the cough, she left Rooy in my care because he was still a child, and when the

319

Baas hired me I persuaded him to take Rooy too. He didn't seem very keen, for Rooy must have looked very small and helpless, but in the end he took us both. And to keep the Baas satisfied I saw to it that Rooy did his bit, even though in the beginning it was only light work like chopping wood, gathering dung, burning scrub and so on. Sometimes Rooy gave me trouble, for whenever he got the chance he would slip away to throw stones at birds, or rob their nests, or catch meerkats, or play around the *vlei* dam; what else could one expect of a child? But I did my best to keep an eye on him and to teach him what he needed to know, the way our mother had told me to.

Which was why I was troubled by Galant's talk. But he wouldn't let me be. Every now and then he would corner me again to ask: "Well, how's it with you and Rooy? Can I count on you? Are you with us?"

"How can we be with you?" I would protest. "We're not slaves that got to be made free. We're Hottentots, we're Khoin. So we're free already."

"Show me your freedom," Galant would mock me. "Where is it? Whose farm is this you walking on barefoot? Who is it gives you food and beatings? Who tells you to come and go?"

"We can go away if we want to."

"Then they just fetch you back. Right or wrong?"

"It's so," I had to admit, beginning to feel very worried about what he said. "But it still doesn't make slaves out of us. It's better for us to stay out of it."

"It's not a matter of better or worse, Thys." Galant was looking right through me as if he could see the Cape far away. "No use you saying you want to keep out of it. When that day comes it's going to be one big flood that takes the lot of us along. So it's better to choose now. Else it may be too late."

"Give me time."

"Time's short, Thys. It's masters on one side and the rest of us on the other. There's no difference between slave and Khoin no more. We all go barefoot."

Then I would stare away into the silence, wishing I could

320

see the Cape as he did. For there was no telling what I would do if that flood came of which he spoke. I was scared. And beside me, from the way he was pressing tightly against me, I knew that Rooy was just as scared. For whatever Galant said it was their business, not ours: a matter of masters and slaves, not of Khoin. Why draw us into it too? Could it really be like he said: that when the flood came no one would be able to keep out of it?

I was scared.

Deep in my heart I knew it would be a wonderful feeling to be marching down to the Cape with a gun over my shoulder, free to go wherever I wished, without having to glance over my shoulder all the time at the Baas standing behind me.

But I was scared. I was scared of the changed Galant. And of that freedom threatening us all.

NICOLAAS

The flood. Taken by themselves—mere bits of flotsam and jetsam in the torrent—the events of the two years between the night we'd sheltered in the mountains and the July night when Galant ran away to the Cape were perhaps unimportant and redeemable; but all the time I was aware of the dark motion continuing, gathering momentum, tearing at my remaining roots. So often I thought: If only something visible and graspable would present itself to grapple with and overcome; if only the adversary had the innocence of those afflictions of the past—Bushmen, pests, droughts or floods—I might confront it and survive. But in this anonymous flood I was helpless. And most ineffectual of all was the Word which had earlier been such an easy and obvious lamp to my foot. The fault, of course, lay in myself, in my sin. God had turned His face against me, rendering His own Word powerless in my mouth. Around us was the groundswell of threats, prohibitions, prescriptions and regulations from the Cape, issued and withdrawn it seemed at random, and the increasing menace of an unknown force from outside, beyond the deceptive protection of the mountains, threatening to overtake our lives. Inside was the growing uncertainty about where I stood, not only on my own farm but in my own life: was I central to it or had I become peripheral? There was this thing inside me, this rage, this madness, breaking out when I should restrain it, causing me to panic when I was supposed to be reasonable and collected.

And there was Hester, too. Even after losing her to Barend I'd clung to her as an image of ultimate salvation: until she turned against me, and away from me: *You're disgusting. I'm ashamed of you.* And when Galant went to her that day, behind my back, what unspeakable dark deed did he perpetrate of which neither he nor Barend would say a word? Impossible to demand the truth from her: I'd already lost whatever "right" I'd ever had to be frank with her and expect frankness in return.

Flogging him for it was a terrible way of torturing myself; and when he ran away, a last grasp I retained on her was gone, since only he could tell the truth. Whatever happened, he had to be retrieved; and killed if need be. Would that remove the menace, the lie, the lack of knowledge? I don't think it really mattered. It was a blind intuitive urge to destroy something in the hope that life would miraculously spring from it. To catch him and drag him back in chains or thongs, to make him run home ahead of our horses, would reassert my paltry authority over him and through him over the life I could feel slipping from my hands. But he escaped, which was the worst insult, I thought, he could hurl at me. Except that there was one still worse I had not expected and which he cannily prepared: his return. Of his own free will he gave up the gun, offering no resistance; he was, in fact, smiling. I tried to beat it out of him, but realized in time the futility of it, and stopped. All night I lay awake beside the gently snoring body of the woman who was my wife: I couldn't even seek solace from Pamela, as she was too far advanced in pregnancy. And anyway, without even asking my permission, she'd left the house after supper to return to his hut, as if it were the most natural thing in the world (and wasn't it?) and I had no say in the matter at all. There was an uncontrollable urgency in my body, and no means of expending it. In a rage increased by disgust I reached down to touch myself, to rid myself of the bitterness that was building up, gathering heavily in my stomach, and in that root of shame at which I tore in hate. Cecilia woke up; she knew what was happening.

"Aren't you ashamed?" she said. "Your hand will wither. Why don't you take me if you have to?"

I turned away, but she would not be denied. Naturally,

when at last I yielded, I was impotent again. Her scorn was even worse in silence, leaving me with a rage more destructive than ever before. All because of this man, Galant, who in voluntarily returning to his serfdom had demonstrated nothing so much as the compass of my own bondage. I had not chosen this for myself, God. It had been Your decision. I was caught in Your inscrutable will.

In the morning I had Galant flogged again. I wanted to destroy him utterly, finally to rid myself of the evil conscience he'd become. But at last I stopped. It was becoming a mockery. Instead of asserting myself I was humiliating myself in all their smouldering eyes; in his.

"Untie him," I ordered Ontong and Achilles.

All day long I sat in the house with the Bible. From now on, God help me, I would never lose my self-control again. If something was in fact gathering to destroy me at least I would have no hand in it: withered or otherwise. Let God be the judge of my intentions.

1 Chronicles 21: *So the Lord sent pestilence upon Israel: and there fell of Israel seventy thousand men.*

And God sent an angel unto Jerusalem to destroy it: and as he was destroying, the Lord beheld, and he repented him of the evil, and said to the angel that destroyed, It is enough, stay now thine hand. And the angel of the Lord stood by the threshingfloor of Ornan the Jebusite.

And David lifted up his eyes, and saw the angel of the Lord stand between the earth and the heaven, having a drawn sword in his hand stretched out over Jerusalem. Then David and the elders of Israel, who were clothed in sackcloth, fell upon their faces.

And David said unto God, Is it not I that commanded the people to be numbered? even I it is that have sinned and done evil indeed; but as for these sheep, what have they done? let thine hand, I pray thee, O Lord my God, be on me, and on my father's house; but not on thy people, that they should be plagued.

Then the angel of the Lord commanded God to say to

324

David, that David should go up, and set up an altar unto the Lord in the threshingfloor of Ornan the Jebusite . . .

And David built there an altar unto the Lord, and offered burnt offerings and peace offerings, and called upon the Lord; and he answered him from heaven by fire upon the altar of burnt offering.

And the Lord commanded the angel; and he put up his sword again into the sheath thereof.

GALANT

There's a silence on the mountain when it snows. In the falling of a stone one hears the silence that comes before it as well as the silence that follows. The men on commando must have gone away a long time ago, they won't be able to stand this cold. In the cave I'm protected against the worst, and I have my kaross with me; but a fire would be useful. When things get too bad I build a small one and light it by rubbing twigs together. But one has to be careful that the smoke will not be seen from the valley below.

Little difference between night and day. Cold. My body grows chapped and dry; scaly like a tortoise. Hands, feet, ears. My ribs begin to show. But I got to survive; it's important. From time to time I trek to one of the more distant farms to catch a sheep, taking care to avoid the dogs and to cut up the carcass and leave bits of skin behind to make it look like the work of a jackal or hyena. They mustn't know I'm right here in the mountains. They think I'm far away in the Cape like I told Ontong and the others.

When one sits hunched up like this, arms clutching oneself, fingers touching one's own hard ribs, there is a new intimate awareness of the body. My fingers move from one scar to the next, some old, others still covered with scabs. I read myself like a newspaper. Here all my life is written up: every callus, every cut and scar and ridge and hollow, every mark telling of something specific; all of it carried with me wherever I go. That's why it's useless to trek to the Cape. At last it is very clear to me: one can run away from a place and from some people; but one's body can never be left behind. And in your body places and people are contained. This bite on my shoulder: Pamela. This callus: handling the pitchfork on Oubaas Piet's farm. This mark: Nicolaas's sjambok. This old burn: Ma-Rose's three-legged iron pot. One cannot escape. And then there are those other scars, those that leave no mark on the body and which are invisible to the eye, but which remain inside: the ridges and marks you discover in your sleep, in your thoughts, your dreams. This word; that look; that gesture. *You can't go swimming with us today, for Hester is with us.* A lion tumbling head over heels as the bullet hits it. Sitting together under a hairy kaross: Hester, Hester.

It's because of her that I'm here. She told Barend: "Galant interfered with me."

High up in the attic I lie on my stomach; and peering through the slit in the floorboards I see the man lying on the big bed; the woman on the chair staring through the window. I cannot grasp it at all. In its total simplicity it eludes me. And now I'm looking down from another height, this time at myself. And once again I fail to understand.

All I know is that I'm here. This is my body: feel it. I am Galant. This, at least, at last, I know. There is no place for me in the Cape. I'm here, in this low deep cave while the snow is snowing outside; and in the falling of a stone I hear its surrounding silences.

My feet will have no difficulty finding the road to the Cape: I've trekked on that journey so many times in my mind. But it will be only my feet: I'll remain behind here, in these mountains. For down there at Houd-den-Bek is a woman bearing my child inside her. Tomorrow's sun waiting to rise. Now it's night; but the sun will rise from her. How can I leave her? I'm not free to go. One enters between a woman's legs and is caught forever. Inside her a child is shaped who holds on to me. I can pretend not to know about it; I can pretend that the road to Cape Town will make me forget. But cornered in the snow, where I have nothing else to do but think, with everything gathered up inside my body, I know very clearly: it is impossible to escape. Running away is the solution of a

327

coward and it gets you nowhere, for your body goes with you and everything is right there in the body.

Hester.

No: through her own word against me that bond, I think, is finally broken. From her I'm free at last. I have to be.

Pamela: from her nothing can set me free, because of the child who will rise from her.

To be free is not going to the Cape. It's not wandering through the mountains either. My feet remain bare: it is the mark that brands me. To be free is to want to be where you belong: to dare to be who you are.

The swallows that stayed behind that other winter: I understand them now.

Back to the beginning every time. The woman; the child. The child.

In the melting snow I come down the mountain, running like water. I give myself up in order to return to the child. It is like reaching the place for the first time. As if it is wholly new. I have chosen it for myself.

Tied to the manger, while the blows break the skin of my back and rip into the already scarred flesh, thought breaks from me like a falling stone. All the endless tales of setting free the slaves. Here I am. My hands are tied. But I shall repeat those tales to them until they believe me.

I am back with the woman in whose belly life is blindly stirring, like a fish. Ma-Rose moves in with us to be at hand when she's needed.

In the night the waters break. The child struggles to swim free. Pamela heaves and sobs and moans to rid herself of the terrible burden.

At sunrise the child lies sleeping in her arm. A child with white hair and blue eyes.

A stone falling endlessly. And in it the silence of before and after.

328

PART THREE

CAMPHER

Surely it can't go on like this forever. How often did I comfort myself with this thought; including the day we were reaping in the fields, and the afternoon on the threshing-floor. Then I would see Mother's face in my mind, old before her time, and worn out, and dog-tired. How many more times? "Joseph," she'd always said, "I can foresee only one of two things for you: you'll either make a fortune or die on the gallows." Adding, with a sigh and a shake of her grey head (she must have turned grey before she was thirty): "I'm sure I don't know who you take after. Definitely not my side of the family." Which, if Father was present, would lead to a new argument. He was from Northern Brabant and we lived not far from Breda; while she was from the south, from the Belgian territory, so that great explosions of temper were frequent in our home. "Just you wait, Mother," I would try to comfort her. "I'll show you. The world will look up to me yet." Perhaps we both had reason for believing what we did, for I'd been born with a cowl, which from my earliest age had prompted a wide variety of predictions about my future, alternately dire and enthusiastic. In the meantime all I could really be sure about was that whatever lay ahead for me wouldn't tumble into my lap by itself; I would have to get out and make it happen. We were like a great litter of puppies, with not enough teats available for all; and the only way to survive was either by outwitting or by outfighting the others.

From as far back as I can remember we were surrounded by wars and rumours of war; and the armies took turns to march through our sandy region—Austrians, Prussians, French; while at Hondschooten and Camperdown the English announced their presence on the coast. One day we would be a republic, the next a kingdom, or part of the French empire. I grew up with the names of the members of the House of Orange; then came Pichegru (his name in our home the equivalent of Beelzebub's; in Father's mouth the account of his progress from Antwerp to 's-Hertogenbosch and Nijmeghen sounded like a voyage of Lucifer; and what his soldiers had done to Mother and my sisters in the house while Father and the rest of us were guarded by bayonets in the pigsty, I only realized many years later, although I'd long suspected that it must have been something atrocious, judging from the way Elsje turned soft in the head, able only to utter unintelligible sounds); and afterwards Louis Napoleon.

On our small farm, where we burned charcoal to make a living for the thirteen of us, and planted cabbages and turnips for our own table and the market—when they were not tending the poultry and the pigs the girls worked inside with Mother, spinning and weaving—all the slogans of those times came whirling past like rags blown by the wind and left fluttering in a hedge; and because they were all in a foreign language they reminded one of the magic chants from the fairy tales Mother used to tell us. *Liberté—egalité—fraternité*: three hot coals smouldering in one's stomach of a winter's night when one lay with a wriggling assortment of brothers and sisters listening to rain and wind or to the silence of snow, while on the other side of the wooden partition the cow and the goats and pigs would be trampling and uttering their low moans or sudden squeals. *Les droits de l'homme. La commune. Vive la république.* The men drinking their gin round the scrubbed table in the evenings—Mother sitting apart from them in the semi-darkness, darning or crocheting, a grey mouse with red-rimmed eyes and a perennial drop at the tip of her nose—and recklessly throwing the magic words about. *L'homme est né libre et partout il est dans les fers.* Father slamming his fist down on the table amid a clattering of plates: "You can bloody well say that again! All the lot of us have ever seen of the so-called liberty everybody is going mad about, is

332

famine and misery. The whole season's turnips carried off by that last bunch of soldiers. A month's charcoal requisitioned just like that. And my wife and daughters—my Elsje—!" There his voice would falter, for Elsje had been his favourite; and then another thundering blow of his fist.

All the time that one name repeated again and again, no matter what the topic of discussion was. Napoleon. Napoleon. The Breaker of Chains. The Liberator. "Liberator my arse!" Father again. "If this is liberation I'd like to see oppression." And Mother's whining, monotonous reprimand: "Geerd, Geerd, not in front of the children."

Three of my brothers joined the army; two of them died within a year, one for Austria, the other for France, and the third came home with one leg missing. Once again Father was cursing to high heaven. "And then they have the nerve to go on talking about Liberty—Equality—Fraternity!" (A spurt of yellowish tobacco juice would come squirting through the gap between his large front teeth.) "All we've seen of it so far is its bloody backside. And that looks pretty grim." "Oh Geerd. Oh Geerd, how can you?"

I had to admit that he was probably right. Still, in the dark nights when the wind was tugging at the corners of the house, the words would continue to reverberate in my mind. *Liberté. Egalité. Fraternité.* Somewhere beyond those words, beyond the misery and poverty, the charcoal and the turnips and the rags and the mumbling sounds from Elsje's open mouth, I believed, a tremendous reality must be lurking. Otherwise I could see no sense in anything.

The outlook became even more bleak after Father's death, just a few weeks after he'd finally decided to leave home in spite of all Mother's protests, and join the army to teach Napoleon a lesson. Unfortunately there was nothing heroic in his death: on his way to Hohenlinden he stumbled over a dog and shot himself in the chest.

By that time I'd already discovered, thanks to the inspiration of Ome Fons, Mother's consumptive elder brother, that war itself could be turned into profit if among all the scattered armies constantly moving about one could turn up with the right contraband at the right time and place. Soon our activities escalated into a broadly based underground resistance movement against the foreign occupiers. My remaining unscathed elder brother Diederik was the leader of our group. Eventually it was decided that on a given Wednesday night we would blow up the barracks of the garrison stationed at Oosterhout. At the last moment my courage failed me: thinking of poor Mother who'd already lost so much in the war I decided I owed it to her not to endanger my own life. So I packed all my possessions into a knapsack and ran off to join the war on the Tuesday night. (Afterwards I learned that the attempt had failed and that both Ome Fons and Diederik had been among the dead: sure proof of the protective powers of my cowl.)

Mother was weepy when I woke her up to say good-bye. "You're not even sixteen yet, Joseph," she pleaded. But I pressed a finger to her lips. "I'm big for my age, Mother. I can easily pass for eighteen. And it's high time I started doing something for the family."

"We're dirt poor, Joseph, but we've always managed."

"It's not good enough for my mother. Besides, I've always told you—I can feel it in my bones—that there are great things in store for me. It's time I set out to find my fortune." Thrusting my fist into the air I whispered proudly in her ear: "Liberté. Egalité. Fraternité."

"Oh Joseph, Joseph, Joseph," she sobbed. "You can't even pronounce them right."

"You'll see, Mother."

And so I went off in search of the Black Angel, firmly expecting history to open like a gate and let me through. I could already hear the trumpets. Stand back for the man with the cowl!

Like hell. All that happened was that for years on end I plodded through the length and breadth of Europe, mostly on foot. Other soldiers around me held forth with shining faces about the great battles they'd been in—Ulm and Austerlitz,

334

Jena, Vimiero, Götschen, Leipzig, a veritable fanfare of names—but all I ever saw of the glory I'd expected was blood and shit, exhaustion, rags, misery, dead horses, curses; and unremitting hunger.

Disillusioned with both sides I finally joined a band of vagabonds and deserters that followed the troops like a pack of scavengers, living off the spoils and leftovers of the armies. When peace was concluded and the talking began at Vienna I made up my mind to shake the dust of a ruined and impoverished Europe from my feet and to try out England.

Mother was inconsolable, but I refused to be dissuaded. "I've tried Europe," I explained to her as patiently as I could, "but it didn't work out. Surely it couldn't all have happened in vain. You've got to keep faith. I promise you, Mother, you'll die a rich woman yet."

"There isn't much time left for me, Joseph. Of the eleven children I had there are only four left, and of those one is a cripple and another an imbecile: now you want to leave me too."

"Not for long, Mother. I know it's just waiting round the corner. England is full of opportunities."

But what with all the soldiers streaming home after the war there was little sympathy for foreigners. I was employed in a succession of miserable little temporary jobs—in a coal mine, in a boot factory, even in the potato fields—but it wasn't the life I'd anticipated or thought I deserved; so I began to show an interest in reports of more distant countries. There was much talk of America where, it seemed, the resounding slogans of my youth had already come true and people lived in freedom and prosperity. Others spoke about Australia. Still others about the Cape of Good Hope. That was a name that appealed to me, and it so happened that when I reached Southampton there was a ship ready to sail for the south, which decided matters for me.

But my arrival was inauspicious to say the least. A terrible wind kept us out of Table Bay for five full days and nearly broke the anchor chains; even when we were finally allowed to

335

go ashore the wind was blowing with such ferocity that it was all one could do to stay upright; and the whole Mountain was hidden under a sullen bank of white cloud.

A couple of Malay slaves in charge of a small cabinet-making business on the Buitengracht offered me lodging in their shop for a week, in exchange for most of the tobacco and arrack I'd been able to smuggle ashore. Thanks to the efforts and connections of the head carpenter Mustapha I was offered work on a wine farm near Constantia. "Do you have any experience of viticulture?" the farmer, Sias de Wet, asked me, openly suspicious. "I learned all about it in France," I assured him. "In the Vendée, in Burgundy, in the Médoc, all over." That was something my late Ome Fons, rest his corrupt soul, had taught me at a very impressionable age: If someone asks you whether you're qualified for a given job, the answer is always yes. For one can pick up any trick or technique; but if you say no, the opportunity is lost. And I did learn the ropes quite soon. If I botched a job I would soon pacify De Wet by explaining that I'd been doing it the French way but that I was quite prepared to adapt to the methods of this remote colony. In the end we got along very well indeed; but I couldn't stand it for more than two years. History was still waiting for me. And Mother wasn't getting any younger either.

Once again I felt drawn to the army, but it was a mistake. What future was there for a soldier at the Cape? Expeditions against marauding Bushmen and Hottentots; sentry duty in the Cape Town batteries; patrols into the interior. After barely a month or two I deserted. But while I was helping out harvesting on some farms near Piquetberg, the Government caught up with me. I'd never expected them to feel so strongly about desertion in a colony still so uncivilized. Damn them all. A severe flogging in Cape Town, and that in public to make it worse; the worst humiliation of my life.

At least it meant formal discharge from the army; so I was free to make a fresh start. That was when I met Herr Liebermann who was in the process of loading his three wagons for a trading expedition into the interior.

336

"I'm looking for a guide and a huntsman," he said when I announced myself. "What do you know about the interior?"

"I know it like the palm of my hand," I assured him. "And I was just about born with a rifle in my hands."

"Well, in that case you can come with me. Provided your price isn't too high, *ja*?"

Once we'd agreed about my remuneration I persuaded him to invest the few hundred rix dollars due to me at the end of the journey in a load of merchandise which we could take with us so that I might sell it at a profit. My chance, it seemed, had finally arrived.

As we trekked along, over the mountains to the Warm Baths and from there through the wilderness to Swellendam and the outlying district of Graaff-Reinet and the Great Fish River, I would ride ahead on horseback every day to trace a route and then come back to guide Herr Liebermann. To the day of his death the credulous old soul never discovered that I knew as little of the land as he himself. And as we reached the more remote parts of the Colony we began to do good business too. Usually we stayed over on some farm or another; early the next morning we would unpack our merchandise and barter and sell as best we could; and invariably we would be offered food and drink as well. There were many days when old Liebermann was so drunk that I had to tie him up on the wagon to prevent him from rolling out. While he was in that state I could do business to my heart's content. Having discovered that in those distant parts one could get much higher prices than closer to the Cape, I felt no qualms about pocketing the difference between what Herr Liebermann had expected and the amount I actually received. It was no loss to him; while every rix dollar brought me closer to that *liberté—egalité—fraternité* which, as I'd now come to look at it, could only be achieved with a substantial amount of cash in one's back pocket.

I persuaded the old man to cross the Fish River into Kaffir Land. He had misgivings as it was against the law. But who would ever find out? And once he'd discovered how much

337

ivory could be obtained from the Xhosas in exchange for ludicrous handfuls of beads and ironware and tobacco, his watery eyes opened into a wide stunned gaze and he promptly drank himself into a stupor.

We only turned back when we ran out of stuff to barter. Herr Liebermann was quite content to go back to Cape Town; but I persuaded him to give it another thought.

"Just think of it," I explained. "If we have the right merchandise we can bring home five times as much ivory."

"What sort of merchandise?"

"Brandy. And ammunition."

"*Aber* Joseph, you can't sell ammunition to the Xhosas. *Gott im Himmel*, haven't you heard the Boers talking about the dangers of life on the border?"

"Herr Liebermann, you can't tell me anything about war I haven't been through myself. Before I was ten years old I'd learned that war meant good business."

"But the people will all get massacred if the Xhosas are armed."

"The best way to preserve the peace is to make sure that both sides are equally strong. Then neither will risk anything against the other."

He still seemed very lukewarm about my proposal, but with the aid of the last draught of brandy left in our barrel I persuaded him to drive to Algoa Bay where we sold our ivory and other bartered goods. The profit was so staggering that he promptly drained a bottle of vile Cape Smoke, which laid him out flat for five days, by which time we were well on our way towards the Fish River again, our wagons creaking under the weight of the guns and ammunition, tobacco, brandy and ironware I'd acquired.

This time business was like a raging veld fire; and thanks to a couple of interpreters I'd hired in Algoa Bay transactions were speeded up considerably. When the iron pots were all sold out I got the idea of selling birdshot to the eager customers. "Pot seed," I explained to the Xhosas. "Just plant one of these seeds and water it for a month, then a pot will start growing: and as

338

soon as it's reached the size you need you can pick it."
Incredible to see the enthusiasm with which the people bought
the stuff, paying half the price of a full pot for every seed. The
wagons could hardly move for all the ivory when at last we
turned back. In order not to alert the militia in the border
area—fortunately I'd been warned in time by one of our
interpreters about a patrol in the neighbourhood—I left Herr
Liebermann with the wagons outside Algoa Bay and went
ahead to make sure the coast was clear.

Right there fortune turned against me again. On my return
to the wagons all I found was one of the drivers who'd
managed to hide in the bush when the patrol had surprised
them.

I went back to farm work, first in the Suurveld of the
Eastern Cape, but after the war of '19, when the Xhosas
crossed the frontier in their thousands, plundering and destroying everything in their way, I returned to safer parts; and at
last I landed in the district of Worcester. By that time I'd saved
a small amount of money, but the farmers were either
downright stingy or unable to afford a liveable wage; more
often than not one was promised part of the harvest—and
when it was a bad year, which happened to me three times in a
row, one was left with barely a rag to cover one's backside.

Far, far away, across the seas, Mother would still be waiting
and pining. Perhaps she'd already gone blind. Perhaps she was
dead. And all I had to show for my life was that I was still a
labourer on one farm after another. The wonderful words of
long ago were beginning to fade in my memory, as if those
bright rags had been dislodged from the hedge again to be
blown away by the wind. Had it really all been in vain then?
The great slogans of the Revolution. Napoleon. All of it. In
vain?

At the humble place of the raving old shoemaker of Houd-
den-Bek I rediscovered a small measure of hope. For it was a
good summer. Dry, but good. The wheat was billowing in the
wind. I was asked to give a hand with the harvesting, not only
at old D'Alree's place, but on several other farms in the

neighbourhood. There was a prospect of earning enough soon to equip another wagon and take the road into the interior again, where the ivory was.

For the first time I'd acquired a touch of prestige too. Not with old D'Alree or the Van der Merwes, who looked down on me as a common labourer, but among the slaves. Amazing how avidly they could gather round me to listen to whatever I chose to tell them. More, more, more, they would encourage me. In their eyes I'd become an extraordinary man. And perhaps, I thought, it was not yet too late. Half my life still lay ahead. Perhaps the cowl would yet show its magic powers; perhaps Mother hadn't been waiting entirely in vain for so long.

All these thoughts were constantly in my mind during those summer days. And especially on the wagon-trip with Nicolaas to the Cape, that late October; and the day in December when we were harvesting the wheat. And again that afternoon on the threshing-floor, just after New Year. For that, I believe, was where everything was finally decided.

GALANT

White. The child was white.

NICOLAAS

It was almost a relief in the uncompromising glare of the early November light to approach from the Rear-Witzenberg, trekking through the tumbled rock formations of the Skurweberge and reaching the summer wind of our highland again, the wagon almost jolted to pieces as usual by the long journey to and from the Cape. I was sitting on the driver's seat with Campher beside me, while old Moses wielded the long whip alongside and little Rooy led the oxen. Relief, since one could never be sure any more about what was happening in one's absence (at least there was a prospect of more certainty by Christmas or New Year); and because it had been a depressing and lonely trip, what with Campher so wholly withdrawn into himself, mumbling from time to time words in strange languages as if possessed by the Holy Ghost. At the same time a familiar oppressiveness closed in on me again. All the way from the Cape I'd had the curious feeling of recapitulating the motion of my ancestors: this was the same road the first Van der Merwe had taken from Cape Town, leading to Roodezand and the valley of Waveren; and after his quarrel with the Landdrost my Great-grandfather and his companions had trekked up the backbreaking Witzenberg and into the Bokkeveld, among the first ever to cross those unconscionable mountains; here he measured off, galloping for a whole day at full speed on horseback, the great farm which after the fight with the messenger of the East India Company he baptized Houd-den-Bek, Shut-Your-Trap; and fifty years after the family had moved on to Swellendam, Pa returned to repossess Houd-den-Bek and Elandsfontein and Lagenvlei. Now I was following these tracks of my own history once again, with a feeling both of fulfilment and of apprehension. For I was not simply the result of my history but also the victim of it. I had no choice to deviate or follow my own inclination: not only because the Government in the Cape was doing its utmost to determine the confines and direction of my life but because this long valley, and these wild mountains, and the people living among them, and my own family, all combined to circumscribe my existence. I was returning to this place, and to my wife and waiting children, because I had no liberty to do otherwise: the prisoner of a land apparently open and exposed but crushing one in its hard grip.

In the absence of any entertainment or conversation, there had been much time for thought on the journey there and back. Rooy usually kept his distance, his cheeky little mug smiling defensively, his big black eyes alert like those of a ground squirrel; old Moses offered little more than occasional grunts in affirmation of whatever I'd said; and Campher would give brief replies to explicit questions but no more—although I'd noticed before that he would be quite loquacious when left alone with the labourers.

Had I really been a failure in life? But what, exactly, was "failure"? Inevitably, it seems to me, one relinquishes whatever one may have presumed to possess; life is a taker away, and ceaselessly it prunes one. The most I could have hoped for was to be respected in my neighbourhood. Not even that: just to be recognized and accepted by my neighbours, to be liked. But it had turned out otherwise. My parents regarded me as something of a wash-out, all the more conspicuous for having settled on the old family farm. My brother despised me as a weakling. My own wife regarded me as a husband not man enough to produce sons, a pursuer of black women. Hester had long ago, and utterly, rejected me. And from the way Galant looked at me or answered back it was obvious that even he had no regard for me: and we'd been so close. Who else was there? Bet, who still followed me wherever I went, clearly biding her time to avenge the death of her child? Pamela, whom I couldn't look in the eyes as she carried her white child from hut to house?

I avoided the vicious if unspoken reproach in Cecilia's attitude about Pamela's white baby. Couldn't God have taken the child away from my sight? But this was undoubtedly His punishment, daily to confront me and force me into abject humility. Unendurable. Leaving me no choice but to throw me on His mercy. There were days when I wished Cecilia would send the woman back to her father's place where she'd come from: at the same time I knew, and Cecilia perversely concurred, that my sin had to be kept in front of my eyes.

The only people unconditionally mine were the children. Helena. Little Hester. Katrien. They never asked questions and never judged. Holding two by the hand and carrying one on my shoulders, I would roam the farm with them. Small arms throttling me with love; fervent wet kisses like a licking of puppies; a smell of sun and dust and bruised flowers. Precarious innocence, and terribly transient. For when the teacher arrived, which was very soon now, I knew the inevitable estrangement would begin. In fact, it had already begun, as gradually Cecilia was taking over, prompted by the consideration that it was "improper" for them to run about wild with their father, in sun or wind. Only a little while longer before they would begin to conspire with her against me and my man's world; drawn ever more resolutely into their mother's. A whetting of loneliness. In the beginning everything must have been whole; undoubtedly. The care of a mother, the awesome strength of a father; a brother's regard; the trust of a friend who accompanied one everywhere, sharing everything. But how soon it was blemished, how inexorably diminished.—*You're too much of a fancy turd.*—*Barend told me about their plans this morning.*—*It's the sort of thing I'd have expected of Barend, not of you.I'm ashamed of you.*—A lion with a great black mane sinking into a wretched little heap: freedom ruthlessly curtailed. The only thing that had helped me to survive had been, ironically, the one thing that had most oppressed me in the beginning: the farm. And here we were on our way back to it, each bitterly turned in upon himself—Rooy; old Moses; Campher; I.

344

I'd resented the whole idea of the journey. When March and April had passed without an opportunity to make the trip—the beans were late and a new land had to be broken and cleared—I'd already tacitly resolved to postpone it for a year. But the produce was accumulating—the soap and hides and pelts and bush-tea, the eggs and feathers and *biltong*—and Cecilia had reasons of her own: "The children are growing up, Nicolaas. I won't have my daughters run about like savages. They need an education. You must find a teacher in Cape Town. Helena is ripe enough for school." And when October brought a brief respite in the work before the full violence of the reaping and harvesting and threshing of summer would break upon us, I had no choice but to pack up.

"You've been pestering me a long time to go to Cape Town with me," I told Galant. "Now it's your chance."

To my amazement he declined. "I'd rather stay. I been to the Cape now and I saw all I wanted to see."

"I really don't understand you, Galant."

"If you order me to go I'll go," he answered in his sulky way. "But if I have a choice I'd rather stay."

The prospect of going without him depressed and frustrated me. I'd been thinking: perhaps, if he accompanied me, on the long road to Cape Town we might retrieve something of that lost night in the mountains. Now it was ruled out. Yet why, even at that stage, should I have thought of it as "a last chance"?

After all, I tried to persuade myself, some good might come out of it if he stayed behind. Perhaps we needed the break, after what had happened in the winter, to clear our minds. And the farm would be safe in his care, in spite of everything. That was, perhaps, the most remarkable of our relationship: that I still trusted him so unreservedly. And, admittedly, he'd changed since his return. Not that he'd opened up; but he was, it seemed to me, less squarely intransigent than before, as if in some subtle way his experiences in the Cape had matured or mellowed him. We might yet learn to live together. We were both older, and who knows a trifle wiser, more seasoned, less absolute. So I went to old D'Alree and persuaded him to lend me Campher for a month. He could hardly refuse, living as he did on our mercy. From Pa's grazing place in the mountains I borrowed old Moses; and little Rooy was taken along to lead the oxen.

"I'll come back as soon as I can," I assured Cecilia, who almost seemed relieved to see me go. If only she would attack me openly, I thought: but her humility was impenetrable. She was always so right in every respect, so exemplary in her devotion to her duty: feeling no doubt that God would appreciate her encouragement and approval for pursuing His inscrutable ways. I did not mean to feel ungrateful to my own wife; but she did make it difficult for a man to live up to her standards.

The produce was sold quickly, and more profitably than in previous years, and soon I could proceed to buy the things on Cecilia's list: linen and hats and chintz; coffee, sugar and spices; ammunition and two new guns for myself, and iron, tar and pitch. I was fortunate in finding a suitable schoolmaster too: a middle-aged, virtuous if somewhat uninspiring man called Verlee who'd recently married a girl not yet fifteen; they were living with her relatives in whose home their first baby had just been born. From the family, and the testimonials he showed me, I gleaned that he'd been an itinerant teacher in the Eastern Cape, spending three years in the environs of Graaff-Reinet before moving to Stellenbosch. The young wife's relatives were eager to see them stay on in the Cape, but he'd set his mind on moving into the interior again, and so we arranged for him to start at Houd-den-Bek in February, by which time the harvest would be home and his wife's baby more manageable; and Helena ready for school.

I was introduced to him at a meeting, one of the many, I'd been told, held in Cape Town in recent months, mostly to discuss the slave question. All through the Colony it seemed frustration was reaching boiling point. And just as well that I was able to attend one of the meetings personally so I could hear for myself what was going on. Hearsay can cause such impossible distortions.

Most of the people present were from Cape Town itself, but a considerable number were wine farmers from the environs and from Stellenbosch or further afield, even from as far as Swellendam. At the back of the hall a number of slaves had also taken up position, including old Moses, who'd always been as inquisitive as a monkey. It was announced, a statement received with great applause, that we'd had enough of ambiguity and prevarication; what we needed now was certainty. A week before, we were informed, a deputation had been to see the Governor; and on this occasion an officer was sent to report back—which in itself was rather extraordinary, as Lord Charles had a reputation for being unreasonable. The officer treated us with a surprising show of deference. In the beginning he was nearly shouted down by the rather unruly mob, but when it became obvious that he meant well he was allowed to continue unhindered. He'd brought a young Hottentot with him to interpret for us—a Pandoer very proud of his uniform, but at the same time as scared as anything in front of that congregation of hostile Boers, which made it quite amusing.

According to the officer (as translated haltingly by the fearful young Pandoer), the Government was aware of our worries and was conducting a thorough investigation of the whole situation. A long report had already been sent to the King in England, and it shouldn't take too long to receive a reply. Should the British Government decide on the emancipation of slaves—in which case there would be ample remuneration—we would be informed in good time. By the end of the year everything should be cleared up. If we hadn't heard any news by then it meant that we would be free to continue as before. Otherwise messengers would be sent throughout the Colony, round about Christmas or New Year, with full particulars.

A number of the farmers present grumbled about the new postponement. Some even threatened to attack the young

Pandoer as if he'd been responsible for it all; but there were red-coated soldiers in all the doorways ready to prevent mischief. Most of the audience were prepared to accept the situation. After all, one couldn't expect a final decision overnight. Personally, I was quite prepared to wait until New Year: then, at least, one should know whether one was to be master on one's own farm and over one's own slaves.

There was a feeling among some of the farmers that we should anticipate a decision and resolve the uncertainty by liberating our own slaves immediately. I gave it much thought on the way back. But it was clear to me that that would be no solution. Suppose I were to free my own slaves—what about those on neighbouring farms? Surely such a position would be quite untenable. One had to consider one's neighbours too: no one was free simply to do what he wished. And the end of the year was close enough to wait for.

So I cannot say that I felt dissatisfied as I reflected on what had been accomplished on the journey. Not satisfied, perhaps: but not outright dissatisfied either.

In the narrow highland valley, pale in the summer light, the wagon seemed to lumber on by itself. The oxen must have smelled the grazing of Houd-den-Bek; the ones in front were playfully tossing their horns so that Rooy had to pull in his back and trot briskly to stay out of their reach.

Naturally I stopped at Elandsfontein. From a long distance off I already kept my eyes open for Hester's skirt. But Barend was alone at home: she'd gone to the veld on her own, he replied to my query—nothing it seemed would domesticate her. The two of us sat in the *voorhuis* drinking some of the new coffee I'd brought with me, while Campher found himself a shady spot outside, with the labourers: through the window I could see him comfortably squatting down with them to answer their excited questions about the Cape while inside, Barend and I discussed the journey—the price our wares had fetched; the two new guns; the schoolmaster.

"Why are you so eager for your girls to have an education? You want to prepare them for town life or what?"

348

"It's Cecilia," I said. "And they're girls, after all. They cannot grow up wild like boys."

He looked at me from under his dark eyebrows, a look both quizzical and mocking. "*Ja!*" he said at last. "I suppose you know more about girls than boys, don't you?"

"I won't exchange my girls for anything in the world."

"I'm sure you won't. Still, it would be a pity if Houd-den-Bek had to fall into strange hands one day for lack of an heir."

Deliberately ignoring the remark I changed the subject: "Everything all right here while I was away?"

"Yes. I went over to Houd-den-Bek every other day. Galant seems to have settled down at last. Perhaps he's finally got over his cheekiness."

"After New Year the world will be a much better place for all of us," I said.

"What do you mean?"

I told him about the meeting. Halfway through Abel came in and interrupted us to discuss something about a hoe with Barend. "I'll be there just now," Barend told him brusquely. Abel hovered impatiently in the background while I resumed my account; then we went outside together and Barend's share of the load was taken from the wagon. Soon afterwards we were on our way again—without Moses, who'd stayed behind with his tobacco and his small keg of brandy and the new trousers I'd given him: he was to take the short-cut back to Pa's grazing place in the mountains.

A new reluctance grew inside me, not so much at the prospect of being home again as at the memory of the very first time I'd been to Cape Town with Pa, when everybody had been so excited about the uprising of the slaves at Koeberg; and when, upon our arrival, Pa had summoned all the slaves at Lagenvlei and had them flogged by way of warning. In his time I imagine that was all the deterrent that had been necessary. But today? I tried my best to shake off the morbid mood. After all, there was new hope. And slowly, as we drew nearer—past Frans du Toit's farm and then eastward to Houd-den-Bek—my mind began to clear. At last the farm was there, ahead of me in the depression between the two ranges of mountains: the farm with its stone-walls and whitewashed home and outbuildings, the kraals, the cluster of trees. In spite of myself a sense of pride returned: almost all of this was my own handiwork. The dilapidated cottage in which Hester had first lived had been changed into a sturdy white homestead with a pitched, thatched roof. There was the elongated dark-blue sheet of water where the marsh had been dammed. The paved irrigation furrows. The orchards; the peach-trees in front of the house; the bean-fields; the deep green pumpkin patch; the tobacco; the expanse of wheatlands already turning yellow. There was a deeply reassuring stability about it all. It had been done well, and solidly, surely. We were no temporary sojourners, all this was here to last and endure. Perhaps the uncertainty was really subsiding now. One had forfeited much; but one had also learned, and become matured. Soon, when I cracked the great whip after dropping off Campher at D'Alree's place, leaving only Rooy and me on the wagon, I would see the children running out to meet me, bright dresses swirling, hair streaming in the wind, shrill voices shrieking: "Papa! Papa! Papa!" My farm; my home; my children.

Indeed, we would prevail.

The Lord was sure to exterminate our enemies ahead of us.

And tonight, after Pamela had washed our feet and cleared away the dishes, we would gather round the table for prayers, the slaves on the dung-floor near the kitchen door; and I would abandon myself to the drone of my own voice as I read in restrained exultation:

Now also many nations are gathered against thee, that say, Let her be defiled, and let our eye look upon Zion.

But they know not the thoughts of the Lord, neither understand they his counsel: for he shall gather them as the sheaves into the floor.

Arise and thresh, O daughter of Zion: for I will make thine horn iron, and I will make thy hoofs brass: and thou shalt beat in pieces many people: and I will consecrate their gain unto the Lord, and their substance unto the Lord of the whole earth.

350

MA-ROSE

It was turning into a dry year, and windy. Some days the wind was swirling and gusty, and unruly in a woman's skirts; but mostly it blew steadily, evenly, for days on end, as if driven by a great hand sweeping everything out of its way and bending down the wheat under its weight, making one wish it was threshing time. For it was a real threshing wind from the west, ready to take away all the chaff and straw and leave only the rich grain behind.

On the surface the Bokkeveld farms had a peaceful look about them that summer. Galant's running off to the Cape and his return in the melting snow seemed to have cleared a stormy sky. And now the days were still and blue, the swallows had returned, the sun came up and trailed across, and went down, and rose again; the wheat was filling out and turning a deep yellow, scorched brown in places from too much sun, yet promising the best harvest in years.

Only the wind brought a feeling of restlessness to what otherwise would have been peaceful. And another wind was rising too. One couldn't see it, or feel it in your face; but I recognized it nonetheless. The first I knew of it openly was the day Galant came to discuss it with me. For I might be living apart from the rest, but all the world came past my hut, and there was nothing I didn't know. Many evenings Galant would come by, and the others from Houd-den-Bek or from old D'Alree's place; even Barend's slaves would look me up—the likeable, irresponsible Abel, ever ready for music, or a swig, or a joke; and the meek young Goliath; and that squirming toad Klaas—and even men from more distant places: Slinger sporting an ostrich feather in his floppy hat, and old Moses with his watery eyes, and the whining old Adonis from Jan du Plessis's farm. Each with his own story to tell: and I listened to them all, for I was old and what they wouldn't dare tell anybody else they confided to me, and why shouldn't they? I was mother to them all.

That evening Galant came over to bring me some soup he'd asked Pamela to pinch from the kitchen; and he sat there telling me all his wild stories of Cape Town.

"The Cape must have changed a lot since I knew it as a girl," I said at last. "I hardly recognize it from your stories."

That stung him. "You think it's lies I'm telling, Ma-Rose?"

"I never said such a thing. What does one person know about another? I can't see the inside of your head, can I? All I remember is the way you used to have dreams when you were small, and I had to drive all the bad thoughts away by rubbing your little prick. But when a man is grown it's not so easy to get the dreams out of him."

"You don't believe me then."

"What's it to you whether I believe or not? As long as you believe it yourself."

For a long time he was quiet.

"You believe in yourself?" I asked him again.

Without looking at me, his eyes still far away in that distance where the *thas*-jackal roams, he suddenly said: "I'm not the man I used to be, Ma-Rose."

"Is it because of Pamela's white child?"

"It got nothing to do with the child!" he burst out.

"Well, what is it then? They finally broken you in?"

"No." He said it very softly. "No. No one can do that." Then he was quiet again before he went on: "When I left here it was to try and find me a place where I could go to live. In the Cape, or across the Great River, anywhere. All my life I been looking for that place; all my life I been wanting to get away from here. But there's one thing I found out and that is that one cannot get away from one's own place. It's stuck to your footsoles. My place is here. This Bokkeveld. This Houd-den-Bek. Before, I was here because I got no other choice. Now

352

I'm here because I want it. I made up my mind and I chose this place. It's mine."

"So you're satisfied at last?"

"I didn't say that." He turned to me and stared very hard at me. "How can I ever be satisfied while I'm a slave? But at least I got a place now that is mine. All I got to do now is to get out from under the masters."

"Why you talking so mixed-up tonight?"

"I know what I'm talking about, Ma-Rose. And I'm just biding my time."

He had me worried. "What time you biding?" I asked him.

But he wouldn't give me a straight answer. Instead, he asked, still looking straight at me: "Ma-Rose, you heard the news that we going to be free?"

"There's been a lot of stories like that over the years, Galant," I warned him. "Don't put your heart on it. It gets you nowhere."

"Christmas or New Year," he said quietly, ignoring me. "That's the way I heard it. This news comes from right across the sea. The newspaper itself said so."

"What do you know about newspapers?"

"I tell you it's true!" He was so excited that he grabbed my shoulders and started shaking me till my teeth were chattering. "You hear me?"

"Of course I hear you. No need to shout at me."

Ashamed, he let go of me. "Well, that's what the newspaper says," he repeated.

"Where did you hear it?"

"Everybody heard it." Stubbornly, he held on to it, the way I'd known him from childhood. "It's Christmas, or it's New Year. Today I know my place; when that day comes my place will know me too."

"Christmas and New Year will come and go," I said. "Like every other year."

"Just you wait. I'm biding my time. And New Year is my time. No sooner, no later."

At first I thought it was just another of his whims. But I kept

353

my ears open, and it wasn't long before I heard the same story from Abel.

"You heard it from Galant?" I asked him.

"No, why should I? Haven't seen him for a long time. I heard it straight from Cape Town."

Shortly afterwards old Moses repeated the same thing; and then I heard it from people who'd come up from Worcester in search of grazing for their cattle. It gave me a dizzy feeling. There's so many things one hears all one's life; and one gets used to going on regardless. Now, all of a sudden, there was this new business. Could it really be true then?

I discussed it with Bet. After the child with the white hair and blue eyes was born to Pamela, things had changed at the farmhouse again and Bet was brought back into the kitchen while Pamela was moved out, even though I knew the Nooi wasn't very fond of Bet. The menfolk really give us a hard time. Anyway, Bet was doing the housework again—except Pamela was still called in to help the Nooi with her clothes and her hair and so on—and I told her to keep her ears open for the newspapers, and to find out whatever she could. It was high time we knew where we stood.

Not that she ever found out much. According to Bet the Nooi wasn't interested in newspapers herself; preferred to let them lie there. And if she did say anything it would be neither here nor there: "In a land far across the sea they say the slaves must be set free, but the farmers won't let them." And when Bet pressed her the Nooi would just tell her to shut up. Then, out of the blue, she would suddenly let fly at Bet again: "I wish we could get rid of all the damned slaves. Why can't somebody go and get our money from the king and pay us out?—then the lot of them can take their stuff and go." What on earth could that mean? But Bet knew as little as I did.

"Do you ever discuss these matters with Galant?" I asked her.

"If I talk to him he just tells me to keep quiet about it. He's a difficult man to get on with, ever since little David died. Ma-Rose, I just don't know what to do any more. I feel rejected by everybody."

354

Then I must go and find out for myself, I decided at last. For it was already harvesting time and the wheat was beginning to fall to the sickles of the reapers and soon it would be Christmas and New Year: I had to make sure before it was too late. Already I could feel it pushing, pushing like a rising wind.

I went over to the farmyard. A blistering day it was, the cicadas screeching in the thin trees fit to burst your skull, all day long from long before sunrise till after sunset. By that time the wind had also died down; not a breath of air stirred, and the world was white with heat. The wheatfields a dark yellow-brown where the reapers stood crouching with their sickles, swishing and moving on, swishing and moving. Galant and Ontong and Achilles, the youngsters Thys and Rooy, the seasonal workers Valentyn and Vlak and others; and old D'Alree's people, the foreman Campher and the big man Dollie; and even some of old Piet's farm hands. The old man's wheat was late that year, so the reaping had started at Houdden-Bek before they were to move on round the mountain. The clouds were swelling out in large white bundles of washing over the mountain ridges, and it was hard to predict when they might grow heavy with black thunder to threaten the lands.

Nicolaas was working in the farmyard, adding a new layer of rushes to the thatched roof of the wheat-loft. Pamela and Lydia were helping him; so I assumed that Bet was still in the kitchen.

The Nooi came out from the shade of the *voorhuis* when she heard me talking to Bet. The smallest girl was with her, peeping from behind her mother's skirts; the two older ones I'd seen playing up and down the stone staircase to the attic.

"Oh it's you, Rose. What do you want then?"

"I come to find out if all is well, Nooi." I gave Bet a quick glance; and she went out into the yard.

"What makes you think all isn't well?"

"One hears so many stories, Nooi."

"Really?"

355

"What about some snuff, Nooi?"

She seemed annoyed at the request, but fetched me some from the shelf in the corner to fill up my box; always been an irritable woman, the Nooi.

"Well, what is it?" she asked.

As I looked outside into the whiteness of the yard, I suddenly noticed a dust-devil far away in the wagon-road, whirling towards the yard. Nothing unusual for that time of the year, especially in a summer as dry as this, but I couldn't help shivering. I knew it was Gaunab, the Dark One, taking on the shape of a whirlwind. In that form his name was *sarês*, my mother had told me long ago; and it was a bad omen. I could see it coming towards us, swirling up dust and twigs and dry leaves into the air; I'd seen it throw up dead frogs and other evil things before. And I was frightened, for I saw it heading straight for the house.

"We need water, Nooi!" I shouted. And when she just stood there doing nothing I pushed her out of the way and grabbed the tub of water from the corner by the hearth; stumbling and splashing I lugged it outside to the gate where I threw the water right in the way of *sarês*. That made the whirlwind hesitate suddenly, and change course, and die down. But I still felt shaky as I went back to the kitchen carrying the empty tub. The little girls had stopped playing and were watching me from the attic staircase. As I entered the kitchen they quickly slipped in after me.

"Rose, are you out of your mind to do a thing like that?" the Nooi scolded me.

"You don't know what you saying, Nooi," I told her angrily.

"But what are you doing? Bet filled up that tub just now."

"That dust-devil means danger, Nooi. If I hadn't stopped him in time there would have been death on this farm, I tell you. Don't you know then?"

"What ungodly stories are you telling again?" she asked, annoyed. "How often have I told you to stop scaring the children with all this heathen nonsense? I won't have it, do you hear me?"

"It's not stories, Nooi," I said. "It's the truth. I grew up with it."

"God will punish you for your bad ways, Rose."

I sighed. "Nooi—"

"I've got a lot of darning to do," she said, turning her back on me.

I raised my hand to stop her, but dropped it again. If she was in that temper it would be useless to discuss what I'd come for. With a heavy heart I went outside and down to the shed where Nicolaas was still working on the wheat-loft. Perhaps he would be more approachable.

"Good day, Ma-Rose."

"Good day, Nicolaas."

His face was flushed with heat where he stood high up on the ladder; and dark patches of sweat showed up on his shirt. Lydia went on stacking rushes, clucking by herself like a chicken making her nest; and Pamela also kept her head down, as if ashamed to face me. Some distance away, in the shade, lay the child. But it was all covered up, and one couldn't see the face.

Nicolaas came down the ladder for another armful of rushes.

"You've come a long way in this heat?" he said.

"Yes. There's something I want to ask you."

"What is it?"

"The people are talking a lot about New Year."

I watched him very closely, but he didn't give away anything. "Oh?" he said. "And what might that be?"

"They say the newspapers talk about it too."

"Baas," said Pamela from the roof, "don't listen to her."

"Everybody is talking about it," I kept on, for I hadn't walked all this way for nothing. "Now I want to hear it from your own mouth. They say the slaves are to be freed by New Year."

"Who are 'they'?"

"Everybody. They all say it comes from the newspapers."

"Ma-Rose, you can tell the people who say such things that

357

I'll shoot the first man who sets foot on my farm to take away my slaves. And if need be I'll first of all shoot the slaves myself."

"That's a bad thing you saying, Nicolaas."

"Then stop bothering me with such nonsense. Whoever has filled your head with these stories is looking for trouble. You better warn them from me. I have enough problems on the farm as it is."

His voice had the sound of fear in it. Perhaps I should have tried to reassure him first, in order to coax from him what I so desperately needed to know; but after the scare *sarês* had given me I was too upset to be patient.

"Just tell me: is it in the newspapers or isn't it?" I said.

"What difference does it make? You can't believe any damned newspaper. Even the people in the Cape don't know their own minds."

"How can a newspaper lie?"

"Ma-Rose." I could see his patience was running out. "I promise you: if ever the newspaper says something I can believe I'll tell it to you outright. But you know how readily the slaves swallow the wildest nonsense. What will happen if we allow every evil rumour from outside to destroy our peace of mind? So please try to understand reason!"

"I understand reason when I hear it, Nicolaas. All I'm asking you is if these stories come from the newspapers or not?"

"I've said what I had to say," he said. "The rest doesn't concern you."

"I won't have you talk to me like this, Nicolaas. I suckled you on these paps of mine."

"You won't get any further with me that way."

"You trying to cover up the truth now?" I asked him. "Then let me tell you: if it's true it will come into the open sooner or later."

He clenched his teeth. "I have work to do, Rose. This roof must be finished before dark."

A whirlwind of anger swept up inside me. "Don't think your roof will keep out the wind, Nicolaas!" I called. "When the

358

storm comes up it'll blow all of this right away."

He shouted something after me, but I didn't hear what he said. My ears were ringing, not just from the cicadas. *Rose.* That was what he'd called me. As if he'd forgotten all about *Ma-Rose.* He thought he could do without her now. What a pity. How could I ever have known, when I'd suckled him as a baby, that I would be rearing him for this!

I went on walking and walking through the shimmering afternoon, unmindful of where I went. All I kept on thinking was: What a pity. The people got to be very careful now. They turning this land into a threshing-floor where they themselves are to be threshed. Tsui-Goab will send his wind to sort the grain from the chaff. He won't allow his people to be humiliated like this. He's sitting up there in His red sky, seeing everything that happens; and when the time comes He will send his great wind.

ACHILLES

It all happened because they wouldn't listen to me. I told them, didn't I, they were asking for trouble. Whenever the man Campher spoke I kept silent, not wanting to set up my word against a white man. Before, when I was young, I tried to do that. But I learned my lesson. All I hoped for now was to end my days in peace, working when I had to and drinking my honey-beer when I could; and dreaming at night, when I was safely out of reach of the others, of the *'mtili*-trees of my land, with their tall white trunks and dark crowns. For that was all I had left; and no one could touch that.

I could never come round to understanding or trusting that man Campher, with his thin white skin that never got brown like that of other white men: it only turned red and scaly; and his unkempt hair and sparse beard. Thin as a beanpole, as if he never got enough to eat; a real scarecrow, all bones, but as tough as a snake. Not that he ever suffered from lack of food. Whenever he was at our place to help out with the work he'd gorge himself like a bloody pig on the thick soup they gave us mornings and evenings, beans and peas in turn; and meat in the afternoons, and the thick slices of bread Galant handed out. And if any of us left over a piece of bread or something Campher would gobble that up too. Real vulture. But he stayed as lean as a stick. And when we teased him about it he'd laugh, baring his bad teeth, asking: "Ever seen a good rooster that wasn't lean?" He was always joking and talking with us like that as if he was one of us; but it didn't change his whiteness one bit. It made me uneasy. A man should stick to his own sort, else there's trouble.

Still, he was a great talker. And when he warmed up even I

couldn't help listening. Once he got started on those countries far across the sea where he used to live, we all listened. He was a great general over there, he told us. He trekked about with his soldiers, one place to the other, to free the people that were slaves. The Breaker of Chains they called him. And as far as he went there were no slaves left behind, and no one was hungry any more, or in need of clothes or stuff, and every man had his own wife; even two or three for those who wanted them, all those good lean roosters, he would say, laughing. And now he'd come from across the sea to find out if there was something he could do for us too. Our time was coming, he said. Just be patient. Wait for the stars to be right. Because he was born with a cowl, so he could see ahead what was coming. And there was a big thing for us.

"Is that what they mean when they keep talking about New Year?" Galant asked him.

"Maybe," said the thin man, looking deep. "The time is getting ripe, just like the wheat."

"What do the newspapers say?" asked Galant, who always had a thing about newspapers.

"The newspapers don't matter," said Joseph Campher. "It's the stars. And I can see them moving into the right position. There's a great freedom coming. Liberty, equality, fraternity." The way he said it he made it sound like the Baas reading from the Bible, Wednesdays and Sundays.

"I still not sure about this man," I used to say to Ontong and the young ones when we were alone at the hut or with the sheep. "If he really was such a big general how come he's so hungry that he gobbles up our bread behind our backs?"

"Perhaps he was fighting so much he didn't have time to eat," said little Rooy, always too big for his size.

"If he was so important why's he reaping wheat with us now?" I kept on.

"Because we're the ones he wants to set free," said Thys. "Don't you remember he told us how he always sided with the poor people?"

"I don't trust him," I said. "I always worry about people who are so concerned about others. He got no need to bother about us. So why's he going on like a fly on a hot day? Do *you* believe him, Galant?"

"Let me be," he mumbled. "We'll see what happens. It's almost time for Christmas and New Year."

Just before Christmas Campher was again with us, reaping on the lands. A terrible day, one of the hottest, the cicadas like thorns piercing your ears. Nobody felt like talking; not even at breakfast time. Only Campher went on.

"You're really prepared to swallow a lot, aren't you?" he said. "Why do you allow yourselves to be driven like this on such a hot day?" And all because in the early dawn the Baas showed us the patch of wheat he wanted us to cut that day; and it was blue murder. But if he said so it just had to be done, even if it meant working till moonlight.

"If the wheat is ready it got to be cut," said Ontong. "It means food for all of us."

"Food for the Baas," said Campher. "Leftovers for you. What do you say, Achilles? You must be a wise man, you're so grey."

"I know nothing about leftovers," I said gruffly. "I'm satisfied with what the Baas chooses to give me."

But he went on and on. By the time Bet came down with the second *sopie* of the day—for when the harvesting was going on the Baas wasn't stingy: no less than four *sopies* a day it was—we rested in the shade for a while; and there the Baas found us when he came down to see how we were getting on.

"How's it going?"

"Not bad, Baas. Just hot, Baas."

"It's too early for malingering."

"No, Baas. We not malingering, Baas."

"I thought you'd be further by now."

"We'll finish, Baas," I said. "Wheat's good this year."

"*Ja.*" He looked round. "Well, I've also got work to do." He grinned at me. "I feel the heat just as much, but have you ever heard me complain, Achilles?"

"That's so, Baas."

362

"Remember what the Bible says about the sweat of your brow?"

"True, Baas."

"Perhaps one day you can go back to your land, Achilles. How would you like that?"

We all looked up at him.

"How can that be, Baas?"

"You too, Ontong."

"I don't understand what you saying today, Baas."

"Just talking. One never knows, does one?" He laughed. "Tell me: suppose you were set free one day: would you like to go back home?"

There was a sudden burning feeling in my eyes; in broad daylight I saw the *'mtili*-trees of my dreams shimmering in the white sky. The long road leading from Zim-ba-ué to the sea. The sun rising among the palm trees.

"How shall I ever find the way back, Baas?" I asked him. My throat was dry with lust, as for a woman. "I suppose my mother and all will be dead by now. Will anybody still know me?" But in my mind I could see myself coming back, walking down the plank from the ship; and the people thronging on the shore to gape at me; and suddenly a voice shouting: "But that's Achilles! That old man there is Achilles who was taken away when he was a child!" Except he wouldn't say *Achilles*, but *Gwambe*, the name that was my own.

"That's right, Achilles," said the Baas. "No use going back, is it? Much better to stay here."

"If you say so, Baas," I said; but keeping my head down so he wouldn't see my face.

Suddenly Galant spoke up. "Don't let them tease you like that, Achilles. Don't let them crush you. Only ten more days—time enough to get this wheat out of the way, and move on to Lagenvlei—then it's Christmas. And soon after that it's New Year."

It was very quiet; even the cicadas seemed to have stopped.

"And what is that supposed to mean, Galant?" asked the Baas.

"You know as well as I what New Year's going to bring," Galant answered in his cheeky way.

"Have you been listening to rumours again?" asked the Baas, in that tone of voice that meant: *Watch it!*

"Nothing wrong with my ears," said Galant. "Nor with my eyes. And I'm just waiting for New Year to come round."

"You still have time for idle talk," the Baas said crossly. "Come on, the work's waiting. And for your impudence you can cut down that patch over there too after the others have done."

Galant straightened his back and looked at him. But he didn't say a word. Just as well. Otherwise we'd have had a fight on the farm again.

All the time the Baas was with us the man Campher said nothing. Keeping right out of it as if it was none of his business. But as soon as the Baas was gone, walking through the young beans on his way home, the man suddenly found his voice again. How much were we going to take from the Baas before we had too much? Hadn't we swallowed enough of his shit? He went on and on, until I asked him straight: "Why didn't you say a word when the Baas was here? Why didn't you talk to him then?" Campher just looked at me, his pale eyes burning in his face; then took up his sickle and started reaping again.

"I can bide my time," he said over his shoulder.

I turned to Galant, for he had really upset me. "You mustn't cheek the man like that," I told him. "You know what'll come of it."

"He won't touch me again," he said. "Has he once laid hands on me since the winter?"

"One day you'll be going too far again."

"No. He knows our freedom is coming close now. What about all those questions he asked you about going back to your land? It's because he *knows*. He's getting very careful."

"What do you have against him?" I asked. "The Baas is good to us. Why do you think he gives us food? So we can work for him. And if you don't work you deserve to be flogged. The Baas is working just as hard as the rest of us."

"Won't someone bring me a handful of grass?" Galant jeered. "So we can stuff it up the old man. He's talking through his arsehole."

"You'll be sorry yet," I warned him. "You saying all sorts of things today—and tomorrow a commando comes to take us away. Then we'll all stand in a row before the gentlemen of the Cape, our hands tied behind our backs."

"Let them come," said Galant, raising his sickle. "The whole Bokkeveld will stand up when the day comes. We'll shoot them all the way back to the Cape. Just you wait: one of these days I'll be standing on top of the Lion's Head with my gun in my hand, and they'll all see me from a long way off."

I hunched my back and got on with my reaping. I had no stomach for that sort of talk. After some time I briefly stretched my back to ease the pain—in the distance I saw Ma-Rose passing on her way to the farmyard, and I wondered what had brought her such a long way on a day like that—and I said to Joseph Campher: "Aren't you ashamed of yourself? You a white man, yet you allow Galant to talk like that?"

"What's wrong with it?" he asked. "He knows that soon there won't be any more slaves. What's the matter with you then? Aren't you man enough?"

"I know what I know," I mumbled.

"The day I gather my army I want only real men. Not shit-scared old wives."

"Say what you want," I said, bending down with my sickle again. "You can't make me do what I don't want to."

As in the shimmering sun of a hot day I saw the *'mtili*-trees of my land.

Perhaps, I thought, freedom is also just a shimmering of lies.

If only they'd listened to me.

HESTER

I could never stand that man. Gross, exuberant, and cruel, he'd cast his great shadow across my childhood ever since the day I'd seen my father fall under his whip. Yet there was no joy, no sense of spite, in discovering him motionless and shrunken when, inevitably, the whole family gathered at Lagenvlei for Christmas, only two days after the stroke had felled him on the land. It was unsettling to see him lying there with his fierce and hopeless gaze. On every previous Christmas he'd dominated house and farm with his boisterous presence, whether roasting the carcass of an ox on a huge spit outside, or grabbing someone's violin to lead a parade of musicians across the yard, or intoning in his patriarchal voice one of his favourite booming passages from the Bible:

While the earth remaineth, seedtime and harvest, and cold and heat, and summer and winter, and day and night shall not cease.

In a way the excesses of his life, however offensive or maddening at times, had been to all of us a bulwark against the end. With him struck down we were all, suddenly, hopelessly, exposed to the inevitability of our own death. Pausing briefly on the threshold of his room to meet his stare, my anguish was not for him but for myself as in a sudden rush—an utter and purifying wind sweeping not past me but right through me—I remembered all the nights I'd lain awake beside a snoring Barend, my nails cutting into the palms of my hands as I'd stared into the darkness thinking: My God, this can't be all: it can't just go on like this forever: somewhere, invisible now but undeniable, there must be something more than this slow ageing, this fatal oozing away of possibilities, of hope.

Somewhere there must be a force so vast that one day it must explode inside me, bursting into brightness and meaning, opening up what now seems stopped, or stoppable.—All the nights Barend had stripped me naked, then avenged himself on me for finding only nakedness; turning resentfully from me to escape into crude sleep, abandoning me in my other nakedness to the dark.

Again, as I left that room with its smell of irrevocable decay to blunder through the familiar rituals of Christmas day, I acknowledged this silent cry in me: *There must be more than this. Something must happen, and soon, while I am yet alive to respond to it.* And only weeks later did I discover, in retrospect, the terrible thing that had been prepared below the surface of that unremarkable day.

It had begun in ordinary enough fashion; there had even been a touch of frivolity in the efforts of our drivers to outdo one another: Abel on the front seat of our four-horse carriage, Galant on that of Nicolaas and his family. I'd enjoyed the chase, the wild clatter of the wheels over the ruts of the wagon-track, the swaying of the carriage, the thunder of the flailing hooves, my hair getting undone in the wind. But Barend stepped in angrily to reprimand Abel; and I suppose he was right, it might be dangerous to go on racing like that, risking our own lives and those of the two small boys who were screaming in the exhilaration of fear; and so we rode on more sedately, just far enough behind Galant to escape his dust.

I had hardly seen him since that wintry Saturday, six months before, when he'd turned up at Elandsfontein in search of his bullock. In fact, I had the distinct impression that he was deliberately avoiding me: he'd always been reticent, of course, especially in the presence of others, but those months there had been something different in his attitude, a bitter aloofness, a pointed sullenness. I'd heard that he'd been flogged again and that he'd run away—to Cape Town, I believe; and once I'd tried to discuss it with Nicolaas, but he'd angrily brushed it off. I hadn't insisted: we'd grown so far apart since the reckless innocence of our youth. And yet—

In the afternoon, when everybody had retired for a nap after gorging themselves on the Christmas meal in that stupefying heat, I slipped out of the house, eluding the ever-alert children who would be clamouring to go with me; and making sure that no one had seen me (the maids were washing up in the kitchen, but the farmyard lay deserted, shimmering in its bare whiteness), I followed the footpath up the incline behind the house, back to the dam I hadn't visited in years. Apart from the shrill of the cicadas there was no sound; even the weaver-birds in their dangling nests were silent, dazed with heat. Muddy brown and green, the dam lay in its hollow, the repository of an entire childhood. Unremitting memory.

He was sitting so still on one of the large boulders on the near side that I wasn't even aware of his presence before, alarmed by the sound of my approach, he jumped up to skelter towards the willows.

I caught my breath, startled by the suddenness of his movement.

"Galant!" I cried.

He stopped, clearly reluctant, almost guilty.

"Why do you run away from me?"

"I'm not."

The insolence of his colour.

"I didn't mean to scare you."

"You didn't."

"I was just—" With a vague, hesitant gesture I pointed towards the water, as if that in itself would be explanation enough.

He said nothing.

Cautiously I went towards him; he seemed ready to bolt.

"Every time I've been to Houd-den-Bek these last months you've kept out of my way."

"Why shouldn't I?"

"But surely—"

Almost in contempt he turned to go.

"What have I done wrong?" I cried.

He turned round to face me, his dark eyes glowering.

"Nothing," he said, "You're a white woman. You *can't* do wrong."

"Oh for God's sake, Galant!"

"Did it really please you to have me flogged?" he suddenly blurted out; it was like the snarl of a cornered dog.

"But I never had you flogged!" I protested. "When? And why should I?"

"It was you who told me to stay that day I came after the bullock. You gave me food. You told me to take the brandy. I didn't want anything. You forced me to."

"What are you talking about?" I asked, stunned.

"When Barend came back you told him I'd interfered with you."

In the oppressive heat I could feel a thin trickle of sweat running down the side of my cheek; but I felt too dazed to brush it off.

"That's not true," I whispered. "How could you think that I—"

"I no longer try to think what you may do. It's not my business. Whatever you do is right. Except that it's Christmas today; and it's only a week to New Year."

I shook my head numbly; he must be mad, I thought. Or I. The madness that had always been lurking just below the surface of our lives.

"Why do you deny it now?" he asked. He came a step towards me. For a moment his voice almost sounded pleading. "There's no need to. If you did it, you had the right. Just don't lie to me. That's one thing you've never done."

"I'm not lying," I said hoarsely. "I swear. I never said a word to Barend. How can you accuse me of such a thing?"

He stared at me. Neither of us moved. Another trickle of sweat found its way down my temple and across my jaw.

"Klaas was there," he said at last in a changed tone of voice; and then it was very still, only the cicadas shrilling.

"I'm sorry," I mumbled.

"Don't say that!" he cried angrily. Suddenly he bent over and picked up a stone, and hurled it into the water; then

369

another, and a third; I'd often seen him do it as a child. I knew he wouldn't speak again, so I turned and went away, a curious mixture of relief and oppressive sadness in me.

I waited for two days. Then, as Barend came back from the lands—our reapers were late that season; on the other farms the harvest had already been brought in before Christmas—I told him: "Klaas was cheeky with me today. And when I scolded him he talked back."

One uses what weapons one has. Yet suffering offers no redemption; and it gives one no rights. In its own way it corrodes, and corrupts. The only significance of the past is that it is past.

KLAAS

What else could I expect of the woman? She was white. That first time she pretended to be so upset about the flogging. When they try to be kind it's even worse than when they're cruel; one never knows when they'll turn round to ask the price for it. She was just waiting for the chance; and a day or two after Christmas, simply because it pleased her to do so, with no reason at all, she had me whipped.

All those years I'd cringed and cowered in their sight. I'd tried to worm my way into the Baas's favour. This was my reward.

And so when Abel came round with Galant's instructions, telling me the time had come to rise up against them, I was ready.

GALANT

New Year's Day. The harvest is in and it's not yet time for threshing. We still waiting for the west wind. It's the one day of the year we're given off: a day of presents for all the labourers for the year ahead; and since as far back as I can remember a day of merrymaking and dancing. Unharnessed, we play about like young horses. Every year. Except this one.

For nights on end I talk to Pamela about it, for she wants to rein me in.

"For Heaven's sake don't put your heart on New Year," she says every time. "It'll hit you too hard if things go wrong."

"All these years I been taking their bit in my mouth and heeding their heels in my flanks," I tell her. "But now we heard the word of freedom. Christmas is past. So it must come on New Year's Day. How can you say I mustn't put my heart on it?"

"Since when can you trust a white man's word?" she says. "What happened when you told them we wanted to get married? How many times have they given their word and broken it?"

"This word is different," I insist. "It comes from far away, from a land across the sea. The newspaper itself said so. I heard it."

"What difference does it make? The people who live across the sea are also white. They're all the same and they all stand together."

"Then it's time for us to stand together too."

"You saying all sorts of things lately," Pamela replies. "But you never say what's really in your head. What do you mean we got to 'stand together'? Suppose New Year's Day comes and goes just like Christmas and nothing happens—what then? It's all just wind."

"Christmas wasn't just wind, Pamela. Remember what happened on the land at Lagenvlei. We all standing there reaping wheat when we hear Oubaas Piet give a shout—and when we look round, there he is, lying like a dead horse. I got a real fright at first: thought he was trying to catch us out. For the man Campher was with us and we were talking the way we always talk on the lands. But afterwards I knew it was a sign that the masters are going to be taken away from us. So we better be prepared for the New Year."

"There's nothing you can do, Galant. There's nothing no one can do. It's not in our hands. We're slaves."

"After New Year no one will be a slave. Old Moses heard it with his own ears when he was in the Cape with Nicolaas. Joseph Campher knows it. And then there was the sign of Oubaas Piet. Ask anybody."

"Galant. Galant." She presses my head against her breasts and her body moves from side to side. "Oh God. Don't you understand?"

"Who are you to ask if I understand?" I cry. "You got a child that's white."

"Don't!" she says, shaking with sobs. Her tears run down from her face on to her breast and on me.

I grab hold of her. Like two animals fighting tooth and nail we grapple with each other. I drive and thrust and pound her, fit to break her bones; while she claws into my back with her nails, shouting like a savage. Are we trying to destroy one another then? Hurting, breaking, tearing, trying to break loose, to break out, to break free. I don't know how or why. All I know is we're fighting, wrestling, clawing at each other in the nights. And what comes of it? Around us the night stays as dark as ever.

The child lies sleeping in a corner; but she remains between us. The little girl with the muddy blue eyes and the frizzy white hair. Sometimes when Pamela isn't there I pick the baby up ready to dash her to the ground, to tread on her so she

373

won't be there any more: but I know I won't. I'll never be rid of her; it's like David who still comes back to me in the night.

I don't understand it. I don't understand it at all. It's as bad as the ants from the newspaper that gnaw at me in my sleep until I have no insides left. David's death cut me off from Bet; I never wanted to have anything to do with her again. But Pamela's baby cannot cut me loose from her. And it should. Deep in the womb of my woman Nicolaas planted his seed and poisoned her. His child. I know I'll never be free from her while the child is alive: yet I can't touch it. For a child is without any defence; it knows nothing; it's tomorrow's sun; and it brings a trembling weakness to me. Now it's Nicolaas's sun that rose from Pamela's womb, and yet it keeps me tied to Pamela. Oh godly god in the blue heavens: I don't understand anything about it. And it gnaws at my heart and devours me utterly.

If only New Year would come. It must come quickly now.

New Year's eve, all the neighbours turn up at Houd-den-Bek to celebrate, bringing their labourers and slaves with them. While the masters are dancing in the *voorhuis* and in front of the house we make merry among the huts at the back, like every other year. Abel is the leader of the dance, as always. But tonight I can't stand their merriment. From the dark stable I quietly lead Nicolaas's black horse and ride into the night, bareback. It's a very still night, but our speed tears wind out of the sky and the sparks fly underneath where the hooves strike rock. I go on riding and riding until the horse is exhausted. It's the last night I have to be careful. Tomorrow it's New Year's Day. Tomorrow I can come and go as I please. Tomorrow I'll be wearing shoes on my feet like a man. That's what the word of freedom means.

Impossible to sleep on a night like this. When the horse can go no further I tie him to a wagon-tree and go up the mountain alone to watch the day break from up there. The slightest dulling of the stars. A grey smear creeping up from below. Cocks crowing more and more insistently. Then a dirty smudge of red. A day like any other day. Except it's New Year.

374

Only when the sun is fully risen do I go down to the horse again and ride home very slowly. The farmyard is deserted. Here and there people have slumped down in drunkenness and exhaustion, sleeping where they fell. Only Lydia is moving about picking up feathers and talking to herself.

"What you doing? Why you not sleeping?" I ask her.

"I got work to do. It's the feathers," she says. "I got to fly."

"No need to go on working," I tell her. "It's New Year today. Just now you'll see Nicolaas coming from the house to tell us. Otherwise there will be a man on horseback from over the mountains."

"I got to fly," she says.

"Then fly to hell!"

In the hut I can hear Pamela's child crying, but I don't go there. First I take the horse back to the stable and brush it down and give it an extra portion of wheat. Have your fill, I think as I go on brushing and stroking the animal. Today's New Year.

It's late morning, while we're all sitting in silence round the breakfast pots, most of the others sulking with headaches, before Nicolaas comes down from the house carrying the bag of presents. Clothes for everyone. Trousers and shirts for the men; dresses for the women. Only Lydia is left out as usual, but what does she know about presents anyway?—she's wandering among the chickens in their run.

After handing out the clothes and the rations of tobacco and sugar, Nicolaas folds up the empty bag again. "Well, I hope it's going to be a good year. Enjoy your rest today. At the first sign of wind we'll have to start threshing." He turns to go back.

The others meekly sit around inspecting the clothes and trying out the tobacco, but I push my bundle aside.

"Is this all we getting?" I ask.

Nicolaas looks round as if he doesn't understand what I'm saying. "Were you expecting something else then?"

On his feet are the new yellow boots the little old man made: the boots that should have been mine. "What about shoes?" I ask.

"Since when do slaves wear shoes?"

The others have all stopped fidgeting and are watching us without moving.

"It's New Year today," I say quietly. "There are no more slaves."

"Galant, I told you long ago not to listen to idle talk."

"We'll see about that," I say. "There'll be a man on horseback from over the mountains before the day is over."

"The sooner you put that out of your mind the better for us all." He changes his grip on the bag. "Here at Houd-den-Bek we'll be going on just as before. And anyone looking for trouble will get it."

"So that's how it is," Ontong says after Nicolaas has gone home.

"The man on horseback will be coming soon. Just wait."

But all day long there is no sign of a messenger. All that happens to break the silence on the farm is Lydia's business. What else can anyone expect of a madwoman? Rolling in the mud of the *vlei*, as naked as my finger, then plastering herself all over with the feathers she's collected over these many years; and climbing into a peach tree, to steal some green peaches I suppose, and losing her grip and falling out. When Ontong carries her off to the hut, covered in mud and blood and feathers, she's crying and laughing at the same time, a sorry sight.

And that was the end of our New Year's Day.

LYDIA

I can fly. Look, I can fly. Why don't you believe me? No man will ever force me down again to ride me. No more beatings that cut me to bits. Nothing. Look, I can fly.

ONTONG

"Now you see what comes from newspapers and New Year," I told Galant. "All I got out of it is that even Lydia isn't what she used to be. There she lies, more chicken than woman."

If she hadn't kept me so busy with looking after her in her sickness—the Nooi came to help, and Ma-Rose came to help, but nothing made any difference: Lydia just lay there—I might have had more time for Galant. But it's hard to say. Perhaps I didn't *want* to be involved with him those days, for I could see there was something brewing. Ever since the day Oubaas Piet got ill on the land I knew there was something coming.

After New Year's Day we had a bad time on the farm. The odd jobs went on as usual; but we were all waiting for the wind to come up so the threshing could be done. All summer the wind had been blowing; but now that we needed it there was no sign of it. The silence pressed down on us. Our tempers were all strained—like a plank that's bent further and further, and you just wait for it to splinter. Nobody discussed it openly, at least not when I was present. Galant mostly just stared away into the distance as if he was still expecting to see a man on horseback. But I knew there would be no one. If anything were to happen it would have happened long ago.

If only the wind would come up.

How were we to know that when at last it did nothing in its way would be spared?

The day on the threshing-floor. There's much that gets
threshed out on a day like this. Ever since my childhood it's
been the best time of the year for me, as if all the lesser days
are brought together in one heap. It's back-breaking work, and
at night one is too tired even to lift an arm; and when you lie
down on your woman the weariness puts its heavy foot on the
small of your back; and the stubble is itching in your eyes and
nose and throat and between your shoulder-blades and all
the places you cannot reach properly. But it's a man's work and
it gives one a proud feeling, as if you're a tree that begins to
grow, roots sprouting down from your feet and discovering all
that's hidden, stone and earth and secret water; and from your
roots it rises up through your trunk, through your body that
bends and sways and swings like a tree in a high wind; and into
the wind one hurls spade upon spade of wheat, for the heavy
yellow grain to fall down and the chaff to be carried away; until
only the pure grain is left and everything else is winnowed
away; and in one's body the good deep ache of a tree.
Fulfilling work indeed, beginning well before sunrise, when
the first light is showing up below the fading stars, until after
the last blood of the sunset has drained away over the black
mountains. The wagon is brought from the shed, stacked high
with wheat; and the hard floor is covered thickly. Then I bring
in the horses, a man's got to know his step right there in the
centre, for the young ones are wild and unpredictable, and the
older ones shrewd, keeping well to the inside where the rounds
are shorter. The others spread out the wheat and beat down
the bundles, as the horses come past, a rhythmic swaying
motion that goes on till the horses are up to their knuckled

chests in straw, when it's time to take them off so the chaff can be forked out of the way, more and more of it, leaving the grain in deep golden banks on the floor. Endlessly, without a moment's rest in the baking sun, the men scrape and sweep, and scrape and sweep, cleaning away the stubble for the last dust to be winnowed out in spadefuls spread out against the steady flow of wind. We've been waiting for a long time for this wind to come up, a wind that goes through the lands like a great man striding. Now at last it's come, rising in the middle of the night and still blowing strongly at daybreak, as if at long last the year has settled into its course. The quiet days are over. Once again the farm has come to life, and in the strong dependable wind we hang out the spadefuls of wheat like washing hung out to dry; and the heavy grain seems almost reluctant to fall back to the floor, streaming down in a steady rustling sound like rain falling.

Every year it's like this. But this year there is an added darkness to the work, a heaviness, submerged thunder. For Christmas has gone; and New Year has gone. Already we're deep into January and nothing has happened yet. The word of freedom has been blown away and all we are left with is the sound of it.

If only I could force something out of Nicolaas. But ever since my return from the mountains he's sealed himself up against me. He is longsuffering and patient with me even if I deliberately challenge him. That makes it unbearable. For if only he were to raise his hand against me it would give me the reason I need. Now he's keeping even that possibility from me.

But if he goes on refusing to give me a reason I shall have to force him. And that is what the day on the threshing-floor is all about.

From early morning it's Campher who's at us again, just like when we were reaping. We're all working together, including the seasonal workers and old Plaatjie Pas and Dollie from D'Alree's place; the sun is beating down on our backs and gradually all talk dies away in the heat; only Campher never stops.

"Galant," he says, leaning on his broad broom. "New Year's come and gone, hasn't it?"

"So?" My stomach contracts like a fist clenching, but I stick to the horses, round and round.

"Weren't the slaves supposed to be free by now?"

There's nothing I can say against that. I know what I feel. Still, I don't like the man. Why did he come all the way across the sea to meddle with our lives?

"Let's finish the threshing first and bring in the wheat," I say. "There's enough time to talk afterwards."

"Well now," says old Achilles, rubbing his sore back. "We certainly have a lot of talk on this farm. Suppose you also found out it's easier said than done, hey?"

"You shut up!" I tell him.

"Didn't you say that if they hadn't set you free by New Year's Day you'd take your freedom yourselves?" Campher goes on.

"That's right," I say. "And that's the way it's going to be." I feel tempted to pick up a fork and bury him under the bank of grain.

"How are you planning to do it?" he asks. "Will you be going up to Nicolaas to tell him: 'Now I'm free'?"

"Maybe."

"Suppose he just tells you to go back to your work?"

I go on steering the horses, chaff burning my neck.

"I'm asking you, Galant," says Campher defiantly. "One can't go on talking for ever, you know. Sooner or later you must do something about it."

"You talking about dangerous things now," warns Ontong, pausing with his pitchfork in the air.

"True," says old Plaatjie Pas who's stopped for a pinch of snuff before he clutches the broomhandle with his small black paws again. "What do we know about freedom? The day the masters say we're free we'll be as free as they want us to be. No more and no less."

"That's why it's useless to wait for the masters," says Campher. "What you don't take with your own hands no one

381

will give you." He's stopped working now.

"Easy for you to talk," says old Plaatjie Pas. "You a stranger here and as soon's there is trouble you can clear out."

"I'm in it with you," he says calmly. "I've come here to stay. If you decide to go all the way I'll be right at your side."

The brooms and forks have all stopped working. In the distant orchard one can hear the birds twittering.

"What's 'all the way'?" I ask him.

"That's for you to say," he answers, turning his colourless eyes to me. "How far are you prepared to go now that they've gone back on their word to set you free?"

"Just give it time," Thys says playfully. "Perhaps the messenger is still on his way. It's a long way from the Cape."

"They said Christmas, and they said New Year. The moon has almost grown full again since then." Campher looks at me again. "Well, Galant? Aren't you saying anything?"

There's a whole world struggling inside me. The mother I cannot remember and the father I'll never know. Early days at the dam, and breaking in horses, and pressing a snake-stone against Hester's thigh, and hunting a lion, and staring at rows upon rows of ants crawling across a page and attacking me at night, and Bet lying to me about being able to read, and my child beaten to death and my jacket torn to shreds; a man with the voice of a lion, and chains on his arms and irons on his legs, and free men living across the Great River, and a woman chained to a rock for life; and a night on the mountain in the fog: things too many to think about separately, but they're all there, all of them at the same time, growing and swelling like a thing wanting to be born; and in my ears the sound of a terrible wind blowing.

"One man can't do it on his own," says Campher. "But when many act together it's possible. I've seen it with my own eyes. There are more than enough of you right here; and there's only one *baas.*"

One by one we put down the brooms and forks. I let go of the horses and they head for the winnowed wheat, but little Rooy chases them off. There are flies. I can hear them buzzing.

382

"What do you want us to do?" I ask Campher.

"It's not for me to say. You must decide for yourselves whether or not you're up to it."

"Over the years they been telling us many things," I say after a long time. "But never as clear as this time. They said there would be men coming from the Cape to free us. But those men never came and now it's past New Year."

"So what now?" Thys asks cautiously.

"Campher is right," I say. "No use just to talk about freedom unless you ready to take it when the time comes. And that cannot be done with words."

"How you going to do it?" asks Rooy in a timid voice.

I look round for a while. Then I grab one of the pitchforks and stab its prongs into the wind.

"Watch out, Galant," says Achilles. "What'll happen if the Baas sees you?"

"Let him!" I shout at him. "Or are you all too scared? You want to remain slaves?"

"Talking about freedom is one thing," says old Plaatjie. "Killing is another."

"What if it's the only way to be free?"

"I won't have anything to do with blood," says Ontong.

Slowly I come across the threshing-floor towards him, crunching the grain under my feet. I press the prongs of the fork lightly against his bare chest. "We're all together here," I say softly. "We all speak with one voice." Inside me something is still pressing and pushing to get out; now that I have begun I can't stop talking. "All these years we been bearing it in silence. Bad food. Harsh words. Floggings. Cold. Heat. Hunger. He took our women when he wanted them and planted his white children inside them. He killed my child. All that I suffered. We all did. But there's one thing a man cannot take, for if he does he got no right to call himself a man." I have a strange feeling of listening to myself from a distance. "And that is if he's promised his freedom and not given it. One can take a lot for a long time. But in the end, like a horse that rears up against the whip, you got to refuse to take

383

any more. When that day comes you say: 'Now I'm taking my life in my own hands. Otherwise I'm a dog or a snake or a worm, not a man.'"

"You allowing yourself to be fooled by this man," says old Achilles. "Can't you see he's white?"

"I'm not fooled by anyone," I reply. "What I'm saying here comes from deep inside myself. All he did was to loosen it up so it could come out. It was already lying there; and I thought I could still keep it down, but now I know it's time to bring it out into the open. For it's past Near Year."

"Here I am!" said Dollie, planting himself beside me, the muscles moving on his bare shoulders and arms and chest, grey with the dust of the chaff, and streaked with sweat.

With my raised fork I go from one man to the other. "Are you with me or not?" I ask them. And as the points of the long fork touch their bodies, one after the other says: "I'm with you, Galant."

"What are we going to do now?" Achilles asks after I've spoken to each in turn; his face the colour of old ash.

"We must provoke the man," says Campher. "Make him angry. It won't take much to make him strike out, it's his nature. Right here on the threshing-floor. Then we have the reason we need."

"Right here? Today?" asks Achilles, gulping.

"You can do it," Campher says to me.

"Yes, I'll do it."

But I can't help thinking: This is the way it's always been. When there are nests to be robbed it is I who have to put my hand in first to make sure there are no snakes; I must test the strength of the willow branches; I must break in their horses or walk ahead when we go hunting: they'll follow with the gun but I must lead the way.

One by one we squat down at the edge of the floor. Some light their pipes; others begin to chew tobacco. Old Plaatjie takes another pinch of snuff. The horses wander off towards the reaped fields. Rooy gets up to bring them back, but I stop him: "Let them go if they want to. We not budging from here."

At lunchtime we watch Bet as she comes down with the food, followed by Pamela with the wine calabash.

"Why you sitting around like this?" asks Bet, surprised and suspicious.

"Just sitting," I answer.

"If the Baas heard you—"

"I want him to hear." I get up. The others remain sitting, but I can see they're watching me closely. Taking the heavy pot from her I put it down on the hard smooth surface of the floor and take off the lid. Calmly, deliberately, I push the pot over with my foot and watch the thick stew spill out.

"What you doing now?" asks Bet, shocked.

The others are still watching, tense as newly tied thongs.

"Look at this dirty food," I say, scraping it with my foot. "You go and tell your Baas we won't have it."

"This will be big trouble, Galant!"

"Just you go and tell him."

Pamela puts down the calabash and hurries over to me. "For Heaven's sake, Galant—!" But I push her off and after a while she also goes away, her shoulders drooping.

Once or twice we see Bet glancing over her shoulder as she walks on through the beanfields and into the trees of the cherry orchard. With a strange feeling of peace I look after her, as if all my life I've been waiting for this moment; and now, at last, it's there.

The cicadas are shrilling away in their summer madness.

Nicolaas stays away so long that I begin to fear Bet never told him. But at last we see him coming down, walking very slowly, carrying in his hand a sjambok with which he flicks the bottom of his trousers.

As he reaches the edge of the floor where the sheaves still lie untrodden, I get to my feet and pick up the long fork again, staring straight at him. For the first time, as I see him coming towards me, I think of him not as *Nicolaas* but as *Baas*.

"Well, Tatters?" he says playfully, stopping a few yards away from me, twitching the sjambok. But his strained, anxious eyes belie his light manner.

"We not eating this food."

"Why not?"

"It's slave food."

Out of the corner of my eye I see the others rising to their feet, one by one. Only Campher remains seated in the shade a little way off, leaned against the wagon.

The Baas looks at each of us in turn, all of us standing there in silence, each with his fork or broom.

"Why don't you beat me now?" I say. "You got the right to do it. You're *baas*."

"What are you up to today, Galant?" he asks, a frown between his eyes.

"Call me Tatters," I say. "For you I'm no longer Galant."

A small muscle jumps in his jaw, a tiny shadow flickering from time to time.

The cicadas go on screeching.

"You shall eat what I give you," he says. "Otherwise you can go hungry."

The handle of the fork is getting sweaty in my hand.

"And you better hurry," he continues. "On Friday I'm going to fetch the schoolmaster for my children. By that time all the wheat must be in the loft."

We look at him in silence.

"Is that understood?" he asks.

Bending over, I pick up the calabash Pamela has brought, and pull out the stopper, tipping over the calabash so that the wine runs out on the hard floor where slowly it oozes in, leaving only a dark stain.

"You've been given food and wine," says Nicolaas. "What you do with it is your business."

With that he turns round and begins to walk away. The hand holding the sjambok is very stiff now. He doesn't stop once to look round.

Long after he's disappeared through the orchard, Ontong says: "You see, he didn't want to take offence."

"You getting scared again?" Campher calls from his shady spot. "I expected more of you."

386

He cannot make me angry any more. It's no longer his business. I've taken over.

"Let's finish the threshing," I tell them. "And when Nicolaas goes to fetch his schoolmaster on Friday I'll go with him and speak to the people on all the other farms we come to. Because it's not just here at Houd-den-Bek we're taking our freedom: it's every man and woman and child who's a slave, in the Bokkeveld and everywhere else. What's begun on this floor today will go on till the whole land has been threshed and winnowed. It's a wild horse we saddled today, but it's the best horse that ever was; and once a man is on his back you can't get off again before he's broken in. On this horse we'll gallop all the way, from farm to farm, throughout the Cold Bokkeveld and the Warm Bokkeveld and over the mountains; through the Land of Waveren and Paarl and Stellenbosch; till we reach the Cape. And if that road is closed to us we'll go to the Great River where the free people live. But whatever we do, we'll ride this horse."

"It's a lot you asking," mumbles old Achilles. "And that on a hungry stomach too."

"We hungry now," I say. "But tonight when the people are asleep we'll take the fattest sheep from the kraal and slaughter it. From now on we'll take whatever we need. All of us will eat together. And then we'll all get on that horse and we'll gallop through the land like the wind itself."

Taking up our tools again we return to the threshing. The hooves of the horses tread out the fat grain, bank upon bank of it, rich and thick; and the chaff is winnowed out, over and over, a fine golden dust disappearing in the wind; and the wheat that remains is clean and pure and good to eat.

In the reddening dusk we go home in a long row, each man carrying his fork or broom over the shoulder. At the *vlei* where we go to wash ourselves a couple of hammerhead birds are standing in the muddy water unmoving, like weird-shaped brown stones, staring at the fish. In silence we hold back, paralysed, too numb to interfere. For we know it's not fish they see in that dark water, but the face of a man marked for death.

387

BET

We all ate of the sheep that was killed that night, and on Galant's instruction each of us washed his hands in the blood at the slaughtering stone. I was against the idea but from the way Galant picked up his *kierie* I could see he meant trouble for whoever opposed him. I felt resentful towards him for having treated me so meanly for so long—and it wasn't my fault, was it?—but there was more pain than anger in me. He'd cast me out. Everybody had rejected me. And I was left alone with the hunger of my body, and loneliness like an illness in my bones. Like death.

Could I still have stopped them had I tried? But who would have paid any attention to me? I was frightened of what I felt coming; and eating the sheep and washing our hands in its blood was but the beginning. And the next night it was the same thing. We were all there. Even Ma-Rose, to my surprise, turned up and held the sheep down when Galant drew back its neck, cutting the throat with a single stroke of the long knife so that the dark blood came spurting over his hands and arms.

After the second sheep I spoke to the Nooi, for I couldn't keep it to myself any longer; and it was all I could think of to try and ward off disaster.

"There's a bad thing coming," I told her. "I thought I'd better tell you before it breaks out, so you can do something about it in time."

"You're just being a nuisance, Bet," she said sharply. "Why must you always sow suspicion against everybody?"

By the Thursday I couldn't stand it any more. I waited for the Baas at the kitchen door when he came back from the wheat-loft where the men had stored away the last bags of wheat; the threshing was all done.

He stopped in his tracks when he saw me and tried to avoid me at the last moment.

"Don't go away from me again, Baas," I said. "I've come to tell you something."

"What is it, Bet?"

"You mustn't go to fetch that schoolmaster tomorrow. There's an ugly thing brewing here."

"And what can it be?"

"It's Galant," I said, glancing over my shoulder to make sure there was no one to hear me. "You better be careful, Baas."

"I know you've been bearing a grudge against Galant for a long time now, Bet. And against me too. But I'm getting tired of it now."

"You don't understand me, Baas."

"I understand you only too well and I won't have any more of it."

"But Baas, it's Galant."

"Galant and I grew up together," he snarled. "We have our misunderstandings from time to time, but we've always been able to sort it out in the past and we'll do so again."

"Baas, you must listen to me. Don't go away from here tomorrow and leave the place unprotected behind you."

"Galant will be going with me. I don't need any advice from your bitchy tongue. Now go away and let me be."

I looked after him as he went into the house and closed the kitchen door behind him to keep me out, as if I was an animal that might attack him. The yard was dark. Inside the oil lamps were burning, and in their glare the windows appeared frank and exposed. The shutters would only be closed after prayers. The windows stared out into the night like eyes: but they were blind eyes, seeing nothing at all; and one could stare right through them from outside.

I had done my best. They wouldn't listen. In that darkness, for the first time, I began to feel ashamed of what I'd been doing, running after him like a bitch on heat. He hadn't

389

understood at all. Perhaps he really was scared of me, because of the child. What did he know about the fire in my body—the fire only his seed could put out? For only by drawing a man into one's body can one get power over him. Now he remained in charge; and I following in his tracks, year after year.

But even a bitch might turn to biting in the end.

D'ALREE

No matter how old I get—and I won't last for much longer; already my health is failing—I'll never forget that journey. While it was in progress I did not pay much attention to what was happening; I was just there, dozing from time to time on the jolting four-horse carriage. There was absolutely nothing unusual about it: not then. Only afterwards, when all the particulars came back to me, did I relive those few days, all sound shut out, witnessing our progress through landscapes of parched veld and bare brown wheatfields, between the rough ridges of endless grey mountains, under a sky from which occasional loosely drifting clouds cast dark shadows below, speeding along swiftly in the wind: a macabre journey on the chariot of the dead, our bones rattling, on the driver's seat Death with his long whip, straight-backed and silent, and the young boy next to him; on the narrow benches I, and the pale blonde girl holding her baby; and the two corpses in solemn conversation, one of them wearing my new boots on his feet.

There was a blankness about it: for who of us at that stage anticipated what was already so close? Only a few days later it would be all over. Two of them would be dead and buried, one widowed the others dispersed or in chains, and I deprived of the little I'd had. And all that remained unmoved would be the veld and the mountains, and the shadows of clouds chased by an invisible wind.

When I heard that Nicolaas van der Merwe was planning to fetch the schoolmaster from the Joostens that Friday, I immediately asked him to take me with him, grasping not only at the prospect of a brief escape from those inhibiting mountains but at the opportunity of discussing, at last, with

Nicolaas the circumstances of his father's stroke. In that, alas, as it turned out, I was inhibited by the presence of Galant —while Nicolaas, in turn, made it impossible for me to air with Galant the unfortunate misunderstanding about the boots. Only two evenings before he'd unexpectedly turned up at my place again—it was in fact he who'd told me about the planned journey—and he'd been in a foul mood.

"I came for my shoes," he announced.

"They're not finished yet. You know I've had a lot to do lately."

"It's my shoes you gave to Nicolaas."

"I'd never do a thing like that. Your shoes are coming on. Just be patient. I've even cut out the soles as I promised."

"Where are they?"

There was so much rubbish lying around that I couldn't find them. I knew they were there; and when I cleared up later, when everything was over, I found the soles. But because I couldn't produce them that evening Galant wouldn't believe me. He insisted that it was his leather I'd used for Nicolaas. "You just like all the other masters!" he stormed. "But you better watch out: if the wind comes up it'll blow you away with the rest of them."

I had no idea of what he might be talking about. Only afterwards I understood. But then, of course, it was too late.

Very early on Friday morning we set out. The woman and her three daughters stood at the front door to see us off; I could see the children waving until they disappeared in our dust.

We went from farm to farm, starting with Frans du Toit's, through the Wagenbooms River and the Elands Kloof, past the Long River and beyond; and, as was customary with these farmers, we stopped at every place for tea, or coffee, or a *sopie*, or a meal, and for some conversation—although I found the latter much too unremarkable to recall afterwards: while they were talking I would occupy myself with my own thoughts. It was already getting dark by the time we reached the Joostens' farm where we found the schoolmaster waiting—Jan Verlee, a thin, stern-faced man, with a pale and learned look—and stayed for the night. On Saturday we rode as far as Buffelsfontein, the farm of Nicolaas's father-in-law, old Jan du Plessis, who insisted that we stay over. The next morning, having slept badly, I rose very early. As it was Sunday, there was no one else about yet, not even the slaves (not surprising, after their carousing until God knows what hour of the night). Remembering the protruding head of a nail on the bench that had rendered the previous day's journey extremely painful to me, I took a hammer from the shed and clambered on the carriage. Having secured it, and as I was getting down, I noticed under the seat a bundle that hadn't been there before; covered with Galant's old frayed jacket. Idly, without much interest, I inspected it and found, somewhat to my surprise, a bullet mould. Still, there was no reason to suspect anything unusual, except possibly in the manner of its stowing. Before I had time to dwell on it old Jan du Plessis came from the kitchen door to ring the slave bell and invited me in to breakfast. The morning passed in a drone of prayers and conversation, and it was only after dinner that afternoon that we finally set out for home. Verlee spoke compulsively about himself, but his wife never said a word—a frail blonde waif who sat absently rocking the baby the way a girl might play with a doll. And at sunset we were back at Houd-den-Bek. I might have broached the matter of the mould, if only I didn't feel so blunted by the heat and the effects of the copious meal. If only the schoolmaster hadn't prattled on so incessantly. If I hadn't felt so uneasy about talking to Nicolaas in Galant's presence, or to Galant with Nicolaas beside us. If—if—if. Where does guilt begin, and with whom?

There is little to tell about it, and yet I remain preoccupied with those few unremarkable days as if somewhere hidden in them I might find a clue to it all.

Briefly and superficially my life had brushed theirs. Alida, old Piet, young Nicolaas, and Galant. I'd scrupulously tried never to become involved, never to take sides, never to give offence. But the merest touch had disturbed the balance: an idle conversation; the promise of a pair of boots. If I'd given

393

Galant the boots he'd wanted—? Or if I hadn't, after all those years, gone in search of Alida again, would old Piet have been spared the stroke? And if he'd been well, would not he have seen in time what was happening and found the means to prevent it? Or was it indeed unavoidable for all of us? Is it the land itself which renders evasion impossible, forcing even the ignorant spectator into a position of complicity?

Passively we drove through that innocent landscape, not knowing that already our lives had been decided.

ROOY

Galant spoke very little on the way. From time to time the Baas would say something, to which Galant would mumble yes or no. And the little old man, Oubaas D'Alree, just sat there, his wild white hair blown in the wind and his unlit pipe in the corner of his mouth, his watery eyes staring far away as if he couldn't see anything that was close by. But whenever we stopped and unharnessed on a farm, as the masters went inside to eat or drink, Galant would open up.

"Come on," he would say. "Time's short. We got to talk to the people."

Only on the first farm, Baas Du Toit's, Galant kept his mouth shut. Too risky, he said: this man was Field-cornet and we wouldn't want one of his slaves to split on us; then we'd have a commando on our backs before a single shot was fired. But at all the other farms we rounded up the people, far and wide.

I just gaped at them. I'd much rather have scrambled into the veld to look for tortoises or meerkats or birds' nests. All that talk was too much for me. But he kept me right at his side, and I suppose in a way it made me feel important. And if anybody tried to question me, I'd just say: "You listen to Galant. He's a great captain and I'm his right hand." Then they'd look at me with new respect, and draw closer to Galant to listen to what he had to say.

"How's things around here?" Galant would ask. "You people heard what was said about Christmas and New Year?"

"Yes, we heard," they'd say, some of them sullen, as if they didn't feel like talking; others more openly. "But New Year's come and gone again."

"We gave them time to give us what they promised," he would go on. "But it was no use. Now we know a thing like this isn't given freely: you got to take it for yourself. The weak ones get nothing. Only those who deserve freedom will get it."

To which one of the older men might reply: "They'll kill us in a heap."

"That's why I'm travelling from farm to farm today," Galant would say. "So that each man can keep his eyes open and make sure he knows where the guns are kept. When the day comes we must get hold of the guns before the masters know what's going on."

"How will we know when the day is there?"

"You'll get word from Houd-den-Bek. From there we'll trek through the whole world and take everybody with us."

"How do the others feel about it?"

"They're all solidly behind us."

"And how far off is that day?"

"It's close. Ten days. Perhaps five. Just keep your ears open and be ready. We'll send the word."

"And if they send commandos?"

"If we work fast enough we'll be gone before there can be a commando. Perhaps it won't even be necessary to shoot." Then he'd give them a while to chew over his words before he added: "This I can tell you: if the Dutch try to resist, there will be shooting. We won't spill blood if it isn't necessary. But we're not afraid of it either." Another silence. "And you better think about your own blood too. For if anyone tries to stab us in the back, his blood will be shed first. You heard me?"

"We heard."

"When it's all over I'll go from one place to the other myself to round up all those who didn't join. And there won't be much of them left when I'm through."

Every time I heard Galant say that a spider would run down my spine: a fright that had pleasure in it too, like the very first time one takes a girl aside to ask her: 'How's it?'; a fright and a

396

pleasure you will never forget again, leaving your throat dry and your chest out of breath and your balls tight, as if they're being squeezed.

At each farm Galant appointed one man to act as his eyes and ears, and to get hold of the guns and see to it that all the slaves stood together. When here and there he came across someone who still felt uneasy about the idea he would start telling them about what he'd seen and heard in the Cape that last winter; and then there wouldn't be any doubts left.

The night we spent at Baas Joosten's farm where we picked up the schoolmaster, Galant entertained them for hours with his Cape stories: telling them how we would all go up the Mountain with our guns, and how the gentlemen would have to come before us to lay down their arms, and how we would take over the whole land. The brandy flowed like water that night, for someone had filched a new half-aum from the cellar, and Galant's tongue was well oiled. The cocks had already begun to crow by the time the people rolled over to sleep. I thought he would be finished too, but he didn't budge from the fire and the two of us remained there all by ourselves, watching the flames flicker and die away and the red coals slowly fade to grey.

"You did a good job today," I said at last to break the silence. "You got the whole Bokkeveld behind you now."

He didn't answer; perhaps he hadn't even heard.

"Will there be a gun for me too?" I asked again.

He suddenly looked at me, his eyes screwed up to see me through the smoke. "How old are you, Rooy?" he said.

"How must I know?" I said, embarrassed. "I suppose about eighteen or so."

He gave me a short dry chuckle. "You're not a day over fourteen, man."

"I been with a girl already."

"That's neither here nor there."

"I can handle a gun."

"I hope so." He turned his head away. After a while he suddenly said: "No. No, I don't think I really hope so."

397

"You can rely on me," I said hastily. "I promise you, I'll stand by you, better than anyone else. The day you go up that Mountain in Cape Town I'll be right beside you."

"Rooy." He shook his head slowly. "I'm not sure you really know what you letting yourself in for."

"Of course I know. I been listening to you all the time. I'll shoot anything that comes in my way."

"You're not a slave. You're a Hottentot."

"But I heard you tell Thys there's no difference. We all under the yoke."

"Still, you can stay out of it if you really want to."

"I don't. I want to hold a gun in my hands, a brand new gun. And I want to trek to the Cape so I can see for myself what it looks like."

"It's not a game, Rooy. It's life and death."

"I'll shoot them so you'll just see blood everywhere, and brains, all over the place."

"I don't want any shooting unless it can't be helped, Rooy."

"I'll do just what you say."

"I wish I could trust all the others like this," he said. "But Rooy, you still a child. And children—" He almost sounded cross. "It's because of the children a thing like this must happen. But I don't want to see you destroyed too."

"Nobody going to destroy me. You said yourself we'll be going from one farm to the other and take everybody with us. You think I can have one of the two new guns the Baas bought in Cape Town?"

He got up before I'd even finished; wandering off into the night. After a while he came back, stopping in the darkness opposite the dying coals. This time he spoke very softly, I could hardly hear him.

"One goes about for a long time carrying something in your heart," he said. "One doesn't want to look at it straight. One keeps hoping it won't really be necessary. Then one day you see there's no other way. Nothing at all you can do to stay out of it. So you go ahead. Yet all the time you keep wishing—" His voice died away. "You just wish it wasn't really necessary."

"That's not the way you spoke to the other people today," I said, surprised.

"To them I got to say the things that will make them come with me, Rooy. But no one knows what's in me. Only I." Once again he turned as if to go; but he stopped. "And it could have been different, Rooy," he said. "I gave him a chance. It got to have been different." He bent over to pick up the tattered old jacket he'd brought with him against the cool of the night. "But this is how it's turned out. And I'll be a coward if I don't do what I got to do."

"You just tired," I said, still uneasy. "You had a rough day. Tomorrow you'll feel all right again."

"I'll never feel all right again, Rooy." He sighed and turned to look me in the face. "Rooy, whatever happens, I want you to remember this: I had no choice."

My eyes were so heavy I couldn't keep them open, so I don't know if he went on talking after that. I dropped off right there, dreaming for the rest of the night about a great war in which we were charging wildly ahead on horseback, shooting and killing everything in our way.

The following night we stayed over at Oubaas Jan du Plessis's place; the people there—old Adonis and Jochem and the rest—we'd known for a long time, so it wasn't difficult for Galant to talk them over. Only Adonis, shifty old baboon-spider that he was, gave us trouble, piling up one excuse on the other. It surprised me to see how patiently Galant kept working on the old man. Oubaas Jan, Galant said, had in his shed a bullet mould, that all the neighbours used to borrow when someone needed to make ammunition: and Galant wanted Adonis to bring him the mould. Some of the others offered to fetch it, especially Jochem who mostly worked with it. But Galant held them back: he wanted old Adonis to hand it over himself. At first I thought it was just to flatter the old man, or to pull his leg; but afterwards, when the mould lay safely hidden under some old bags and the tattered jacket on the carriage, Galant explained to me:

"It's because I can't trust the old bastard."

"Then why didn't you just keep him out of it? Suppose he splits on us?"

"That bullet mould will keep his mouth shut for him. You see, whether he wants to or not, he's right in it with us now. Only way to keep him quiet."

I grinned. "You'll get them all right in your hand."

He sighed again. "We got a long way to go still, Rooy."

"You said it was only a few more days?"

"Each day is as long as a lifetime."

"What about all the other farms and places?" I suddenly asked. "We been to a lot of them now, but what about all the others that don't know about our plans yet?"

"Don't worry," he said. "They'll join the moment the thing is under way. It's like a veld fire: once it's started it burns all by itself. As long as the wind is right." Then he was silent again, in his customary way—and in the roof of the hut where we sat a grasshopper chirped—and after a long time he said again, more softly this time, and more to himself than to me: "So long as the wind is right."

PAMELA

He was very quiet the night before they went to fetch the schoolmaster. The wildness that had been in him since the birth of the child at last seemed to have left him. I was particularly aware of it, as it was the last night we ever spent together. When they returned on Sunday evening Abel was there and they sat talking all night; the Monday night he rode out on the Baas's horse and only came back at dawn; and on Tuesday I went to sleep in the kitchen so that I could keep watch inside. And so that night was our last.

But he didn't want my body. Not that he lacked the desire. It was something else. He said: "Just let me lie beside you and hold you. I want to feel your heart beating in my hands."

"What is my heart to you then?"

"It's so alive. It goes on and on."

"Galant, what's the matter with you?"

"Just lie still."

For a long time we lay like that; and he fell asleep with his hands still on my breasts. I was the one who stayed awake.

But deep in the night I couldn't bear the loneliness any longer; in his sleep I felt abandoned by him. I touched him, and called softly: "Galant."

He woke up, confused with sleep, moaning lightly, and chewing as if he could still taste his dreams; and said: "Is it time to get up then?"

"No. But you going away tomorrow."

"It won't be for long. You heard what Nicolaas said: we'll be back on Sunday."

"And then?"

"You know what then."

401

"You sure you want to go through with it?"

"I got to." Suddenly he asked: "Pamela, you remember the first night I was with you? You asked me something I couldn't answer then."

"What was it?"

"You said: 'Galant, who are you?'"

"Did I?"

"Yes. Don't you remember? I been going about with that question in my head ever since."

"What makes you think of it now?"

"Because I want you to know that for the first time I'm getting closer to an answer."

"What is the answer?"

"Don't ask me yet. Only a free man can answer that. But it won't be long now."

"Don't say it's I who forced you on to this road."

"No one forced me. My eyes are open."

"What can you see? It's so dark."

"You must stay with me, Pamela. I don't know what's going to happen yet. No one can know that. But you must stay with me."

"There was a time I almost left you," I said softly.

He grew tense against me; I could hear him holding his breath. "What made you do that?"

"After I had the baby," I whispered, "there were many days I just couldn't bear it." The darkness made it easier to confess, but it still wasn't easy.

Gently his hand caressed my nipple. I shut my eyes and pressed my head against his shoulder.

"The other day," I said, "when the Nooi's father came to visit her, I asked him to take me back. Because I'm still only on loan to Nooi Cecilia."

"What did you say to him?" His breath was on my face.

"I said they were not using me well, I wanted to go back."

"What did he say?"

"He spoke like the Bible. 'You've been christened and everything, Pamela,' he said. 'Why are you so small of faith

402

then? Don't you know we will be rewarded in Heaven? The best that can happen to us in this world is to suffer. The Lord Himself set us an example.'"

"Why didn't you tell him about Nicolaas?"

"Because that wasn't the reason I wanted to go back." I could barely say the words; but the dark made it possible.

"Why was it then?"

"Because of you."

"You wanted to go away from me? Do I use you badly then?"

"No. It's different. All I can bring you is misery."

He didn't answer straight away. I thought it was from anger; I was waiting for him to take it out on my body again, but he made no move. At last he said: "It's because we're still this side, Pamela. We can't see properly because we got the eyes of slaves. But once we reach the other side we'll know for sure. There will be a sun rising. Then I'll tell you who I am. For the first time we'll really know each other."

"I don't understand what you saying about this side and the other side. You talking just like Oubaas Jan now."

"No, it's something else I'm talking about. We're still chained to the rock, like that woman I told you about. Just a few more days and we'll be free. We'll cross that Great River that keeps us from the other side. Our eyes will see properly then. Everything will be different." And after a silence he added: "I need your help, Pamela."

"How can I help you?"

"We going away tomorrow. The house will be open. I want you to get hold of the guns and hide them for us."

"It'll cause bloodshed, Galant."

"It's to avoid bloodshed I want you to steal the guns. Hide them away."

I was afraid. It was one thing lying there in the dark talking: stealing the guns was different. A gun is a dangerous thing, and all it brings is death.

I put out my hand and touched him. "Come," I whispered. "The night is almost over."

403

He grew stiff in my hand, but I felt him shaking his head against me. "Not tonight, Pamela," he whispered. "I want you. But there's too many other things. When I come into you again I want to be a free man. Otherwise it'll just be the same again."

At sunrise they left in the carriage; the horses were prancing as if they knew it was Galant who held the reins; they always did their best for him.

That first night I had the guns in my hand. I took both of them from the shelf above the bed where Nooi Cecilia lay sleeping, and I stroked the smooth wood and the heavy brasswork, the cold hardness of the barrels. Then the smallest child moaned in her sleep. Without waiting I thrust the guns back on the shelf. Not because I was scared the Nooi would wake up; but because of the child.

The second night, after everybody had gone to bed, I wandered through the dark house like a ghost. I knew it so well I could move about without bumping into anything in the pitch dark behind the closed shutters. But I just couldn't get past the doorway into the bedroom. At last, when the cocks began to crow I realized time was running out. I just had to get those guns, or the chance would be lost for good. Cautiously I drew away the bolts of the kitchen door so that I could slip out quickly and unnoticed. Then the Nooi spoke behind me.

ADONIS

It's a bloody lie. They all lying if they say I stole the bullet
mould and gave it to Galant. He was always against me, that
Galant: remember how he attacked me with the axe when Bet
was new on the farm. Did he think I'd forgot about it? Now he
wants to put the blame on me. We only found out about the
mould after they was gone. He must have taken it himself. I
don't know anything about it and I don't want to know either.
My Baas was always good to me. What will become of me
without him?

CECILIA

In the darkness before dawn, awakened from the dream (always that dream), I heard something in the kitchen and found, when I went to investigate, Pamela standing at the back door.

"What are you doing?" I asked.

She started and swung round to face me. "I—I'm just going out, Nooi," she stammered. "My stomach is upset."

"I've been hearing you moving about all night," I said. "Are you ill then?"

"No, Nooi. It's just the stuffiness, I think."

"Well, go then. And bring me the tub when you come back. It'll soon be light."

She went out. It was a strange feeling: an awareness, for the first time, of her not as a slave, as the servant who'd attended me all my life, but as a woman. Her restlessness was no doubt caused by Galant's absence. I almost envied her: if only I could be so concerned about Nicolaas. It made one look at things in a new light. They can give one so much trouble, always underfoot like domestic animals; yet somewhere, it seems, lurks a strain of human feeling.

If but she could restrain her baser nature in my husband's presence. Then that child would not have been lying in its wraps to shame us all. But they have an animal cunning that guides them, knowing exactly how to provoke the weakness of a man.

I remembered the dream again. Thank God Pamela had awakened me before it had run its usual course; even so it was enough to make me feel sick. How often it had returned to me in my life, innumerable variations of the same nightmare. I would be alone somewhere, sometimes in the veld, or in the house, in a shed, or wherever; and then I'd become aware of another presence. I never saw his face; only that he was black. I would try to send him away, but each time I was unable to utter a sound. My throat would constrict as he came closer. Then I'd try to shout, knowing no one could hear me for there still was no sound. In another moment he was tearing the clothes from me and forcing me to the ground where he would grapple with me and perpetrate unmentionable horrors on me. "Please kill me," I would plead with him. "For God's sake, I'd much rather be dead." Anything except what he was doing to me. It was the worst that could possibly happen to one.

And when at last I would wake up from the dream, feeling more nauseatingly besmirched than with mud or slime, I would immediately get up to wash myself, my whole body, scrubbing and scouring, yet unable to rid myself of the stain of that memory. And usually it would take days before I felt I could face Nicolaas and the world again.

It had been the same that night; but Pamela had averted the worst and set me thinking. In the early dawn, after I'd washed myself in the tub and long before the farm stirred to life, I went to the outbuilding we'd prepared for the schoolmaster and his wife and sat down in the part we'd partitioned off with a cupboard to form a schoolroom for Helena. I took the Bible on my lap, but I didn't read. For a while I paged through it, but soon gave it up, leaving the book open on my knees. That in itself restored a measure of peace to my mind.

Perhaps the dream was a visitation of God, I thought, to make me reflect on the grudge I felt towards Nicolaas. God had given us three daughters; it was clearly His will for us not to have sons, and if I continued to murmur against it I might be responsible for driving Nicolaas deeper into sin. I should be more humble in future.

In his absence, as in October when he'd gone to Cape Town, I usually felt more composed, more contained (except for the dream): then I was in charge, and house and farm would be run according to my wishes and my orders. There

407

would be nobody else to defer to. But this time, that early Sunday morning, I had to admit that I was lonely too. Perhaps it was only natural: God has made man upright so he couldn't easily touch another at his side; loneliness is his condition. Yet there is comfort in the knowledge of another existence next to one's own.

In the restlessness of a slave woman unable to sleep because her body's urge for a man had kept her awake, and in being saved from the worst of my dream, I'd learned to face again something of the nature of my own need.

Outside, the children came running from the house, filling the yard with their shrill voices. I picked up the Bible and went to the door of the schoolroom to assume my responsibilities for the day in the name of God.

VERLEE

From the beginning Martha had been against the idea of returning to the interior. Life was so much easier and safer and more enjoyable in the Cape she'd known since birth, she said. And all her relatives were there. But their very proximity added to my resolution to leave. Ever since we'd got married—a decision not taken lightly after I'd been on my own for forty years—her family had been around to admonish and advise; and the birth of the baby had made it immeasurably worse. Which might account for my rather precipitate acceptance of Van der Merwe's offer to become schoolmaster on his farm.

Almost all the way from Cape Town she sat crying in the wagon, which upset the child too. Fortunately things improved somewhat once we'd reached the Joostens': at least he was a distant relative of hers, and his wife knew remedies to ease the child's colic. During the two weeks we spent there Martha grew more resigned to her lot, but she still didn't say much when we left in Van der Merwe's carriage on the Sunday. She wasn't crying any more, but she wasn't very communicative either. Only once, very softly, so that the others wouldn't hear, she turned to hiss in my ear:

"Jan, I won't ever forgive you for doing this to me."

"Just give it time, Martha," I pleaded. "Once we have a place of our own to live you'll soon feel at home again."

"Whatever happens will be your responsibility."

"Obviously." Perhaps I sounded a trifle too acrimonious, but my nerves were beginning to feel rather frayed.

Neither Van der Merwe nor the little old man who'd come with him said much, so I had to make an effort to keep the conversation going by telling them about my experiences in the Eastern Cape—enough to make anyone sit up, I'm sure—and everything I'd witnessed in my life as an itinerant teacher. I thought it was wise for them to realize as soon as possible that they'd done well to choose me. Their children would be in good hands, strict but reliable. What a pity they were all girls: education is wasted on females, really. What could Martha show for all her exposure to governesses and finishing school? It certainly was no help to her as a house-wife. She couldn't even feed the baby and we would have to get a slave woman for that purpose: fortunately Van der Merwe had indicated that he had one in milk at his place. However, if I had some success with the Van der Merwe offspring some of the neighbours might be prevailed on to send their sons to me as well. It still meant something of a comedown for me, but after the year with Martha's family—however kind their intentions—at least it was a new start, independence regained. In the end she, too, could only benefit from it.

From time to time Van der Merwe made an observation. More often than not it had nothing to do with what I'd just been saying, as if he hadn't been listening; but I was careful to subscribe to whatever he said—even though he held some startling opinions, especially in connection with slavery at the Cape. Truly an uninformed person; but I preferred not to contradict him at such an early stage: he was my employer and I had to remain in his good books, especially for Martha's sake. There would be ample opportunity in due course gently to coax him towards a greater degree of enlightenment. I was even beginning to look forward to it.

"Please don't worry," I repeated to Martha when we set out from Du Plessis's farm on Sunday, hoping my voice would convince her of my own confidence. "We're embarking on an entirely new life this week. You should think of it as a great adventure. Not so, Mr D'Alree?"

The little old man just stared at me in mild bewilderment.

410

BAREND

Hester was bloody impossible again that Sunday morning. One of the black moods that just descended on her without any reason on God's earth; and it wasn't even the time of the month. We started quarrelling the moment we woke up; and when I suggested we drive over to Houd-den-Bek to meet the schoolmaster Nicolaas had gone to fetch for his children she refused point-blank.

"But it's Sunday," I said. "It's fitting that we should look up the family."

"Your family, not mine."

"What you need is a damned hiding."

"If it'll make you feel better."

"You're as stubborn as a bloody mare in heat, and that on a Sunday."

"And you like to think you're a good stallion, don't you?" she countered with that familiar little nasty smirk on her face.

A low blow; after the night before. And damn it all, it hadn't been my fault. It was she who'd started the quarrel knowing very well it could only lead to one conclusion. But our brief skirmish that morning did, after all, shed some light on her mood. It had indeed begun with the mare: the beautiful stray mare that had turned up on the farm the Saturday afternoon, a spirited wild creature nobody had seen before. It was Abel who finally managed to corner and catch her, but not without a ferocious struggle and only after being thrown twice (Klaas could kill himself laughing and I had to flick him with my sjambok so that he could stop his nonsense and help Abel subdue the animal); and when at last he brought her back to the yard my stallion broke out of his stable. We had to run for

411

cover as the two horses started cavorting, breaking down everything in their way, right through the fence of the kitchen garden; the wooden lean-to against the shed was kicked to pieces, and they tore a great gap in the quince hedge before, at last, the stallion cornered her against the stonewall between the gate and the stables. For a considerable time they still went on fighting, biting and kicking and rearing; but in the end the mare gave up and the stallion covered her. When I turned round I saw Hester standing in the back door, pressed against the frame as she leaned forward, her fists clenched in her lap; the strands of hair hanging down in front of her ears were moist, and her mouth was half-open. When she saw me she immediately swung round and disappeared into the house. Neither of us referred to it afterwards. But after we'd put out the light that evening, while the smell of oil was still overwhelming in the stuffy darkness behind the closed shutters, she started the bitchy taunts that inevitably led to her forcible subjection. She must have been excited by the horses; and it was carried over to Sunday.

"Well, if you won't go I'll go on my own with the boys," I said.

"Pieter is too small."

"I said I'm taking the boys with me. It's up to you whether you want to come with us."

I knew she wouldn't change her mind, of course. Neither would I.

"Inspan the cart," I told Abel. "You can come with us on horseback and bring the mare along."

"Where are you taking her?" asked Hester, looking piqued at the idea of seeing the animal go.

"I can't have the place trampled to pieces again like yesterday. I'll make enquiries on the way to find out where she came from. Perhaps she belongs to old D'Alree. He's the only farmer around who'll let a horse like that run away. I wish he'd pack his bloody junk and leave the Bokkeveld."

"Why are you so unreasonable with the poor man?" she asked.

412

"In your eyes I'm unreasonable with everybody." Out of spite I added: "You didn't think I'd leave the mare behind so you could put the stallion on her again the moment I turned my back, did you?"

Hester's cheeks were suffused with the redness of rage; and without another word, without even saying good-bye to the boys, she went into the house.

We passed by Frans du Toit's farm without stopping to greet him: I knew the mare wasn't his, and to off-saddle at his place went against my grain. Only Nicolaas was pusillanimous enough not to want to offend the man even if he couldn't stand him.

As it turned out it wasn't D'Alree's mare either. Plaatjie Pas told me: he was the only living soul I found at the place, as Campher and Dollie, I presume, had gone somewhere in search of drink again. How a white man could be so thick with a lot of slaves was beyond me.

Nicolaas wasn't home yet when we reached Houd-den-Bek.

"We can wait," I said. "We're in no hurry."

"Why don't you stay for dinner?" Cecilia invited me.

"If it's not too much trouble."

I sent Abel to stable the mare: Nicolaas could take her over from there. I'd had my share of trouble.

It became an extraordinarily long day. Cecilia was an exemplary housewife, but she couldn't offer much in the line of conversation and we'd soon exhausted all that could be said about the harvest, and Nicolaas's journey, and Pa's illness, and the children, and the school business. I was beginning to wonder whether it might not be better to go home after all, but that would just be grist to Hester's mill.

After dinner we retired for an afternoon nap, Cecilia to her own bedroom and I to the children's. But I found it too hot to sleep. A deadly silence in the yard. The buzzing of flies inside. The children were playing in the outbuilding prepared for the schoolmaster; later it seemed to me they slipped out to the orchards. They'd been ordered to stay indoors, but I was reluctant in that oppressive heat to go after them: and I

413

remembered our own swimming on such scorching afternoons in the dam at Lagenvlei when I was a child. Without really dozing off, in the heavy stupor following Cecilia's enormous meal, I abandoned myself to the memory of a lifetime of Sunday afternoons. Those days at the dam. The afternoon I'd tried to force Hester to take off her clothes; and her refusal. The way she'd always resisted me in everything: even her acceptance to marry me had been a way of frustrating me. I remembered our excursions in the veld; in the mountains. The day we'd been surprised by the thunderstorm, when Nicolaas and I had run off ahead of them: and the panic at the thought, afterwards, that she and Galant might have been struck by lightning or something, while in fact they'd been sheltering cosily in Ma-Rose's hut. Thinking back to it all I had an impression of our growing up among all sorts of threats and dangers—yet we'd got through them all unscathed, until we were here now, so many years later. Safe and secure: only somewhere along the road the sense of adventure had disappeared. Everything had become so even and predictable, and perhaps it was a good thing; perhaps inevitable. But how infinitely less than it might have been if—If what? I couldn't tell. And yet other possibilities must have existed once. What tremendous event would be required to restore adventure and significance to our lives, to change Hester into one of the possibilities of my life again? Years before there had been the grownups, Pa and Ma—and then us, opposite them: the children who on Sunday afternoons could enjoy themselves at the dam without a care in the world. And now, suddenly, we were the prematurely middle-aged, and the children enjoying themselves were ours. A few more years and it would be their turn again. Would there never be an end to it? And no fulfilment either?

I tried to restrain the thoughts. Sundays had never been good for me. The inertia made one think too much. All week long one was working hard, and in control of all that happened; and that brought a feeling of security. But on a day like this the world seemed to be slipping through one's fingers.

One no longer knew for sure what was happening in the heavy silence; one felt a stranger in one's own place, threatened by a panic one couldn't subdue because it remained beyond comprehension. *There is no man that hath power over the spirit to retain the spirit.*

From outside I once heard Abel's boisterous laughter. What carefree exuberance. In spite of myself, like so many times before, I had to admit that I envied him. How I would have wished to be like that myself!—and I might well have been if I'd not been weighed down by responsibilities from too early an age.

I remembered the occasion when he'd accompanied me to Cape Town; the exhilarating evenings when he would play his fiddle beside the fire. So far away from home a burden fell from me; some evenings I even joined in the singing, and we took turns with the jug of brandy. But in the end it was always I who had to decide where to stop when things threatened to get out of hand. I was never free to abandon myself completely to the music and merriment like him.

Afterwards he lost his violin in the Cape. He could give no coherent explanation of the loss. But the truth struck me: it had been his way of spitefully depriving me of something he knew I liked, a slave's petty manner of correcting his master. And it would forever remain a stumbling block between us. Once, after the upheaval caused by Goliath, he'd even threatened me with a spade. Only momentarily, but that shock of fear would always remain with me. *For they have sown the wind, and they shall reap the whirlwind.* What outrageous thoughts the Sunday afternoon was stirring up in my mind! I felt impotent against the heavy burden of the heat. There seemed to be no end to the day.

It was sunset before Nicolaas came home at last. The schoolmaster looked a real fart; his wife a slip of a girl with a sweet, strained, harmless face. The baby was whining; Cecilia called the slave woman Pamela to take the child and suckle it.

We sat down in the *voorhuis* for coffee and a desultory chat. Old D'Alree came as far as the door, but as soon as he

415

recognized me he offered his apologies and went off again.

"He's really becoming a bloody nuisance," I said to Nicolaas. "There must be a way of getting rid of him."

"Pa won't like it."

"Pa's lying there like a corpse. What does he know about what's going on?"

"He'll know."

To avoid trouble I changed the subject. "What does the world look like the way you came?"

"Some farmers are still threshing, but most have finished."

"You satisfied with your harvest?"

"Yes indeed. It's been such a dry year but the harvest was one of the best ever."

"Did you by any chance come across someone looking for a stray mare?"

"What stray mare?"

I explained.

"No," said Nicolaas. "But you can leave her here if you want to. Sooner or later someone'll come to claim her. As it happens I have an empty stable, and if she's as fiery as you say she is I'm sure Galant will enjoy looking after her. If no one comes for her I'll just keep her. Then I needn't go to Tulbagh to buy another."

"Yes, it's much better to stay out of the towns," I approved. "Those English are just a pain in the arse."

"I don't think they'll be giving us much more trouble," he said. "I looked in at Frans du Toit's place on the way and he told me there's been no sign of commissioners or messengers yet, and it's almost the end of January. It can only mean that they've given up the idea of liberating the slaves."

"I suppose he had a lot to say, as usual?"

"Yes, he held forth on things like justice and order again."

I laughed. "A lot of hot air." I said. "It's because of that face of his. It's always easier for a man with some blemish to feel holy. Only thing he's good for is big words."

The young blonde girl came in to call Verlee—something about the baby—and he left with her.

416

"I really don't see the need for messing about with school-masters," I told Nicolaas. "He'll just stuff your children's heads full of nonsense."

"Now don't start on that again." He got up. "Come and show me the mare."

Abel was waiting at the back door.

"You want the cart, Baas?"

"Aren't you staying over?" said Nicolaas.

"Thank you, I'd like to." I turned to Abel. "Find yourself a place to sleep with Galant or someone. We won't be going home till tomorrow." It would make Hester properly worried, I thought, if the boys and I stayed away for the night: just the medicine she needed.

From the stable we took a walk through the orchards and the beanfields down to the worn-out threshing-floor.

"Why's it still looking like this?" I asked, annoyed by his negligence.

"I haven't had time to have a new floor laid since the threshing." Nicolaas said apologetically. "But I already told Galant to make sure it's repaired and smeared again tomorrow."

We took a detour past the kraals and the *vlei* on our way home. Dusk was deepening. A new sense of peace had invaded the place, filling the valley like cool clear water. From the *vlei* we looked towards the farmyard with its solid home-stead and its outbuildings, the schoolhouse and stables and sheds; the kraals and huts; and, to one side, the small square of the walled graveyard, empty but for the single grave of Hester's father.

I remembered the restlessness I'd felt all afternoon. I'd been wrong, I thought now. All hadn't just been whirlwind and vanity. Look at the peaceful solidity of the place. Like my own. In Pa's youth, and in the time of our great-grandfather, all of this had been wild and untamed. But fighting against savages and wild beasts our race had conquered it, and now it was ours, forever. We'd known danger and disorder too: all the annoyance caused by the slaves in recent years. But at last it

417

was over. With strong action to show them who was in command, we'd kept the whip in hand, and now everything was under control. As far as the eye could see the land was ours. Looking out across it I could understand the profound satisfaction with which at the end of the week of creation God had surveyed everything He had made, and had seen that it was very good.

I even felt a brief tinge of longing as I thought of Hester. After all, we'd been created man and wife.

CAMPHER

I never thought it would get beyond the stage of talking. How often in my life hadn't I witnessed something similar?—a wind rising, then wavering and dying down again. Even the day on the threshing-floor I still thought Galant was only showing off to hide his chagrin when his master refused to rise to his baiting. (While surely anyone should have known in advance how the man would react.) The first indication I had that their threats might in fact be translated into action was on the Sunday night just after Galant and Nicolaas van der Merwe had come home with the schoolmaster. I'd gone over to the huts as usual for an evening *sopie* with the slaves. Dollie wasn't there—thank God, I thought afterwards, otherwise everything might have gone awry—as he and old Plaatjie Pas had to repair a sty where the pigs had broken out in old D'Alree's absence.

I was shocked to discover how far Galant's plans had progressed. On the journey he'd actually begun to prepare the slaves on the neighbouring farms for rebellion; the air was thick with it.

"Are you quite sure it will work out?" I asked him, very cautiously so as not to arouse any suspicion.

"Of course," Galant said quickly. "Isn't that exactly what you said? You been with us right from the beginning."

"Indeed. I just wanted to make quite sure that you're serious."

"You think I'm joking?"

"No, no. You can depend on me, Galant."

He stared at me very intensely, trying it seemed to see what was hidden inside me; at last he said: "All right then.

We agreed on Tuesday night. It gives us two days. You better tell Dollie too. We need every man."

Back in my hut that night I couldn't close an eye. In the end I went outside, leaning back against the doorpost, staring up at the stars. Light, almost transparent clouds swept through the sky in a high wind. The moon was up. The motion of the clouds made it seem as if it were the moon and stars passing so swiftly and soundlessly overhead. More than that: as if the earth itself, the farm, the yard, the hut, I, were sailing through the void. I had to steady myself with my hands pressed to the ground in order not to fall, feeling quite dizzy.

I shut my eyes. And in my imagination I saw the rebellion succeed: I saw us rising here at Houd-den-Bek and claiming Nicolaas's guns and taking over. I saw us setting out, trekking from one place to the other, to ever more distant places across plains and mountain ranges, adding to our ranks as we went, until a vast army was following us, an army greater even than Napoleon's, changing into a hurricane that swept everything out of its way. I saw us marching through the streets of Cape Town, cheered by the multitudes, and sweeping up the side of the Mountain like an enormous wave that nothing could stop any more, until we reached the top, where we shouted those glorious words for the whole world to hear: *Liberté —egalité—fraternité!* In my dream I saw my mother joining me, suddenly young again, her hair blonde and a smile on her face; and I took her to a new place of our own where we might live with my father and all my dead brothers and sisters, including Elsje, restored to normality. I could hear her say: "Joseph, my son, I'm proud of you. I always knew you had it in you."

But then I called up another vision—the image of a failed rebellion. I saw a small bunch of men caught unawares and overwhelmed and dispersed; I saw corpses littering the earth, and maimed men crawling like spiders with broken legs, like the hundreds I'd seen on the battlefields of Europe. I saw conquerors riding over us on horseback, threshing us under their terrible hooves; and I saw a handful of survivors rounded up, wretched and tattered, and in their eyes the hopeless

420

hungry stare of defeat; I saw us stumbling along in a long row, hands tied behind our backs, one chained to the other, and guards on horseback driving us on with their whips; I saw us hanging from the crossbeams of a row of gallows, swinging in the wind, eyes staring and black tongues protruding from our mouths; and birds coming down from the sky to consume the bodies until only the white skeletons remained; and I heard the wind making a sound of desolation through the empty eye-sockets and the ribs. I saw my mother buried old and worn to the bone, without even a coffin to receive her, and her gnarled hands folded on her chest, her eyes staring upward in one final reproach for all I'd promised and never done.

It was a balmy night; but I began to shiver as I sat there. Never in my life had I been quite so scared and hopeless. My teeth were chattering. And overhead the thin clouds still drifted past, as if the world itself were falling, an endless unstoppable fall.

All the wonderful slogans of my youth resounded in my ears again. But I could see nothing but the failure and defeat and misery resulting from those ideals: a world covered in battle-fields and armies, rags, maimed people, corpses and skeletons, famine, crying children, hate, violence, terror, fear.

Was it really inevitable then for all dreams to be no more than illusion? And did I have any right—in the tenuous hope that it would prove more than illusion—to join Galant and the others in this desperate adventure? Or would that be the surest way of finally forfeiting everything, even hope?

But it was too late now for any attempt to stop it. They'd already committed themselves, and I was involved in it: they were looking up to me as one of the instigators. If I were to go to them now and say: "Look, it's madness, I'm pulling out," they would tread right over me and turn me into the victim of something I myself had set into motion. But what could I do then? Was there really no other way?

I was scared. God alone knows how scared I was.

But it was too late even for fear.

What, moments before, had been only a vision, a nightmare from which it was still possible to wake up, had now assumed absolute certainty: nothing but failure and defeat could come from it.

Two sorts of people I'd known in my life: those born to oppress, and those born to be slaves: and each was the condition for the other's existence. In their midst, from time to time, there were those individuals, like me, who were dissatisfied, proclaiming other possibilities—but we were the exceptions (the way one sometimes found a child with a club foot or a calf with six legs) who only succeeded in causing a measure of discomfort to the others. Our only possible victory lay in defeat. And that turned us into an abomination. It had taken me a long time to reach this clarity—and God knows, a dream is not relinquished easily—but at last I'd learned my lesson; and that night, on an earth falling like a shooting star, there was no doubt at all in my mind.

There was no hope of preventing it: at least not through direct intervention. But *something* was still possible. Call me cowardly; call me anything. I feel no shame to admit I was afraid. But even if I could save no more than myself it would already be something. For my mother's sake, perhaps: I couldn't inflict on her the blow of yet another failure and another dead son.

Very early the next morning, while old D'Alree was still fast asleep, I called Dollie and told him Galant had arranged with us to wait in the mountains where they would join us for the big day. To make it sound more plausible I suggested we take one of D'Alree's two guns with us.

It was like inviting the man to a feast. He pulled back the great shoulders that had begun to droop of late; and his eyes were aflame. It took all my powers of persuasion to keep him from going on the rampage there and then and destroy everything on the farm. Old Plaatjie shouldn't get wind of anything, I warned him: he was too untrustworthy and could tell on us.

"So why don't we just cut his throat straight away?" asked Dollie.

422

"Then the farmers will immediately know we're on to something. It must be kept secret."

"But won't they guess something if they see the two of us are gone?"

"Galant will explain to them," I said. "We discussed it all last night."

"I should have been there."

"Don't worry, Dollie. You're here now."

We waited until Plaatjie had taken the sheep out to the veld and D'Alree had begun to potter around in the yard before Dollie slipped into the house to steal a gun and some food. We fled into the mountains where we hid until nightfall. "Wait here," I said to Dollie. "I'm going to fetch the others now." May God forgive me: I didn't mean to do Dollie any harm; but someone had to be sacrificed in the process, and in any case it shouldn't be for long. Waiting outside in the yard until old D'Alree's light went out, I crept to the house and hammered on the door; and when he opened, scared and flustered, I told him that Dollie had absconded with a gun and that I'd been following in pursuit all day. Now I'd finally tracked him down, and I needed the other gun to overpower him before he became a menace to the neighbourhood.

D'Alree suggested that we call in the Van der Merwes to help us, but I persuaded him that too many pursuers might spoil the hunt; and with the gun, a length of chain, and old Plaatjie Pas ostensibly to give me a hand, I returned into the mountain. In a safe spot I told the old man to wait, while I went on alone.

Dollie was pleased to see me again.

"Where's the others?" he asked.

"They're on their way." Then I brought the butt of my gun down on his head as hard as I could, and tied him up with the chain. The gun he'd brought with him I hid among the rocks before I called old Plaatjie to show him that I'd apprehended the deserter. "Now go home and tell the Baas not to worry any more. I caught the man and he's dangerous; so I'm taking him to the Landdrost right now."

I wasn't running away. In that terrifying night I'd thought it all out very lucidly. I knew that Galant and the others were all looking up to me as a leader; and they needed Dollie's great strength. With the two of us out of the way, I hoped, they would reconsider in time and abandon the whole insane idea.

Let them blame me if they must, I thought. I'd been blamed for many things in my life. But I'd always acted with the best intentions. I'd always believed implicitly in the enchanting slogans. But now I'd finally seen what resulted from them and I owed it to myself as well as to them not to soil my hands with such a venture.

If the others really were reckless enough, after my clear warning, to proceed—then it was their own responsibility.

Mine lay with my life, and my aged mother.

ABEL

At last I was going to get my fiddle back. That was what I told them on the Sunday night when we were all sitting in front of the huts making the final arrangements, after Galant had come back from the farms. All I needed was a good gun to shoot my way open to the Cape; there I'd go straight to the betting place and put my gun on the cocks and win back my fiddle. "The rest of you can do what you want," I said. "But I'll lead the way up the Mountain with my fiddle and make your feet itch so much that the whole world will start dancing."

"We talking about serious things," Galant said. "This is no time for joking."

"You think I'm not serious?" I laughed. "You all talking about freedom. Right. So let me ask you: just what's this thing you call freedom? It means eating when you hungry and drinking when you thirsty and riding a woman when you got the feeling; and it means taking up the music when you happy or sad, with no one around to make you shut up or move away. As for the rest, I shit on it."

Right after dark, as soon as the white people had withdrawn into the house, we gathered round the cooking fire: everybody from Houd-den-Bek; and Campher from old D'Alree's place—Dollie and old Plaatjie, he said, were held up by work, but he promised to take them our message—and I. Even Ma-Rose was there, shrivelled up like an old quince. Everybody that mattered was there that night.

In the beginning all seemed to be holding back, each waiting for someone else to say the first word, because it was such a big thing; and when you suddenly know it's right there and there's no way of stepping past it any more, it makes you

425

slightly short of breath. Ma-Rose had brought an apron full of late sweet peaches from the orchard; and for a long time we just sat munching them as if we had no hurry in the world. Achilles was nibbling the softest ones with his toothless gums, chewing like an old tortoise, the sweet juice running down his chin, which made us all laugh.

"You look like a man who hasn't got a care in the world," I told him.

He looked up, the firelight gleaming on his wet face, his tongue still licking the last drops of sweetness from the corners of his mouth. "And why not?" he said. "There's nothing better than a peach."

"Maybe," I joked. "But I still think the best kind of peach in the world is a fig."

Our talk annoyed Galant. "We got more to discuss than just figs and peaches," he scolded us.

"Fig is king," I said. "But you're right. Now's the time to talk, for there's a big thing coming." I couldn't help laughing from pure joy. "Just another day or two, then we'll be running free through the world, and take whatever we want. I can already see myself'—another laugh broke from my stomach—"I can see myself sitting on the stoep at Elandsfontein, *sopie* in one hand, pipe in my mouth; and taking out the pipe to shout: 'Hey, Barend! Move your arse, man. Bring on that wagon, I'm going on a trip.'"

The eyes of the young ones were beginning to twinkle; they were tittering. It was like taking out my fiddle and tuning it for the dance.

"Otherwise I'll be calling Barend to tell him: 'Hey, Barend, I want you to ride over to Houd-den-Bek and tell Baas Galant it's time he gave that useless Nicolaas a proper flogging again.'"

The others were beginning to join in the fun; I was really getting into my stride now.

"And if I get the feeling," I said, "I'll just walk over to the huts and say: 'Open up, Hester, your Baas wants to come in.'"

Galant came at me so fast, like a lynx from a bush, that

before I properly knew what was happening he had me down on my back, his hands on my throat, throttling me.

"Now you shut up!" he shouted. "Or I'll kill you!" His face was right against mine, and I'd never seen him so mad. "If that's all you can think about, Abel, it's your brains I'll be blasting out first of all. You hear me?"

"Dammit, man," I gasped when he eased up a bit. "I was just joking. What's life if there's no place for laughter any more?"

"You think we planning a feast?"

"And you make it sound like a funeral."

Campher was the first to get up and pull Galant off me; then the others kept us apart.

"Have some more peaches," Ma-Rose said drily. "They juicy and sweet."

"I'd rather have something to drink," said Ontong. "I know Achilles still got some honey-beer hidden away."

"What do you know about my beer?" mumbled Achilles; but in the end he relented and fetched a calabash. And after some time the thunderstorm had passed and we got talking, right through the night until the cocks began to crow.

I thought of the only occasion when I'd been on the point of taking on Baas Barend, on account of Goliath. That afternoon his gun had kept me off him. But one doesn't forget a thing like that; and afterwards it begins to gnaw at one and make you feel ashamed. This time no gun would stop me. This time it would be all the way.

Achilles was the only one who still shook his head doubtfully from time to time, as he sat chewing quietly on his shrivelled gums in search of the taste of the peaches.

"You looking for your own death," he mumbled.

His cowardice angered me. "Right," I said. "Then at least I'll die with a shout in my throat, knowing I tried to do something worth while. And who knows, perhaps death is just like a woman: all deep and strange in the beginning, fit to make you weak in the knees; but once you're in you don't ever want to pull out again."

427

"Easy to talk about death when you young," the old man grumbled. "I was just like that, I know all about it. But when you got to where I am death looks dark."

"Don't worry, I'll stand in front of you to protect you," I mocked him.

He went on mumbling to himself, but we ignored him.

To begin with, we checked the men we had: the group of us beside the fire, and Dollie and old Plaatjie Pas; and the slaves from the farms Galant had been to, all equipped with the guns of their masters. That seemed enough for a start, and the general feeling was that we should go ahead as soon as possible, before the news could leak out. Some were in favour of launching the attack the very next night but there was still too much to be done and we couldn't risk going into such a venture unprepared. Galant ordered Ontong and Achilles— much against their will, but they were scared to resist him openly—to make enough bullets in the mould he'd brought with him; while I offered to spend the next two days working on some more people from the other farms Galant hadn't been to, so that we would be protected on both sides.

"How will you do that?" asked Campher. "You're working at Elandsfontein all day. Your master won't allow you to take off just as you wish."

"Leave it to me," I said. "I'll find a way."

And so we all agreed on Tuesday night. And the next morning, Monday, on the way back home, I waited until we were about an hour from Houd-den-Bek before I said to Baas Barend:

"Dammit, Baas, now we left that mare's reins behind, and we need them for the tie-rod in the milling shed."

"Why the hell didn't you think of it before?"

"Sorry, Baas. But I can go back and get them. You can ride home so long."

"All right, then."

It was easier than I'd thought. Whistling gaily I rode back to Houd-den-Bek where I slipped into the stable and fetched the reins. When I came out I saw Galant in the distance and

428

greeted him, waving my clenched fist. He did the same, a gesture saying: *Tomorrow night!*

Once I'd passed D'Alree's place again I turned off the wagon-road and made a wide detour round the mountain to Lagenvlei. On the day Oubaas Piet had fallen on the lands we'd already been discussing the possibility of taking our freedom; but I had to bring the people up to date so they would be ready the next day. From Lagenvlei I rode into the mountains to the grazing place where Moses and Wildschut and Slinger were tending the old man's sheep. By nightfall I was back at Elandsfontein, but without showing myself to Baas Barend. I knew he'd be furious about my staying away; and he was probably already working himself up for another flogging. But I couldn't care less: only one more day, then he would have no more say over me.

That night I had a last talk with the people at our place. I even spoke to Klaas: and much to my surprise he immediately and eagerly agreed to join us.

"You just say one word to the Baas and you're dead," I warned him.

"What makes you think I want to have anything more to do with that man?" he said. "I been waiting for this ever since the Nooi had me flogged without any reason."

On Tuesday morning, after instructing Klaas to tell the Baas I'd sent a message that the mare had run off again and that I'd been sent in pursuit, I set out for the lower farms. I had to watch out so that the masters wouldn't see me; but that was easy. On one of the farms I was told about a man, one Hans Jansen, who'd passed that way with his Hottentot Hendrik in search of the runaway mare. But I paid no further attention to it: how was I to know that I'd find them back at Houd-den-Bek? And even if I'd known it could have made no difference. They had nothing to do with us; and I had my work to do.

Shortly before dusk, after a hard day's riding, I was back at Elandsfontein. In a small kloof at some distance from the farmyard I tied up the horse and sat on a rock watching the place slowly come to rest for the night. The Nooi coming down from the chicken run, her apron filled with eggs, followed by the two little boys each carrying a basket. The Baas making his last rounds to the kraals and the pigsties, the hayshed and the stables; then up to the huts, no doubt to find out whether I wasn't home yet, and back to the house. I saw Sarie coming from the back door for a last armful of wood. Now she would go in to wash their feet. Then supper. Prayers round the dining-table. The dishes. At last the doors barred and bolted and the light disappearing from the windows.

For the last time.

Only then did I go down to the huts for something to eat. I had a last talk with the people to make quite sure everyone knew exactly what to do. It was very close now.

Then I took a spare horse from the stable and led it back to the kloof, and mounted mine. In the moonlight I took the well-known road along the valley, past Wagendrift, and up to Houd-den-Bek.

In my mind I was already holding my fiddle to my chin and stroking the strings, drawing from it the sound of a woman in the night. Without thinking, as in the early days when I'd been courting Sarie, I brought my hand to my nose and sniffed my fingers. It was the smell of freedom.

HENDRIK

We had trouble with that mare before. A devil of a horse. My body was still raw from the beating—because I got the blame for it, of course, as always—when the Baas ordered me to set out with him to look for the bloody thing. For three days on end, including Sunday, which was the day I usually got off to visit Dina and the children over the mountain. We'd meant to get married long ago, we'd both been brought up with the Scriptures. But what's the use? I'm Khoin; Dina is a slave. And the Baas wasn't interested in buying her so we could be together, while her master didn't want Hottentots on his farm: said we were just a lot of thieves and vagabonds.

On the farm where we finally found the mare on Tuesday, a place called Houd-den-Bek, I saw the people eyeing me rather suspiciously. At last one of them, the *mantoor*, Galant, came to me.

"What's your name?" he asked. "And are you a slave?"

"I'm Hendrik. What makes you think I'm a slave?"

"Who's your *baas*?"

"Hans Jansen," I said. "We came all the way from there, from the hills of the Karoo."

"You staying for the night?"

"I suppose so. The Baas isn't a young man no more and he's had his backside in the saddle for three days." I screwed up my eyes. "But why you asking all these questions?"

"Because I'm glad you came. We can use you well. Unless you're one of those arse-lickers with the masters."

"An arse-licker, me? Look what Hans Jansen's whip done to my back." I pulled up my shirt to show him. "And on Sunday he kept me away from my wife and children."

"Then you very welcome here."

"What d'you mean?"

"Tonight the people of the Bokkeveld are rising up. They promised to set us free when the New Year came round, but the farmers stopped it. So now we breaking out. Just like that mare of yours."

"A breakaway horse gets caught again."

"A man is not a horse. We got it all worked out. Or do you think you can stay out of it because you're of the Khoin?"

I didn't answer right away. I went to the stable. The mare whinnied softly as I pushed open the top door. For a moment I felt an urge to let her out again so she could run free into the wide world. But my back was bruised enough as it was. Carefully I closed the stable door again and went back to Galant.

"Yes, I'm of the Khoin," I said. "The Dutch call me Hottentot. But what does that mean? On one side you have the masters. On the other side the slaves. What about us? We're in between. We get trodden on from both sides. The masters came from far across the sea and so did you. We're the only ones who have always been here. And what do we get for it?" I pulled up my shoulders. A shiver ran down my raw back. "Just give me a horse."

"You can have your master's horse."

"The big one?" I felt the shiver again, this time of delight. How could this man have guessed that I'd desired that horse for years?

I took Galant's arm. "You're right," I said. "It's a good thing I came. You can use me well."

JANSEN

I only came to fetch a horse. In what conceivable way could that implicate me?

GALANT

On this farm we've seen everything. Burial, as far back as the death of Hester's father. Marriage. Children who get born and who die. There's the stable. From its beams I'm still hanging, waiting for Hester to untie me. And in the night Pamela whispers: "Galant, who are you?" We know about sowing and planting, and ploughing and reaping and harvesting. We know suffering and joy; and summer and winter. We know about wind.

But now the wind has died down and it's very quiet. Nothing stirs. Everything is in suspense, waiting.

A single worry gnaws at me: ever since the day on the threshing-floor Nicolaas is refusing to take offence and to give me the reason I am looking for. All is ready; but my heart remains heavy for that lack of a final reason. Already it's Tuesday. Tonight it must happen.

Quite unexpectedly, when the sun is already down, Nicolaas comes out towards me, holding his daughter Helena by the hand. The visitor Hans Jansen is with him; also the tall thin schoolmaster Verlee.

"Galant," he says sternly. "It's Tuesday already and I told you on Sunday to repair the threshing-floor."

I shrug. "I had other work to do."

"You know very well that every year as soon as the harvest is home the floor is laid and smeared again." He glances at the visitor. "Baas Jansen here told me they had a lot of trouble with disobedient farmhands in his part of the world lately. I told him I was proud of my people, they can set an example to all the others. Now you let me down like this."

I wait in silence.

"At sunrise tomorrow I want to see that floor smeared and done."

"The sun is down already."

"Then you can damned well do it in the dark. I've given you enough time. Tomorrow morning when the sun comes up I want to show Baas Jansen what you've done."

"The sun will come up and it will go down too. I can't stop it."

"Galant." How well I know that little muscle flickering in his jaw. And just because he's trying to show off to this stranger. "We'll be coming down to the floor first thing in the morning."

"You can come down if you wish."

As they walk back to the house I suddenly feel like laughing; my heart is light and carefree. Now I know what Abel feels when he's talking about his fiddle. Everything is very quiet now: there is an openness, all tension released. Like a new sun rising from the threshing-floor. Now I have the reason I was looking for.

For a moment I am a boy again. I am alone behind the stables in the grey drizzle where a mare is giving birth. There is no one near, and she is in pain. I thrust my arm into her as far as it will go, shoulder-deep, feeling the trembling hot wet life inside and dragging it out. It is a foal, stumbling about on sticks of legs, but soon as fierce and free as the lightning, the wildest grey horse in the world. It is mine forever. This horse I shall ride into the mountains of the night, into the day already breaking, into the heart of the sun.

I know now: horses are tamed, hope can be shackled, the dream is crippled.

But it is a new foal I'm dragging from its dark mare-mother today. It's a new horse I'm mounting bare-back to ride into the world. And this one no man will ever take from me. A stallion like the wind, like lightning, like fire, life itself.

In the silence of the night we hear the sound of Abel's horse coming to the yard. It sounds dull and muted, like far-off thunder.

But actually it's very close.

HELENA

The Lord is my shepherd, I shall not want.

Tomorrow I'm starting school. I don't like Master Verlee's breath. But his wife is sweet. She lets me hold the baby.

Mummy has already started teaching me things. Daddy thinks I'm very clever. I can plait my hair myself. And two and two make five.

PART FOUR

MA-ROSE

I was told by my mother, and she by hers, and she I should think by hers again, that one day, long ago, the Moon sent the chameleon to the people newly created by Tsui-Goab to give them this message: "Even as I wane and disappear and wax again, so will you all die and be born again." But the hare took over the message from the chameleon and ran ahead to tell the people: "Listen to the words of the Moon: Even as I die, so shall you also die." That was how death came into the world. And now it is right in our midst, in this Bokkeveld. Not just the death of those who have been murdered. There is another kind of death, a deeper one, the death of the heart, and that is something which will be with us for a long time. When I stare into the dark I can see with my old eyes the dying of my people's fires and the cold ash turning white. I see no longer the smoke curling from our fireplaces. I hear no longer the songs of the women as they come home with wood from the veld. The antelope that used to roam these plains have gone and all the wild animals have disappeared. Only the wail of the jackal is heard, and the cry of the hammerhead bird treading the waters of death. My heart is cold inside me and my eyes are growing dim. My end is drawing near now that I am bowed down by the death of the one who could have been my child, by the death of both who were suckled on my paps.

It is a death that comes from far off. There is one kind of lightning that one sees with one's eyes, the lightning that announces the storm which lays waste the wheat but which also brings new life to the earth for next year's harvest. But there is another kind of lightning, invisible, and inside you, leaving its mark on your heart; it lies there waiting for years, curled up, as patient as the egg of the Lightning Bird in the darkness of the earth; and suddenly one day it breaks out to burn and scorch you inside, driving you into a madness until it has destroyed you; and only then, perhaps, can you be fertile again for a different kind of harvest.

You, Tsui-Goab
Father of our fathers
Our Father!
Let the thundercloud stream.

There is nothing more I can do about it. I cannot change the world. When the fire broke out here that night, blown up high by Galant and the others, I could neither stop them nor encourage them. I couldn't join in with them; but I couldn't stay out of it either. All that was left for me to do was to be there: to see what was happening; to look with my old eyes and listen with my old ears—so that it wouldn't just pass like a summer storm on the horizon of which you remember nothing when you wake up in the morning. I did not sleep. I was there. I was among them. I was too old to do anything, but one thing I could do and that I did: to be there.

And all that was left in me was pity. For all of them. For those killed as well as for those who had no choice but to kill. For the parents as well as the children. For white and black.

When, afterwards, the wagon came to take away the bodies, I rode with it. I helped to wash them and lay them out: Nicolaas and the schoolmaster and the stranger Jansen, all three. It was a long and shaking journey on the slow wagon from Houd-den-Bek back to Lagenvlei where we'd all started, where old Piet had been lord and master in the old days. Now he was finished, wasted away. For the last time I washed him too; and to my surprise Nooi Alida did nothing to prevent me. He was still alive, but I washed him the way one washes a body for burial; the way a mother washes her child. Death lies in wait for all of us. And all that remains will be the rough cliffs and the plains of our highlands, with their black wagon-trees and their red-grass, and the smell of buchu in the evening breeze, and the sweet tea of the mountain.

440

And all I can say about what has happened is that I was there.

In the beginning I thought it was not enough to know: one needed also to understand. Now I'm not so sure. Is it enough to understand unless you also try to change it? That was what Galant tried to do. But where did it land him? Only his head will come back to Houd-den-Bek.

This Houd-den-Bek. All these years we believed it was cut off from the world, a region apart and contained within these mountains. We thought we were on our own here, that nothing could touch us from outside. But it was a delusion. Like that lion, so many years ago, that arrived here from nowhere and disrupted our quiet lives, all of us, too, came in here with our yesterdays and our worlds clinging to us. Now, out of the shadow of death we're all looking back over the past. And perhaps someone will hear us calling out, all these voices in the great silence, all of us together, each one forever alone. We go on talking and talking, an endless chain of voices, all together yet all apart, all different yet all the same; and the separate links might lie but the chain is the truth. And the name of the chain is Houd-den-Bek.

We're looking back; and I can say that I'd seen it coming from far off, through years and seasons of sun and snow and wind. Indeed, I saw it all. I understood. But is that enough?

No. In this ache that remains of everything I've witnessed I know it is not the answer. It depends on *how* you understand: on how you *reach* understanding. What is important is not just to understand with mind, but to live through it all. To avoid nothing. Not to judge. To suffer without presuming that pain gives one a right to anything. To pity. To love. Not to give up hope. To be there: that is what's important. We're all of us human, and I pity us all, for I'm the mother of all.

Ma-Rose is my name.

I was there.

DU TOIT

I thought I knew what had happened. I did what was expected of me, neither deterred nor encouraged by our several histories. Beyond the passions and terrors of our personal involvement lay, small and sordid, what seemed like irreducible fact. Now, having taken down all their statements, each the summary of an existence, I am perplexed by the obscurity of the truth. Where does it reside? In these affirmations and contradictions, this incipient pattern, or somewhere in the wild and senseless groping of that initial action preceding the word? Does it evolve from the litany of repetition, or is only the unutterable true? Can the virgin be celebrated except in the act of violation, or innocence established except in its corruption? But if it is such a precarious undertaking to arrive at the truth, how does one find the way to justice, of which I am supposed to be the officer and instrument?

Justice: a word as profound and passionate as that faceless naked woman I burn for and will never possess, kneeling head down at my disposal, offering the cleft flesh I feverishly dream of, a fire in which to sheath and engulf myself—forever unattainable because of the shameful mark of Cain I bear upon my face. A word as disgusting and noisy as a pig held down by slaves for my furious entry, briefly to assuage the searing of a different flame. Pig-woman, loathed and loved, confirming a base need, an innate incompletion; girl-sow, degrading, risible, and indispensable. Justice: I pursue and espouse you, accepting that to find you would irrevocably change woman into sow.

The facts, then. On the morning of Wednesday 2nd

442

February last the old man D'Alree accompanied by Barend van der Merwe arrived at my place Wagendrift with a message that murder was being committed on the farm of Nicolaas van der Merwe. I forthwith, with their help, assembled as many people in the neighbourhood as I could collect, whereupon I led a commando of about a dozen men to Houd-den-Bek.

On arriving there we found the said Nicolaas van der Merwe, as well as Hendrik Jansen and the schoolmaster Johannes Verlee lying dead on the floor, Van der Merwe at the front door of the house, and the two others in the kitchen. We immediately examined the bodies, and found on Van der Merwe three wounds, one through the back of the shoulder, one in the right eye and one through the head, but the one in the eye had only grazed it. On the body of Verlee we found a wound in the left arm, another in the left side, and a third through the left hip. The left arm was almost entirely shattered. In addition, he had received a wound in the stomach. On the body of Jansen we found a wound in a slanting direction along the right breast, and one in the left side, but whether they were both occasioned by the same shot or by two different ones I cannot tell.

The wife of Van der Merwe was also wounded and lay on the bed in her room; the wound was in the lower part of her abdomen, and she would not allow us to examine it.

In the back yard, on a small patch of grass, we found the young woman Martha Verlee sitting with her knees drawn up and staring into the distance; her baby was lying in a bundle of blankets beside her and was crying, but she paid no attention to it. She appeared equally oblivious of our presence and would only, in response to our questions, shake her head from time to time. I believe it was not before she was taken to the farm Lagenvlei and delivered to the care of old Mrs Alida van der Merwe that she recovered her speech, and even then she was unable to give any coherent account of what had happened.

In and around the house we also found two elderly slaves of the late Nicolaas van der Merwe, namely Achilles and

Ontong, and a female Hottentot by the name of Bet who was tending the wounded lady of the house and comforting the three small girls we found huddled together in the loft.

After a brief inspection we rode thence to the place of Barend van der Merwe, but finding it deserted we proceeded into the mountains where, about three-quarters of an hour's distance from the farm, at a grazing place of old Piet van der Merwe, we caught sight of the murderers who immediately mounted their horses. Two of my commando fired at them, and they also fired some shots at us, without however anyone being wounded on either side. I specifically saw Galant turn his horse round, stop, and fire. What made him conspicuous was that he had a blood-flag tied to his hat and was wearing shoes, presumably stolen from his late master, whose body had been found barefoot.

The servants and slaves belonging to old Piet van der Merwe immediately approached us on foot to surrender themselves, informing us that they had not had anything to do with the murderers. An old man named Moses took us to his hut where we found Hester van der Merwe in hiding with her two small boys, in the care of a young slave Goliath who, it appeared, had aided her to escape the night before. She was restored to her husband and although she appeared somewhat reluctant to be reunited with him, they thereafter returned to their home while the rest of the commando pursued the criminals.

At the sheep kraal we found a horse which we were informed belonged to Klaas, who had run away on foot. Jansen's servant Hendrik had likewise been thrown by his horse and was soon recovered by the commando among the rocks where, like Klaas, he had fallen down in a state of inebriation.

The same evening the youngster Rooy was also apprehended in the vicinity of the grazing place. Abel was caught the following day as he tried to make his escape through the mountains in the direction of Tulbagh.

I immediately proceeded with a preliminary examination of the four prisoners in our care. All of them reported incitement

444

by Galant to the effect that the slaves had been promised their freedom a long time ago, but that this had not taken place, so that they now felt they had no choice but to make themselves free. Thereupon I drew up a memorandum which I sent, with the prisoners, to the Special Heemraad. I was subsequently informed that the Landdrost had met the prisoners at Goudini, from where he had sent them on to Worcester.

The other accused were all apprehended in the course of the next fortnight. Initially Achilles and Ontong had been allowed to come and go as they pleased, but after some clothing belonging to their late Master had been found in their huts I gave orders for them to be arrested as well. The slave woman Pamela was not apprehended until six days later when she was driven back to the farm by the pangs of hunger, she having taken only a small crust of bread with her at the time of her flight into the mountains. Galant himself was only taken on the thirteenth day, soon after members of my commando had come upon him and Thys in the mountains. Thys offered considerable resistance and had to be subdued by force; but when Galant eventually surrendered he did so without making any effort to defend himself. At that time we lay encamped in a remote part of the mountains above Houd-den-Bek, and it is not inconceivable that Galant might have killed several of us under cover of darkness had he so wished; yet he came down to us unarmed and with raised hands. He was barefoot once again, with the shoes of his late master, laces tied together, slung over his shoulder. At first we thought that he must have run out of ammunition, but following our inquiries he led us to a place a few hundred yards away where he had concealed his gun and a leather bag filled with powder and shot.

I had to restrain my men from doing him too much harm, since they were understandably enraged about the brutal murders for which the prisoner had been responsible and for the many days he had forced us to continue our hunt for him in that rugged terrain; and having, in the end, bound him hand and foot I thought it wise to send the members of the commando back to their homes. Galant and I proceeded

445

through the Bokkeveld and down to Tulbagh alone, I on horseback, he on foot. Our progress was slow, owing to the injuries he had received at the time of his arrest. But in a sense time seemed no longer of much importance. What had happened belonged to the past; and what was still to happen, however predictable, belonged to a time and a place we had not yet attained. This was a moment in between, a suspended existence in which we were accountable only to one another.

The man intrigued me. I tried to prod him, but he was very reticent. Not that he appeared sullen or recalcitrant, or that he seemed deliberately to withhold anything from me; and I doubt that it was a matter of incomprehension. In fact, he made the impression of a man at peace with himself and with the world. He offered no complaint about the manner of his treatment at the hands of the commando at the moment of his arrest, or about the rigours of our journey. He simply did not seem to find it necessary to speak; and when he did, he offered little more than the briefest responses of a commonplace nature.

Or is it that in these extremities, and beyond redemption, beyond the entire compass of our ordinary existences defined by right and wrong, only the commonplace has the right to exist, acquiring for itself, perhaps, that small bare simplicity of truth it must originally have possessed?

I made many attempts to draw him into conversation, to extract some meaningful answer to my questions.

"Galant," I would say, "why did you do what you have done? Why such a terrible thing?"

He would look at me with a blandness that shook me, as if he found the question wholly redundant.

"To be free," he would reply.

"But was it necessary to go to such an extreme?"

"What else could I do?"

"Surely there were many other possibilities you could have tried first."

"I tried."

"But *murder*?"

446

"We murder every day, in our hearts."

"You grew up with Nicolaas. He was your friend. Did you not find it almost impossible to do such a thing?"

"Before you do a thing it looks difficult. Then you do it and it is done. It is like digging, or chopping wood, or riding a horse. When you're a boy you think you'll never be able to do it with a woman. Then you do it and it's easy."

Were his eyes mocking, defying me? I felt my face burning with rage and shame.

But I persisted: "With a woman, there are children. With this murder you haven't gained or earned anything. Except more deaths."

He shrugged.

"How can you not feel horrified by it all," I asked, "now that it is all over?"

"It is not over. It will never be over."

"You've lost. It has ended in defeat."

"There is not defeat," he said quietly. "For the moment you are stronger that's all."

"We shall always be stronger."

"To be strong will not make you right," he said.

I got angry. "You think you had right on your side when you left that house strewn with corpses?"

"There was not right or wrong there," Galant said. "There was only the killing, doing what had to be done. If there is right it will be for others, one day." More softly he added: "Perhaps."

"What use is that to you?" I said. "You don't even have children to survive you."

"There may be a child," he said.

"Where? How?"

He smiled and looked down, not bothering to reply.

"There's nothing but ruin and waste," I insisted. If only I could take him by the shoulders and shake some sense into him.

"There's always the children," he said, not looking at me. "On us they can trample. They can winnow us in the wind.

447

They can blow us away like chaff. It doesn't matter. The wheat remains. The grains. The bread. The children."

He must have become deranged, I think, by what he'd done; I discovered no sense in his ramblings, and his silences were disconcerting.

As we proceeded we spoke less and less frequently.

"Don't you feel any remorse?" I asked on our last night together. "Did you really hate Nicolaas so much?"

He looked up, as if in surprise. "I did not hate him," he said.

"You killed him in cold blood."

"I loved him," he said. "So I had to kill him."

"You're not in your right mind any longer."

"I loved him." For once there was a hint of urgency in his voice as if it was important to him to make me understand (but what? am I not simply transferring my own confused wishes to him?). "He grew up with me. Ma-Rose was our mother. We were together. Then he turned away from me. He became not Nicolaas but a man I didn't know. A man strange to himself. I had to free him from that man. I had to break into his whiteness to make him my friend again. That Nicolaas."

"I don't think you know what you're saying."

He stared at me for a while. His eyes were burning like embers. He probably hadn't had any sleep for many nights. But he didn't reply.

"It will soon be over," I said, prompted by an incomprehensible urge to comfort him. "Tomorrow we shall be in Worcester and from there they'll take you to Cape Town."

"Yes," he said. "At last I shall go to the Cape."

"You've been there before," I said. "Last year when you ran away."

He didn't answer.

"Why did you come back?" I asked.

"I had to."

"You really were very stupid, Galant!" I cried, exasperated with the man.

"Who are you to say that?" he asked. "You do things with pigs."

448

In a fury I grabbed a piece of firewood and hit him in the face with it. A thin black line of blood trickled from his left eye across his face. He made no effort, with his chained hands, to brush it off.

I couldn't help feeling a tinge of regret.

"I'm sorry," I mumbled. "But you have no right to taunt me like that."

"My hands are soiled," he said. "So are yours. We are alike. Yet you are taking me to the gentlemen of the Court so that they may kill me. That is your justice."

"There's a big difference," I said hotly, "between murder and—" I stopped short.

He only shrugged.

It was the last time we spoke.

Everything has gone its predictable course from there. And now, when it is all over, when the truth has been established and justice done, when some have been killed and others imprisoned, we shall be free to go home, history our only burden.

I have nothing more to add. It is, it must be, the truth, the whole truth, and nothing but the truth.

THYS

Then Galant gave me a blow that landed me flat on my arse.
"I thought I could depend on you?" he said. "Well, if you so
shit-scared, you can just stay here!"

That was what persuaded me to go.

I'd been with him all the time we spoke about what was
going to happen. It was only that night, when at last we heard
Abel's horse coming round the huts, that I got scared.
Suddenly it was no longer just talk; it was real. That's why I
said: "You really sure we got to go through with this? It's fire.
And fire burns."

"What do you know about fire?" asked Galant. "You got to
feel it before you know it."

"Then it's too late."

That was when he struck me and Abel spat at me. And only
much later, after the fire had died down again, when I came
back from the Karoo and joined Galant in the mountains and
the commando got us—and I gave them a hard time before
they finally took my gun from me and beat me down—I
discussed it with him again; and by then he was quite changed.
Is such a fire really worthwhile, I asked him, if it just burns
itself out like that?

"You mistaking the flame for the fire," he said, without
looking at me; in those last days he always seemed to look right
past or through one. "All you see is the outside. The real fire is
different. It's inside, and it's dark, like the heart of a candle."

I'm not sure about what brought the change in him. It was
there even before I came back from the Karoo where I'd
escaped to from the grazing place where they found us after

450

the killing. If I think back now, it seems to me the change was already there that night on our way back from Baas Barend's farm. He was the one who kept us going, but by that time I think he was already changed. Perhaps that was the darkness inside the flame he spoke about. Right in the beginning, before we set out from Houd-den-Bek, he had an argument with Abel who wanted to take the road to Lagenvlei first so we could start with Oubaas Piet; Galant would have none of it.

"You leave the old man out of it," he said. "He's already dying in his bed, he got nothing to do with this."

"But he's their father," said Abel. "That's where they all come from."

"His time was different," Galant said. "He understands nothing of all this. With him one always knew what was right and what was wrong; he may have been a hard man, but he had a good heart. Our war is not against him."

"You getting soft?" asked Abel.

"Take out your *kierie*, then we'll see who's soft."

So we obeyed him. Right, he was different from Abel, but that's not what I'm talking about. The war was in him, same as in us. But by the time we rode back from Elandsfontein that other darkness was in him that made him different; I don't know what it was: a darkness that made light, the way Ma-Rose's Lightning Bird lies brooding in an antheap, showing only its gleaming eye. And afterwards, in the mountains, he was changed even more. I know, for we spoke a lot those last days.

"All the others are rounded up now," I said to him then. "But they'll never find the two of us here in the mountains. We can tackle one farm after the other at night until there's no *baas* left in the Bokkeveld."

"You think we'll be free then?"

"That's what you said."

"Yes, Thys, I suppose that's what I said."

"So what's wrong with you then? You not beginning to regret that you killed Baas Nicolaas, are you?"

"I'm not regretting anything. I had to do it. But it makes no difference."

451

"Galant, I really don't understand you."

"No, you won't." Then he would look at me for a long time before he added: "Thys, you just a boy. It'll be much better for you to give yourself up to them; then you still have a chance."

"I'm not a boy." I felt hurt and humiliated. "The night we set out you said I was shit-scared. Didn't I show you? I stayed with you all the time. It was I who brought Baas Jansen back when he tried to escape on his horse. It was I who broke Baas Barend's front door open with the spade. It was I who helped you take the guns from the Nooi. And when the women and children went to hide in the attic I went up with my sabre to bring them down again—"

"I know, Thys. You did a man's job. But that's not enough."

It scared me to hear him talking like that. And in the end I let him be; I could no longer understand him. He tried to stop me when we saw the commando coming towards us, but I charged down the side of the mountain on my horse, shooting as hard as I could. When there's only death left one puts everything into it. And charging towards them like that, right into their guns, was all I ever understood about this freedom thing we'd been talking about so much. Everything was over for me. There was nothing I could go back to: I could only go on, deeper into the veld fire. It was a strange feeling, the way one feels when one gets drunk; the way I felt that first night we rode out.

That night, when Abel arrived with the horses from Elandsfontein, Galant said: "You all ready? The time for talking is over. Now it's war."

And I rode out with them into the dark. The hooves of the horses were thundering in the night. Where they struck rock they sent sparks flying like swarms of fireflies. Let them set the red-grass alight, I thought. Let the whole world catch fire. Here we come!

HESTER

It was the time of the month when desire sears my womb like a flame. Yet I fought Barend off when he approached me: for that very reason I fought him, as the acceptance of his assuaging seed would seal my submission, a humiliation more unbearable than my physical need. It was made worse by the fact that, for once, he had refused even to turn out the lamp. In its yellow light, heavy as dust, we fought and tossed on the bed and as he tore the nightdress from me I could see our shadows staggering grotesquely on the blank enclosing walls and ceiling. Forcibly, as often before, he entered me; but feeling his frenzy approaching I managed to wrestle myself free from him, feeling his futile seed spurting against my hip—his cry of rage, his fist crashing against my skull—burning my skin, liquid fire. A child whimpered in his sleep, a sound heard not with the ears but the guts. In disgust and frustration he turned away from me, and snarled, and slept. Defeat and victory were irrelevant in themselves. What mattered was that my revolt had become unavoidable lest in my continued subjection I became as corrupt as he in the exercise of his male power.

The heavy body of the night crushing the house after the lamp was turned out; the smell of paraffin stinging my nostrils. The shutters shut; the wide world unattainable outside, and we imprisoned in that oppressive heat, he in obtuse oblivion as I remained awake, lying on my back and staring at the ceiling, every muscle in my body tense in lust and hate, my clenched hands pressed numbly against my mound. Until at last, in some nameless hour, I heard the sound of sheep breaking from the kraal and then the barking of the dogs.

KLAAS

Truth is in the Bible; lies lie about on the ground. All I can say is what I know. I'd arranged with Abel that, when he came back from Houd-den-Bek with the others he'd repeat the hoot of an owl three times; then I would drive the sheep out of the kraal to lure the Baas outside, where we would take over.

I was waiting for the owl. Already in the early dusk, when the Baas made his last rounds through the yard in search of work half or badly done, and the Nooi moved in and out through the kitchen door to bring the children in, I could feel my heart contract. Not long now, I thought, and that man would be out of the way for good. Then I'd have a go at the woman to avenge myself on her both for that flogging of long ago, and for the recent beating for which she was responsible because she felt guilty about Galant. She'd be soft in my hands. She would scream when I broke into her. All these years I had to accept a woman standing over me. Now at last my chance would come to prove to her I wasn't just a slave but a man. I'd teach her to say please. And after I was through with her I'd throw her to the next like a used old skin.

The shutters were closed for the night. After the washing of the feet, and doing the supper dishes, Abel's Sarie came from the kitchen; then the doors, too, were closed. The farmyard grew silent. In the shed one could hear the cows gently chewing their cuds. I sat waiting for the owl to call.

Then everything went wrong. Before I knew what was happening the sheep came breaking from the kraal by themselves. My efforts to stop them just made them more bewildered; soon the whole flock was streaming out in the moonlight, and the dogs were barking frantically.

I heard the bars drawn away from the kitchen window; Baas Barend leaned out to call: "What the hell's going on there, Klaas?"

Before I could say anything the men and their horses were all round me. In the confusion I hadn't even heard them.

"Help me!" I said to Abel. "The bloody sheep all broke out. We got to round them up again."

"But that's as it should be," he said.

"Don't argue, man. It wasn't I who let them out. They broke out by themselves. For God's sake, help me!" Only afterwards it struck me how ridiculous it had been of me; but at that moment I was too bewildered to think properly. All I knew was that things were going wrong and we had to get those sheep back to the kraal. The Baas was already on his way across the yard when I glanced up to see Galant and Abel scrambling through the kitchen window—it could only have been they; the others were still with me—and disappearing inside.

Then I heard the Baas calling from the shed: "Klaas, you bloody bastard, why are the dogs going on like that?"

"I got visitors, Baas," I stammered.

In the house someone must have lit a lamp, for suddenly there was a glow behind the kitchen window, as Galant and Abel came jumping out again, each with a gun.

"Baas," I began; but then they fired and he stumbled like a wounded buck and fell down. For a moment I thought he was killed, but the shot had only grazed his heel. On all fours, his backside up in the air, he came scrambling towards me in his flapping white nightshirt, grabbing hold of me: not to throttle me or attack me, but in panic. "Help me, Klaas!" he shouted. "For God's sake, help me! Klaas, I'll give you anything you want. I've always been good to you. Please help me!"

I hadn't expected ever to see a thing like that. This man, ruling over us all so cruelly for so long, now whimpering and grovelling like a scared dog. I was so flustered—and from the house I could see Galant and Abel coming towards us; ready, no doubt, to shoot us both—that I could only stammer: "But

Baas, I got no gun. How can I help you?"

I don't think he even heard me. Seeing the others approaching with their guns he let go of me again and ran away, round the nearest shed, back to the house.

"Klaas," Galant said sternly, "listen to me. If you help Barend tonight I'll kill you with my own gun."

We all ran back to the house, but just as we came round the corner the door was slammed shut. Thys went out ahead of us and, finding a spade somewhere, started hammering on the front door with it. It shuddered under his blows, and soon we heard the sound of splintering wood.

"It's down!" shouted Galant.

At the same time, we saw the Baas scurrying away into the dark from the back door, still in his nightshirt, disappearing up the quince hedge. Abel ran after him for a few yards, aiming a wild shot—but the Baas only gave a little jump of fright and went on running. Galant also aimed a shot but the cock of his gun got stuck, and so Baas Barend got away in the mountain. Thys was all in favour of going right after him, but Abel held him back. "Let's take the house first," he said.

We all rushed inside, struck by a new sort of madness. How often had I been in that house before, meekly holding my hat in my hands—*Yes, Baas. All right, Nooi*—and now suddenly it was all ours. We started smashing everything in our way, tables and chairs, cupboards, shelves. We tore open the pillows and strewed the feathers all over the place. Abel found the brandy jug and passed it round from mouth to mouth. It was like a New Year's festival. All that was visible of little Rooy through the feathers clinging to his clothes and sweaty face was his big bright eyes.

After a while I remembered about the woman again. It was time for it now; my blood was hot. I went in search of her but she was nowhere to be found. I stripped the bed and turned it right over, thinking she might be hiding under the down-mattress in fear, but there was no sign of her. In disgust I poured the contents of the piss-pot over the bundle of crumpled sheets and blankets.

456

"What you doing?" the others asked behind me.

"Looking for the woman."

"She slipped through the front door long ago," one of them said. "Galant told Sarie to take away the children."

"Where's Galant?"

"Have another drink," Abel insisted, thrusting the jug into my hands.

I drank deeply. The others returned noisily to the front room, leaving me behind in the bedroom with the broken remains of the big stinkwood bed. My head was reeling. Nothing seemed real any more. A terrible numbness slowly sank into me as I stood looking at the mess in the room. The Baas had run away, I thought; so had the Nooi. And sometime soon they would be coming back bringing all their neighbours with them to avenge this ruined house. I should have foreseen it when the sheep broke out. Already it was all over for us: and yet they were dumb enough to go on drinking and breaking up the place.

Stumbling to the middle door I began to shout at them in panic and rage, but no one heard. I was shivering. Any moment now, in another minute, in an hour, the horsemen would come streaming over the hills towards us.

"What's the matter with you?" Abel suddenly asked me, taking me by the shoulders and shaking me. "You look like death itself."

"We got to get out of here. Quickly."

"Why?"

"Can't you see? They all got away. Even the woman."

Then, to my shock, I saw the woman standing in the darkness outside the broken front door. I stared at her. I was still shivering; but I gulped. She was wearing her nightdress and it was torn. I began to move towards her like someone walking in his sleep.

"Let her be!" I suddenly heard Galant say as he appeared in the darkness behind her.

"That's right," Abel said. "Our war is against the masters. Let her go."

"I need someone who can take her away to safety," Galant said. "Over the mountain to the grazing place of Oubaas Piet, where Moses and the others are."

"Klaas?" said the woman, not sounding very sure of herself.

"Yes, Nooi," I replied, thinking of the long road over the mountain in the dark. There wouldn't be anyone near us. But I also thought of the commando which would surely be coming to this place to seek retribution: if I could lead her away from there I wouldn't be among the victims. They might even be grateful to me.

"I'll take her," I said hastily. "I know the way."

Galant stared at me. *What you looking at?* I thought. *What you seeing in me?*

"I'll take her," I repeated as urgently as I could.

"Where's Goliath?" asked Galant.

"I want to stay with you," pleaded Goliath. "I want to be with you all the way."

"You heard me!" Galant irritably cut him short. "Goliath, you take her away over the mountains to Moses's place. Make sure she's safe. Look after her until we come back. I'm holding you responsible."

"But—" Goliath seemed ready to burst into tears.

"Let me take the woman," I insisted.

"I'm sending Goliath!" Galant shouted. And as Goliath went off into the night with the woman Galant turned to us. Kicking at a broken chair in his way, he snarled: "Is this all you can think about? Is this your freedom?—breaking and drinking and arguing?"

We all felt rather crestfallen as we followed him back to where Rooy was holding the horses. He ordered me to saddle Baas Barend's horse and ride beside him, as if he'd seen my hidden thoughts and wanted to make sure I wouldn't escape on the way.

I kept thinking about the woman going into the night with her torn nightdress. It felt like the morning after a night of much drinking. And if one feels in advance what should only come later one has really had it.

458

GOLIATH

Since the day I allowed myself to be talked into complaining I was stuck. There were some who never seemed to care a damn about beatings and floggings, but I was different. And that was what weighed me down. Not the Baas, but my fear of him; my fear of pain. That evening when I saw how even Abel was too scared to raise a hand against him, my own fear got worse. And when the word came that we were going to rise up it was like being given another chance. It was not so much the masters but fear itself I was going to root out. In that big fire, I thought, my fear would be burnt out, leaving me a new man, a free one, for the first time in my life.

In order to rid myself of the burden I would have to do something that almost didn't bear thinking about: I would have to kill, and cover my hands in blood. Preparing myself for it I forced down the terror I felt, swallowing it like a lump of dry bread as I dashed about through Baas Barend's house with the others, shattering whatever we could lay our hands on. The brandy made it easier. I was working myself up to a state where I knew I could do what I'd most dreaded. Freedom was very close now.

And then Galant appeared and ordered me to lead the woman through the mountains to old Moses, and to take responsibility for her safety.

It was the last thing I wanted to do. I knew that if he took away from me this chance to murder my way to freedom, I would never again have the guts to throw off the fear which had so long paralyzed me. But he told me to lead the woman to safety; and I had no choice.

Not a word was said between us all the way. I knew I had

lost the only chance I would ever have. Now the others might become free, but not I. And the resentment I felt against Galant was one of the fiercest and bitterest feelings I'd ever had in my life.

Only afterwards, when the others were arrested and taken away to Cape Town, I began to wonder whether perhaps Galant had known me better than I had myself. Had he already seen what I'd been blind for: that I would never really have enough courage to root out the fear in me? Had he realized long before the rest of us that it could only end in defeat and disaster; and had he wanted to save me from it?

Because of the woman. But of her I cannot talk. I am not free to say what I know.

PLAATJIE PAS

In Ma-Rose's hut near the place of old D'Alree I hid away that night when the horses came past. As soon as I heard them I crawled under her skins and lay in the corner, too scared to move. I heard Ma-Rose say to them: "No, I don't know anything about Plaatjie. If he's not at his hut he isn't there, that's all."

The night before Campher had taken me into the mountains and shown me the runaway Dollie. He ordered me to tell the Oubaas they were going straight to the Landdrost. Which gave Oubaas D'Alree quite a fright. "If the Van der Merwes hear about this," he said, "especially that Barend, they'll never let me hear the end of it." So he told me to keep quiet about it until the Landdrost had finished with the case.

It scared me too. Wouldn't the others take it out on me when they came for Campher and Dollie and me? What would become of the whole business without those two? All day long I went about with this fear in my mind. And when the sun set I left my hut and went to hide with Ma-Rose.

All right, so I'd told them I would join them. But I was an old man. I didn't want to leave them in the lurch; but I didn't want to die either. I had few enough days left to spend in peace. My tobacco and my *sopie* and my draught of tea was enough for me, and a patch of sunlight to warm my old bones in, and an occasional breathtaking ride with Ma-Rose. This madness was too much for me.

At last I heard the horses go away again.

461

BET

My hands were tied. Old Ontong and Achilles stayed behind with me when the others galloped off to light their fire at Elandsfontein; and Galant instructed Ontong to keep an eye on me as he didn't trust me. But saying Lydia was not feeling well Ontong soon left me, and so did Achilles.

"Bet," he said uneasily, avoiding to look at me directly, "now you're on your own. Do what you think best."

But my hands were tied, faster than any thong or rope could hold them. It was like years before on the Eastern border when our small band of Hottentots had also been caught in the war of others, Boers on one side and Xhosas on the other. Would there be no end to it then? Could one never live one's own life?

Through the deserted yard I crept to the house, to the back door where I thought I might find the courage to knock and shout to the people sleeping inside: "For God's sake, wake up and get ready, for death is running about barefoot in the Bokkeveld tonight." But I didn't knock. What was the thong that bound my hands? Surely it was more than just the memory of those other times when I'd tried to warn them only to be ridiculed and abused?

I turned back again. There was no peace for me that night. At the hut which had been mine and Galant's, when David had still been alive, I stopped. Those had been good times: he'd been so besotted with that child. Why should it have ended, and in such a way? I remembered how he'd rejected me as if I'd carried some disease in me. Just like the Baas. Everybody's mongrel bitch. At the door of the hut I stooped to look into the past. The days at Bruintjieshoogte, and the long road to the Cape. The child I'd buried in the hard earth on the way; growing more and more empty inside as the years wore on. And here I was, with my bare hands tied. Where could one go on such a night?

I set out on the footpath to Ma-Rose's hut. Through the years we'd all trodden that path to ask her help when everything else had failed. From a long way off I could see her fire burning; and from the smell I knew she was brewing herbs. It made me feel better to see her quietly go about her business in spite of all. But she already had a visitor. From a distance it seemed like old Plaatjie. And so I turned away again. But it wasn't only because of him: it was because I knew that in spite of all her herbs and stories and advice she would be unable to help me after all. It was a different and more personal sort of remedy I needed that night.

The *vlei* lay gleaming in the moonlight, a dull sheet of water in the dark. Behind it were the mountains, its ridges black against the sky, like an enormous sleeping beast.

Back to the kitchen door. With my head pressed against the smoothly worn wood I stood for a long time trying to make up my mind. It might have been my imagination, but I seemed to be hearing the muted sound of voices talking softly together inside; and the moan of a woman. Pamela; the Baas was with her.

—When I followed you begging you with my body to put out the fire you'd kindled with the killing of my child, you rejected me. But you don't mind taking her, to plant your white children in her womb. Then, for all I care, you can die like the scavenging dog you are!—

The huts again. Looking back I saw a shooting star drawing its stunning white line across the house.

I couldn't bear to be alone. My breath burning in my throat I went to Achilles's hut and lay down with him, simply to feel a human being close to me. For I no longer knew what to do, and my hands were tied.

Deep in the night I heard the horses coming back.

463

DOLLIE

The bloody bastard Campher cheated me. How could I ever
have trusted the shit? Because he was a labourer that worked
with us? The hell. He was white. They always stand together.

From my chains I spoke to him. "Why don't you just run
away if you so scared? Why take me with you, you scum?"

"It's for your own good," he said, which just showed how
mad he was. "What Galant is planning can only lead to ruin.
I'm keeping you out of it. You'll thank me for it yet."

"I won't ever thank nobody for a chain."

"It's just till we get to Worcester. Then I'll set you free."

"I can't wait to get my hands on that chicken neck of yours.
I'll break you to bloody pieces."

So he didn't free me. Told the Landdrost without batting an
eyelid that I'd deserted and he'd caught me. That meant the
cat o' nine tails and a year in chains.

"A year's better than hanging," Campher said. "If I'd left
you behind with Galant and the others you'd have hanged."

"If you'd let me be they would not have put out our fire so
easily. But a year passes quickly," I told him. "Then I'll come
to look for you. No matter where you try to hide, from the
Cape to the Great River, I'll hunt you down. You won't have
any peace day or night. For sooner or later I'll find your tracks
and follow them. And if I don't get you in time my children
will. Some day. For these chains you going to pay. You started
a fire inside me that day you first lied to me and it'll burn for
ever till the veld is scorched black and you along with it."

464

ONTONG

It was a long night, after the men came back from Elandsfontein. That was where everything was finally decided for us. Not in the rage and murder and confusion of the next day; not afterwards, when the dead were taken away on the wagon to be buried; but that night, when we all sat together in Galant's hut.

The following day, when the people barred their doors and windows against us, I stopped Galant from setting fire to the place (he was acting like a man in a daze then, as if he wasn't properly aware of what he himself was doing or saying: in a way, although he was right there with us, he was absent from all that happened, and when I spoke to him he almost looked surprised as if I was accusing him of something he didn't even know about): it was wrong, I said, to burn the women and children with them, and to destroy everything we might otherwise have had. But it was not enough. There was another fire I should have put out in the night; and I didn't. And with that I allowed the man who might have been my own son, how shall I ever know?, to be burnt to death. Galant, my son, born from my body of the girl Lys whom I'd known.

They came back like men tired of feasting and with the bitter after-taste of too much drinking in their mouths. Galant very quiet. Abel with a clenched fist in the air. Hendrik with his head bowed, as if he'd been caught in some mischief. Thys brandishing a sabre, like a small boy beheading flowers with a stick. Klaas scowling. Rooy sleepily dragging his feet. All of them round the fire. And not a word.

At last Achilles asked, in a voice that said he wasn't really keen to have an answer: "So did you kill Baas Barend?"

"No," said Abel. "He got away into the mountains."

"Then it was bad work."

"We'll get him in the morning, don't worry."

"Perhaps it's just as well he got away," said Bet, standing away from the others in the door. "Perhaps a bad thing has been averted."

"What do you know about it?" Galant flew at her.

"If you want to do a thing like this," Achilles went on, "then you either do it well or not at all. To let him get away makes it worse for us. Now it's a mess."

"Shut up!" said Abel. "Or would you like us to start with you?"

Galant stepped between them to stop a fight. "No, Abel. Let him say all he wants to."

"You said, when we rode out, the time for talking was past."

"Yes. But now it's different. Things have happened. We can see better now. And we got time. It may be our last. So I want each man to speak his mind."

"You want us to sit around talking while the Baas rounds up a commando?"

"He won't get far in the night," said Hendrik. "And he was scared as hell."

"Why don't we set on the masters of Houd-den-Bek right away?" said Abel. "They all asleep now. Before they know what's hit them they'll all be dead."

"The house is full of guns," said Galant. "We must get hold of the arms first, and for that we got to wait till morning. So we have time to discuss it now, after what's happened."

"Why are there so few of you?" I asked when they fell silent. "Where's Campher and Dollie and Plaatjie?"

Abel mumbled something.

"I can't hear you," I said.

Galant looked up. "We went round to their place. Ma-Rose says Dollie ran away and Campher went after him. Old Plaatjie just disappeared."

"Then there's not enough of us to do the job, man," I said. "We can't do without Dollie."

466

"And what about Campher?" said Achilles. "He started it all. He's the master of the whole plan."

"Maybe it's just as well," said Galant. "I never trusted the man anyway."

"But Dollie?"

"It's a bad blow. But we can manage without him."

Thys sat digging into the dung-floor of the hut with the point of the sabre he'd brought back with him, hacking out small bits, like the ants got into the place. "If they already backing out now," he said, not looking at anyone, "what'll become of us in the end?"

"What'll become of us if we stop here?" Abel was quick to ask. "You think they'll just let us be if we don't do anything more? What happened at Elandsfontein is done. Now our feet are set on a burning road. If we stand still our soles will be scalded. All we can do is go on. And I spit on those who stay behind."

"I know everybody's hand is against us now," I said cautiously, to calm him down a bit. "But you sure it's really necessary to kill? Can't we just take our stuff and run off to the Great River? Galant said there's a lot of free people living there. Why can't we also be free like them?"

"Free?" said Abel behind me. "Running off to live in a strange place like a criminal or a deserter?"

"I'm already living in a strange land," I said quietly.

"But don't you understand?" he asked in a tone of exasperation. "As long as there are masters we'll never be free, no matter where we live. Running away won't set us free. It's right here we got to tread them into the ground."

"You make it sound like everything's just right for treading," I warned him. "But it's no use going into something knowing it's hopeless."

"No," said Galant suddenly, turning his eyes away from the fire to look at me. "That got nothing to do with it."

"Oh really?" I said, stung. "Just look at what's happened so far. Baas Barend got away. Some of our best helpers deserted. And you think it's not hopeless?"

467

"I tell you it got nothing to do with it."

"You want to make war knowing you can only lose?"

"I don't care about losing or winning any more."

"Now you talking like Lydia," I jeered. "You lost all your senses then?"

"Perhaps Lydia isn't so mad after all," Galant said, paying no attention to the sniggers of the others. "There was a time when we needed to talk about winning or losing, about taking our freedom. Even earlier tonight, as we rode out to Elandsfontein, it was fitting to think of that. But now it's different. Now I got to think of my son looking back at me one day to see if his father chose to be a slave or not. It's not for myself I'm doing it. It's for him. On the lands we're burning down today there got to be soil for him to grow one day."

"Now I know for sure you must be mad," I said. "Where's that son you suddenly going on about?"

He shook his head like he was despairing about me. "I know what I know. And you're old."

"True," I said. "I'm old. So I've learned to be patient. I know it works out better to bow and take it. By talking to your *baas* about what's wrong, by showing him the yoke's too heavy, you can persuade him to make your burden lighter. There's no need for murder and killing."

"Oh sure," said Abel, in a passion. "He'll always make your load lighter for you. He'll shorten the hours you got to work, or give you more food, or a better hut, or an extra *sopie* when you please him well. But we remain slaves, Ontong! That's what we want to change now. Not a life that's a bit better than before, but not to be slaves any more. To be free. I'm not an ox under a yoke. I'm a man. I got hands and feet just like the Baas. I walk like him, I eat like him, I take a woman like him. I get tired just like him. I get hurt like him. So tell me: Why should he be the master and I the slave? Let me tell you one thing, Ontong: if a *baas* tries to keep me under the yoke—fine, that's his job, that's what he's *baas* for. But if I *let* him put that yoke on me, that's unforgivable. Then it's I who turn myself into an ox. And that's much worse than just to be harnessed."

468

"You're young, that's why you can talk like that," I repeated.

It was Galant who spoke again. "After what happened this night no one can call me young any more."

"And what made you so old?"

He looked at me from across the glare of the fire, as if first to test me thoroughly, holding very tightly in his hands the small bag of bullets I'd made for them that day. At last he said: "You won't understand, Ontong."

It was a long discussion, that night, in the dark hours before daybreak. All of us took part, except for Bet who just sat brooding on one side after serving us something to eat, meat and bread and honey-beer; and Rooy who fell asleep in a corner. My heart lay heavily in me, like a great lump of clay. I didn't say anything against Galant again, disheartened by those accusing words, the worst he could have said to me: *You won't understand, Ontong.* He'd shut himself against me for good. We had become strangers and there was no hope for me ever to understand.

Galant, Galant.

You might have been my son. But have I been a father to you?

BAREND

She never was mine, yet I'd always clung to hope. But that
night I finally lost her. I knew that for sure when the next day
our commando cornered the gang of murderers at the grazing
place in the mountains and old Moses brought her and the
children unscathed from his hut. Neither of us spoke. It wasn't
necessary. Together, beside each other, but strangers, we rode
off, away from the rest, back to Elandsfontein.

As we rode, from time to time, I glanced at her. Once or
twice I even spoke her name: "Hester."

She didn't give the slightest sign of having heard me; she was
too remote even to appear resentful or on her guard. She was
simply not there. At another time it would have made me
furious. It might even have provoked me to assault her. But that
morning I rode on meekly beside her, depressed by a feeling of
doom. She was, I thought, more beautiful than before. Even
after that terrifying night in which God alone knew what had
happened she appeared serene, wearing her torn nightdress as if
it were a wedding gown. There was a silence about her that was
different from her usual aloofness: a silence suggesting that she
no longer needed anything from outside to sustain her, no
person on whom to lean. Erect like a flame she sat on the back
of the horse, holding the younger boy in front of her; burning in
that burning day like a flame without smoke.

I loved her. But it was unthinkable to utter it. Even my
relief at seeing her unharmed—and God knows, in the course
of that unworthy night I'd sometimes, in my demented rage
and shame, wished something terrible might happen to her—I
couldn't express: it would sound irrelevant and trite.

Why hadn't she escaped with me? There had been time

470

enough. Even when they'd started hammering down the front door she could have got away through the back with me. I'd taken her by the hand. But she'd torn herself loose as if the contact had soiled her. I could hear the front door splintering under their blows. "Hurry up, for God's sake!" I shouted. "They'll murder us all. Come with me!" But she stood unmoving, her arms crossed over her breasts to cover up the dress I'd torn earlier. "Let me be," she said calmly, a pallor visible through the familiar sultriness of her skin. She almost seemed to relish the thought of remaining behind. The door was giving way. I turned and fled. It was not even a conscious decision, just something happening in my legs.

From the outset the night had been like a runaway horse I could in no way control; and that eventually I would fall had been as certain as, on a distant day in my youth, the fall from the great grey stallion; only the exact moment and nature of that end had yet to be decided. First there had been Abel who hadn't come back. Then Hester humiliating me in a way even she would earlier have regarded as outrageous.

When I heard the noise at the kraal I did not immediately suspect something wrong. The merest touch of suspicion when Klaas responded so strangely to my shouts. Then came the gunshot. I felt no pain. My foot just gave way under me. As I looked round I saw Galant and Abel taking aim at me through the kitchen window. And all of a sudden the night was shaking with sound and movement. On a previous occasion my gun had saved me; now it was Abel's turn. And it struck me very suddenly that ever since that earlier day this night had been predestined, an appointment neither of us could avoid.

I fled blindly into the dark. But it still felt like a dream, impossible to believe. Because it was the unimaginable, the entirely inconceivable that had suddenly come true: the slaves had risen; they were armed; they were firing at me.

Since my earliest childhood I'd been surrounded by them. I'd often quarrelled and even fought with Galant. Many times I'd seen them angry, sometimes trembling in such a rage that I knew they could murder me. If only they hadn't been slaves

471

and I Baas Barend. But this, precisely, had been the determining element in our relationship, all those years: that they were slaves and subject to me; that there existed an invisible but unmistakable frontier separating us which they could never even conceive of to overstep. They might snarl, and grumble, and growl like vicious dogs. But they would never bite. They couldn't. That had always been excluded; that had been wholly unthinkable. Only once had Abel approached to the very edge of that line; but even he hadn't been able to cross it. Now, in one impossible moment, all that had been changed.

Whether they'd hit me or not wasn't even important. Only the fact of their shooting: a slave firing at his master. That frontier crossed, there was no end to what might yet lie ahead.

This was what I'd feared. Not just that they might kill me or massacre my family: but that a single shot would shatter an entire way of life, a whole world. God's own established order, God Himself, was now threatened. Everything was at stake; everything could be destroyed: nothing was inviolate to their flames. And it was in the nature of fire not only to burn but to change utterly in the process: wood into ashes.

It was like standing on the slope of a mountain and suddenly finding myself threatened by rocks tumbling down, not one or two, but a whole landslide of them; the mountain itself was subsiding around me, above me, below me, everywhere. What had always been firm earth had suddenly begun to flow like water; and water was turning to fire.

Would that be what it felt like to go mad? Or to die?

It was indeed a form of madness; and a form of death. The death of everything I'd always taken for granted; everything that had made me what I was; everything that had kept me alive and secure.

I left Hester in the house and fled. Not from the danger that threatened me physically; but from the ruins of an entire life crumbling around me. And if that was cowardice, I would accept being a coward.

I fled. Into the mountains behind the house. It wasn't even necessary to go far. No one could possibly find me there. My

472

bare feet torn and bruised by rocks. Hours of waiting, listening to the din of their destruction below. And Hester? I was expecting at any moment to hear her stumbling towards me, soiled and torn and wounded, at last to acknowledge me. I should have known it was a futile wish. Until long after the noise had died away I kept waiting, but she never came. Did it mean that she was dead? I would deserve no less. But what would then become of me? And the boys? God forgive me, but I only thought of them much later. The future, after all, had already been decided, whether we lived or died.

Everything was very quiet when I descended to the farm in search of my family. The house was in ruins, plundered and smashed to bits. No trace of her or the children. And I didn't dare to tarry as the murderers might come back at any time. In a deep depression I returned to the mountains for the remaining hours of the night.

Would it have made any difference if the next morning I rode to Frans du Toit first so that he could round up a commando? His farm was the nearest. But on my way there I realized I was still wearing only a nightshirt; how could I, in that humiliating condition, face a man I'd always despised and answer his inevitable questions about my wife and children?

I rode past to old D'Alree's place. He gave me a pair of trousers, rather tight and much too short, but at least sufficient to cover my shame. He wanted me to proceed directly to Houd-den-Bek where, he said, he'd heard shots just before my arrival. But neither of us was armed and I was shaking so much that he had to help me mount my horse. He accompanied me back to Wagendrift where Frans made me lie down and gave me some essence of life before he set out to call up his commando.

There are moments when I wonder whether Nicolaas wasn't perhaps more fortunate than I. Surely the three shots they gave him would have killed him very quickly without causing much suffering: and then it was over. Now he's dead, and he is remembered as a martyr, while I must go on, for the rest of my life, with Hester's silence beside me.

If only I could have laid hands on Galant afterwards.

But it was too late. I should have got hold of him long before. And Abel. And Klaas. Every one of them. It was because we'd been so soft with them that they dared to do what they did. No. No: now I'm talking like Pa again. It may have been true before; but no longer. It is too late now; it has gone too far. And I have answers to no more questions.

On the surface the world seems peaceful and under control again. Nicolaas's farm has also fallen to me now that Cecilia has returned to her father. I am the new master of Houd-den-Bek. I affirmed without delay my ownership by doing what I'd long wished to do: ordering the useless old D'Alree to pack up and leave. For him to have witnessed my shame had been the last straw. How could I regain even the semblance of self-respect with him around?

I must confess that in a way his reaction was unnerving. No recriminations, no sentimental pleading. He merely bent his unkempt head and mumbled: "As you wish. I suppose it is no more than I deserve." He must have reached the age of dotage.

But even his going made little difference. Indeed, Houd-den-Bek is now mine, but it can never be the same again. Neither the farm nor being master over it. Once the earth has given way under one it can happen again at any moment. Today. Tomorrow. In a hundred years. I'm here now, and my sons with me. But it is no longer safe; nor will it ever be again.

I have survived. But perhaps it only happened for me to be brought face to face with an even more terrible truth: the death of the world that made me possible; the death of the future in which I believed—in which I had to believe in order to survive.

Could I have prevented it? The question is redundant. Even my flight implied a choice in the consequences of which I am irretrievably caught. Link upon link. Hester. I. Our sons. Living next to each other; but our solitude is absolute. Each can really talk only to himself. And in the silence we are all listening intently for the turbulence to start again.

HENDRIK

From the stable I stood watching them as, in the fading of the stars, they went out to take up their positions in the yard, shadows flitting through the first signs of dawn. The youngster Rooy accompanied old Ontong and Achilles to the kraal —more to get them safely out of the way, it seemed to me, than for any reason of strategy; for Galant obviously didn't trust them very much. Galant himself led Abel and Klaas and Thys (with his sabre!) to the peach trees near the front door. I'd asked to be posted in the stable to bring out the horses should it become necessary. In the back of my mind I'd decided that should anything go wrong I would be the first to get away. And in case of doubt I could always let out the wild mare and explain that I had to go out after her; then no one could possibly pin any blame on me.

There seemed to be no end to the waiting. The cocks were crowing their heads off. In the cowshed one could hear the cows moving about and mooing softly. In the stable where I stood the horses were sniffing and snorting, stretching up their necks, straining at their thongs, eager to be brought out. Down by the furrow the muscovy ducks were hissing and fighting. At last I saw Thys fetching the milk-pails, probably just to keep himself occupied and steady his nerves. There was an uneasy silence in the early dawn as if the day was holding its breath.

Just as the sun came out at last the kitchen door was opened and I saw the two men emerging together, my Baas Hans and Baas Van der Merwe. They stopped in the yard to look up at the sky, stretching arms and legs; then leisurely walked across to piss against the wall of the outhouse where the wagons were kept. The kitchen door was left open.

It gave me quite a shock to see Galant coming out from behind the trees and walking casually over towards them. But of course it wouldn't strike them as unusual. What did they know about what was going to happen? I saw Van der Merwe talking briefly to Galant. There was no sign of a quarrel.

Very slowly the two men strolled away from him in the direction of the kraal. To them it must have seemed a day like any other. Skirting the kraal they went on towards the threshing-floor just beyond.

I saw the men emerging from their hiding places among the peach trees and running swiftly round to the back door. They took off their hats before they went inside.

Nothing would stop them now.

CECILIA

If only there had been thunder in the night; or lightning. It was my habit at the first sign of a storm to wake up the household and cover the mirrors and gather the family round the dining-table for prayers until the violence outside had subsided. I'd been brought up to mind the weather. And had that happened we might have been warned. But it was another kind of lightning, dark and secret, that struck our farm that night.

The humiliation of it. To have to struggle bodily with slaves for the possession of the guns they'd taken from the shelf above my bed; to be pushed and pulled this way and that by men smelling like animals. Hadn't I always warned Nicolaas, God rest his soul, about Galant?

My familiar nightmare seemed suddenly and terrifyingly to come to life. The black hands grabbing me. The sweat-streaked faces. The whites of their eyes. The grunts coming from their throats as they struggled and panted. Animals. I fought like someone possessed. Not this, dear God. Not this most terrible of abominations that could be perpetrated on a white woman.

When the gun went off I didn't feel pain immediately. In fact, I only realized what had happened when I felt the sticky warmth and looked down and saw the blood. For a moment I almost laughed and cried at the same time, in a shock of relief: because he'd shot me rather than commit the horrible thing of my dream.

Only much later did I realize that what he'd done was, if possible, worse: to have despised me so profoundly that he had no desire even to inflict on me that other shame. He'd had no wish to kill me. This wound had been deliberate, aimed right

477

there, down there, the most degrading humiliation of all.

Was this his answer to the sin Nicolaas had been committing for so long? But why take it out on me? Hadn't I always lived a devout and Christian life? Why avenge the flesh on me in such a way?

My nightdress was covered in blood, like my wedding dress so many years ago. Already on that far-off day, soiled by the blood of the dead ox, I'd known that something terrible would yet result from it. Blood unto blood, one chain from beginning to end.

Wounding me was still not the end. The humiliation continued in my efforts to drag myself somewhere to hide from them, only to be torn from one shelter after the other like a bundle of bloodied rags—shot from the baking oven in which I'd ludicrously tried to conceal myself; picking myself up from among the broken plaster and rubble, to hide in the hearth; under the dining-table; at last, crawling up the stone stairs outside to the attic above, leaving a trail of blood behind. God, how disgusting. And afterwards I had to lie back and allow the slave women to wash and bind my wound; no end to the degradations.

For the sake of my children I bore the suffering in the face of God. For their sake I pleaded with the murderers: not for mine. To cringe before a slave and ask for mercy!

Nicolaas dead on the lion-skin in the *voorhuis*, arms and legs spread out, the boots torn from his feet. Bodies and blood in the kitchen. Verlee's bedraggled young wife clinging dumbly to me in the attic, too shocked even to cry, smothering her baby against a barely nubile breast. Degrading. Humiliating. Unworthy. How could a white woman be forced to suffer thus in front of the eyes of blacks?

I still cannot understand it. How could they so bite the hand that fed them? We'd cared for them and taught them the commandments and decrees of God; every Wednesday and Sunday we read the Bible to them, and prayed with them, and sang with them. Food and clothing we gave them according to their needs. When they were ill we looked after them. When

478

they had problems we solved them. They had neither want nor worry. There was no need for them even to be concerned about the morrow: we'd take care of everything.

Then this. Our adversary, the devil, as a roaring lion, walking about, seeking whom he may devour.

Give me the strength, Lord, to survive this ordeal. To be an example to my children. Never to bend or yield. So that I may triumph over these tribulations to the greater glory of God. I have been tried with pain and suffering, but I am not broken. It is hard, God knows it's hard; but I know He is on my side and will give me strength. From the suffering of His martyrs His name is glorified. And in His fire are we purified.

If only He'd chosen to leave His mark on my forehead rather than in this wounded flesh, branded in my very womanhood.

We must relinquish the flesh in order to live more purely in the spirit, in this land the Lord has given unto us, to us and our children, for ever and ever.

Yea, though I walk through the valley of the shadow of death, I dare fear no evil.

ABEL

I regret nothing. Except that we weren't able to carry it right through. But that's just too bad. Better try and make a mess of it than not try at all. All one's life one treads so softly, sniffing about like a dog happy with whatever food he's given, taking one's safe little chances as they come: but once in a lifetime one got to have the guts to put everything at stake and break out. Once, even if it's only once, you got to do something just because you know its time has come and fuck the rest. If it breaks you, you die. A bit sooner or later makes no difference anyway. As long as you know, when your time's up, that you took that chance when it came. I regret nothing.

I've lost the fiddle for ever. It would have been good to take it up again and bring the bow to it, to hear that wail of woman and catch the smell of resin. But what's done is done. At least I tried.

All my life I lied to them, about everything: the wood I was supposed to chop, the axe that got lost, the horses that had to be watered, the empty half-aum. I had no choice. The lies were the only thing I could hide behind so they couldn't touch me. All I had was theirs: body, hands, work, days, nights: bought and paid for. Except they never had *me*. Behind my lies I always escaped from them. The only problem is that one begins to lie to oneself too. It's a habit hard to shake off. You start convincing yourself that life isn't really so bad. That's when you get all tangled up. That's when, one day, you just realize: Now I got to break out. Even if it doesn't last. At least it gives you the courage to look the world in the face when they tie the noose around your neck.

In a sense you might say it was like a wedding. Right in the beginning it gave one the bitter taste of aloes to see Baas Barend get away, though that bare-arsed trot of his made me laugh so much I missed the next shot. Run, I thought, run, you bastard. Soon we'll see all the white masters running like that, like a herd of baboons scared by a leopard and scattered in all directions, leaving their yellow shit on all the rocks.

But the real fun only came at Houd-den-Bek. When Galant and I came from the bedroom that morning in a tug-of-war over the guns with the woman it almost felt like dancing. If I'd had my fiddle I'd have tuned it up right there. Bang on the cunt when he shot her. Real wedding feast.

We should have kept the Dutchmen outside; that would have rounded it all off much sooner. We should never have given them a chance to get back into the house and shut the doors; but that shot had warned them. Didn't take long to get Nicolaas though. I fired first, soon's he poked his head through the door. Next shot was Galant's. That finished him off neatly. But the man Jansen bloody nearly got away. It really was a close thing. If Ma-Rose hadn't called out from the nearest shed as he galloped off, we would have lost him. As it happened, we'd posted Hendrik in the stable, so the horses were ready and Thys and I went in pursuit. A proper race, just like I saw in the Cape; we headed him off from old D'Alree's place before he could raise the alarm, and pushed him down towards the thickets of the dry riverbed. When he saw he was cornered, he plucked his horse round and galloped back, right into the house, horse and all. Fit to split one's sides laughing.

Then it was cat and mouse with the people indoors. The schoolmaster and his pale wife also slipped in through the back door. Galant wanted to set fire to the roof to smoke them out, the way one does with snakes, but Ontong stopped him, the old spoilsport. At last little Rooy peered through the small high window in the kitchen that had no shutters, and he said the Nooi was crawling into the oven. We all started firing into the oven from behind, and Galant began to break down the kitchen door with a crowbar from the shed. We were just in time to see the woman rolling from the oven in a pile of muck

481

and rubbish. From then on it was just shooting and breaking and shouting all the way. Both men, Jansen and Verlee, shot to bits. One of them, I think it was Verlee, still tried to crawl away, but someone shouted: "Hey, the shit's still moving!" And it was Rooy who gave him the last shot, right on the button of his waistcoat. No sign of fear in that little fellow. Fought like an old soldier; and if we hadn't stopped him he'd probably have tackled the women and children too.

That was the real joy of it. The way we all did everything together. Not one man doing something over here, another over there: but the whole lot of us together. And afterwards we brought out the brandy and made merry till the walls were shaking, what with all the shouting and laughing and battering and breaking that went on and throwing target at the bodies and scaring the children—in the end the schoolmaster's little wife, Martha Verlee, just flopped down flat on her backside on a patch of grass, staring away as if she was seeing ghosts in broad daylight—not even crying, just sitting there like she felt tired so early in the morning—and hunting for ammunition, and tearing up the bedding and turning over the tables and stuff. I hadn't had such fun in these parts for years. When we were too tired to think up anything new, we started kicking the two bodies in the kitchen: Take this, for that hiding you gave me. Take that, for the bad food. And that, for the way you shouted at me. No matter we didn't even know those two— after all, who the hell was this Jansen? who was Verlee?—they took the place of many others, over many years. Kick them right into the dust. Take this; and that; and that. And have another *sopie*!

482

NICOLAAS

The others never really mattered; they were bystanders. From the beginning it has been between Galant and me and now caught in this timeless moment.

In the early daylight I see him coming towards me just as Hans Jansen and I prepare to go down to the kraal. There is nothing servile in his attitude; but I'm used to that.

"Good morning, Galant."

He says nothing.

I prefer not to mention the threshing-floor—it would be asking for trouble so early in the morning—but to my annoyance Jansen broaches it; and in order not to lose face in front of a stranger I turn to Galant to ask: "You finished the floor?"

He grins. "All ready for the threshing."

"But we're through with threshing!"

He doesn't answer. My heart grows leaden. He mustn't try to humiliate me in front of Jansen: that would leave me no choice but to punish him again. Must we always be driven back to that? Why can't he accept that it would be in his own interest for us to be on good terms?

"We're on our way to the floor now," I say tersely. "Come on, Hans." As we walk away, I turn back to Galant: "I'll see you again later."

He shrugs.

The threshing-floor lies crumbled and exposed as it was last night; as it's been since the threshing was done. Bare and cracked, worn out by the heavy hooves of the horses that milled round and round to separate chaff from wheat—the clean rich grain winnowed in the wind and scooped into the bags, loaded on the wagon and stacked on the loft, ready for the mill: food for everybody on the farm.

"Well!" says Jansen beside me, pipe in his mouth, a smug look in his eyes. "Just shows you, man. They're all the same."

I turn away from him, trying to come to terms with the burden of knowing that Galant and I will soon be facing one another again. All that is still to be decided is when and how.

While we're still standing at the floor, before we've had time properly to inspect the kraal, there is the report of a gunshot from the house. Both of us instinctively start running at the same time. There is a second shot as we reach the gate to the enclosure of the farmyard; I feel a curious jerking in my arm, but only after we're safely inside the kitchen Jansen says with a shocked voice: "My God, they hit you. Look at your shirt."

Soon afterwards, as I try to reason with them at the front door, I suddenly hear Galant shout: "Shoot him, Abel!" Yet another shot. Luckily it only grazes me as I jump back and slam the door.

Inside the *voorhuis* I lean against the wall, closing my eyes briefly in a sudden dizziness.

From the bedroom I hear Cecilia calling. Covered in blood in the crumpled stained sheets she insists that we first sit down with the children to have prayers. "Do you realize what you're doing?" I feel like shouting at her. "Is this all that matters to you?—to have a decent death, to do everything the right way? Did I ever matter to you? Do you care in the least that I may be shot dead in a few minutes?" But I restrain myself.

I listen absently to my own voice reading: "—that through death he might destroy him that had the power of death, that is, the devil; and deliver them who through fear of death were all their lifetime subject to bondage."

Long before we have done the hammering on the front door becomes so loud that I cannot continue. Without bothering to say Amen I get up from my knees beside the bed.

"You cannot leave me here alone, Nicolaas."

"I must speak to Galant first."

"Your place is with your family!"

484

I return to the front door on tiptoe and cautiously draw back the bolt that bars it. He must have been standing there all the time, waiting for me: but I don't think he was expecting me so suddenly. All the others are there too, but further away, indistinct, a blur, as if my eyes cannot properly focus on them. It's only he and I, as if we're alone on the earth, naked as two boys in a dam: my shadow and I.

I wait for him to speak first. In a minute, in a few seconds, I realize, I shall be dead. Surely, in this extremity, there should at least be *something* we can say to one another. But I am drained of thought and feeling, unable to think of anything to say.

This I find the worst of all, this silence preceding death, this act of denudation, this experience of total strangeness in the face of the man who has been my only friend. This inability to touch one another in any way at all. This expanse through which we can do nothing but stare at one another. A savage silence.

Life against life.

What, in such a silence, remains of an entire life? How can one grasp its beginning, its course, its end? Bare children in a dam below the swinging nests. A tunnel into an earthen wall caving in. Evenings in a smoky hut. A timeless old woman telling stories. A girl. A horse broken in. A lion: a great predator that appeared miraculously from another world and brought life to the darkness with its roar; an incomprehensible freedom in the deep sound of its breathing, in and out. And when Galant's shot hit it, life left him with the suggestion of a sigh, something of a groan, as if he almost pitied us who were left behind. In a silence just as complete as this one I stood opposite the lion that day. But I lied to Pa about it. Since then all has turned to lies. And today I finally fall victim to the lion.

The silence persists, crammed with images. A wedding. A wife. Children on my shoulders. Hester's wordless resentment. A journey to the Cape. A lost night in the mountains. Sundays at Lagenvlei. Never-ending work: clearing new lands, building walls, digging furrows, planting and sowing, reaping, threshing.

485

Earth. Water. Wind. Fire.

What is there of all of this I can share with you in this final moment? We've been in all of it together: nothing remains. Not even a word.

I here: you there. Master: slave.

It was the moment, the irreparable moment, when I changed from your mate into your master that I finally destroyed my own freedom. That was the moment when the stone wall, the high rough mountain, rose between us, so high that we were left with only the illusion of seeing one another. We can no longer hear.

Is it a matter of choice, then, to become a master—or is that no more than a sign of being a victim of one's world? Immaterial, now. *This* is where we are.

And now that we've got as far as this—*because* we've got as far as this—only the most elementary acts can still be committed between us.

You will kill me. Afterwards, if the law runs its course, you will be killed in turn. That's the pity of it. Not the killing as such—in this silence one is even beyond fear—but the knowledge that it is too easy: for both of us it is an evasion, a denial of responsibility. We should have learned to live with it.

This is not a truth, but a final defeat—for both of us. It's a lie. Like the skin on which I can feel myself falling.

We're back at the slaughtering-stone then. And once again my fervent futile wish is not to be here. But I am.

ROOY

They all thought I was still wet behind the ears, but I showed them. Thought they could just let me hold the horses and things like that, but I was with them all the time. In the kitchen, when they shot the schoolmaster, the man suddenly gave a snort; he was lying against the wall then, behind a chair. "Come on," Galant said. "Give him another shot." Thys was right behind him, but when he heard it he quickly ducked in behind the others. Big mouth he had, but when it came to killing he was scared. So it was I who took the pistol someone gave me, and aiming right on the button I pulled the trigger. The body jerked, and that was that. Easy.

The way I see it: if we hadn't decided to break out I'd have had to spend the whole dreary day out in the veld with the sheep again; and that time of the year the sun burns the shit right out of you. So it was a bit of a change.

Pity it couldn't go on for longer.

MARTHA

Schoolmaster and all, where did your cleverness land you? Now you're dead and I must fend for myself. I'd been used to a better life. It was you who insisted we should cross the mountains to start again. You said that once I'd had a taste of real life I'd come to like it.

It was you who saddled me with a child too soon. I'd still been playing with my dolls when you married me. Then you turned me into your doll. And now there's the baby.

Do you really expect me to manage on my own in this place? In the Cape everything seemed so nice and civilized. It took a thing like this to make me see how crude this land really is. A savage wilderness, not fit for whites to live in.

If this is the life you spoke about I'll have none of it.

HELENA

It's the nicest smell the attic has. Dried fruit and raisins, tobacco leaves, and tea. But only the weekend before Mummy said I was getting too big for games in the attic; a girl ready for school should know her manners. So in a way I was glad we could all come up to the attic again; it was like playing hide-and-seek.

Of course I knew it wasn't really a game. But when I lay flat on my stomach to look through the chink in the boards everything seemed so confused down there—the shooting and shouting and breaking of the furniture—that one couldn't really believe it anyway. I felt far away from it all, looking down from very high up, into a strange world that just made me stare and stare. A grownup world I knew I'd never understand and to which, anyway, I didn't belong. So it didn't seem to matter so much really.

Little Katrien cried from time to time; and Mummy was making funny little noises. I knew if I looked at her dress I'd see the blood again. So I didn't look. I just lay on my stomach and stared through the chink, knowing that even if I grew very old one day I'd never ever forget it. I still get bad dreams from it at night. But as I was lying there looking at it all it was no different from a dream anyway.

Sometimes I'm not quite sure, actually. Was I awake then, or am I now? And if it's only a dream, will I wake up again?

I'm not sure I want to.

PAMELA

I would have preferred to stay in the hut with Galant that night, in case something happened. But he was sullen and withdrawn towards me since he came back from fetching the schoolmaster, blaming me for not stealing the guns for him. But how could I? I'd tried, but the woman had stopped me. So I thought: All I could do to prove to him that I was with him would be to sleep in the kitchen that night. If the Baas wanted to have his way with me again, just too bad. At least I would be inside to keep my eyes open and perhaps to open a door for the men if it became necessary. My desire was with Galant; but for his sake I went to the kitchen. And to me that was the worst: not the killing, then and later, but that they'd moved in between Galant and me, for the two of us had been together.

"Yes, go," Galant said when I picked up the child in the hut. "I suppose it's your place now."

"Don't you understand then?" I pleaded.

"I got work to do," he said, turning away from me.

Halfway to the house, when I looked back, I saw him still standing there, staring at me and the baby on my back. I wanted to call out to him: but what could I say? That is how I shall always remember it: I here, he over there, and the silence of the yard between us.

After I'd done the washing and cleaning for the night I put the child to sleep in the corner by the hearth and then lay down myself. But it was impossible to sleep. I kept listening to the sounds of the house, beyond the small gentle snoring of the baby. A house has a life of its own after dark: beams creaking as if a slow heavy man is walking along them; the bed in the bedroom when someone turns over; a sigh of wind in the chimney; the bolt of a shutter. I pricked my ears for what was happening outside, but it sounded no different from usual. A dog stirring at the kitchen door, or cracking a bone, or licking its balls. The laughter of a jackal or a ghost, very far away. A squeaking of bats. And a small screech-owl once. That was all. And yet I knew the night was filled with men on horseback riding to and fro. Blood welling up in silence. The wind holding its breath before the storm would break loose and white lightning would crack the dark sky.

Then I heard Nicolaas coming to me on his bare feet. I tensed up but didn't move.

"Pamela? You sleeping?"

I tried to breathe deeply and evenly, hoping he would give up.

His hand on my bare shoulder. I still didn't move.

You starting again, I thought. *Isn't it enough for you to know that child is sleeping right here beside me? And the man I want is outside. But what does he know about me? What does anyone know about anyone?*

"Why can't you leave me alone?" I suddenly asked. "Don't you know what you're doing?"

"I want to talk to you, Pamela."

"There's enough time to talk in the day. I'm sleeping."

"There's no one I can talk to."

"Talk to your own sort. Let me be. I'm a slave."

"You listened before."

"Because I had no right to say no."

He was silent for a while. Then he said: "Pamela, what's got into Galant?"

It shook me. Before I could stop myself I sat upright next to him. In the dark one couldn't see anything; the coals in the hearth had turned grey.

"Galant has changed," he said.

"Why ask me?" I said fiercely. "It's between you and him."

"He doesn't talk to me. And you're his wife."

"One wouldn't think so, the way you lie with me."

"I said a bad thing to him tonight."

I didn't answer. But I waited very tensely.

491

"I told him to make sure the threshing-floor was ready in the morning. It was because of Baas Jansen I lost my temper."

"It's your business, not mine."

Why should it have upset him so? He was the master: he could do as he wished; there was no need for him to feel sorry or guilty about anything. However, he suddenly got up from beside me and went to the back door.

"It's bothering me," he said. "Perhaps I should go and talk to him."

On hands and knees I crawled after him, shedding my blanket on the way, trying to stop him.

"He's sleeping now," I whispered urgently. "There will be time enough tomorrow."

He hesitated, his hand already on the bolt.

I put my arms round his legs.

"What's the matter with you now, Pamela?"

"Stay here." I moved my hands to reach under his shift. He moved in my cupped palms. Then he bent over.

Take me, I thought. *Take me any way you wish. It's the last time. Tomorrow I'll join them when they kill you. If you call for help I'll laugh in your face. I'll bury my heel in the place where I'm holding you now. I'll spit on you and your brood.*

It was for Galant I did it. But the next day when they all came streaming from the house in the high white sun, from the rubble and the bodies and the blood, across the yard where I sat waiting for him with the child at my breast, he didn't know me. With the sun in his eyes he stared at me as if I wasn't there.

"Galant, I must talk to you."

"We're past talking."

"I helped you."

"You kept out of it all the time. I don't need you any more. Look at the thing you holding to your breast."

"Is it my fault then?"

He suddenly got so angry he couldn't speak. Grabbing his gun by the barrel he let fly at me with the butt. I tried to stop him, but the child's head got in the way.

Long after they'd gone, but before the commando arrived on their horses—I watched them from a distance—I came down for a crust of bread from the mess in the kitchen, and fled back to the mountains again with the child: deep into the tumbled Skurweberge where they'd never find me.

Towards nightfall the child died. I buried her myself. The earth was too hard to dig a grave, however shallow; but I covered her under a mound of stones to protect her from the vultures. The child who'd looked at me with the eyes of the Baas as she sucked my nipples. Yet she'd been mine too; how could I deny my own?

There were no tears in me, not even while I was stacking the heavy stones: and after that it was too late. The emptiness was too big.

In a terrible way I also felt relieved; cleansed. If Galant were to come to me now, I'd go to him, my breasts heavy with milk, and say: "Look, my arms are empty again."

But he never came. The bread was soon finished. I began to wander aimlessly, driven by hunger, my breasts aching. In the end I had to go down and give myself over.

So the masters had won after all. They'd separated Galant and me for good. He would never come back now. I'd been wrong thinking the child's death would change anything. Even in death it tied me to something I couldn't help but in which I'd had a part and for which I had to bear the guilt. I don't know why. I don't understand any more. But that's how it happened. What had been ours only had got out of hand and was now common to everybody.

They even refused to hang me with him. Even that they denied me. Yet we had been man and wife.

ACHILLES

Bleeding, and in agony, the Nooi promised Ontong and me that if we helped her she'd plead with the gentlemen in Cape Town to make sure we would be looked after till the day of our death; and after the others had left on their horses we helped Ma-Rose to care for her. Later, when the wagon came, we rode with her to Buffelsfontein, her father's place. For that she gave us each a shirt and trousers of the Baas. But when the commando found the clothes with us afterwards they accused us of having taken part in the murders and we were put in chains with the others. The Nooi didn't stop them. Perhaps she was too ill; perhaps they never told her. But I know white people forget easily anyway.

And perhaps, who knows, it's better this way. Because the hardest thing to live with is hope. And now at last that is gone.

MOSES

No use saying one should have done this or that. You got to take a chance when it comes, but you also got to know where to stop. The world isn't as it should be, sure, but who am I to try and change it? Rather enjoy a bit of life than lose it all. What's the use hanging on the gallows like them or working in chains for the rest of one's life? I could have been there with them if I hadn't kept a clear head. The important thing is to see the lightning in time, so you can duck. Else you get blinded.

When I was in the Cape with Baas Nicolaas I heard with my own ears that our freedom was promised for New Year or thereabouts. And I spread the news when we got home, and I was pleased. But when nothing happened I resigned myself. The ways of the Dutch are different from ours.

Then, when Abel came to the grazing place to tell us that the whole Bokkeveld was rising up, I stood with them like all the others. It seemed the right thing to do, and I began to polish the good gun Oubaas Piet had given me to protect the sheep. The bullet I blessed with spittle. I was ready for action. In the band of my hat I stuck a new guinea-fowl feather.

But when Goliath arrived in the night with the Nooi and the children, it took just one good look to know this thing was turning bad. And when I heard that Baas Barend had also got away, I said to Wildschut:

"No use, man. Whatever Abel told us, the world has now bent over to show us its backside."

And to the Nooi I said: "At your service." So she could know on whom to rely.

Still, when daylight came things looked different again.

495

When we got to Elandsfontein and saw how the place had been thrown upside down, I couldn't help feeling a touch of excitement. Just then Galant and the others turned up—he was wearing new yellow boots on his feet and a blood-flag round his hat—and they told us about what had happened at Houd-den-Bek. So I looked at the men and cried to Galant:

"Here we are, Captain! Just say the word."

One had to stay on the winning side. Else there would be trouble.

We went into the farmhouse with them. In the daylight we found a barrel they'd missed the night before, and Wildschut and Slinger and I joined in the drinking. In my mind I could see us riding to Cape Town, our numbers swelling all the way until there'd be hundreds of thousands of us on the march. Who in the wide world could stop us now?

But we'd barely reached the grazing place again when I heard Slinger shouting: "They coming!"

One glance at the commando on their horses and it was clear which way it was going to go. I had no desire to get caught there with a gang of criminals and be shot to pieces for a thing in which we'd had no part at all.

So I was right in front, and I admit it with pride, when we ran to the commando to surrender. Galant and Abel started shooting as soon as they saw what was happening; one bullethole right through the rim of my hat. But by that time the commando had already drawn up and the gang had to run for their lives. I'm glad to say we helped the farmers round up some of the evil-doers. I've always been a man for law and order. Ask Oubaas Piet. He wouldn't have given me all the responsibility of his grazing place if he hadn't trusted me well.

Now life is peaceful again. I'm not saying it's the way I like it. But I'm not complaining. It could have been worse.

PIET

There's nothing my hands can hold on to any more. Powerless my talons lie on the bed beside me. Before, I had everything in my grasp: farm and people, earth, mountain, slaves, wheatlands, cattle. Now it's pulled away from me like a sheet, exposing my shame. Bare-arsed one comes into the world and bare-arsed one leaves it. There used to be giants in the earth, but their time is past.

Damn old D'Alree. When I got home for tea that afternoon and saw him idly sitting there it annoyed me so much that I just turned back to the lands. The reapers had already started on the wheat. Moses and my other hands, and all Nicolaas's labourers; his wheat was already down. They probably never expected me back so soon. No one saw me. Right behind them I stopped when I heard what they were talking about. Murder and mutiny. A terrible rage got into me. I gave a roar and grabbed a sickle to mow them down. Then it just got dark very suddenly. Since then I've been lying here like a baby. I could have stopped them. But what's the use of good intentions? God doesn't consider them. When the ark of the Lord came to the threshing-floor of Nachon and the oxen stumbled, Uzzah put out his hand to prevent it from falling. Yet God killed him right there. That was all the gratitude he got. Vanity, vanity, all is vanity.

GALANT

The masters are dead, but we are not yet free. Is an ox free just
because the yoke is taken from its back? A man who's lonely
goes to sleep with a woman: does that make him any less
alone? So much could have been avoided had one known in
time. But how can one know without going through it? Never
in advance; always only afterwards. Is it the same, I wonder,
with death?

Still, there was the hour in the loft.

Here I'm hiding in the mountains and time is running out.
I'm sitting very high up, beside the human footprint trodden
into stone for good. All the others are gone now. Just before
sunset Thys also left me; he was the last. I suppose he got tired
of wandering about with me. He must have expected something different from me, some great action which might have
justified everything; something to carry to the grave and make
death less terrifying. He's so very young.

Down in the valley, after he'd gone down, I heard shots.
Perhaps he was killed. Perhaps he killed some of them. More
bodies.

They know I'm here. Only darkness holds them back. At
daybreak they'll be coming up; I'll be here still, with Nicolaas's
shoes, tied together, over my shoulder. It's so much easier
barefoot; I'm used to it. Anyway, they hurt me. I don't know
whether there'll be another shooting when they come for me.
Nor do I know whether they'll kill me or try to take me alive.
To be caught or not is no longer important. It has nothing to
do with freedom any more. That is what Thys couldn't
understand.

Down in the valley lies Houd-den-Bek, even though I

cannot see it now, in the dark. Beginning and end. I'm very high up here, close to the stars. The sky is clear. Only in the distance, in the direction of the Karoo, there is from time to time a flickering of summer lightning. Storms passing far away. But here it's very clear.

How well I know my mountains. Yet tonight they feel distant, although they're all around me. I'm here; but I'm no longer with them. Already I'm on my way. Tomorrow when I leave, and later when I'm dead, every rock and crag and tough shrub will still, I'm sure, be here; without me. They've always been here. Holding me like cupped hands they've sheltered me all my life. Beyond all my comings and goings, beyond fun and floggings, work and rest, suffering and uncertainty and brief happiness, they've always been here, good and solid. I needed them.

Yes, they can go on without me, forever. And yet I feel a strange doubt: What I know of them no one else can ever know; and if I die something of them must die as well: that knowledge I have of having seen them, of having hidden in them, of feeling them around me. They require me for that knowledge. This footprint in the stone is like my own.

Another glimmer of distant lightning. For a moment it's there; then it's gone: so quickly that I'm left wondering whether I ever saw it, or only dreamt it. Still, it was there.

Did I dream the hour in the loft?

In its own way the lightning is as everlasting as the mountains. Deep in the earth the Lightning Bird lays its egg; and when its time comes it hatches in the dark and fire returns to the world: a fire that burns and scorches and strips away all that is superfluous, so that life can sprout anew in red-grass and scrub, in small yellow flowers, in everything that grows. Like life in the womb of a woman the egg of the Lightning Bird lies waiting in darkness to be born.

Perhaps there'll be a child after my death; a son.

Alone. From the beginning, and forever. I thought, when we were children, that Nicolaas was with me; but he wasn't. Later I thought the same of Bet, but she turned against me.

Pamela, closest of all: then came the white-haired child. I thought the others were with me, Abel and those, but that didn't last either. Not that I'm blaming them in any way —some got frightened, others were stopped—but that's what happened. Each man was fighting his own war. We were not really together. We never really understood each other.

Hester.

Has it all been in vain then? Was it too much to think we could take our freedom? I have only this night left to find the answers. Tomorrow I'll be going down the mountain; and what will happen afterwards I do not know.

Usually one lives like a man walking with a candle in the dark. Behind him, where a moment ago it was light, darkness closes in. Ahead, where it will soon be light, darkness still lies undisturbed. Only where he is right now is there light enough to see by, for a moment; and then he moves on. But in a night like this it is different: then the darkness that was and the darkness that is to be merge in the light of what is now. I can close my eyes and see inside. Everything is alive in the heart of the flame. Within the falling of the stone lies the silence of before and after.

That is what it was like in the loft. Except there was no thought then, only the blindness of the act. Now I must bring the light of thought to it. That is why I allowed myself this last night; it would have been too easy to go down with Thys.

I have come as far as I could. On New Year's Day, when Nicolaas gave us the clothes and nothing more, a light died in me. What else could we do but kindle a new fire to warm us? All of us, even those who were scared, even those who later turned against us, stood together then. It was important. In that fire we had to burn out the weeds closing in on us. But soon we were dispersed. And then there was only Nicolaas and I.

Poor Nicolaas: you thought I had it against you. You thought it was you I wanted to kill, for some reason or another: because you'd lied to your father about me when we were children; or because you'd kept me away from the dam when you went swimming with Hester; or because of floggings or quarrels; because you'd landed me in the Tulbagh jail; because of shit. It wasn't you. It was all those whose places you took as you stood in that terrible silence in the door. Not your father, not Barend, not Frans du Toit. You had no name then, no face. You were all the white men, all the masters, all those who had always set themselves above us and taken our women and called their farms *Shut-Your-Trap*: Houd-den-Bek.

And poor Galant too! You thought you were rooting out the masters from the earth to bring us freedom—and all you did was to shoot down one man. Lying dead on that moth-eaten old skin were not the masters of the earth, smothering in their own blood: it was only one man, you, Nicolaas, who used to be my friend and should have been it still.

Lightning trembling on the horizon.

In the loft we were together. A single hour.

Has it really been in vain?

We're not yet free. But does that mean that freedom doesn't exist?

All right, I suppose we lost. But what we fought for still lives on, without beginning or end, like the mountains, like fire. And for that it was worth while. Perhaps there are things in whose name it is better to lose than to win. Provided you try.

This I could never have known unless I'd tried, my handful and I, to break the chain called Houd-den-Bek.

This I could not have known except through the fire of that hour in the loft. Dark lightning.

When Thys called: "There he goes!" we all broke away from the front door and ran after Barend. Abel fired a shot. So did I. The dogs started barking madly. We followed Barend up the quince hedge for some distance, but he got away. In that darkness it's useless to look for a man; once he's escaped into the mountains he's gone. I know.

They all trundled back to the back door which he'd left open behind him. I remained outside for a while before I went round to the broken front door again. At the side of the house I found Abel's Sarie with the children; one by the hand, the other, wrapped in a blanket, in her arm.

501

"Where you going?" I said.

"They breaking everything inside," said Sarie. "It's not good for the children. They're small. So the Nooi said—"

"Yes, take them away from this place."

Then Hester came round the corner after the children. She stopped when she saw me, barely a yard away, clutching the front of her white nightdress with one hand. In the moonlight I could see something of her face; but her eyes were shadows.

She seemed frightened.

"I told Sarie to take the children away," I said.

"Thank you. I—"

I looked at Sarie. The elder boy was tugging anxiously at her hand, half hiding behind her to keep out of my way.

"Go on," I said. "You can wait behind the shed. No one will find you there."

They went away.

"Thank you," Hester said again. I think it was what she said; she spoke so softly, as if her throat was dry.

Then she said: "Galant."

Nothing more. We didn't move, dark in the moonlight, close enough to touch; but we didn't touch. She dropped her hand and stood quite still. The top of her nightdress, I noticed, had been torn open. One flap hung right down. Unmoving, she, I. With everything of all those years exposed between us. The dark was like a kaross sheltering us; like so many years ago in Ma-Rose's smoky hut. I could feel all those stories moving invisibly around us. Once again we were in the veld where she'd been bitten by a snake; and I took out the poison with a black snake-stone. We were in a stable in the heavy odour of horses and straw, bleeding weals on my back; and she untied my hands and washed my broken body. In a dusky kitchen we stood together by the glowing hearth: "Stay here, don't go, don't leave me, I'm alone." Everything: naked. She moved. Her face, it seemed, was wet with perspiration. I know mine was. Her breast exposed without shame. Behind us, far away, inside the house, the night was reverberating with their noise;

502

but I scarcely noticed it. It belonged to another world. Here were we. Time had stopped. Nothing happened. Nothing passed. She. I.

Until—how, I don't know, I don't remember—I raised a hand towards her as if to touch her breast, but I didn't dare, I wouldn't ever, no I did, but only just, a finger on the small shadow of her breast, and said, I think it was I:

"Come," I think it was I: a single word and even that seemed superfluous as we walked, leading and led, but who by whom?, round the house and up the broad stone steps to the loft above, grass sprouting here and there, a gentle caress to the bare soles. —Utter darkness here, the world obliterated and irrelevant as it breaks and flounders below; remote from this intimate burrow in the dark, confined yet limitless, ours, now, and everything reduced, as in recovered childhood, to touch. The rough grain of wood, prickliness of straw, a half-open bag with wheat spilling from it in a gentle cool hard stream running through open fingers. Clothes torn or fiercely thrust aside. Invisible, night grows dense, hard and definite, to assume the shape of a man. I mould him in my hands, fierce and gentle and in awe: the hands that clawed at Barend in rejection and disgust, now affirm the shape of a man-body, coarseness of hair, bone of shoulders and rib-cage and hips, the surprising insistent swell of buttocks, hard knees; that member always denied, now discovered in wonder at its brutal hardness and vulnerable softness, coaxing, insistent, violent; the mysterious bag at its base, swaying, swollen, a peculiar coolness. I'm crushed by his full weight, my legs helpless and apart, kicking to find some hold; the surface of a back gnarled and marked with seams and welts, calluses, old scars. This must be the end, there can be nothing beyond it, darkness, blinding light, as he pushes down on me, crushing me, breaking me, giving me being, a name, an inseparable existence, a loneliness, excruciating fulfilment. He lunges, thrusts, hammers, pounds in silent frenzy, impaling me, cleaving me, sundering and slaughtering me, setting me free

504

forever, unbearably. For Barend I had only the nakedness of a body exposed by clothes torn from me: this was altogether different, the nakedness of a child in a dam, shameless affirmation: I am—I am—I am. Thresh me, break me, shape me: running with fire.—

Gasps, cries, sobs, an uncontrollable panting, surrounded by silence: not a word. Impossible, unthinkable to articulate. All we could do, all we had to offer one another, that is the horror and the miracle of it, was that brief brutal sharing of bodies, avenging and celebrating everything we'd lost, everything we'd never had, everything forever beyond our grasp, a desperate groping towards the only thing not yet denied to us because it did not yet exist, the future. The day in the stable decided this: his pain and my rage, and the untying of his hands: it is no choice of our own, we can but submit to what we, ourselves, have made unavoidable.

—Will the world condemn me for this and cast me out? But it will never know. I myself shall deny it, because this is mine only. And yet, looking back one day, long after he is dead perhaps, will not I too find it incomprehensible, despicable, risible? No. I cannot. I am two things that can never be risible: a child, and a savage. We recognized it in one another, from the beginning. And only this once, liberated from the corruptions of both power and suffering, in the madness and violence and destruction of our familiar world, in this terrible merciful total night, are we free to admit and share it. Never again. But having shared it now, it remains forever ours, beyond death and the mountains.—

He is dead now. In me he lives. Time thwarted.

Such a brief hour, so dark, so light. But in that most private of acts, unacknowledged by the shamed world, we entered history: we are here. Look, we are free. We can reassume the burdens of our separate conditions. A brief shout against silence, a parenthesis, an almost imperceptible stay—between the vulgar irruption into the house and the flight into the stern innocence of the mountains—but that was life enough: a vision, an illumination, forked lightning, agony, terror, joy. I bear the future in my womb, predestined in that insignificant moment when I dared expose myself to him and he said, I think it was he:

GALANT

"Come," I think it was she, and together we went up to the loft. How many times had we approached this moment?—but always thwarted, not from outside, but by ourselves. Free woman; slave. But this time it was different. In that loft I was free: a man; and she a woman. And for this moment, so fleeting and simple, it was perhaps worth while to be born, to live, to suffer, to be in the dark, and then to die.

All right: so it was not the freedom we dreamed of, open and visible, and shared by all. In that sense we failed. But perhaps freedom can never really be other than this, a small and private thing? If this is so, we had indeed no hope of succeeding. And yet we had to do what we did! No doubt about that. We had to. Take that away, and what happened in the loft would have been no more than a man-and-woman thing. And without her our rising up together would have been madness and defeat.

For the first time I think I'm beginning to understand what the lion man in Tulbagh meant. I have committed the greatest crime of all: and even if they never find out about it that would still be the reason why they will have to kill me in the end. This is the one freedom that truly threatens them.

Murder is easy. Any man who works himself up into a rage can commit it. But to choose, with open eyes—even if it is in the dark!—willingly to bind oneself to that tomorrow which does not yet exist, but which is brought into being by the choice itself: that is perhaps the most difficult thing I've ever done in my life. Perhaps this is freedom. When I was a slave the Baas took care of everything. I never worried about tomorrow: there is neither yesterday nor tomorrow for a slave.

Now, in that moment when, in the silent loft above the thundering house, I found the woman who had always been mine, I freely took up the burden of yesterday as I chose tomorrow for myself.

This is what I know now. My last night in these mountains has not been in vain. What lies ahead is that end Nicolaas told me about: the death of the man who'd run amok with his axe. To be hanged on the gallows with its three crossbeams; and then the beheading, and the head stuck up on a pole in the place where the man comes from, until only the skull remains, staring into the wind. Let it be so. I can get up now and wait for them to come, whatever lies ahead: Cape Town, and death.

Only through killing can I, perhaps, be heard. I have no other voice.

Free? No, I'm not free. But at least I know what freedom is; what it might be. I have glimpsed it.

The sun has been pushing up from below for a long time. Now the plains are filling up with light, like a great dam, burning in transparent fire.

There are many swallows about. They've always been here, since the mountains began. When I go down the slope just now, they will still be flying overhead, this way and that, darting and swerving and skimming over the rocks, free to go as they wish. Later, as the summer reaches its end in the first frost that shrivels up the brittle grass, they'll gather in flock upon flock. And one day, all of a sudden, all of them at once, they'll take to the open skies and fly away. I don't know where they go when it grows cold. Perhaps there are distant places where it's warm. All I know is that they leave—and that they come again as soon as it's summer. Dependent on the seasons, they freely come and go.

And some defied the seasons.

My time to go is nearly there. I won't come back. Not this Galant that's sitting here. And yet all cannot be over when I die. Perhaps I planted my life in her womb. I'll never know for sure. But whether it's so or not, whether we have a son or

508

not—and if he's born he shall be free, for she's his mother-
—something of what is now departing will return. Something
remains on the earth. Something will come back. My skull
will stare across these highlands even if its eyes are empty. The
eggs of the Lightning Bird remain in the earth for a long, long
time: but one day they'll hatch and bring the fire back over
these mountains without beginning or end, where my footprint remains forever proudly trodden in the stone.

I'm going down now. In a way I suppose I'm burnt out. But
the fire: the fire remains.

VERDICT

After due investigation and having heard the claim of the R.O. Prosecutor together with the prisoners' defence, and having taken into consideration everything which deserved attention or could move the Court administering Justice in the name and on behalf of His Britannic Majesty in this Colony of the Cape of Good Hope, we the undersigned members of the Court declare as follows:—

It is a lamentable truth which experience has taught us, that when once the idea of being oppressed has entered into and taken root in the human mind, whether groundless or not, it will oftentimes carry men to unthought of extremities.

As long as every man is satisfied with his station in life, peace and contentment reign in the mind, and no rupture of the existing tranquillity is to be feared, however unequal the situation of the one may be from that of the other; but scarcely does man feel that his inequality with those whom fortune has placed in more favourable circumstances affords him reason of discontent, and that he conceives he has to bear a burden which is unjustly imposed on him, than his passions begin to work, peace is banished from his mind, and he will leave nothing undone to find an opportunity to throw off his load.

The Country in which we live has alas! already in our time afforded proof of this truth, and Heaven protect us from witnessing any more.

Can a greater inequality of the human station exist than that between the Freeman and the Slave?—the latter bound, without his consent, to appropriate the entire portion of his life to the service of his free Master—and yet we have not found in the whole history of the Colony a single instance, previously to

513

the year 1808, of the Slaves ever having cherished or entertained the least idea of breaking their bounds by force.

Taught by the moral lessons of our Holy Religion to obey their masters, they did not withdraw themselves from this obedience without well knowing to have failed in their duty; and the punishment of their offence left no other impression on their minds than that they had brought it on themselves by their own bad conduct. This impression was necessary as tending to preserve order and tranquillity in the Land.

We by no means speak as advocates for slavery in the abstract, but we speak under the circumstances of the Colony as they actually exist, a Country which is cultivated by the labour of the slaves, and of which the free Inhabitants, or Colonists properly so called, have been allowed by the laws from the earliest period of its colonization, and encouraged by the example of their own Magistrates, to invest a very important part of their means and their welfare in the purchase of Slaves. Under such circumstances that impression by which Slaves are bound to obey their Masters was and is absolutely necessary for the good order and the well being of the State.

In the year 1808 however some evil disposed and wicked persons, whose evident object was to involve the whole Country in Anarchy and Confusion and hence to derive great advantage to themselves, found means to remove that impression from the minds of many of the Slaves here, whom by a most culpable and criminal perversion of the benevolent object of the British Legislature to abolish, not slavery, but the slave trade, they made believe that they were kept in Slavery contrary to the will of our Sovereign in England, where no Slaves are.

It is not yet effaced from the memories of the Colonists what a dark cloud hovered over their heads when the pernicious poison of strife and discontent was infused into the minds of the slaves by those wicked men, and how easily it penetrated and corroded their bitter feelings.

The example which was made of the ringleaders of those Criminals, and the inability to execute a plan of general Rebellion, withheld the Slaves from again attempting a similar

514

enterprise, but whether the spirit of discontent at their situation which then began to reign among them was quelled is a point which one has much reason to doubt. At least since that time the complaints of slaves against their masters for ill-treatment have considerably augmented; and notwithstanding that much has been done on the part of the Government to ameliorate considerably the state of Slavery in this Colony, still however the fire of discontent at the frustrated hope of a general freedom appears to have been smouldering under the ashes, so that the smallest blast of wind is but necessary to make the flame burst out again more violently than ever.

This disappointed hope was the cause in the year 1808 of the rebellion among the Slaves which we then witnessed. But whereas on that occasion the lives of the Christian Inhabitants were spared, it was but a short time since the cause of those disasters which befell one of our South American Colonies of Slaves; and now we hear for the first time in this Colony also the cry of murder at the disappointed hope of freedom, raised by a slave, who speedily collected a gang of adherents, and who, had he not been timely stopped in his career, would perhaps at this very moment have plunged this Country into the deepest mourning and sorrow.

Three victims of his fatal rage were already felled when he was stopped in the progress of the murderous tragedy which he had but then commenced.

It is necessary that we should take a nearer view of the causes that have led to the crimes of which the prisoners have been accused, not only because they may be considered to have an influence on the culpability of their acts, but also that we may not be thought to have been mistaken in our judgment of the case.

We shall begin with the head of the gang, the slave Galant, accused of having laid the whole plan and instigated the gang to commit the most murderous and bloody scenes, and to make a beginning with his own master, the playfellow of his early years, and whose life he has now brought to a termination in the most cruel manner. When we hear his statement, one will

515

be easily led to suppose that he had been obliged to sigh under a continued chain of successive ill usage at the hands of his Master. How unfortunate it is for the impartial investigation of the truth that the man whom these accusations regard, now lies low and cannot refute them, and that his widow, who is likewise implicated in the charges, although she still lives, cannot possibly appear before this Court without suffering too much under the consequences of the wound so cruelly inflicted on her. However, we have the evidence of the prisoner's co-accused and of those witnesses who have appeared before us, to stop the mouth of the slave Galant about these charges. The Landdrost to whom he complained in the past about the bad usage to which he had allegedly been subject, found him in the wrong; his fellow prisoners declare that he was favoured above them all by his Master, and who, when warned by the Hottentot woman Bet that Galant had laid a plan against his life, paid no regard to the information because he could not conceive it possible that such a dreadful thought could enter into the heart of a slave whom he so favoured, whom he considered as it were a member of his family, for whom he felt an attachment in his own heart because he was brought up and had grown up with him, and to whose irregularities he had even shewn indulgence by allowing him to have two Concubines instead of one.

Of victuals and drink the other prisoners complain nothing, although they signify that it would have been by no means disagreeable to them if they had got more than they were actually allowed. But let us hear what Joseph Campher says, a free man and a Christian and consequently entirely trustworthy and who, all accusations against him having been found groundless, is herewith discharged unconditionally. He states that in harvest time the slaves got wine four times a day and more bread than they could consume, besides soup with peas and beans twice, and a little meat. Is that want of victuals and drink? How many thousands are there among the fortunate Inhabitants of free Europe who would not thank the Almighty on their bare knees had it fallen on their lot to suffer the same

516

kind of want? Yet this food was too mean for Galant and because they were not allowed during the Harvest as much meat as would satisfy their appetites without bread, he stole no less in the short space of six days than four sheep, and certainly not the poorest, from his Master's flock, which he and the other people belonging to the place Houd-den-Bek consumed by night.

But it was not the ill treatment which Galant alleges to have suffered that brought him to the step, as he calls it, of fighting himself free; no, it was his disappointed hopes of freedom that induced him to it. We take his own words. When in his confrontation with the Witness Bet she says that Galant told her before the commencement of the present year that he should wait until the New Year, and if he were not made free then he would begin to murder, what else did Galant do then but to acknowledge the truth of what Bet said and to refer to persons unnamed from whom he had heard last year in Cape Town that at the New Year a general freedom of the Slaves should take place? See there the pivot upon which the whole machine guided by his hand turned.

Such like false reports appear to have prevailed for some time. It is impossible to say how long they have been in circulation, but they have been communicated not only to the slaves but to the owners of slaves. No wonder then if some credulous and misled Masters, imagining that their right of property to their slaves, which next to their lives they considered as most sacred, would be disputed, now and then expressed themselves in language characteristic of the bitterness of their internal feelings; and that the slaves who listened to such discourses or found an opportunity of getting a knowledge of them should on their part become exasperated against their owners from the opposition to their freedom which they supposed they met with at their hands. It is in this point of view that we consider the statement of Galant with regard to the reluctance of the Masters to communicate to their slaves the news contained in the papers which they received from time to time, and also with respect to his fishing out discourses which

517

he says were held between his Master and others. For why should we doubt that such discourses have actually been held by slave owners who, supposing that they were at once to be deprived of all their slaves, were driven by such an idea to the very borders of rage and despair?

It is not our task to endeavour to trace out the authors of such evil reports. It is sufficient in the present instance that such reports did prevail, and that they were the leading cause, as Galant states them to have been, of his undertaking.

The second of the gang, namely the prisoner Abel, who says that he was the Corporal while Galant acted as Captain, although he chiefly screens behind the information which he received from Galant and therefore knows of no other propagators of such reports, or does not think proper to name them, he however did not hesitate to say (as appears from the deposition of the widow Cecilia van der Merwe in the preparatory information) at the moment he was about to give the death shot to Jansen, that no Christian should have pardon, for that the report was that the slaves were to be free at New Year and that this not having taken place they would make themselves free. Nothing more is necessary for us to accept that this prisoner was also led by the same misguided cause to take a principal part in the tragedy.

It is true that he states other reasons also, such as ill usage and that his master had threatened to shoot him; but as he was apprehensive that his body would be examined and his lies thus detected, he cunningly adds that his master flogged his slaves in such a manner that no marks were left; and the threat of shooting refers to one occasion when his Master in a moment of passion threatened to fire at him merely to frighten him into obedience. Many a free Servant has heard a similar threat from his Master in a moment of anger, without attaching the smallest weight thereto, because they well knew it was not meant.

How much less can the hasty expression to a Slave from his master, whose property he is, and with whose loss he must lose a part of his means, awaken any fear or anxiety? We do not say

518

that Slaves have never been killed by their Masters; but there are also examples of fathers having murdered their children, and yet where can a child be safer than in the arms of his father? Or how can a father be better protected than by the love of his own offspring?

If we compare the examples of murders committed on slaves by their masters with the number of those committed on and by others, we shall soon see that the Slave is almost as safe under the protection of his Master as the child under that of the father; and especially those slaves intimately attached to the home, of which description both Galant and Abel are, with respect to whom the natural feeling of affection combines with self interest to make them find true friends and protectors in their masters.

With respect to the other Prisoners we do not need to say much. They were all seduced. The Hottentots among them, namely Rooy, Thys and Hendrik, could not have been driven to their crimes by a sigh after freedom, for they were already free. No desire for revenge for long protracted emancipation could have actuated them, for that was no case of theirs. It is true they were under the subordination of masters, and that fired by the hope of being Masters in their turn they might have been induced, by the craft and subtlety of Galant, to become the enemies of their masters, from whom they undoubtedly enjoyed fewer privileges than are allowed to slaves in general. The hope of plunder and booty may also have had some influence on their mind, but essentially we consider them as instruments only of which the ringleaders Galant and Abel availed themselves to attain their object.

In respect of the 3rd Prisoner Rooy there is an additional factor to be considered, namely his age, which to this Court appears to be as under fourteen, or at all events (as we are obliged in rebus dubiis, in primis in criminalibus ad admittendam benigniorem sententiam) much nearer 14 than 18. This Prisoner appears really to deserve more pity than contempt for the acts which he has committed, and which he has not only openly and frankly, but even with a childish fear and anxiety,

519

confessed. And should he have committed a premeditated crime, even then must be applied to him what we find in Lex 37 ff de minor *in these words*: In delictis autem minor annis vigintiquinque non meritur in integrum restitutionem, utique atrocioribus; nisi quatenus interdum miseratio aetatis ad mediocrem poenam judicem produxerit. *Besides this, we have seen how this prisoner Rooy from the very beginning was obliged and compelled by Galant to ride after him as his postillion and coerced to shoot the wounded Verlee. Who will for a moment doubt what would have been the lot of this Prisoner (whom we may well call a child) had he not complied with the order of Galant?*

The 6th, 7th and 8th Prisoners, Klaas, Achilles and Ontong, as being slaves, shared in the same interest with the two first prisoners Galant and Abel. It appears that with deeply troubled hearts the last two acquiesced in the plan to fight themselves free, although they foresaw all the danger of the enterprise and were slow in joining the others, without polluting their hands with the blood of their Master or of the other two murdered persons, and without following the others to the place of D'Alree on the road to Barend van der Merwe where it was intended to shed more blood. On the contrary, the instant the gang left the place Houd-den-Bek they joined their wounded Mistress and remained with her till the Commando arrived. In addition, the two prisoners Achilles and Ontong have not been proved to have made slugs for the gang as charged in the Act of Accusation and they are consequently found not guilty on this count. It has been established, however, that they shared in the deliberations which preceded the execution of the plan and took some part in the execution itself at their Master's place. That certain items of clothing belonging to the late Nicolaas van der Merwe were later discovered in the huts of the two prisoners, is a further and decisive indication of their complicity.

The charges against the 9th Prisoner Adonis not having been proved sufficiently, there is no need for the Court to dwell on the evidence in this respect and, like the 11th Prisoner

520

Joseph Campher referred to earlier, he is herewith discharged unconditionally.

We must now say a few words about the 10th Prisoner Pamela, who is accused of having by her passiveness and silence co-operated towards the disasters which befell the family of the late Nicolaas van der Merwe. It is indeed true that she seems to have had the will to provide Galant with one or more guns belonging to her master, which she as housemaid and sleeping in the house had more than one opportunity of procuring, but there is no conclusive evidence on this point. It would appear that by a careful silence when the storm was approaching, although she was in the house and had slept there the whole of the night, she exposed her master and his family to the danger that threatened them and consequently contributed as well to his death and that of the other two persons as to the wounding of her mistress. But let us ask ourselves who is this prisoner Pamela, and in what relation does she stand with the Prisoner Galant? As his wife, could she truly be expected to smother the feelings of nature (if indeed she had been previously informed of the plot by her husband)? She felt too sensibly the relation in which she stood with the Prisoner Galant, to accuse him (had she in fact known his intention) of a crime through which she should in all probability be severed from him for ever. Furthermore, if ever one may venture to acquit a person of guilt for passiveness during the commission of a crime, then certainly it is Pamela, for she already knew the passionate nature of Galant, and that it would perhaps cost her her own life if she endeavoured in the least to interfere. How real such a fear may have been was proved only too cruelly by the way in which, after the carnage in the homestead at Houd-den-Bek, Galant assaulted the baby she was holding in her arms and of whom we must imagine himself to have been the father. The Court consequently absolves the 10th prisoner Pamela from this instance.

Proceeding now, in conclusion, to the grounds of the criminality and punishableness of the several points of accusation in respect of those Prisoners found guilty, we remark that *the most heinous species of High Treason consists in taking up arms against the State, and that all those are justly considered guilty of this crime who combine to oppose the existing order of public affairs with violence and arms.*

In a Country where slavery exists, a rising of the slaves to fight themselves free is nothing else than a state of war, and therefore to such a rising the name of war has been given more than once in the Roman history, and justly, for hence States can be, and we know have been, totally overthrown; and the remark Nullum esse genus hominum unde periculum non sit etiam validissimis imperiis *can be here very properly applied. (See also Mattheus de Criminibus Lib. 48, Tit. 2, Chap. 2 par 5.)*

Even those Prisoners who acted primarily as instruments of the ringleaders cannot be absolved from complicity in this respect. When Galant consulted with the other conspirators about the execution of their plan, not one of them had any arms. Not only the two guns, but the two pistols also, were in the possession of his Master; who of them could at that period have prevented any one of the gang from throwing himself on his Master for protection, informing him of what was going forward, and in this manner preventing all that has happened? When five of them, among whom were three Hottentots, were on the road to Barend van der Merwe's place, all on horseback and unarmed, who could have prevented any one of them taking the first opportune moment to separate from the others and, favoured by the darkness of the night, concealing himself in the Fields or in the Mountains?

Why did they not follow the example of the slave Goliath who withdrew himself from the gang after Galant and Abel had got possession of his master's guns, powder, and ball, and even fired at them?

The 7th and 8th prisoners Achilles and Ontong have with much emphasis maintained that they used their endeavours to dissuade Galant (whom Ontong moreover refers to as his "child") from his purpose and to represent to him the danger to which he was about to expose himself; but when Galant persisted in his intention, what did they do? They sat down to supper with the gang, every one of them went to rest for a time, without availing themselves of yet another of many opportunities which they had of informing their Master of the threatened danger or, if they could not or would not do so, of making their escape while the others were gone to Barend van der Merwe.

The prisoner Klaas can just as little as the others screen himself behind the pretext that he was compelled by fear to join the gang. When his Master, who was awakened about 10 o'clock at night by the barking of the dogs, enquired from him what it was, Klaas by keeping silent enticed his master to come out of the house, and thereby afforded Galant and Abel the opportunity to rush in and seize the guns and ammunition. The situation of the place in the mountains, and in the darkness of the night, would have no less afforded him than his master an opportunity to escape; he could just as well as Goliath have remained with his Mistress. But the active part that he took with the other members of the gang sufficiently proves, were proof necessary in so clear a case, that he was a voluntary and wilful accomplice in the whole business.

Even the prisoner Rooy, in spite of his extreme youth (to which we referred earlier), took an uncommonly active part in everything that was done by the gang, prompted no doubt by his own bloodthirsty curiosity to be at the very least a near spectator of the murderous scene that afforded Galant the opportunity of putting a loaded pistol into his hand and obliging him to give the death shot to the already mangled body of the dying Verlee.

Not one of the Prisoners attempted to avail themselves of the ample opportunities that presented themselves of averting the dreadful action by warning his Master. No owner of a slave is any longer safe in his own house if a slave can conceal with impunity from his master any danger with which he may be threatened, were it even at the risk of such a slave's own life.

The eagerness to shake off the yoke of slavery, which had never before led to such excesses in this Colony, cannot be considered in any other light than as a desire to withdraw themselves from the laws of the land and from obedience to Government; a desire for blood, war and confusion leading to the most disastrous anarchy. And the desire for freedom, thus directed, is a reason, not for the mitigation, but for the aggravation of the punishment.

Or can it be said, when so many have to suffer, humanity requires that the example to deter should extend to all, but the punishment to only few? Of this we find instances in history where great crimes have been committed by many persons. But this belongs to the rights reserved to the Sovereign. As Judges we cannot go farther than the right with which judicial authority is vested with regard to crimes and punishments.

We therefore declare the eight first Prisoners in this case Guilty, the 1st and 2nd Prisoners Abel and Galant of conspiring to commit and of actually committing the crimes of High Treason, Murder, and Armed Violence; the 3rd, 4th, 5th, 6th, 7th and 8th prisoners, Rooy, Thys, Hendrik, Klaas, Achilles and Ontong, of being accomplices in the execution of the plan previously framed by the first two Prisoners, aggravated with respect to the 3rd and 4th prisoners Rooy and Thys, on the part of Rooy by having assisted in the murder of the late Johannes Verlee, and on that of Thys by the particularly active part which he took in all the acts of violence that were committed; taking into consideration however the youth of the 3rd prisoner and the circumstances in which he fired at the late Verlee;

and therefore condemn all the said Prisoners to be brought to the usual place of execution and being there delivered over to the Executioner;

the 1st, 2nd and 4th prisoners, Galant, Abel and Thys, to be hanged by the necks till they are dead; the heads of Galant and Abel to be then struck off from their bodies and thereupon stuck upon iron spikes affixed to separate poles to be erected in the most conspicuous places in the Bokkeveld, there to remain till consumed by time and the birds of the air;

the 3rd, 5th and 6th prisoners, Rooy, Hendrik and Klaas, to

be exposed to public view made fast to the gallows by ropes round their necks, and together with the 7th and 8th prisoners, Achilles and Ontong, tied to a stake and severely scourged with rods on their bare backs, to be then branded, and thereupon confined to labour in irons on the public works at the Drostdy of Worcester—Rooy, Hendrik and Klaas for life, and Achilles and Ontong for the term of fifteen years;

while the Court reconfirms its verdict of finding the 9th and 11th prisoners, Adonis and Joseph Campher Not Guilty, and of absolving the 10th prisoner Pamela from this instance, with rejection of the greater or other claim and conclusion made against the 3rd, 4th, 5th, 6th, 7th, 8th and 10th prisoners in this case, and condemnation of all in the costs and expenses of the prosecution.

Thus done and decreed in the Court of Justice at the Cape of Good Hope on this 21st day of March, 1825, and pronounced on the same day.

(Signed)   J.A. TRUTER
W. HIDDINGH
W. BENTINCK
J.H. NEETHLING
J.C. FLECK
P.J. TRUTER
P.B. BORCHERDS
R. RODGERSON

In my presence.   (Signed)   D.F. BERRANGÉ,
secretary.

1979–1981